CINDY'S DIARIES · VOLUME I

# BEHIND THE
# BLUE DOOR

A Vade Mecum on Tipping the Velvet

CINDY'S DIARIES - VOLUME I

# BEHIND THE
# BLUE DOOR

## A Vade Mecum on Tipping the Velvet

# SAMI GOLDHURST

This book is dedicated to the memory of Jessie Moisa, grandmother and philosopher.

# Contents

*Few phenomena are as mysterious as the female orgasm.*
- Carl Zimmer

# Prologue
## Behind The Blue Door

*Standing outside an anonymous* blue door *in an anonymous back street, I read the nameplate, an unpolished brass plaque - a reminder of better times:* Felicity Mynar MCSP.

*I used my phone to google the qualification:* Member of the Chartered Society of Physiotherapy.

*Really? I googled* Felicity Mynar. *From her LinkedIn profile, it appeared that she had retired about five years previously. I assumed she had sold her practice to the new owner, who wished to remain anonymous. Or, perhaps, the owner of* Felicity's Tantric Massage, *as she styled her business in the advert, had simply acquired the premises. The new Felicity had certainly changed the business model. In exchange for sports massages for injured athletes, it seemed there was a better market in the art of Tantra.*

*It was my fascination with Tantra that had led me to this* blue door. *But it had been a three-month journey to pluck up the courage or maybe a lifetime's journey to arrive at this anonymous* blue door *in an anonymous back street, pondering:* Do I have the nerve to cross the threshold, and, if I do, will it lead me up a path towards spiritual bliss, or down an alley towards degradation?

*I'm not even sure in which direction I was hoping to travel. Whatever the truth, I wasn't ready. So I picked up my phone:*

"Hello, Felicity's Massage."

"Er, I think I need to cancel my appointment."

"What's your name, love?"

"Er, Vishti. I have an appointment at 4 pm."

"Who's that with, love?"

"Cindy."

"OK, that's a one-hour Tantric massage. It's five to four. You know that, right, Sweetheart?"

"Yes, I'm sorry for the short notice. Is there a cancellation fee?"

"No, darling. But - and I'm not trying to be funny - I can see you outside on the CCTV."

*I looked up at the door and saw the spy camera.*

"B-b-but…"

"Look, love, Cindy is here waiting for you. She really won't bite. Didn't

I tell you, on the phone, how she'd give you the best massage of your life? I'm going to buzz you in now. Just chat to her, and if you still don't want to, no sweat."

*With that, I heard a buzzing and the latch released.*
*I thought to myself:* One small step for man...

# PART I

# 1

# Dixie

"Why are you always on your phone? Is that a spreadsheet?"

Dixie, my college roommate, seemed to have a mission in life. She was more worldly than me. Same age but had sort of been around the block a few times - streetwise. I felt like a school kid beside her, but we got on fine. Shared interests: music and boys (they might have been in their twenties, but still boys at heart).

Food as well. Surprising, since I grew up with a kind of *mish-mash* of Eastern European from my Jewish mother, Fidget Pie from my Shropshire farming father and steak & chips from a very English step-dad.

Dixie (well, if your name was Dorothy you'd also want to change it) was the daughter of the clergy, who'd grown up in the North with traditional fayre, like Black Pudding. I thought she was kidding when she told me the ingredients.

But, as soon as we arrived in College, we experimented with Asian cuisine. Now it's Indian or Thai or whatever Asian food the Uber Eats algorithm happens to recommend.

Dixie's mission: *Save Rachel.* I wasn't then sure why she felt the need to save me, why she wanted to spend so much time on me, but, at this point, I needed a mentor and saviour. I needed someone to help me sort out my finances, and Dixie provided some stability in my otherwise chaotic life.

"The spreadsheet helps me to plan. You never seem to be short of cash, but I'm really struggling on the student loan."

Dixie presented me with three options:

"Sponge off your parents; get yourself a job; or take the easy way out."

When Dixie said *the easy way out*, she was referring to the little side earner that was keeping her in clothes and more. I couldn't do that!

Dixie had referred me to the website *www.college-escorts.co.uk*. I didn't get further than the home page. The deal was 50/50 with the Agency. The Agency claimed to *screen* all clients, for your safety. The big plus, as Dixie had reassured me, was that you could choose the profile. Dixie had specified thirty-five to fifty-year-olds and university education a must. She was adamant that she had to be able to have an intelligent conversation with her companion. The thirty-five to fifty category was in case sex was on the agenda. She was fed up with fumbling college students. If she had to, she wanted someone with a little more maturity, who could ensure a mutually pleasurable experience.

"I keep telling you, Rache, you don't have to sleep with them."

"It's not the sex that puts me off. To tell you the truth, I wouldn't mind a casual fling with a real man. I'm quite fed up with my current squeeze. He picked me up at the Freud lecture. He's not in our group. I think he just went to the lecture thinking that anyone attending the Freud lecture would be into kinky sex."

"What does he do, tie you up?"

"...trary, I have to tie him up... and then toss him off."

"...ou get out of it?"

"Fuck all. Well, actually, he's a good kisser, and we have had sex, but he doesn't come unless he's tied up. Funnily enough, it kind of turns me on. I wouldn't mind so much if his tongue knew its way around, but he's an embarrassment in that department."

I had tried to explain to Dixie that my problem with the escort deal was that I wouldn't know what to say. Dixie seemed to be genuinely interested in her clients. Her curiosity meant that the conversation just flowed. I knew that I'd just clam up. I was really worried that the client would ask for their money back, and then the Agency wouldn't book me with anyone else.

"If you won't escort, what about erotic massage? You know June, Skip's friend? She can clear £500 for a day's work. She has to work there from midday to 10 pm, does maybe six to eight clients during that time. She says most of them are happy with a quick wank, the *happy ending*, as they call it. She also has a regular who gives her a £50 tip for a blow job.

That was how it started.

£500 would mean the difference between scraping by or having enough for the trip to Thailand that we were planning for Easter. I could easily spare one day a week for a couple of months. The coursework wasn't too taxing and I could borrow Dixie's notes for any lectures I missed.

I set up a meet with June.

*******

"Tell me, does everyone have a happy ending?"

With that, June gave me the ins and outs of what was *de rigueur* in the world of erotic massage.

The first thing was the vocab, a whole lexicon:

*Tantric massage* meant they expected special emphasis on their erogenous zones.

*Lingham massage* required slow massage of the penis, with special care that they didn't come too quickly.

*Nuru massage* was fully naked, using Japanese seaweed gel. The naked bit was alright. Most clients were sufficiently turned on with you sliding over their body and didn't take any liberties.

*Body to Body* is what it says on the tin. Naked, and the client is massaged by various parts of the masseuse's body, including her breasts.

*Mutual massage* could get a bit tricky. The client is permitted to massage you, which invariably means playing with your nipples, but the rules say they don't touch you down there. If they do, it's usually enough just to wriggle away.

The blow job, June explained, was her own choice, and could get her the sack. It was a regular client who she quite fancied. She had asked if he wanted any extras and offered him the blow job.

Apparently, a lot of clients will ask for extras, but will generally take *No* for an answer. There's always someone else on the premises, usually Fiona, known as Fi, the owner, who works on reception. The rooms actually have a panic alarm, though June had never come near to needing to use it.

"Oh, you need a new name. Your stage name. Doesn't matter what you choose, unless there's another girl already using it. Never tell your clients your real name. You should keep your two lives separate."

"My friends used to tease me and call me Rochelle."

"OK, but I'd say that's a little close to Rachel."

We carried on chatting for a while, reminiscing about when we were kids.

I told her a funny story about when I overheard my Catholic stepdad talking to my Jewish mum, trying to explain about Original Sin. There was a kid at school called Cynthia, who we nick-named Cyn. I thought they were talking about her.

I suddenly had a *eureka* moment: "That's it! Cyn."

"Not sure. We're supposed to do Tantric, very spiritual, not sinful at all."

We giggled.

"Wait, I've got it. I'll call Fi and tell her that she's going to be interviewing her new therapist: my mate - Cindy!"

I'm not sure I'll ever understand why, but when June named me Cindy, I had an image, a flashback, of a young girl, licking an ice cream. It wasn't the school friend Cynthia. The image wasn't one of innocence. I felt a shudder. I hesitated. I could see June had made up her mind, so *Cindy* it was going to be. But I did wonder. June's casual rebranding of this gauche psych student was supposed to set me on a path towards financial stability, but had she also, unwittingly, unlocked the lid of a Pandora's box?

# 2

# Training

June said they'd train me. That's a laugh. At my interview, Fi said that I'd have full training. The problem was I'd be getting no salary. I was to be on a 50/50 split with Fi, but Fi would not be earning anything while I was in training. By her reckoning, she was losing £500 for each day of training. She would front up that cost and then deduct it from my commission over the next three months.

I couldn't work out the figures, but it sounded to me like I wouldn't earn any money in the near future. So, when Fi asked me how long I felt I needed for training, I said just a week and I'd be ready to start earning.

The irony was that there was no real training at all. My role was to shadow another therapist but, as the client wouldn't be happy having someone watch, Fi had to sell it as a four-handed massage. Fi was quite helpful in one respect:

"If you play with his cock, he won't notice that you don't know how to give a massage."

So, most of my so-called training involved massaging the client's penis, while ensuring that they didn't climax. The other therapist would focus on the Tantric element and take care of the Lingham towards the end.

The real fun came with my first prostate massage. I was with one of the more experienced therapists. She went under the *nom de plume* of Shirley.

She gave me the down-low:

"I've been working here for five years, but it took me two years before I'd do prostate. In the end, it wasn't about money. The extra cash in your pocket is neither here nor there. It was the number of clients who requested it. If you ruled it out of your menu, you could be sitting on your backside half the day. But if you include prostate, Fi will keep you fully booked."

I took the plunge, literally. My rationale: I was there to earn money, the £500 a week I needed. It looked like my choice would be one day a week if I did prostate or two days a week, half the time sitting on my arse if I couldn't handle it.

I asked June whether she was happy to do prostate massages. She pulled a face.

"I wouldn't exactly say *happy*, but I sort of challenged myself. You see it's not just sticking your finger up their arse. You have to find their prostate. If you get it right, they can actually have an orgasm. I started using gloves, but to be honest, it's better all-around riding bareback. Just use a lot of Dettol when you wash your hands after."

I decided to follow June's advice and dispensed with the gloves after my first go. It was one of Shirley's regulars, who liked to be referred to as Willy. After the preliminaries, we got down to business. Shirley worked on his top while I worked on the bottom. Shirley knew what he liked, which involved talking.

Mostly Shirley, instructing me: *Go on, I'm rubbing Willy's willy. Finger him deep inside. Is that deep enough for you, Willy? Go on Cindy! Give him two fingers.*

Willy had a shuddering orgasm, so I guess I'd hit the right spot.

I soon came to realise that most of the clients were less interested in the spirituality of the Tantra and more interested in satisfying their individual kinks.

By the end of the week's training, I must have done over 40 clients. I did seven days on the trot before the start of the new college term. I think I'd covered the whole menu of services plus quite a few things that were *off-piste*. No one had asked for, or been offered, blow jobs, or full sex, but I'd had plenty of quirky clients requesting fairly kinky things.

My biggest education was in the variety of shapes and sizes. My experience to date had only really been boys. Maybe I hadn't paid much attention, but, with younger guys, they all tended to look the same. I mean apart from the obvious difference between the Cavaliers and the Roundheads. But looking at 40 or so cocks in quick succession made me realise the variety out there. I had to confess to a guilty pleasure at the thought of getting up close and personal to examine some of the differentiators.

*******

I must have done something right over that week, because on my first day of work, when I'd be starting to see paying clients, Fi invited me into her back office.

"Now, the training seemed to go well. No client complaints. The girls said you were a fast learner. I told you I'd need something to cover the lost income, so I'm suggesting £500. I'll deduct £100 each day off your first five days. How does that sound?"

I considered that a result. It would actually mean I'd be earning from day one. I had eight clients booked on my first day, who were due to earn me about £500 commission, less the £100 for the training. June had said that a lot of clients will tip you if they have a nice climax, without you having to offer any extras.

Funnily enough, I was quite looking forward to my first client with the slightly odd name. He sounded Indian. Minutes before he was due to arrive, Fi knocked on the door of the staff room.

"Your client is here already. Sort of a cross between Steve Jobs and Mahatma Gandhi. Go easy on him. He looks like he's drawing his pension already and sounds as if he's still a virgin."

# 3

# The First Session

*After crossing the threshold, I edged past the* blue door. *I half turned to close it, I couldn't see a spring, but it had a mind of its own, self-closing. It was as though it was making a statement:* No turning back now Vishti!

*A rather threadbare carpet ushered me along a dimly lit corridor, at the end of which there was a staircase leading down. Above the staircase, on the ceiling, was positioned a naked light bulb, dangling from a twisted wire. Like the door, the lightbulb seemed to be making a statement. But I wasn't sure what it was trying to say. It was definitely there to brighten up the gloom, but did it want to warn:* Trip hazard ahead?

*I found myself in a basement, my path blocked by a counter, which I'd supposed was the reception desk. In front of me, wearing a botoxed smile with a lit cigarette seemingly glued to her upper lip, stood a wizened vixen.*

"Hi, darling. Cindy will be out in a mo'. As I said, talk to her, and if she don't charm you off your feet, you can go home, no charge."

*Of course, I was going to stay. If I was too embarrassed to press the doorbell, how easy was it going to be to leave the young lady in the lurch, after meeting her face-to-face?*

*But I wasn't expecting what happened next. I had been ushered to a seat by the over-made-up platinum blonde, who went under the name of Fi. I thought short for Felicity, although it was pretty obvious that she was not the Felicity Mynar MCSP on the brass plate outside.*

*Whilst I was waiting, she had removed herself to a backroom, but I could hear her on the phone through an open door. I later discovered that Fi was actually short for Fiona, so all vestiges of the original Felicity were really only a reflection of past times.*

"Yes, it's £100 for Tantric, Love. Yes, she will be topless... No, if you want naked... Naked is usually Body to Body or Nuru. If you want Tantric with your masseuse fully naked that will be £20 extra... Look, Darling, I'm not going to answer that over the phone, but I will say all our clients leave with a smile on their face if you know what I mean... Yes, the Lingham massage is exactly what it says on the website... Don't jack me around, Darling, I'm going to book you in with our newest girl, Cindy. You won't have seen her here before, but she has loads of experience and will charm the pants off you..."

*And so she went on, but I never found out if Fi got the booking, because there she was standing in front of me. My first visual impression: she was, not beautiful, attractive, yes. She wore her hair short, a kind of rough, uneven cut, easy to manage. Here was a young lady who wanted to be ready to wash & go. Fair-haired, or streaky to make it fair. Highlights, I think they're called. Did she do that at the hairdressers or at home? It looked quite uneven, so probably did it herself in front of the bathroom mirror. She was quite petite, 5ft 3 I would guess. I'm not sure why, but I expected someone maybe a bit taller. The face, though, was very much what I'd imagined, almost eerily so. I hadn't pictured Asian features to fit in with the Tantric experience, but I was anticipating exotic. This young lady was not from the Far East, but perhaps traces of the Middle East, or Eastern Europe. So I assumed she'd have a foreign accent.*

*But it was her smile, a sort of cheeky smile that was somehow so disarming. She was wearing a kind of loose-fitting smock, which suggested nothing underneath. Actually, I'm not sure why I thought that. I'd booked a Tantric massage, and having overheard Fi on the phone, I now had to presume that Cindy would be topless. Of course, I could request fully naked as an extra, so now even more embarrassment was on the way.*

"Hello, I'm Cindy. Fi said this was your first time."

*Her heavy cockney accent dispelled any thoughts that this young lady was anything other than locally born and bred.*

*With that introduction, she held out her hand and led me to the massage room, wearing what I later christened her* trademark smile.

*There was a small chair in the room, a massage table, one of those folding ones that mobile therapists take with them for home visits. I used to have a physio when my back was bad. He looked quite strong yet even he complained about the weight of the folding table. How a female therapist could cope with carrying that around all day was beyond my comprehension. At the back of the room, there was a mattress on the floor. The website was very clear. For my Tantric massage, I could opt for either table or mattress. The mattress didn't look uncomfortable, but I'd given up sleeping on the floor in my student days. It struck me as a little odd to have the treatment on the floor, until I recalled that some of the treatments involved a naked masseuse moving her body over the client. Clearly, doing that on the table, especially a portable folding massage table, might be a bit rickety.*

*The room was a little cramped, poorly decorated, but not seedy. Cindy seemed to sense my nervousness. She asked me to get undressed, pointing to the hooks on the back of the door. Then she checked herself.*

"Vishti, is it alright if I call you Vishti? That was the name on my list."

*I nodded.*

"Sorry, I should have said that I'll leave the room while you get undressed."

*Then, to my surprise, she sat on the chair, took my hand, looked up at me with pleading eyes and, in a soft voice, which I could hardly hear:*

"Don't tell Fi or she'll sack me. You're my first *paying* client!"

*Cindy then proceeded to tell me her background. She told me that* Cindy *wasn't her real name but wouldn't tell me what her real name was. She explained that she was a psychology student at Greenwich College and needed to make some extra money to pay her fees. Her friend had recommended the job and she'd spent the past week in training. The training comprised being second fiddle in four-handed massage sessions. The fact that, during these training sessions, she didn't know what she was doing didn't seem to bother the clients, because they were getting a 50% discount on the normal rate for four-handed massages.*

"So I know what to do, it's just that you will be my first solo client, so to speak. But Fi said don't tell the clients or they will take liberties with me."

*Then, sheepishly, Cindy explained that she had to ask for the money upfront. I took out £100, and I'm not sure whether it was the shock of what she had just told me, but I found myself saying to her:*

"£100 that's for fully naked, yes?"

*Cindy nodded. But her look told me that she knew that I was taking a liberty, exactly what Fi had warned her about. I relented with:*

"Sorry, I'm supposed to pay an extra £20 for that."

*I took out a £20 note and gave it to her. She turned around, leaving the room, while I got undressed.*

*I didn't know whether to get on the massage table or the mattress. Since I wasn't expecting her to be writhing all over me, smeared in seaweed gel, the table seemed appropriate. I also considered it more professional and less intimate. I had come for a Tantric massage and, although I expected there to be a sexual element, I wasn't looking for anything that could remotely be considered illegal. I got on the bed and lay on my stomach, so I didn't notice her when she came back into the room. The first thing I felt was a warm towel, placed over the lower part of my body, which was somehow reassuring. I was feeling quite relaxed and ready to enjoy the massage.*

*My only trepidation:* How would I react when the moment came?

*The moment came after about 20 minutes when she asked me to turn over. Still very professional, she held the towel so that I could turn over without my privates being in Cindy's eye-line. But when I saw her standing there naked, with that cheeky smile,* the trademark smile…

"Don't worry, we'll get to him later."

*After about another ten minutes of quite pleasurable massage - head, face and across my chest, slowly working down my body, Cindy asked me if she could remove the towel. She proceeded to massage lower down my body and, as she approached my loins, brushed her hands across my penis.*

*We weren't speaking, but each time she brushed, it was as though she was asking me if it was alright to go there. Each time lingering a little longer. Each time sensing my reaction. The embarrassment had gone. She was not going to ask me if I wanted a happy ending, full relief, or any other euphemism. She just kept brushing and lingering until she knew she had my permission.*

*This was my first time. Well, not my first, how shall I call it, hand relief. I mean my first professional experience. Daphne would take me to hand when she was not in the mood. She was rarely in the mood and she always presented it as a chore. A wifely duty. No sense of erotic arousal. I had, of course, taken myself to hand. The quality of my orgasm depended on the creativity of my fantasy. If inspired by the sight of a young woman, a short skirt, or a furtive glance, I could build a whole scenario in my fantasy that would help to bring me off. I'd used porn a lot. But never right up until climax. I wondered whether I was unique in that regard. The porn, still shots, or video, were a stimulation, but only to stimulate the fantasy. I'd always set the graphic material to one side when I moved to the business end of my solo erotic experience, as I brought myself to climax.*

*But this was altogether different. Cindy's touch was welcoming, almost tender. The fact that she was young and attractive obviously enhanced the experience. And, although I was paying for it, she seemed to be getting pleasure out of it herself.*

*I was concerned that I'd come too quickly, but too embarrassed to ask her to slow down. Her hand moved faster, and I was about to come. I wanted her to look at my face as I was coming, but she seemed intent on watching my explosion, as my seminal fluid spurted out into the air and landed on my stomach.*

"Just lie still, and I'll clean you up."

*She said, in quite a matter-of-fact tone.*

"I can't believe I'm your first."

"Sshh, I said Fi can't know. I told you. Anyway, not my first. I said my first *paying* client. I've had plenty of boyfriends, so I know what I'm doing down there."

*There were so many questions I wanted to ask her. Did she really enjoy it? The watching, I mean. Or was she watching just so that she'd know when I'd come? Would she look at me with her smile, her* trademark smile, *next time, while I was coming?*

"Can I ask you a question?"

"As long as it's not personal."

*I thought my questions, the ones I wanted to ask, were too personal, so I went with:*

"No, strictly professional. If you give me the hand relief with a Tantric massage, what's the difference between that and the Lingham massage?"

"I'd recommend that for our next session together; less time massaging your body and more time down there on the pleasure centre. Just a moment, and I'll run the shower."

*That's how it started. I knew, from that moment, that Felicity's Tantric Massage would be having a new regular client, as long as Cindy continued to work there. What I did not know was how much I was going to learn from that college student, nor did she know much she was going to learn from me.*

# 4

# Mission Statement

Dixie wanted to know how my first day went.

"Believe it or not, I actually enjoyed it. I kind of enjoyed wanking my boyfriends before, kinda gave me a sense of control, but, with this, it was more about proving that I could really turn these men on. I don't think I'm that good a looker, and I'm quite self-conscious about my body, but every one of these clients told me how great I was. I don't think they were being polite. I reckon it was more about the fact that, as they were paying for it, they were going to persuade themselves that I was gorgeous. Everyone was friendly. What I mean is that they didn't try anything on. The only weird one was the first guy. Not weird kinky, but it was his first time and he seemed more nervous than me. It wasn't just his first time at our place. He said he'd never been to a massage parlour. Fi said he was hanging around outside and wanted to cancel, but she told him to stop being so stupid. After the session, he told me that he wasn't a virgin. He was actually married, but his wife never enjoyed their sex. I wasn't sure, but I almost got the impression that he wanted to see if he could learn any techniques to improve his sex life at home."

Dixie was confused. She didn't understand how I was going to improve his sex life at home. If I was massaging him, that wasn't going to help him give his wife an orgasm. It didn't sound like he was the kind of guy who was going to give his wife instructions on how to give him a Tantric massage. I realised that Dixie was right. I hadn't thought it through. There was the Mutual Massage on the menu, where the client could massage us, so maybe that was an option. But I hadn't even talked about that with this Indian guy. I might be able to give him good orgasms, but how was that going to help him in the bedroom at home?

That was when I came to the realisation that, if I was going to help some of my clients to have better sex, I really needed to plan how I was going to do it. It needed to be a proper project, sort of like a mission in life, which would make the job more interesting. Job satisfaction was important to me.

I decided that the first subject for this mission should be Vishti.

24

*******

*I arrived on time. No hanging around outside. I was quite looking forward to the Lingham massage that Cindy had scheduled for me. It was everything I'd imagined and a bit more besides. It had been two weeks since our first session, and, from the way she was touching me, Cindy seemed to have gained a lot of experience. That was a bit of a surprise, as she'd told me that she was only working one day a week, so she couldn't have done much more than a dozen massages since we first met.*

*Cindy explained that, as part of the Lingham session, she would massage my perineum, which in turn would stimulate the prostate. It wouldn't be a prostate massage because there's no penetration, but it would improve my climax. I found it quite exciting how she explained what she would do, in quite a clinical way.*

*It made it seem more professional, almost like sex therapy. But I was taken aback a little bit when she said I could touch her breasts if I wanted to. I felt quite self-conscious, but she always had a way of putting me at ease. I didn't know how far to go, but she invited me to rub her nipples. I got a kick out of seeing them erect. I had often tried to stimulate my wife's nipples, but she always shied away. Now here I was, actually making this young woman excited, or, if not, then she was certainly doing a good impression.*

*I was less embarrassed than at our first session, so I asked her the questions I had wanted to ask her before.*

"You were watching me down there as I was coming, rather than looking at me. I was wondering…"

"Oh, shit, did I get that wrong. Of course, you're the client. Just tell me what's good for you. You want me to look at you when you're coming?"

"Well, yes, I suppose. Will that interfere, with, I don't know, your technique?"

"Oh, bugger me, really Vishti! Don't be daft. It's just a turn-on. I get turned on seeing you spurt. No, I don't just mean you. It's like, I don't know, maybe a kink. I like to see men come. I like to watch as their cum spurts out."

"Like watching porn."

"Well, I suppose, but I'm talking about real life. You know, with my old boyfriends. Ever since the first time. At school. Bit of a bummer, the boys wanted blow jobs, but I'd get more of a kick giving them a hand job and watching them come. As I said, you're the client. I'll try and get it right this time. Any other requests?"

*As she talked, I watched her…*

Trademark smile.

*I couldn't believe how open she was in talking about her sexual experiences, but since she wasn't at all embarrassed, I thought I'd carry on.*

"Well, since you asked, perhaps a little slower, you know, draw it out a bit."

"Yeah, already onto that. I was going to apologise. My job is to spot when you're coming. You took me by surprise last time. I've been OK with the other clients, but, well, you just seemed to come without warning. Look, Vishti, I'm happy to talk, but we are on the clock here, so let me relax you. Close your eyes. You're allowed to open them when you start to come and I'll be looking at you with, what do you call it, my *trademark smile.*"

*She just took control. She gently held her hands over my eyelids to make sure they were closed. Then I felt her lips give me a gentle kiss on the forehead. Next, her hands were running down my body, tickling my arms, circling my nipples, then running over my stomach, and circling my belly button.*

*Her hands move down, avoiding my penis, and now her fingers are tickling my inner thighs. As she's tickling me, I can feel another sensation. Her fingers have moved to my lower ball sack and she's starting to tickle my perineum. Wow! But the sensation is still on the inner thighs. It's her tongue. She's licking my inner thighs, and the anticipation is tantalising. Is she going to… we hadn't discussed… just anticipating was bringing me up to… now her hand is starting to massage my erection. Her tongue has moved away. I hear her whisper in my ear.*

"That was a little surprise, just to say sorry that you came too soon last time. Just picture my tongue, all the places it could go."

*Now she's sucking my ear lobe, and now her tongue is inside my ear, gently, rhythmically, making love to it.*

*Her hand is massaging faster, and now I'm coming, I'm breathing harder.*

"Cindy, yes, yes…"

*She stops rubbing and grasps my hard member, squeezing it tightly.*

"Not yet, not yet. Not this time. Cindy's in full control."

*The moment passes, but she's keeping my erection hard. Holding my attention. Now she's bringing me up again.*

"Now?"

"Sshh. Let me do my job. Just quiet. I'll know when you're ready."

*Again she brings me up to a point when I can feel I am coming. Again, she stops and squeezes. Two, maybe three times more, until I can stand it no longer.*

"Cindy, please, please now!"

"Open your eyes, then."

*And as she holds my well-oiled shaft tightly, rubbing it up and down vigorously, faster, as my muscles are involuntarily tightening around my anal sphincter, as I am shuddering in the most explosive climax that I have ever experienced, as I open my eyes there I see:*

Trademark smile.

*I think Cindy was quite pleased with herself. No words were spoken. I didn't need to tell her that she had just given this elderly gentleman the most wonderful erotic experience of his life.* I looked into her eyes, I looked at her smile, and *I thought:* I want to take you, Cindy. I want to take you to places you've never been. I want to explore your body. I want to pleasure you, just as you've just pleasured me.

*Cindy was back in therapist mode, offering me the towel to shower and tidying up the massage table.*

\*\*\*\*\*\*\*\*

*As I was leaving the salon, Cindy gave me a friendly peck on my cheek and whispered:*

"Book a Mutual Massage next time, where you can rub me all over. It'll be on the mattress, so we can get down and dirty!"

Trademark smile.

# 5

# A Conundrum

My chats with my roommate now regularly reverted to my experiences with clients.

Dixie wanted all the skinny on what I was doing to, or with, my clients. I wasn't going to give any graphic details.

*Client confidentiality*, I explained. But, for some reason, because I'd already told her about Vishti, and, because he was my special project, I was ready to share some of what went on.

"I can't tell you his name, so I'll call him Q, like in James Bond. He's the guy I told you about, with the frigid wife."

"The Indian?"

I suddenly had a premonition. I didn't want to say anything that might reveal his identity, so I made something up.

"Yes, Sikh, I think. Turban and everything," I lied.

"I'm trying to get him used to touching a woman's body. I started with my nipples, but next week I'm going to give him some lessons on how to massage."

"You're kidding! You're going to let him paw you?"

"We call it Mutual Massage, and it's not pawing, it's like you're caressing each other in a sensual way."

Dixie wasn't persuaded. She still thought it weird that I'd let someone massage me when they were paying for me to massage them.

"I can understand having a guy massage you if he knows what he's doing, but what? You're going to teach him?"

I couldn't really get it across to Dixie that I found that clients massaging me could be quite stimulating, even if they weren't professional masseurs.

"How far will you let them go?"

"Well, officially, between the legs is strictly off-limits and no one has ventured there yet. But with Q, well, he's my project. I'm not sure how I'm going to improve his love life at home if we don't go down that road, so to speak."

Dixie laughed out loud. Not sure if it was humour or embarrassment. She had started me on this road, with the escort thing. I knew she was sleeping with a lot of her clients. I couldn't understand her hang-up if I was planning to let Vishti touch me intimately.

Dixie said that she had a relationship with her clients, you know, talked to them, dated them. She only slept with the ones she fancied. I kind of saw her point. But I had a totally different approach. I didn't want to have a relationship with my clients. Not in that sense anyway.

My relationship was strictly as a professional masseuse. OK, it was erotic massage and involved bringing my clients to climax, but that was it. Their climax. I didn't need to like them, fancy them or, above all, get to know them. I wasn't dating them. Heaven forbid. That would be strictly out of bounds, as far as I was concerned. I'd even borrowed a phrase in order to keep my world with clients completely apart from my social life.

Cindy's first rule: *Never date a client. Separation of Church and State.*

But my question was, and I didn't know the answer yet: *How far would I go with Vishti?*

If I ended up letting him give me an orgasm, would that lead me down a path I didn't want to go?'

*******

I saw the booking. Mutual Massage was £150, and I felt a bit of a cheat. In the business, it's called up-selling. We'd gone from £100 Tantric to £150 for the Mutual. But I wasn't doing it for the extra commission. At least, not with Vishti. I had a genuine desire to help this guy.

I suppose I could have asked him if he wanted my help. Somehow, though, from the moment I heard about him hovering outside, not sure whether or not to come in, it seemed that Vishti was looking for something more than a massage. I was going to make sure that his sex life at home improved.

For now, things were going fine. For the first Mutual Massage session, I took things very slowly. We were on the mattress. I started off with a normal Body-to-Body massage. I was rubbing my naked body over his. I invited him to suck my nipples and encouraged him to caress my breasts. I wasn't sure if that was within Fi's regulations but didn't see the need to ask. I rolled over onto my back.

"Massage me. I want you to start on my shoulders, gently caress my breasts and work your hands over my abdomen."

I started to guide his hands down my legs and drew them between my thighs. He was hesitant, at first, but I widened my legs and arched my back. I guided his hands across my pubic bone, put a little oil between my legs and placed his hand over my vulva.

"You're looking for my clitoris. It's very sensitive, so go slow, just gently sandwich it between my lips using your thumb and finger."

He was doing pretty well, but I wasn't going to come, and I realised that I might have misjudged the situation. I was trying to help him to pleasure a woman, but, if I didn't come, I'd have failed. He would be disillusioned. I'd probably end up losing a client. I thought about faking it, but, if he realised, that would be even worse. I wasn't going to come with Vishti's fingers, but he had got me horny, so I thought: *To hell with it...*

"Vishti, would you like to watch me play with myself?"

I didn't need an answer. I could see the look on his face. I normally masturbate with my eyes closed in some erotic fantasy, but I wanted to see Vishti as he watched me play with myself. It heightened my experience.

I was just rubbing myself the way I'd normally masturbate, directly on my clit, then squeezing it between my lips when it had become very sensitive. I was watching Vishti get aroused.

"Play with yourself, but don't come. I'll give you an explosion later."

No more talking now, Cindy. I am struggling to keep my eyes open as I feel myself coming. I can feel my breathing getting deeper.

Now I'm riding a stallion, feeling the throbbing between my legs as the stud is trotting, then cantering, now galloping, through the fields. I'm alive. I'm breathing the air, the smell of sweat against my naked body. My senses are aroused. The soft music, in the room, Zen Massage, has only a faint drumming sound, but, in my state of arousal, I'm hearing the drums playing louder and louder. The pounding in my ears, the throbbing stallion between my thighs and the pungency of the sweat combine as I start shaking. My contractions have started, I'm quivering, I'm coming. I cry out:

"I'm gonna come. I'm gonna come."

My volcano erupts. The quivering lasts several seconds until I settle back down, my breathing calms, and I feel completely relaxed.

He was so sweet afterwards. He just lay next to me and caressed me lovingly. This man is far more sensitive to a woman's needs than I gave him credit for. All I could think of was his wife: *Why won't she let him pleasure her?*

It took me a few minutes to gather my composure before providing the Lingham massage. As I was stroking his perineum, I circled around his anus and asked whether he was ready for a prostate massage. But I wasn't ready for his answer:

"Do I have to pay you the extra twenty pounds now?"

He caught me completely off guard, so I simply said the first thing that came into my head:

"Not this time, consider this a free sample."

# 6

# A Cry for Help

The call came after midnight. My phone was off, but there was a knock on my door. We still had a pay phone at the end of the corridor. A fellow student had picked it up on their way back from a party. From outside my door, their voice in distress:

"It's Dixie! She said your phone was going to voicemail. She sounds desperate."

I sleep naked, but there's always a robe hanging on the door. I grabbed it and ran down the corridor. The phone receiver had been left dangling.

"I'm in A&E. I didn't know who to phone. Can you come?"

"Where?"

"Charing Cross"

"Strand?"

"No, Charing Cross Hospital, it's Hammersmith."

I'd been to the Hammersmith Hospital, but that's in White City. I was confused and Dixie wasn't making much sense.

"Of course, I'll come, but I don't know if the trains will still be running and an Uber will take well over an hour."

Dixie was crying:

"Please just come. I've been so stupid. I don't know what they're going to do to me here."

"Dixie, you have to calm down. Is there a nurse or someone I can speak to?"

I'd barely finished when I heard another voice on the phone. They asked if I was a relative: *No.* They asked for Dixie's name: *I gave it.* Next of kin? *OK, but I didn't have their contact details.*

Then the voice explained that Dixie had been attacked. She wasn't seriously hurt but was in a state of shock. They would be giving her some sedatives and dressing her wounds, but she couldn't travel home on her own. I asked for the address, and the voice - I assumed it was the triage nurse - cleared up my confusion. It was the Charing Cross Hospital, which was in Fulham Palace Road, Hammersmith, not in Charing Cross and, yes, there was a Hammersmith Hospital that was in White City.

I booked an Uber.

The car was close to the hospital when Dixie called me again. She said she'd been discharged, so I asked the driver to wait while I went in to get her. By the time I arrived, Dixie had calmed down. Her left eye was really swollen, and her head was bandaged. They said it was a superficial cut on the head. They didn't think there was any concussion, but I'd have to take her straight back to A&E if there were any signs, like feeling dizzy or blurred vision.

Dixie filled me in on the details on the ride home. She'd broken a cardinal rule of the Agency. She'd given her phone number to one of her regular clients. She then got a call from a guy who said he'd got her number from that client. No checks, no security. She'd gone to the hotel. She thought she was being clever by cutting out the Agency. She met the guy in the hotel bar. The St Paul's Hotel isn't 5-star, but sort of boutique. They ordered drinks. He gave her £400 to cover two hours and took her to his room.

"He spiked your drink?"

"Don't know, Miss Sensible hardly touched it. He wasn't trying to get me drunk. That was sort of why I trusted him. He seemed nice and genuine. He said he only wanted to have dinner with me in his room and watch TV together. On reflection, I don't know what I was thinking. I assumed he wanted to have sex, and I thought: *What the hell. It's £400!* He was good-looking, dressed well, I don't know… He smelt nice."

Dixie went on to say that all had been going well.

"We had ordered from the room service menu. He encouraged me to order a whole load of shit that I didn't want. He wasn't a chatter. Then after we'd eaten, out of the blue, he just blurts out that he likes anal intercourse. I gave a sort of nervous giggle and told him that I didn't, and his whole demeanour changed. He looked a bit angry. I thought that I had to calm him down. I found myself saying I'd do anything else; he could even come in my mouth if he wanted. I don't know why I said that, just that most men I've met rank that higher than a fuck. Anyway, he just looked at me and said it was my choice. I could take it in my arse or take a slap. I thought he was kidding so I said: *I'd take the slap, thank you very much.* Without hesitation, he hit me right across the face. Fortunately, I was sitting down next to him, so his hand didn't travel far. It was more shock than pain. I knew I had to get out of there. So, I jumped up but stumbled and hit my head on the room service trolley. I fell to the floor and felt his shoe hit my eye. I don't think he deliberately kicked me, just that he chose not to move his foot. It hurt like hell. I got up, ran out of the room, down the lift and, as I fled from the hotel, I jumped into a taxi that had just dropped off a guest. I told the driver to take me to the nearest hospital which, by luck, was only about five minutes away."

By the time we got home, Dixie seemed to have recovered her composure, enough to conclude her soliloquy with:

"The irony is I don't mind anal with my boyfriend, but it's a bit different with a stranger."

I helped Dixie into bed, stroked her face and kissed her on the forehead. I lay down with her until I knew she was asleep, and then moved to my own bed.

As I drifted off to sleep, I kept repeating Dixie's words to myself: *It's a bit different with a stranger.*

All I could think of was the massage parlour and how many strangers' arses I'd finger-fucked for money.

*******

A few months later, Dixie's physical scars were all healed. However, I was still worried about the psychological impact. We'd covered PTSD in one of the modules on the course, so we both knew the signs. She said she was OK.

"Then why haven't you gone back to escorting?"

"What do you mean? I never thought it would be you encouraging me back into sex work," she joked.

"I'm serious. You used to enjoy it. If you tell me you've decided you'd prefer a barista job at Starbucks, I just won't believe you. You admitted it was your own fault. I don't mean you deserved it, but you told me you broke protocol. If you'd followed the Agency's rules, you would have been safe. I don't want you to go back unless you're ready. But you know you're not ready. And that's PTSD."

"OK, Clever Clogs, I accept your diagnosis. What's the prognosis?"

"I don't know. We haven't finished the PTSD course yet!"

We shared a laugh.

"And your prescription, Sigmund?"

"Give it time, change your lifestyle, I don't know."

Then she hit me with a bombshell. She was thinking of dropping out of college or maybe deferring. Dixie and I had become close. The thought of her not being around was quite distressing but I couldn't stand in her way if that's what she wanted.

"Dixie, I know Professor Sharpe's a pain. I can tell him to stop hitting on you."

That was a private joke from our first week together when we did the girlie thing of scoring our lecturers and Sharpe scored *nul points*.

"Seriously, Dixie, since I've stepped up my days at the salon to three a week, I need you for those lecture notes."

"You cow. I thought it was just my body you were after."

"Come on, Dixie, level with me. You love the course. What's the matter?"

Then she explained it was the money. She'd been stupid and hadn't saved anything from her escorting and couldn't afford next term's fees. It was three grand. She didn't want to rack up more student debt.

I didn't hesitate.

"You're such a bloody fool. Why didn't you ask me? I'll give it to you."

She immediately refused, but I told her I wasn't taking *No* for an answer.

"Firstly, I owe you for the lecture notes. I couldn't do my part-time job if I didn't have you covering my arse with the lecturers, keeping me up to speed with the coursework. Secondly, you have no idea how much I'm earning. I clear that in a week."

"Seriously?"

"Yes, I'm doing three days a week and my daily commission has doubled since I started."

Dixie quizzed me on the maths. I went on to explain how Fi had put up my rates. The canny sod had turned around to me one day and said all my clients were going to pay more. She had told them I was fully booked and they had a choice of paying the new rate or having another girl at the old rate. That was an instant 25% uplift. 90% of my clients stayed with me. On top of the rate hike, I'd become good at the up-selling. Assisted showers were £25 and didn't stretch the appointment time because they were going to shower anyway.

"And I added my own extra: for another £25 they could watch me shower."

Dixie looked bemused: "You're kidding me. They've already seen you naked. Why would they pay £25 just to watch you shower?"

"SUI."

"What?"

"Stress Urinary Incontinence."

"I know what SUI means, most women have it after they've had kids, but what are you talking about?"

So, I explained how it all started. A client was chatting to me. He asked if I believed the story about Donald Trump and the Russian prostitutes peeing on him. The conversation took a surprising turn when the client just came out and asked if I'd pee on him. I said I didn't think I could. It wasn't a judgement thing. Not even embarrassment. Not that I wouldn't, just that I didn't think it would actually happen. You know, I'm used to sitting down on my own in the loo.

His suggestion was that we shower together and the running water would likely make me want to pee. Well, he had a point. The only time I do pee standing up is in the shower.

I had previously decided that, if I was going to enjoy this job, I was going to have to have fun.

As long as no one's getting hurt (I don't think I could do the pain thing) and I'm not totally revolted by the suggestion, then:

Cindy's Second Rule:
*In olden days, a glimpse of stocking*
*Was looked on as something shocking.*
*But now, who knows,*
*Anything goes!*

I told him I was up for it. Either way, I wouldn't charge him this time, but, if it was to be a regular extra, I'd up the assisted shower rate from £25 to £50 to cover the special.

He was more than happy with that. The running water thing worked a treat. After we'd finished, he confirmed he was happy to pay £50 next time but wanted to sit in the shower while I peed over his face. He was serious, and I wasn't fazed by it. I just told him to book the assisted shower with Fi, but make sure she didn't know about the special service.

Dixie was intrigued but still didn't understand where the SUI fitted in.

"I call that my up-selling technique. It was my way to ask if they wanted to watch me in the shower. As you said, why pay me an extra £25 when they'd already seen me naked? I couldn't ask them outright if they wanted a golden shower. It would be too embarrassing if they said *No*.

I thought I might start to lose clients if they didn't have that particular kink. So I asked if they want to see me shower, but said I had to warn them about my SUI. If they'd be awkward seeing me pee, then we shouldn't do it."

"They fell for that?"

"Fell for it! They were all over me. I had no idea how many men were into that. About a third of my clients now have my special assisted shower, though only a few go for the full mouthful."

Dixie was laughing, and it was good to see that she was perfectly relaxed again when talking about sex. But I did wonder whether her delight at the thought of me pissing on men had anything to do with her unfortunate experience at St. Paul's Hotel.

"How do you know you'll have enough pee?"

"Dixie, I'm a professional. I always prep for my clients. If I see one of my specials booked in, I make sure I drink plenty of water before the session starts."

Dixie started quizzing me on other kinks.

"Tell me about the BDSM. How far will you go?"

"Well, I do have my red lines. Literally. I won't do bloodletting."

"You mean that's a thing?"

So, I told her about the Wartenberg Pin Wheel, a medical device used by neurologists for testing nerve reactions. The small wheel has spikes which run gently over the skin. In soft bondage, a lot of clients like the tingling sensation, especially when they're blindfolded and gagged.

"Do you use safe words and stuff?"

"Oh, yes. I keep it simple with traffic lights: red, amber, and green. I couldn't cope with different words for different clients. I had a client that chose the names of fruits, but I got confused between peaches and bananas and he was screaming *Peaches*. I carried on until he said: *Peaches means Stop! You stupid bitch*. We kind of fell out after that. I lost a client and decided to stick with the traffic lights."

We were giggling like schoolgirls.

"Do you get a kick out of it? You said about the wheel thingy?"

I explained about a client that liked the wheel and asked me to press harder. I broke his skin and the blood oozed out. I rushed out of the room to get an antiseptic wipe. But when I came back, he wasn't annoyed and simply asked if I'd cut him next time. I thought he was kidding, but he said he liked to be cut with a penknife. I freaked out a bit. I'm not sure whether I said *Yes* or *No*, but, after he left, I told Fi to block him."

Dixie wouldn't stop with all the questions and, somehow, I knew she was going to get around to the prostate. In a way, I was glad that we were talking so openly. Although her nightmare experience was about anal sex, she'd already confided that she indulged with her boyfriend and also gave him prostate massages.

"My boyfriend is fastidious down there. He washes, I mean an actual enema-type douche before I give him a prostate massage. Do you make your clients clean themselves out first?"

"Well, it doesn't quite work like that. Yes, I'm happy to do enemas, but that's chargeable as part of the BDSM sessions. Prostate massage is usually for a Tantric session, so, no, there's no flushing beforehand, so to speak. You just take it as it comes."

"Isn't that messy?"

"Surprisingly, no. You use a lot of oil, which kind of acts as a barrier, so your fingers are usually pretty clean. Actually, I don't mean clean, but not covered in you-know-what."

"Your fingers! You don't wear gloves."

"It's strange. One of the few things the girls will talk about at work is how to give a good prostate massage and whether to use gloves. It's odd but we do want to please our clients, and there's a technique to prostate massage. We're happy to learn from each other."

Dixie agreed: "I kind of get what you're saying. It took quite a few times and a lot of guidance before I got it. So, if you've only seen the guy for the first time, you need to know what you're doing."

"Exactly, and with the glove thing. There's five girls at the parlour. I've not met them all, because we work different days, but as I say we chat, and my survey revealed 60% ride bareback."

"Not sure if that's a representative sample across the population."

"No, but remember I'm only talking about the professionals, can't speak for amateurs like yourself."

We giggled.

I didn't know whether to mention the toys, so, in my mind, I gave her a trigger warning and decided I'd spare Dixie the messy details that follow next.

# 7

# Down & Dirty

My life was moving on quite well. Things were fairly straightforward. I was a student who would come out with a degree that should lead to a decent job. In the meantime, I had part-time employment that was earning me more money than I could ever have imagined.

There were two people in my life that I cared about: Dixie, my roommate, who looked after me. She helped me catch up with the lectures I missed when I was working my sideline, but also she was a comfort to me. I think that was a good way to say it. We both liked each other. I think it was just roommates, but could it be more?

The second person in my life was Vishti, my client. That was rather a different issue. I wasn't really sure what that relationship was or where it was going. It worried me a bit. But *hey ho!* Life's what you make of it. I kept telling myself not to be so *introflective*.

*Que sera sera.*

Now back to the toys!

The toys started when I saw a butt plug and another anal toy in the staff room. Fi told me that Daisy had left them when she went back to Poland. I'd never met Daisy. I'd heard that she was quite sweet, but a bit marmite. She spoke a lot to her clients. When I say a lot, she never stopped. Some clients loved her for that, but others refused to book with her again. Being an erotic masseuse is no different from giving an ordinary massage, in the sense that you always need to be conscious of the client's boundaries. If you're talking and they're chatty - fine. But if they want to lay there in silence, they're paying the piper.

But, anyway, the toys. I wasn't sure about using them. There was a hygiene thing. Obviously, we cleaned them, but how would a client react knowing it had been inserted up someone else's back passage? So the idea came when a client brought in his own butt plug, and at the end of the session, he mused:

"There's a restaurant I go to that keeps bottles of whisky for me. Puts my name on the label and stores it for my next visit. They're happy to buy any bottle of any whisky you want because you're paying in advance for the whole bottle. The clientele can have an unlimited range to choose from and the restaurant doesn't have its capital tied up in stock. They'll only do it for the most expensive stuff. The cheaper whiskies get ordered all the time, so those bottles aren't sitting around."

He wanted to know if we could keep his toy. I was fascinated at how he was comparing a twenty-year-old Macallan to a £30 Lovehoney butt plug, but *hey ho*!

"I'm sure we could come to some arrangement. I'll have to ask Fi whether I need to charge corkage."

"Are you serious?"

"Oh please, butt plug, cork. I thought that was a good one."

The client finally got my joke. Then he mentioned that he had a few different toys, but needed to know that they wouldn't be used by anyone else.

"That's a bloody insult. Do you ask your restaurant if they dip into your whisky bottle?"

"No, that's different. I trust them."

"Sod off and take your bloody arse plug with you."

"Are you serious or are you kidding again?"

"I'm not fucking kidding. If you have to ask that, I don't want you as a client."

I got the message across. My *faux* outrage worked. But I was bloody annoyed. Whatever anyone thought, this was not a knocking shop. I always tried to be professional and he insulted my integrity.

He apologised. I accepted his apology, as well as his larger-than-usual tip, as compensation for upsetting me. I kept his butt plug but wasn't quite prepared for the toys he brought next time.

When I mentioned the storage to Fi, she thought it was a great idea.

"The whisky thing means the clients are more likely to keep coming back. I'll buy some small lockers and send you some links to the stuff on *lovehoney.com*. Tell the clients we'll have the toys delivered here and keep them in their own lockbox. I don't know, what do you think? A 20% one-off handling charge which I'll split with you 50/50. Maybe a small surcharge as an extra on the prostate price. Let me think about whether I'll put it on the website or just leave it to the girls to suggest to their clients. You don't mind me mentioning it to the other girls?"

I put on a slightly pained expression.

"No, you're right. It was your idea. Let me speak to the girls and I won't take a cut of the handling charge on your clients."

"Nor the toy surcharge on my prostate fee."

Fi held out her hand to shake on the deal. I was quite chuffed at how good a businesswoman I was becoming.

The client came back with his selection of anal toys. He had two varieties of anal beads. One plastic and the other rubber.

"What am I supposed to do with those? I mean, I know what they're for but how far up can I go?"

They were about three times as long as my finger, and since my finger reached his prostate, I was a bit confused about the anatomy.

"You do it slowly easing each bead in until it's gone right up the anal canal. Cindy, I want to ask you something, but after last time I don't want you to think I'm disrespecting you. What I like, what I'd like you to do, and only if you're prepared …."

I was wondering what he was going to ask. I thought it would be a blow job or touching my pussy. We'd already danced that dance and he knew my limits.

"…I like to get right in the dirt. It's you humiliating me, making me squirm, if you like."

I still wasn't sure what he wanted, so I suggested that he simply guide me during the session and if it reached somewhere I didn't want to go, then we'd stop, and I promised no more tantrums from me.

We started the session as usual and then I got around to the anal beads. I thought the idea was to whip them out at the point of climax, supposedly to enhance the orgasm, but he had another idea.

Well before he was close to climax, he held my hand, which was holding the beaded flexible rod. He gently moved my hand, guiding me to pull out the rod. Then, still holding my hand, he guided it towards his face. As I pulled it out there was a bit of shit on it. I say a bit, enough to cause quite a whiff that almost made me retch.

"Are you ok?"

"I'll be fine. I just wasn't expecting that."

He kept guiding my hand so that this shitty rod was smearing some shit on his face, and then he opened his mouth.

"Tell me to clean it before you put it back up."

Well, now, that's why I spared Dixie the details. Thought she might freak if I mentioned that kink. I told myself to stay professional and not to be judgemental. He'd given me an out if I couldn't face it (no pun intended!). It was my decision.

I went back to:

Cindy's Second Rule:
*In olden days, a glimpse of stocking*
*Was looked on as something shocking.*
*But now, who knows,*
*Anything goes!*

Of course, Cindy's Second Rule did have a caveat:

*As long as… I'm not totally revolted by the suggestion.*

So, I just had to gauge my level of revulsion. Once I got over the whiff, I think I surprised myself. It was pretty awful, but I went back to my mission statement. I was here to help these wankers, sorry, clients. When I reflected on it, I think that was just an excuse. The client told me that he wanted to be humiliated. I realised I got a kick out of humiliating him. The first time he was guiding me, 'cos I didn't know what he wanted me to do. Once I got the hang of it, I was dangling it over him, then urging him on. *Go on clean it, you miserable shit!*

I started to realise that in truth it wasn't that I wanted to help the clients. It was the control. Controlling my clients, teasing them, playing with them, was turning me on. Not just the kinky ones. Even the straight guys who just wanted a happy ending, they would also get the Cindy treatment.

Whereas, when I started out in this game, I just wanted them to come as soon as, now my shtick was to draw it out until they were literally begging for me to let them come. It made me horny watching them squirm. If the guy was a half-decent looker, I'd actually get wet while I was working.

Back to the dirty guy. I couldn't understand his kink, but there must have been a reason for it. I don't know, some childhood issue. I couldn't ask any of the lecturers at College. They'd want to quiz me as to why I was interested. But I did do a bit of homework at the psych library to see what Freud had to say about it.

At the end of the session, we had a slight impasse.

"Are you ok with that?"

"Yes, I don't mind. Can we just call it a bit of fun? I don't want to force you to eat your shit, but if that's the game, I'm ready to play it. But I hope you're not expecting me to clean it?"

"Well, you did agree that you'd be keeping the toys in a lockbox."

"You have to be bloody joking. Here's the deal. I'll bring the disinfectant. Take it into the shower with you. I have a plastic bag to put the stuff in and, because you don't trust me, we bought a wax seal so you can make sure it's still intact next time you come."

"That last bit was a joke, wasn't it?"

I gave him what Vishti liked to call my *trademark smile*, to let him know that we were on the same page.

The lock box was going great, maybe twenty clients using it for toys we bought for them. I couldn't speak for the other girls, but, fortunately, none of my other clients appeared to be into the fudge-eating kink.

# 8

# River View

*I felt I had a real connection with Cindy. After stumbling through our first sessions, we started to explore each other's bodies. I don't think she was more than twenty but seemed to be so mature sexually. I got slightly confused. She told me she was twenty-three. She confided that her first sexual experience was when she was eighteen, so I thought five years of experience, maybe. Young women today were far more sexually active. But then she let slip the year she was born, which made her twenty. I didn't pick her up on it. I didn't know when she was telling me the truth. She'd admitted her given name wasn't Cindy but wouldn't reveal her real name. I went through what she told me over again. The five years of experience fitted in. If the birth year was accurate, that would mean she lost her virginity when she was sixteen. Plausible. I'm not sure why it was important to me. This girl… this young lady was more than my masseuse. But I hadn't worked out what she was to me. I just felt I needed to understand more about her background. Why do kids… why do young women go into the sex industry? Obviously, the money, but:* Some do. Some don't. Some will. Some won't. So what?

*All I knew was that my sessions were getting more and more intimate. But, as always, Cindy led the way.*

*Even then, when I invited her to my home, for the first time, she had seeded the idea. I didn't know if she intended to or was just playing with me. We had finished a session, which, by now, always included an orgasm for her. She chose, or maybe she made me choose, to let her come first. She probably knew that, if I came first, I might lose interest. But I started to see that I had a role in these sessions. Usually, I'd start her off and she would finish. Sometimes there'd be mutual masturbation. One time, she brought her own favourite vibrator. I used it on her, but she took it off me to finish and had an explosive orgasm. My orgasms just got better and better.*

*Before I'd experienced what Cindy offered, my climaxes were just that. Reaching an endpoint and then ejaculating. But with Cindy, the experience wasn't just explosive, it was just ecstatic, it was… spiritual. After the explosion, then the ecstasy, then… bliss!*

*The experience continued to improve. She introduced me to prostate massage and she was keen to experiment, try new things, explore innovative techniques, not just in masturbation. She would probe the erogenous zones, just to see if there wasn't a new area of my body where she could pleasure me. She would use her hands, her fingers, her tongue delicately licking, just touching my body hair. All over, except for my penis. She wasn't a prick teaser. She had explained it to me jokingly:*

"I have to save something for when you leave your wife to shack up with me."

*It was a private joke between us. She knew that Daphne was unable to satisfy me in that way, but I had made it very clear that I would never leave her. Likewise, Cindy had often remarked:*

"Much as I like you as a client, I could never move in with an old codger like you!"

*I had wondered how I'd spent my whole life with missionary position sex. My wife turned away every time I tried anything new. Talking about sex was certainly off the agenda. With Cindy, it was the complete opposite. We would actually spend twenty minutes of the sixty-minute session talking sex.*

*One day, she just blurted out:*

"I'm doing an outcall!"

"What do you mean? Going to someone's home. Is that safe? I'd worry about you."

"Don't be silly. He's a regular client. I've been seeing him as long as you. He lives close to the salon. About ten minutes' walk. I normally start work at midday, so I'm seeing him at ten thirty. I'm charging him the same rate, so I pocket double the money. I won't let him tip me on top, so he gets a better deal. My rail fare's on peak, so that costs a lot more, but I'm still quids in. Don't know why I'm telling you this. If you tell Fi, I'll get the sack."

"Don't worry, we're even. If you tell my wife about what we get up to, I'd get more than the sack!"

*Whatever her motive, it seeded the idea.*

*My wife was away for a week. Her sister was not well. She lived in the West Country, a small village in the Cotswolds. Daphne was going off to see her sister and her brother was joining them. I don't think her illness was serious, although I was a little concerned that her family seemed to be gathering. I suppose you could say it was serendipity, but Daphne announced her intention to spend a week with her sister on the same day that Cindy mentioned her new outcall service.*

*I didn't stop to think.*

"Would you be prepared to visit me?"

"What do you mean?"

"You know, like your other client, outcall?"

"Not sure if I have the time."

*I felt let down. I didn't know why she mentioned it. I thought maybe that's how Cindy was. She was just a youngster who said the first thing that comes into her head. She was not a scheming vixen at all. Or maybe she was playing a long game. Keeping me dangling*

"Sorry, I don't mean to brush you off. The other client, he's local, so I'm just stretching out my day. I don't know where you live, so I don't know how it would work."

"I'm about a twenty-minute walk. It's a five-minute drive. I could pick you up after work one day."

"When?"

"My wife's away all next week. Pick a day."

"Friday. I knock off at nine. I'd need you to drop me off at the nearest underground and I couldn't stay later than eleven."

"That's great. Would you do that for our normal two-hour rate?"

"No, let's do the ninety-minute charge. I absolutely must leave at eleven prompt, but I can't guarantee I'll be ready at exactly nine, because I have to tidy up the rooms and stuff."

"Thank you. That's perfect. What do you drink? I'll make sure there's wine in the cooler."

"You actually have a wine cooler? You're so posh!"

"Posh? Doesn't everyone have a wine cooler? Don't do that!"

"What?"

"Don't give me your *trademark smile*. You know it drives me crazy. I just want to give you a big kiss."

*I'd never kissed Cindy before. Well, not a real kiss, just a peck on the cheek. I know it sounds daft, but I was still a novice at this. We'd explored every part of our bodies, but somehow kissing seemed against the rules. It was more like passion, and this was supposed to be, I don't know, Tantra, spiritual or maybe mechanical sex. Whatever it was, a passionate embrace wasn't part of the deal. But she kept looking at me, with that* trademark smile. *When I told her I wanted to kiss her, she kept smiling and sort of moistened her lips. I grabbed her close and started to kiss her. Our tongues wrapped together. She didn't break away. It was probably seconds but seemed like minutes. When our lips finally parted, we stared at each other.*

"Sorry, I don't know what happened. Are you OK?"

Cindy smiled: "Vishti, it's OK. We're still on for Friday. Just don't do that again."

*I didn't know if she was serious or not. I was afraid to ask.*

********

*She said 9 o'clock outside. I got there at about a quarter to. I parked around the corner and turned on the car radio. It was five past when I got a knock on the car window. I wound the window down.*

"I'm just throwing out the rubbish. I'll be back in five minutes."

*I could feel my heart beating quickly. It reminded me of the first time we met. I was waiting outside the blue door, reading that brass plate. So much had happened since then. I felt a whole new chapter of my life had opened.*

*After what, maybe twenty encounters, thirty? I wasn't counting. But it was an asymmetrical relationship. Cindy had a real life, as a student somewhere. Actually, she'd told me: Greenwich College, studying Psychology. I think she'd forgotten she told me, because a few weeks later, when I asked her how the Psychology course was going, she looked puzzled and told me not to believe everything she said. I think she'd let it slip by accident. In some respects, she was very open, but there were some things she didn't want to go into. Her childhood for instance. A broken home, so common nowadays that the actual expression has gone out of fashion. Apparently, she had a reasonable relationship with her mother. Less so with her dad, but she still communicated with him. Her half-brother, or was it her stepbrother, who was about 10 years her junior.* Get an exact age for the brother, and the age difference and I'd be able to confirm Cindy's age. Do I need that information? Does it matter?

*But there was something about her grandfather. Was there some abuse? She'd sort of alluded to it, but very indirectly. I chose not to press it.* Again: Do I need that information? Does it matter? What's my agenda here?

*The tap on the window came again to wake me out of my musings. I unlocked the car door. She got in, then leant over and gave me a peck on the cheek. That was sweet, and a first, for Cindy to take the initiative in the kissing department.*

*We got to the underground car park at my riverside apartment.*

"Do I have to put my hoodie up?"

"Well, there is CCTV in the lift."

"Does your wife check the CCTV?"

"Hardly, but the security people can see you."

"I'll keep my head down, then, or will that look more suspicious?"

"Just act normally."

"What about the neighbours?"

"Probably not around this time of night."

"It's only 9 o'clock"

"They're my age. Probably watching TV."

"Well, you're your age and you're out and about."

"If they're in the corridor, I'll just introduce you as my niece."

"Seriously?"

"Don't have a niece. A couple of nephews. One's married, but they live in Scotland."

*By the time we'd finished the conversation, we were already in the apartment.*

"You said Chablis?"

"In the wine cooler? Posh boy!"

"In the wine cooler, Madam Smirk."

*The dynamics had changed compared with our time in the massage room. The banter more relaxed, if slightly juvenile. I felt we both needed a drink to loosen us up.*

"Wow! That's a nice view."

*As Cindy entered the living room, she saw the river and the lights from the apartments on the other side of the Thames. On this stretch of the river, there's still a little bit of traffic, pleasure boats or river buses guiding tourists along a glistening waterway.*

"I'd like a view like that."

"Where are you living now?"

"Flat hunting. Moved out of the college halls at the end of last term. Going to get a flat instead of sharing a room in the dorm.

"Still Greenwich?"

"Yes."

"I'll send you some links. Rightmove."

"Rightmove?"

"It's a property search portal."

"Are you in property or something?"

"Sort of. Property management. Boring stuff. Don't want you to get the wrong impression. Not the Candy Brothers."

*I looked at Cindy. She flashed me her* trademark smile, *but then she just seemed to be in her own world, some kind of daydream. I wondered if what I'd said that had sent her to a different place.*

*******

Funnily enough, I'd heard of the Candy Brothers, billionaire property developers. Not that I followed high finance, but I used to watch *Neighbours* re-runs on TV when I was a kid. I followed one of the cast, Holly Valance, on Instagram. She'd long left the TV Soap, but I saw her wedding photos on her social after she'd married one of the Candies. Vishti triggered a moment's reflection. I was suddenly in the Caribbean, on a super yacht, wearing a sexy bikini, with all these young men letching after me. I was brushing them off, playing the snotty bitch, sexy but aloof. Then the owner of the yacht appeared on deck. It was Vishti, but it wasn't him. It was a younger version of Vishti. Someone I could genuinely fall in love with. He approached me and picked me up in his arms. He carried me along the deck. As I passed all these young, handsome guys, I looked down my nose at them with a derisory smile, not my *trademark smile*, more of a sneer. Then with a triumphant chant:

"See who you need to be if you want me, guys. I only fuck billionaires now!"

\*\*\*\*\*\*\*\*

"Cindy! Cindy!"

*She snapped out of her daydream and was back in my flat.*

"Sorry, I thought I'd lost you for a moment. I was saying that I'm always looking. I have to keep in touch with the rental market for my property management business. Agents send me things. You can do it yourself on the internet, but it's easy for me. What's the budget?"

"I need two bedrooms because I'm sharing with Dix…, er, Dorothy. I thought about £250 a week between us."

"You are kidding, right? Two bedder, river view, Greenwich, gym, and pool, like we've got here. My guess starting at double that.

"Bugger me!"

"Can we do that later?"

*We shared a smile. Cindy had told me some time ago that anal was off the agenda. She wasn't referring to our relationship, just generally. This was the first time I'd even joked about it since.*

"It's alright for a posh boy, but I'm just a poor working girl."

*I told her that I wasn't trying to embarrass her, but she'd given me some numbers on her earnings and it was well within her reach.*

"Look, Cindy, it depends what you want to spend your money on. What's important to you. You're working hard. You said you're upping to four days a week plus the studying. Don't you think you deserve a nice place to live? The *River View* is what makes this apartment.

*Cindy was staring out of the window admiring the view. She seemed to be back in her daydream.*

\*\*\*\*\*\*\*\*

I've left the yacht. Now in his helicopter. Just landing on the roof of the building. A private lift takes us straight down to his penthouse. The whole wall of the living room was glass. I'm now staring out across the River Thames. Is he going to invite me to move in with him, so I could have this view all day. Yes, I can hear my lover, but I don't understand:

"Do I want the property details?"

What's he asking?

*******

"Sorry, I was saying I can send you the property details on pdf, or just send you some links."

"My turn to say *sorry*. I was back in dreamland. Yes, you're right. The *River View* makes the flat. I think I'd like a slice of that."

*We finished our wine. I offered Cindy a second glass, but I could tell she was fidgety, so I suggested moving to the spare bedroom, which I'd prepped for the occasion. We'd talked about BDSM and she was adamant that she wasn't into pain. She was happy to do something with me, whipping and stuff, but she told me outright:*

"I'll be the judge of how hard the punishment. I like to take control and dominate but that means I decide how severe. So, I'm telling you, from the off, that I won't hurt you, even if you beg."

"Do you say that to all your clients?"

"Vishti, if we can be serious for a moment: I'm playing. I'm into titillation. I may be OK with some weird shit. But I tell you now, anything that looks like serious damage and I'll run a mile. It's not me. It's not fun, and, if you go too far, it might spoil the evening."

"Noted. Fun. No serious pain. But I did have a little surprise for you. Do you trust me?"

"Yes."

"Seriously?"

"You're making me nervous."

"Don't be. There's nothing that you don't like, but if for any reason you want to stop…"

"Say RED. Yes, I know."

*We were in the spare room. Cindy had mentioned before that she'd let her boyfriend tie her up and she was OK with that.*

*She basically wanted to stay in control but would let someone she trusted take over for a while. I thought I'd test her on that. I asked her to close her eyes. I tied a silk scarf around them. Made sure she was comfortable. I was going to be very gentle.*

*I'd done the prep work and it would be a shame if RED spoiled the evening. I started to undress her. I guess she knew she was going to end up naked, as there was no fumbling over clasps and zips.*

*Her clothes were easy to slip off. No bra or panties. I held her while I sat her on the bed. I lay her back gently. I'd put some restraints under the mattress, with Velcro cuffs for her hands and feet. I kept them fairly loose. If she wanted, she could easily struggle free.*

*I had listened to her. It's a game. She would feel restrained but never in jeopardy. I started to tickle her with a feather tickler and then took out my whip, again very gently drawing it over her body. I whipped the bed hard so she could feel its strength, but then, when I lashed her body, the strokes were very mild, merely a tickle. It was all about expectation.*

*I was keen to ask her if she was alright, but silence was necessary to keep the mood. I just laced the whip's lashes over her pubic area, allowing the lashes to settle over her mons. I drew the whip up over her vulva. I sensed a change in her breathing. I was confident that Cindy was relaxed and ready. I knelt on the bed, spread her thighs a little more and started to open her labial lips. This was the moment. Now or never.*

*I buried my head between her legs and started to lick her clitoris. First a circular motion, then sucking slightly, then alternating the circling with the sucking. Her breathing was getting deeper. I'd never made her come; she had always had to finish herself off. Her breathing was getting deeper and faster. I felt it was going to happen this time. I kept up the motion. I could feel her reacting to my tongue. She seemed to be getting excited, but it was taking longer than I'd expected.*

*In my mind, I pictured Daphne, and how she recoiled whenever I mentioned oral pleasure. Everything I was doing had come from the Kama Sutra, other texts, and some popular guides. So far this had been an academic exercise. This was the first time I'd put it into practice.*

*I persisted. Cindy's breathing was getting deeper. Then, as I thought she was coming, the moment seemed to slip away. I wondered if she was actually stopping herself from coming, because she was enjoying it so much, or had my tongue strayed away from the right spot. I wanted to ask but knew that would kill everything. I had read that it could take anything from 2 minutes to 30 minutes. Not terribly helpful. I wanted to stop for breath, then I heard Cindy crying out.*

"I'm gonna come! I'm gonna come! I'm coming! I'm coming! Don't stop!"

*Her back arched in an orgasmic spasm.*

"Don't stop! Don't stop!"

*I kept licking and sucking. She managed to break a hand free and she pushed my head away while continuing to tell me not to stop. Her body kept jerking. I'd read that for some women, the orgasm would be one explosion whilst, for others, there could be a series of contractions. Cindy went through three, four quite powerful spasms. I carried on until she physically pulled back to separate my head from her pubic area.*

*I moved away gently, then lay beside her. She sensed my body and her intuition struck, she knew I was about to ask her how it was, so she mouthed softly.*

"Don't say anything. Just lie still."

*I was quite pleased with myself. I'd seen her come when she played with herself. I'd seen her have a great orgasm with her vibrator, but this was something else. Although I was still paying her for this evening, this felt like lovers. The way she responded to me, letting me take control, and the quality of her orgasm. I could sense how much she had enjoyed the experience. Now she was satiated.*

*Since I met Cindy on that first day, when I tentatively crossed the threshold of* the blue door, *it had been my goal, my mission, to completely satisfy her sexually. Something that I had been denied by Daphne. So, I had chosen Cindy or Cindy had chosen me, or the gods had simply done their thing to bring us together.*

*We lay there for about twenty minutes, and she suddenly came to life. She had removed the blindfold and restraints.*

"Sorry, I got a bit carried away. That was… simply… simply… er… simply… oh, fuck! Just lie on your back… it's your turn."

*And with that, she took my erection into her mouth, took her mouth out again and proceeded to lick the length of my penis in several strokes, then took me again into her mouth, deeper, until my glans was pressing against her tonsils. I don't know how she didn't gag but the sensation was incredible.*

*The adrenaline flowing. I'm sitting in my Merc, on the motorway, my foot down, hitting past 70 mph. I'm accelerating to 80, 90 past the ton. The exhilaration! I felt I was coming already.*

*Then the foot is off the accelerator. Cindy had slowed me down. She was licking my glans. Just like she used her grip, to stop me coming when she was masturbating me with her hand, so she had a technique to keep me going, when she was sucking my penis.*

Back on the accelerator again, past 70, 80, over 100, 110…

"Now!"

*Then off the pedal. Licking my glans. No words were spoken. But the message was clear:*

"You come when I think you're ready."

*I'd read about edging. The technique of bringing you to the edge, but holding it off, repeating the process. Now she was off again, only this time we were up over 120 mph.*

*I'm approaching the car in front, in the fast lane, I have to swerve inside to avoid him. I'm charged, I'm supercharged. Cindy's my passenger, head in my lap, mouth on my cock, foot on the accelerator, I'm reaching top speed, 140 mph, faster, faster approaching the climax. Another car in front, no time to stop, a huge crash an explosion of ecstasy, as I come.*

*I had ejaculated inside her mouth, and I could feel her swallow my semen. She wanted to keep my penis in her mouth as it became flaccid, but I wriggled it free. I lay on my back and just muttered:*

"Wow!"

*We didn't say much after that. We both knew what the time was, and I was determined to respect Cindy's self-imposed curfew.*

********

*It was a silent drive, just a few minutes to the underground station. As she got out of my car, she gave me her* trademark smile *and blew me a kiss.*

*All I could think to say was:*

"*Rightmove!* I'll send you the links."

# 9

# The Prime of Miss Jean Brodie

Dixie was more settled and looking forward to getting back to College for the new term. We'd already moved out of our shared dorm room at the end of last term. Dixie spent the hols with her parents. I crashed at June's, so I had a buddy for travelling to work.

We were about to trade up and move into a new flat along the Upper Riverside. It wasn't that near the College but had a nice view of the Thames, a pool and a gym. Plus, we would now each have our own bedroom. It was going to cost around £600 a week, but I would soon be pulling down almost four grand a week, all cash in hand. I could pay for the whole thing myself. Dixie insisted on paying her share, which she couldn't afford. So, I suggested she pay me the same as she was paying last term. When she complained that wasn't enough, I suggested she cover the heating bill and that would be quits. We were quite excited to be moving to the new place. For the first time, my side-hustle, which was originally just to help me through college, was now having a positive impact on my lifestyle.

The four grand would come from upping to four days a week. Actually, with my creative extra services, plus tips, and Fi always upping my prices, I could top £1,200 on a good day.

Fi was a bit desperate, as one of her long-time girls had left. I didn't know if there had been a falling out. Some of the girls thought it meant more clients for them, while others said that the girl would be taking her clients with her. Whatever the truth, Fi was urging me to do a fourth day. I baulked at first, told her it was impossible with my studies. She told me that I'd get an extra 10% on top of the 50% on anything I took on the fourth day. I countered with 60% across the board. She said I must be joking, and she wasn't that desperate but offered me an *override* of 10% if I introduced a new girl. I didn't understand the concept of an *override*, so she broke it down. For the first year, the new girl, my intro, would sort of be under my wing. I'd train her, show her the ropes (if you'll excuse the pun) and give her some of those upselling tips that had worked so well for me. The girl would get 40%, at first, Fi would still get her 50%, leaving me with the other 10%. After twelve months, I'd have broken her in - an unfortunate expression - and my 10% would then end up in the girl's pocket instead.

It all made sense to Fi, who, of course, was using me as a free recruitment service.

I took the deal. Probably, if I had thought it through, I would have argued for the 10% to last beyond a year, with Fi actually reducing her cut. As I didn't have anyone in mind to introduce to Fi, it didn't seem that important. I did make a mental note to ask June whether she'd ever been comped for recommending me in the first place.

I was still nominally on the Psych course but knew that giving up the side hustle was going to be difficult. I was now earning more than the lecturers and probably more than the Principal. It gave me quite a kick to know that. The Principal, a dour Scots lady, was dubbed Miss Brodie, after the Maggie Smith character in the film from the seventies about this Scottish school teacher. We'd seen it at the College film night. After we'd watched the film, we ran through the corridors giggling like schoolgirls and shouting the Maggie Smith line: *I'm in my Prime*, imitating our Principal's Highland drawl.

Miss Brodie wasn't my favourite person. I was called into her office once for a dressing down when, apparently, I had groped a male student in the corridor outside our dorm room. I had no recollection of the incident. He was supposed to have found me, sitting on the floor completely out of it. When Dixie opened the door, so I was told afterwards, he asked her who Cindy was, commenting that I kept groping his crotch and saying: *Let Cindy have a look. Cindy will mend that for you.*

Dixie was worried about me having a meltdown. The following day she suggested therapy. As I couldn't remember anything about the previous evening, I gave her a rather flippant reply:

"It's that bloke that needs therapy. People normally pay me for that, and, instead of thanking me, he's gone and complained to Miss Brodie."

When the Principal gave me my ticking off, she commented that if it had been the other way around, the male student would be immediately suspended and possibly reported to the police. I looked at her and was about to tell her that didn't seem fair. They always claim they're *an equal opportunities College.*

Then I thought: *Don't push your luck.*

Dixie wanted a de-brief, so I told her about how Brodie would have treated a man more harshly than a woman.

"I should hope so too."

"But don't you think it's double standards? I basically got a rap on the knuckles, and a warning about the epidemic of drinks being spiked."

"And that was it?"

"No, not quite. I've got a mandatory with the College Counsellor, and I'm on probation till the end of term."

Dixie nodded in approval.

"To be honest, the only thing that bothered me was when you told me about Cindy. You know that's my work moniker, right? If people around College knew about my sideline, I would just die."

"Just go easy on the alcohol, girlfriend, or give up the day job."

The trouble was, I was actually enjoying the job. I wanted the fourth day and got a kick out of negotiating with Fi. I would have taken the fourth day on the same 50/50 deal.

All seemed to be going well, when, out of the blue, I got a call from the estate agent, who asked me if I could come to his office immediately. Apparently, I'd failed the credit check. I was a bit worried when they asked me for a P60 from my employer, bank statements, and wage slips. I was rather naïve. I told him just to put the credit check through as normal, as I've never had a bad debt. I didn't realise that not having any debt was a bad thing because there was no evidence that I could pay my way. The student loan didn't count either way because there were no payments until after I graduated.

When I walked into the estate agent's office, I explained that I was a student working part-time in a bar, and they didn't have wage slips. Again, completely naïve. I just assumed they'd take my word for it that I could find £600 a week. What, from bar tips?

He nearly fell off his chair when I told him I'd pay 6 months' rent upfront. He looked at me weirdly with:

"I hope you're not intending to pay in cash. We have very strict anti-money laundering protocols in place now."

I'd mouthed an immediate response, in my best posh voice:

"Oh, Gawd no! I'll just ask Daahddy."

As soon as I left his office, I called June to see how she launders her cash.

I chose not to involve Dixie, as I didn't want her to know that there might be a hitch with the flat. It turned out that June wasn't in my league. She managed to spend most of her cash in dress shops that didn't seem to know about money laundering protocols. She gave herself a decent clothes budget of £500 a month and paid cash for her holidays. The few hundred she had left, at the end of the month, the bank could accommodate without any suspicion.

I'd saved a hundred grand, kept in newly minted £50 notes, which I collected every week from the bank in exchange for the random notes from my clients. I kept it stuffed in envelopes in my knicker drawer back in the dorm. I then took the cash across the road to another bank to put it in the bank's safety deposit box. I felt grown up. Just coming up to my 21st birthday and I had my own deposit box. I was escorted down to the vault by a handsome young man who always seemed to be on duty whenever I came by for my weekly visit:

*Just picking up some jewellery for a party*

or

*Granny just gave me a lovely brooch and Mummy said I had to keep it somewhere safe.*

I'm not sure if he believed that twaddle. We would go downstairs. He would usher me into the vault. We each had a key to unlock my cubby hole. Both keys were required, simultaneously. He would take out the metal deed box, then lead me to an anteroom, put the box on a table, and then leave me in private, while he waited outside. When I'd finished, I buzzed for him to escort me back upstairs.

One day, we were alone, waiting for another customer to finish. We were outside the vault. While we were waiting, I looked at him, wondered what he would be like in bed and decided I'd like to fuck him. I wanted to impress him, so I just blurted out:

*Actually, they're not the family jewels. I've just made over £100,000 as an erotic masseuse. If you invite me back to your place, I'm going to fuck you like you've never been fucked before!*

Of course, what I actually said was:

*Do you get a lot of people my age coming here for their deposit boxes?*

He rather nonchalantly replied:

*To be honest, quite a few, but mostly Chinese students from Greenwich College. Do you know the place, not far from here?*

Fortunately, the door buzzed. An elderly lady was then escorted out of the room by another young man in his pin-stripe suit. I was just thankful that it wasn't Maisy Cheng from the Psycho-pathology study group. I would have died.

I made a mental note to check the class schedule to make sure there was no risk of bumping into any classmates down in the vaults.

I realised that, for all my street smarts, changing the cash in one bank and opening the deposit box in another served no useful purpose. I was utterly clueless as to how I was going to launder the money. I did know it was illegal, and anyone helping me could get into serious trouble.

I didn't even know who to ask for help. I had plenty of clients who were in finance and talked a good game about currency swaps and share deals. I think they were trying to impress me, even though it left me cold. How could I ask them? I sort of trusted them, because I had a secret that they wouldn't want to be revealed. Or maybe they didn't give a shit if their boss knew they frequented tantric massage parlours. No, I couldn't trust them at all.

There was, however, one client that I did trust. But was I ready to ask him for advice?

# 10
## AML

It was his idea in the first place. The fucking Rightmove links. I knew I should have stuck with something more down-market. They wouldn't have been so fussy about references and all that shit. I had no idea if he could help. He talked a good game about property, but other than his swanky flat, and a few quirky sex habits, I knew nothing about him. I thought he was weird when we first met. Shy, wouldn't even come into the salon.

But after visiting his flat... where did that come from? He told me he learnt the whole technique from books. No one had ever pleasured me like that. Even my trusty vibrator never got close. I once screwed a personal trainer who worked for David Lloyd. He got me close to a vaginal orgasm. He seemed to touch my G-spot, but he came before I got there, and I had to finish myself off.

I now had to admit that the best orgasm of my life had come from a client who paid me for sex. How weird was that?

Back to reality. I didn't even know how to approach him.

I couldn't ask him during a session, but, on the other hand, my rule, Cindy's First Rule: *Separation of Church and State. Don't mix business with pleasure.* How did that work out for you at Vishti's flat, eh, Cindy?

So, I was pondering how to approach Vishti without breaching my stupid rules, when a WhatsApp popped up. I'd given him my phone number when we arranged the outcall appointment at his flat, so he'd be able to get hold of me, just in case he was running late or something.

*Hi, any chance of a longer session, at a hotel? Maybe dinner first?*

~~*Hotel Ok, BUT I DON'T DO DATES!!!!*~~

*Hotel OK, but I don't do dates.*

I deleted the first message. On reflection, there was no need for the exclamation marks, and the capital letters were OTT. They are *my* stupid rules, not his.

I couldn't believe I wrote that. I wanted to pick his brains on the money laundering and here I was, blowing him off. I was running on adrenaline.

*Him: Not a date, I just want to have a chat first. Time to talk over a meal or a drink. Like normal people.*

I didn't reply. I needed to think it through. Cindy's rule: *Don't date clients* and whatever he was saying, this felt like a date.

*Me: Talk about what?*

*Him: I don't know. You choose.*

*Me: My new flat. I followed your advice, but I think I'm digging a hole for myself.*

*Him: Tell me more.*

*Me: ~~NO. THAT'S WHAT WE'RE GOING TO TALK ABOUT OVER A MEAL OR A DRINK!~~*

*Me: No, that's what we're going to talk about over a meal or a drink.*

I hate all this messaging. No nuance. And, when I try nuance, I seem to fuck it up. Dixie uses emojis. Well, I also use emojis on social, but I don't think it's professional. This is business not social, so no emojis.

Should that be Cindy's third rule? *No emojis on DM's with clients.*

I couldn't believe that I was having a conversation with myself over whether or not to use emojis when messaging clients. *Get a grip, Cindy!*

I was getting fed up. I don't like texting and I had hoped, by putting everything in capital letters, that he'd understand. I hadn't noticed that he'd blue-ticked the message, so he read the one with capital letters before I could delete it. But he did seem to understand my attempt at nuance.

*Him: Sorry, just give me a time, date, and rough location and I'll find a place.*

*Me: OK, I'll get back to you later.*

I signed off with a smiley face, but it could equally have been a growl.

Just broken Cindy's third rule, before it even made the cut!

My '*later*' ended up being around 11 pm. I was working and could have texted between clients, but I thought: *Let the bugger wait.*

*Me: I'm free Tuesday afternoon. From 2-6. You pick the place as long as it's fairly central and close to an underground station.*

No blue tick meant: *Delivered not read.* Maybe I'd blown it. Should have gone back sooner. Maybe he's gone to bed.

It was about 3 pm the next day when he sent me the details of a hotel near Kings Cross. He said he'd got *day use.* I didn't understand what he meant, but it turned out that some hotels rent out rooms during the day. Not knocking shops. Proper hotels, where people are coming to London for conferences and things, not staying overnight, but want rooms to freshen up or hold small meetings. It was all new to me, but I googled the St. Pancras Renaissance and it looked nice and smart. Had a pool as well, not that I'd be using that. Should have realised: Posh Boy wouldn't go cheap on me. I confirmed the time and date. I mean the time and the *day.* Definitely not a *date.*

I was quite excited. It could be fun. But I had a nagging feeling. I didn't want to lead him on. I kept saying to myself - *keep it professional.*

Shit! We hadn't even talked money. Did he think this was a freebie? Now I was screwed. I'd confirmed already. I couldn't go back and start negotiating. That would be so cheap, more like a whore. Sod it! Follow your instincts and go for broke.

I sent him a short WhatsApp.

*Me: Thinking again about Tuesday. Not comfortable. Too much like a date. Can we just stick to the salon?*

He replied with a sad face. I just hate this emoji shit. Grow a pair!

Hold your nerve girl. Whoever messages next loses. I gave him 24 hours. Again, I thought I'd blown it. Then it came:

*Him: I didn't mention the fee. My bad. I thought four hours £300. How does that sound?*

If he wanted me for two hours at Fi's, it would cost him at least £300 maybe more, but then, I'd only see half of that. He'd be paying for the hotel on top. Anyway, it wasn't the money. It was the principle, and I'd just won that round.

*Me: Sounds good to me! Look forward to seeing you at the hotel Tuesday at 2 pm. I'll DM you when I'm in the lobby.*

Got back a smiley face. *Grrrr!*

*******

Tuesday couldn't come soon enough. Because I couldn't pass their stupid reference check, the estate agent had come back with a requirement to pay the rent upfront for the full 12 months of the lease, which was £32,000. The agent nearly fell off his seat when I wanted to give him the holding deposit in cash. That was a lousy £600. He'd probably have a heart attack if I tried to hand him £32,000 in readies, even if they were in newly minted fifties. I needed to sort this out within the next 7 days, or I could lose the flat. I had no idea how long it would take to launder £32,000. All I knew was that it was illegal, and I could go to jail, and anyone who helped me could go to jail.

I had to wonder what the fuck I was doing. But I also had to work out how to ask Vishti for advice without crossing over my self-imposed boundaries on the masseuse/client relationship. It seemed a lot to do, and I hadn't even worked out whether to start with the bedroom session, get sucked off by what had turned out to be the best cunny merchant around or leave the sex until I had propositioned Vishti to risk jail for me.

Hmm, difficult choice!

*******

Vishti was waiting for me on the steps at the entrance to the hotel. I was quite nervous. I realised that I hadn't really prepared the ground. I hadn't rehearsed the scene. I heard a voice inside my head. It was my voice, or rather it was Rachel's voice speaking to Cindy: *Get your act together, girlfriend. Oh and by the way, don't do this to me again. Next time I want you to prep for the scene.*

He led me through the hotel lobby up some stairs to the cocktail bar. I was feeling giddy with apprehension.

"So, tell me about the flat. It sounds exciting."

Now we were sitting down. Vishti was drinking gin. I stuck with mineral water. I needed a clear head. I had realised this was the biggest deal of what might turn out to be the very short business career of Rachel Levinson aka Cindy.

I still didn't know how to approach the topic, so I changed the subject.

"I normally drink G&T, but it's during the day. Don't want you to think I'm a lush."

Then we had a random chat about gin, martini cocktails and shit.

"Oh, so the dirty martini is just, like, with added salt water?"

"Well, the brine, from the olive jar, yes… Cindy, what's the matter?"

"What do you mean?"

"Something's wrong. You keep smiling at me, but it's not your *trademark smile*. It's sort of a nervous smile. We don't have to do this if you don't want to. I mean go up to the room. We can just sit and talk. Don't worry, I won't ask for a refund."

He was trying to crack a joke. Not bad for him. I finally thought I'd better get it out.

"No, it's not that. Actually, it's about the flat. It's become a nightmare."

"Why?"

"Well, I can afford the flat, but you know where my money comes from. It's all cash and my credit is shit and I need to launder £32,000."

I looked at the expression on Vishti's face. He thought we were going to have a quiet chat about the gym and the *River View*, and I dumped that on him.

"Err, have you heard of the Sanctions and Anti-Money Laundering Act 2018? We call it *AML* for short. The last time I looked at that, you could be liable for 5 years in jail, but it's worse than that. If I were still a registered financial adviser, I would now be liable to report this conversation to the authorities or risk going to jail."

The last time I was in handcuffs, I was blindfolded while Vishti sucked my cunt. This time the handcuffs were more likely to be from the Metropolitan Police, and I was going to get well and truly fucked!

"Look, I didn't mean I was going to do it. I can cancel the contract. I think I put down £600 holding deposit, which might go down the Swanny."

"Don't be so hasty. Let me know exactly what you need and how much you've got."

I realised it was all or nothing. The first rule to break was actually telling Vishti who I was.

"My name is Rachel Levinson. I'd prefer it if you kept calling me by my working name when we're… you know, in the massage sessions, bedroom et cetera."

"Alright by me. Would you mind telling me your real age?"

"Twenty, but as far as work is concerned, I'm twenty-three. Same with my college friends. Oh, I'm a second-year Psychology student at Greenwich College. The College knows my real age, of course. I bank with HSBC. I've probably got a couple of thousand in a current account, and maybe five hundred in a savings account. I have £100,000 plus change in a safety deposit box with MetroBank. No credit cards, just a debit card with each of my banks. That's the sum total of Rachel Levinson's assets. Maybe some premium bonds."

"Parents?"

"Mum, Jewish, lives with a Catholic stepdad."

I don't know why I said that.

"I didn't have a Jewish upbringing. I don't feel Jewish but don't want to deny…"

"Those aren't the details. Not that I'm not interested, but to solve the problem, is there any way you could look to them?"

"No, they're out of the picture. Even if they could help, how can I ask them to lend me money for an apartment that I can't afford."

"But you can afford it."

"So, what am I supposed to tell them? That I earn four thousand pounds a week in a massage parlour while pretending to read for a Psychology degree?"

"OK, parents are out. I've a fairly simple solution that breaks no laws."

My eyes lit up.

Vishti told me he was ready to guarantee the lease, but that would surely break all my stupid rules. I told him that, while I appreciated his offer, I couldn't possibly be beholden to him. It just didn't feel right.

"So, let's make it a business transaction. You said you've got the cash. We draw up a legal agreement. You simply give me control of the cash. I guarantee the lease. As long as you pay the rent, there's no problem. If you stop paying the rent, and the landlord calls my guarantee, then I can use the cash to cover the money I have to pay to the landlord."

I was a bit nervous. I got the general principle, but I didn't understand how the legalities would work. It seemed that I would need to place a lot of trust in Vishti. Could he pull a fast one on me?

"If we have solicitors and so on, don't they need to know where the money comes from?"

"It can be much easier than that. You said you have the money in MetroBank, in a safety deposit box. I open up a box there in my name. You put in the £32,000 or whatever the value of the guarantee is. We then have a one-page document that says I will guarantee your lease. As soon as my guarantee is no longer needed, I go to the bank, give you signing rights over my box, and you go in and take the money. Other than us, no one needs to know what's in the box. If you want, I can give you my details now, so that your Agent can run credit checks on me. As soon as that is OK-ed, we'll write the paperwork and go to Metro to sort the boxes."

"That sounds great, but I'm still reluctant to accept. It seems like a huge favour. I don't want to end up working it off in massages."

"Don't be silly. This will be completely separate. To make it commercial, I'll charge you for the guarantee. What's reasonable, 2%? Works out at £640, renewable every year, for as long as you're in the flat. Not bad for a day's work. Would you be open to paying an extra £640? It's like an extra week's rent."

"OK, let's do it. Shall we shake hands on the deal?"

"I've got a better idea, let's go to the room and see if you can make better use of your hands."

Yes, I thought, and maybe you can make better use of your tongue at the same time.

*******

In the hotel bedroom, ever the gentleman, Vishti asked, or rather offered, to pleasure me first.

"You're so sweet, so thoughtful. I'd like to give you a big… come here, Lover!"

With that, I pull him towards me, planting my lips on his. I have to stand on tiptoes, but I want to snog. I almost lift myself off the ground. I want to use my tongue. He kisses me back. I break away.

"Can we sit on the couch? I want to kiss you properly. Just for the next hour, I want to be your lover."

I am kissing him passionately; our tongues are circling each other. I'm not really sure what is happening. Physically, I never really fancied him, but I'm so drawn to him emotionally. He's so kind, thoughtful, and good company. The sex is so much better than those stupid college boys I usually end up with. Just for the next hour, I can pretend that he isn't old enough to be my father. Shit, my stepfather is about 20 years younger than him.

"Vishti, can we make love?"

"I thought we'd already decided that."

"No, I mean can we fuck? Look, when you brought me off before, you gave me the best orgasm I've ever had. Yes, I want that again, but not now. I want you to fuck me. I may not even come like that, but I just want you to hold me in your arms and fuck me. I want to feel you inside me. I want you to take me. I want your spunk to fill my cunt."

I don't know if I'm deliberately trying to excite him with my dirty talk, but something is working. We are now on the bed naked. He is on top of me, and I'm drawing him in. For a control freak, I'm doing pretty well at just submitting to his physical domination. Now he is grinding. I'm just letting him have his way with me. Letting him ride. No clit action, nowhere near my G spot. This isn't physical for me. No fantasy, no billionaire, no super-yacht.

"Fuck me, lover, I just want to feel you deep inside. Hold me tight. Love me, fuck me, love me, come for me, come now..."

As he moves faster and faster, his face is getting redder. He is panting. I think he might be having a heart attack, but he comes with a huge exhaling of his breath, then sort of collapses his hands so that he is kind of lying right on top of me, and I can't move.

We lie still for a few minutes. Then he moves off me.

"Sorry, I'm not sure what came over me. Definitely not tantric."

"Please, no talking. You gave me what I asked for. Exactly what I wanted, really. My pleasure was feeling your pleasure."

"But you didn't come. I know you didn't come. Do you want my tongue?"

"Always, Vishti, your tongue is the best. But just not today. I wanted you as my lover. I had you as my lover. Really, that wasn't just for you, it was for me as well."

"I'm glad you described it like that. I thought the fuck might have just been a thank you for helping out with the lease on your apartment."

"Lucky you were smiling when you said that, otherwise you just might have earned yourself a two-fingered prostate massage without any lube."

# 11

# At the Confessional

Everything is fine. Making more money than I could ever dream of. A good relationship with Fi. Clients were OK, Fi lets me pick and choose.

College, still managing to cope, despite working four days a week at Fi's.

If I came out with third-class honours, it wasn't going to matter much for my career. Certainly, Fi wouldn't be waiting on my final exams.

My social life was OK. Working late four nights a week meant I wasn't the greatest partygoer. Moving to the new flat, away from the campus, meant I'd miss some of the student functions. But, for my social life, I was looking to the gym and the pool in the basement of the apartment building, wondering whether I'd be meeting some City slicker to whisk me off to a desert island. Sounded a better option than a snog and a fumble with a spotty under-grad.

Everything looked good - except for one client. I seemed to be getting more deeply involved. I kept kidding myself that he was simply a client, but we were now having sex on a weekly basis, and, whatever we called it, the sex was preceded usually by lunch and drinks. I wouldn't allow myself to say we were dating, but what else was it? Then, he was married, and he'd made it clear that he had no intention of leaving his wife. But what if he did? I wasn't going to move in with him. He was old enough to be my father, or even, I'd hate to think, my grandfather. I still didn't fancy him physically. Well, not in the sense of some of the college guys I'd dated. But they were only good for two dates and then I got fed up with them. They were so shallow.

There again, with Vishti, we didn't fuck. Well, actually, we had fucked, but we both enjoyed better orgasms orally. We were open about our sex together. We got on over our lunches. He was amusing, charming.

Then there was the financial attachment. How he helped over the flat. Yes, I was still charging him for my services, but that was the only thing left. If I let go of that, I suppose I'd have to call him my boyfriend. I just wasn't ready for that.

We'd talked openly about a sugar-daddy relationship. We both agreed we weren't at that point. Nor did we want to go there. For me, I wouldn't want to be beholden to someone who required my presence just because he was funding my lifestyle.

(Note to Ed. I just re-read that last sentence. I'm not even sure if I meant that. I'm pretty confused. I think Cindy wouldn't mind being beholden, if it meant she could live the high life, but Rachel wouldn't like it. Or is it the other way round. Now I'm really confused. Leave that bit in. One of us doesn't want to be beholden. I guess I'll work it out later.)

So, how could I define this relationship? I kept trying to put him off by telling him that I didn't want any emotional attachment. But clearly, that was bullshit. I *was* emotionally attached.

Friends with benefits? Even that didn't match. I look at my friends. People my age. People I hung out with. Maybe had sex with. They were friends. Vishti was, well, I was happy to call him my favourite client. But if I dropped the client label, what would I call him instead?

I had another benchmark. We never included anyone else. Obviously, I wasn't going to meet his wife. He had not indicated that he had any intention of introducing me to his friends. I was certainly not going to let him meet mine. If I did, how would I introduce him?

I decided that the only way was for it to end. Vishti had already told me that he really wasn't interested in seeing me for a session at Fi's. Nothing to do with the money. He was quite blunt; he'd had many better conventional massages. Apparently, that wasn't my forte. But he balanced that by complementing me as his best sexual partner and, of all his acquaintances, he enjoyed my company the most. I suppose that's flattering, but face it, with that age difference, I was probably just making him feel young again.

So, I made up my mind that the next meeting was to be our last. I would tell him over a drink, and if he still wanted, we'd have a final fling in the hotel room.

We were meeting at the Renaissance. Of all the hotels we'd been to, that was our favourite. If you believe their website, I was approaching one of the trendiest rooftop bars in the whole of London, or maybe just amongst the rooftop bars along that pollution-ridden stretch of highway north of the Marylebone Road. *RoofGarden St. Pancras* is, and again I quote: *a botanical haven and hidden gem of Kings Cross and an all-weather hangout.* I mention the traffic pollution, because, unlike my soon-to-be host and lover for the afternoon, the *RoofGarden St Pancras* is a fraud. One expects a roof to be located on the top of a building, rather than merely perched above the ceiling of the ground floor entrance lobby to the hotel. So no, not to be sitting in a rarified atmosphere a hundred feet above the fray, but rather within sniffing distance of the red buses, the HGVs, and those commuters who'd rather sit in jams than spend £12.50 in congestion charge to take a short cut south of the grid-locked inner circle.

But *hey ho* a *botanical gem*. So what's a bit of carbon monoxide between friends?

********

He was already sitting waiting when I walked into the bar. The potted ferns of this *botanical gem* were now but a mirage, for my attention was focused solely on him.

He was already sitting, waiting, but he had no idea what was in store for him. No idea that I was about to bring our non-dating dating relationship, our non-emotional emotional friendship, to bring this sexual union, *indescribable* in the literal sense of the word, to a sudden halt. But unlike the last time I had something important to say to him, this time I had listened to Rachel, and had prepared my script. I just had to pluck up the Dutch courage.

We ordered drinks. He asked for a dry martini, and I opted for a pink gin. When the drinks arrived, I knocked mine back immediately. I asked him for another.

As I sipped my second drink, he looked a little anxious.

"Are you OK? I haven't seen you drink like that before."

"Well, you haven't seen me when I've been really drunk. I don't think that's a pretty sight."

"Why would you deliberately set out to get drunk?"

"Can we not go there? I don't like your moralising. I get drunk with my friends. That's what friends do. I don't get drunk with you because you're not my friend."

"Where's this coming from? You're not yourself..."

I cut him off and just blurted out that I was ending it. This was the last time that we would meet at a hotel. If he wanted to see me again, he'd have to book to come to Felicity's Tantric Massage.

I was quite relieved. Once I'd got the words out, I was able to relax.

I softened the blow with: "We've still got today, so let's have fun."

He sat there. Didn't say a word. We sat there in silence. I remembered the sales motto that he'd taught me: Whoever speaks next loses.

Don't look him in the face. Or maybe I should, you know, give him, what he likes to call, my *trademark smile*.

The *trademark smile* that I didn't know I had until I met him.

The *trademark smile* that, ever since, I had started to use to beguile.

The *trademark smile* that was to become so important to me.

The *trademark smile* that was to define my life.

The *trademark smile* that would tell my story.

I looked up and was about to smile that *trademark smile*, but he broke first.

"Look, Cindy. You know I respect you. I'll do whatever you want. Whatever you say. Except... I'm not going back to seeing you at Felicity's. We've moved on from there. I won't see you again if that's what you really want, but I'm not going back to the beginning."

I looked down. I couldn't look him in the eye.

"Whatever!"

"Don't *whatever* me. That's not you talking. What's the matter?"

I looked up and rocked back in my seat. Vishti was angry. The whole time I'd known him, he'd never raised his voice. I didn't know his heritage. I'd always assumed Indian. He had that Hindu calmness. Like he meditated every day. This anger scared me. But scared me into action.

"Why are you being mean to me? That's exactly what I didn't want."

Vishti sensed my distress.

"Look, I'm sorry. I didn't mean to upset you. I have a genuine, a real concern for you. Something's the matter. There's something you're not telling me."

"Can I have another drink?"

"No. We're not going down that route. And please don't take this the wrong way. I'm not going to restrain you..."

I had to smile, thinking of another session of being restrained. The last one was with bondage tape all over my body.

"Sorry, poor choice of words. What I was going to say is that I don't want you to leave until I find out what's going on. Inside your head. Please just look at me and listen to what I am going to say. This is serious. This might be life-changing - for you, not for me."

I looked straight at him. I didn't know what was coming next. But I kind of knew that this man:

- who I'd known for, what, 18 months
- who I'd only meet when we had sex, in some shape or form
- who I'd never slept with, I mean not overnight
- who was, and still is, a client, not a friend
- who I'd dated with my stupid non-dating rules

- who was old enough to be my father, my grand… my grand-fa…
- who was posh
- who - fuck - who guaranteed my fucking lease
- who! who! who!

I didn't have a fucking clue who he was, who he was to me!

This fucking idiot who was too scared to ring the bell the first time he visited Felicity's. This inexperienced creep - no, not creep - but sexually inexperienced I don't know what, who read a fucking book and has given me the best orgasms in my five years of sexual adventure. My twelve years of sexual awareness.

This man had the audacity to sit in front of me and tell me he was going to tell me something that was going to change my life. Fuck you! Go fuck that frigid wife. Keep your fucking tongue away from my precious clit. You sanctimonious stupid arrogant S.O.B.

And, and yet I knew deep down that what he was going to say in the next five minutes was going to change my life. No turning back now:

"Go on, Sunshine, give me your best shot!"

"OK. Here goes. Please wait till I finish…"

Vishti hesitated, as though he didn't know how to begin, but once he started, it was as though he'd planned this speech from the day we'd first met.

"I don't know much about your background, your family life. You've told me very little. But I know there was damage."

I moved to get up.

"No, please sit. We have to do this. I had to wonder why a twenty-something attractive young woman would go into the sex trade."

I was going to object.

"Yes, I know it's tantric massage and all that. Not prostitution, but face it, there is a sexual element to your job."

I nodded sheepishly but still didn't know where he was going with this.

"Of course, the money. The money's good, struggling student and all that. Shit, you're earning more than I am with your tax-free cash."

We shared a smile.

"But it's more than the money. Your job, if I've got my sums right, involves holding 30 male members a week, and providing 30 orgasms. Probably more, since Felicity's website advertises double pleasure on your menu for a two-hour ritual massage.

Another shared laugh.

Your job involves controlling men. You hold them, quite literally, in your hands, and, at that moment, decide: "Shall I? Shan't I? To come or not to come."

"That is the question," I quipped.

Another shared laugh.

"Don't think I'd keep many clients if I couldn't give them a happy ending."

I was feeling more relaxed but was still waiting, in trepidation, for the moment that I knew was coming.

"Back to your family. Something, something in your background, in your childhood maybe, has left you wanting, no, needing, to control men. Someone, a man, has made you hate men. No sorry, that's not true. What I should say, is that you transfer your hate for that person to your clients. Not while you're doing a massage, but, just at that moment when you're bringing them to orgasm. You are thinking to yourself that you are in control. You're not that little girl anymore that had to give in, to put up with …."

Shit! The bastard hit the button.

Tears were welling. Vishti could see my distress. I think I was visibly shaking. He grabbed me, almost manhandled me, and was half dragging me to the lift. I don't know how I got there, but my next memory was Vishti sitting me down in the chair in the hotel bedroom. He was perched on the bed opposite.

"I'm really, really sorry. But we've got to get through this. I needed you somewhere private. Please, please trust me. I'm not going to hurt you, but you have to get this out. Who was he?"

Finally, 12 years of hidden emotion, 12 years of bottled-up feelings, came rushing out. I was almost screaming but, at the same time, I couldn't mouth the words.

"Grand-g-g… grand-dad…"

I was an emotional wreck. He picked me up gently to move me out of the chair and sat me on his lap. And I just screamed: "NOT YOUR LAP!"

He quickly adjusted me back on the chair with him kneeling in front of me, holding my hands.

"When did it start?"

I was calmer, still sobbing, but able to get the words out.

"I don't know. My first clear memory was when I was eight. But I'm sure it was going on before, just that I didn't understand what it was. I have a clear memory of sitting on his lap."

"Yes, sorry about that. It was so stupid of me."

"You weren't to know. Well, on his lap. That's why I'm sure it had been going on for some years before because he would bounce me on his knee. But this time, I could clearly feel his erection. Of course, I didn't know what it was or what he was doing, but I remember fidgeting, telling him something was sticking up my bottom. I mean he wasn't penetrating me or anything. Just his cock prodding me as he bounced me up and down. And then he whispered: *Shall I show you what a clever girl you are? I can show you how you can make that hard thing go soft."*

A fucking eight-year-old! I went on to describe to Vishti how he got me to put my hand on his cock, first over his trousers, and then to unzip his fly. All this time, he knew he was safe. Mum was at work. She'd split from Dad, and Granddad would pick me up from school and take me home for tea. His fly unzipped, and with reassurances that ice cream would follow, as soon as I made his stick - he called it his stick - as soon as I made his stick go soft. The ice cream wasn't a metaphor, there was ice cream for dessert after tea. Or, maybe, it was a crude metaphor, a little joke to himself, that soon there would be cream on the menu. So, he showed me, he actually showed me, how to masturbate him. Fucking hell! He could have got a job as a trainer at Felicity's. Bloody better than the training I got there.

Vishti held me tight. We shared a smile. Things were getting much easier now I'd started my confession.

"Please go on. Believe me, this will help you. You brought him to orgasm?"

"Yes, of course, it was messy, and I knew it was wrong. Well, I'm not actually sure that I did know. But, fuck, yes, Christ, fucking hell!"

"What! Are you OK?"

I suddenly had a flash. A memory that had been buried so deep that I had completely obliterated it from my subconscious mind. Buried so deep because it was so vile.

"It was the fucking ice cream. I had completely forgotten. When he came, his spunk was on my hand, and he told me to lick up the salty ice cream first and then I could have the strawberry ice cream on the table. Can you believe the motherfucker?"

"If there's anything else, now's a good time to get it out. The more you can tell now, the better later, believe me."

I went on to describe the many sessions that we had. Never sex. Just me tossing him off. Vishti asked me when it stopped. That was a very clear memory.

"As I got older, I was able to make more excuses, and, as soon as I was going to senior school, aged what, eleven or so, I'd be going to school on my own, so no need for granddad to babysit. I realised that it was coming to an end. It had become a routine. If he picked me up from school, I knew it was going to happen. I guessed he had groomed me to accept it as, well, not exactly normal, but, you know, the way it was. Our secret, that kind of thing. So, not sure, eleven or twelve I suppose, but he knew I was due to change schools, so this was probably going to be the last time. By then, I was no longer sitting on his lap. The evil bastard had trained me like a circus monkey. I'd kneel down on the floor and unzip his fly. No, sorry, I forgot. The circus monkey was trained, once she came home, to go straight to the bathroom, get some toilet paper and Vaseline - can you believe, the chutzpah - my mother's word, it's Yiddish, meaning the absolute cheek - he had the audacity to get me to prep for his sordid session. So, I came down with the tissues and Vaseline and he said there was no need for that today. I had no idea what he had in mind, even when he told me that today's treat would be licking his lollipop."

"Are you sure you're OK to go on?"

"Yes, I've gone this far. Up until now, the worst was that I found it all a bit messy, but I'd got to an age when pre-pubescent girls would talk about willies and stuff. My guilty secret was actually making me feel grown up, so although I was being abused, he hadn't actually forced me to do anything. But that day was different. I didn't want to suck his cock, but he wasn't going to let me off the hook.

First licking and then, when I pulled away, he thrust his penis down my throat. I was gagging and he was fucking my mouth. He started shouting, calling me a whore and telling me to make him come. He'd never done that before. It was like he knew it was the last hurrah and he was going to get his perverted way. I tasted his spunk as he came, and I was coughing and spluttering. He let go and I puked on the carpet. He showed no remorse. He just said that I'd better clear that up before Mum came home and, if I breathed a word to her, he'd tell social services that I came on to him and I'd end up being taken away from Mum and put in care or in a foster home."

I stopped speaking. There were still tears on my face. Vishti, who had been kneeling all this time, got up, picked me up from the chair, cradled me like a baby, lay me on the bed. I was emotionally drained. Crashed out.

My next memory was being gently stroked on my arm.

"I'm really sorry to wake you, but I've only got the room till five o'clock. I'm really sorry, I wanted you to sleep."

"How long have I been out for?"

"A couple of hours."

"Must have been the gin," I quipped.

We both knew what had really knocked me out.

"Will you do me a favour? Well, do yourself a favour?"

I smiled.

"That's great, the *trademark smile* hasn't left you."

"Go on, but I think I know what you're going to say."

"You're the psych student. I'm not even an amateur shrink. I didn't know what on earth I was doing, I just knew you needed catharsis. You needed to get it out. But you should still consider counselling."

"I knew you were going to say that. Don't you think you just did the job for me? I couldn't open up to a shrink. I think I'm OK now."

"I'll pay."

"Fuck off. How dare you. I don't need your money."

"Hey, hey, sorry. Look, I am just concerned for your welfare."

I suddenly realised that I was no further on with the whole purpose of today - cutting Vishti out of my life because of my confused emotions.

"Wait a moment. Where are we?"

"What do you mean?"

"I mean where are *we*? You and I? I gave you an ultimatum, remember?"

"Yes, I remember clearly. And here's where we're at. I don't accept your terms."

"You what – what the fuck!"

"Listen to me. I don't accept the terms as you set them out. But here are my terms for our ongoing relationship. Firstly, I want to thank you. Thank you for what you have taught me. You have helped me through my own crisis. You have shown me sexual fulfilment. Now that I've seen how wonderful sex can be, I don't think you can just tell me to stop,"

"No… don't do this."

"Hear me out. I will always be grateful to you. I'm very fond of you, and I want to - no, firmer than that - I *will* continue to see you. But - and here's the change - no more sex. I'll see you for lunch and a drink as often as works for both of us. And no, it won't be a date. And no, as of today, I am no longer a client. But I will be there - for you. To help and guide - if you want me to. To advise - if you need it. To be a shoulder to cry on, for example, if you split up with a boyfriend. Like it or not, I will be there for you. I'll be there for everything. Everything but sex. Feeling horny, use your vibrator. Want a shag, look for the nearest hunk. Oral pleasure? Probably suggest a female lover. You've already told me that most men suck at it, if you'll excuse the pun. You said we weren't friends, maybe not before, but we are now. You said you wouldn't know how you'd introduce me to your friends. I don't know. Try: *an old family friend* or *a distant uncle*. I really don't care."

"Cindy or Rachel?"

"What would you prefer?"

"My friends call me Rache."

"Rache it is, then."

We were holding hands. He let go of my hand as I started walking down the stairs from the hotel entrance to the pavement.

"So, what do I call you?"

"I like being called Vishti. That's my name, that's what my friends call me. But my close family, just my immediate family still use my childhood name, Vish."

"So, Vish it is, then."

With that, I skipped down the stairs until I was standing on the pavement before half-turning to sort of give him a girlie wave goodbye. I took about three steps then turned around and ran back up the steps. He was still standing there. I put my hands around his neck. Looked at him and planted a kiss on his lips. No tongue. And then, my parting shot:

"Will you do me a favour? Don't waste that tongue. There are too many women out there needing your skills."

"Will you introduce me to some?"

"You are kidding, right?"

And with that, we smiled a last smile as I skipped down the stairs again.

In my head, the words of Martin Luther King were ringing:

"Free at last! Free at last! Thank Vish almighty, I'm free at last!

# PART II

# 12
## Free at last?

"Fi, I just need some time off."

"I understand, love, but I'm running a business, so I need to know how much time you need."

"I don't know, a week maybe."

"It's just that I've got to do the rotas for the girls."

"Yes, I know, but I'm not sure."

"Look, love, it's none of my business, but could you just give me an idea?"

"I said it's personal. Family. You shouldn't be asking."

"Sorry, love, but is it like a procedure?"

"What? Fuck, no! I'm not pregnant."

"Sorry, but look, let me be frank. If it's a week, that's not a problem, but if it's indefinite, then I'll have to bring someone else in to cover. You know that you're my best earner and I wouldn't want to lose you. But, if you're not going to be here, you don't earn me anything."

"What do you want me to say? OK, this is what you'll do. Book me out for a week. But I'll call you Wednesday, and then I'll give you a definite time frame."

I was glad to get that over with. It had been two days since my *epiphany* with Vish. I skipped work the next day. I didn't know if I could face going back. If Vish was right, the whole reason I was doing this job is because of my past abuse. But, if I was cured, did that mean I wouldn't be able to do it anymore? I was feeling alright otherwise, but totally confused about work. Of course, there was only one person I could speak to. I picked up the phone. I'd never actually called Vish before. Only DM. There was once when I was running late for a meet, but he was expecting me. I was a bit nervous about whether it was appropriate, but I didn't have time to set up a meeting.

"Er, Vish?"

"Hi, Rache. Lovely to hear from you."

It was a bit odd using our new monikers. But it was very symbolic. It meant we had both moved on, to our new relationship.

"I've got something to ask. It's about work. I need your advice."

I then went on to explain my dilemma. How, if I was cured, I wasn't sure if I could still do the job. If the only reason I was good at my job was because my granddad groomed me to toss him off, does that mean, now, I wouldn't be able to do it anymore? I asked him directly:

"Should I quit my job?"

"Rache, I can't make that decision for you. I'm happy... I'm more than happy, to give you advice. I was serious when I said that. Happy to guide, where I can. But these have to be your decisions. I can't tell you to go back to work or quit. But I can tell you that you're not cured. Have you booked the counselling yet?"

I was silent.

"Exactly! But let me explain. Because you're able to face your past, doesn't mean you can't do your job. When I said your abuse made you want to control men, especially controlling their climax, I was talking about your motivation for doing the job. As long as you stay relaxed, that's what made you so good at your job. You were relaxed, so you relaxed your clients. As long as you haven't lost that, you'll be fine. But my point was motivation. To enjoy your job means you can get home at the end of the day and not be exhausted. I don't mean physically, but mentally, emotionally. The question isn't can you, should you, do the job? The question is whether you want to. My guess? You'll either find you're not enjoying it anymore and cut down your days and finally quit, or else you'll just carry on as before. So don't worry about going back to work. Do it when you feel ready. See how it goes, and then you'll eventually realise what's right for you. That's what Cindy would have done. Taking it easy, taking life as it comes, one day at a time. You haven't changed, Rache. You're the same person as two days ago. It's just that you're not, and here's one of those Yiddish words your mother might have used, you're not *shlepping* all that baggage around with you anymore."

Wow, that was heavy, but, as ever, he was so right. Vish, my mentor, my amateur shrink. But I suppose someone who can teach himself to become Mr Cunnilingus by reading a few books can certainly pick up enough psycho-babble from the library.

I knew I was going to go back to work. Take the week off, like I told Fi, but I'd call her Wednesday, to tell her to rota me for the following week. But now I had a reason. Before the epiphany, the old Cindy used to get turned on watching them come. It was the one downside of a blowjob or even a fuck: actually watching them ejaculate. I'd done some sessions with Vishti where we'd watch each other masturbating. He got turned on seeing me excited, and I could see his sperm flowing when he came, which brought me to my own orgasm. Now, I couldn't wait to get back to work and see if my catharsis would leave me unfazed at the point of their ejaculation. The more I thought about it, the more excited with anticipation I was becoming. Would I get turned on or not?

"Rache, are you still there? You've gone silent."

"Sorry, miles away with my thoughts. Anyway, thanks. You've helped me a lot. I'll go back and see how it goes from there. Oh, there's something else. Have you got some time to listen?"

"Go on."

"I'd like you to meet my friend. She's actually my flatmate, Dixie, well Dorothy, but everyone calls her Dixie."

"Rache, when we left each other, on the steps, and you made that remark about not wasting my tongue, I was joking when I asked you to introduce me to someone."

"Oh, Christ! No, not that. No, no, no. She had a bad experience and I thought you could work your psycho-babble magic on her."

"Don't tell me, another psychology student that's spending a fortune on college fees and needs an amateur shrink to sort her out."

"There you go. Spot on. She's a classmate as well as a roommate. See how perceptive you are."

"You know I'd be happy to help you out any way I can, but I don't know this, er, Dixie. Why should she open up to me, a complete stranger? I'm not sure that's a good idea, for either of us."

"Just meet with her. We'll make it casual and, if you don't hit it off, no biggie."

"How can it be casual? It would just be odd. What, out of the blue, meet this old guy and tell him your problems? Not a good idea. How's the flat by the way?"

"Flat's great. Another thing I have to thank you for. Love you to see it. Hey, that's what we'll do. Come over for a meal. I'll cook. Dixie will be there anyway. An evening, a few glasses of wine. If Dixie wants to talk, she will, and, if not, she won't."

A pregnant pause.

"No problem with that. But who am I? How are you supposed to know me?"

"I don't know. We'll make something up. An old family friend. That's what we said."

"Keep it close to the truth or you'll get caught on a lie."

"OK, how about this? Old family friend, more like an uncle, someone

I used to confide in as a kid. That gives me an in. Look, Dixie's worked as a part-time escort. She was into the, how do you like to put it, *sex trade*, before me. She introduced me to June who got me the job at Felicity's. She knows I nearly lost the flat because I couldn't tell the agent how I could afford the flat. I told her I got help from a friend. There's the truth. I couldn't tell my parents where my money was coming from, but good old Uncle Vish came along. I could trust him not to tell my parents. He came to the rescue. How about that?"

"Yes, that could work."

"You found me the flat. It all fits. You know all about my massage work. There's no reason why she should think you're a client."

"Former client."

"Yes, sorry, former client. Talking about that. Have you booked any of the other girls?"

"Rache, can we not go there? Believe me, it's only been two days."

"Two days? You didn't take advantage of me while I was sleeping, did you?"

I heard Vish laugh.

"If my recollection is right, it was nine days ago. Same hotel room, yes, definitely nine days. I remember because I came so quickly that you carried on for another ten minutes and made me come again. I've got a good memory for these things. *Double pleasure!* Straight off Felicity's website."

"Whatever!"

I laughed out loud. Vish's *whatever* was a throwback to my off-hand comment at the roof terrace bar when he said he wasn't going back to seeing me at Felicity's. *Whatever* was a code word we both used to mean *I get you*, like we were on the same page. That was why Vish took umbrage when I used our code word in the bar because we clearly weren't on the same page at that moment.

"When?"

"Any evening, I'm off work the whole week. Wait, how about Thursday? No lectures. Dixie has to go to them all because she's my cheat sheet."

"Thursday, 7 pm? Text me the address. Is parking easy?"

"Owh, just ask the *con-cierge*." I mouthed in my best posh accent.

I used to take the piss out of Vish about him having a concierge for parcel deliveries, dropping off laundry et cetera. I was only half joking, letting him know that I had joined the ranks of posh society. I was quite getting used to it.

"Thursday, then."

"Thursday, look forward to it."

I was so glad that I phoned Vish. It was so natural. This new relationship might actually work out. But I was still going to miss his tongue.

# 13

# The Best Laid Plans of Mice & Men

I was beginning to have an obsession with tongues. I had come before with a boy sucking my clit, but never anything like Vishti. Maybe it's because all my boyfriends had literally been that - just boys. I didn't think I'd dated anyone over thirty, and it was like being with children. All the talk was about football. They either insisted on having enough drink to stop them getting a proper erection or, if they were sober, whined in apology, when they came too soon. I am exaggerating, but I think I can count on one hand the number of really pleasurable encounters - excluding my former client.

So where was I going to get my oral pleasure?

"Why do men suck at cunnilingus?"

"Isn't that a tautology or something?" Dixie quipped.

"I'm serious. The boys I go out with, I don't know, it's like they skipped the clitoris in anatomy class."

"Don't think they teach that in school, do they? Anyway, nowadays, anybody can learn as much as they need watching porn on the internet."

"You're kidding me, right? The only thing kids learn from watching porn is that women can only come if they have three men at the same time: one in the mouth, one in their pussy, and one up their arsehole. Oh, and yes, double-D silicone tits. Whatever happened to subtly and romance?"

"Where's this coming from? Didn't you tell me you were getting great orgasms from the guy who invented cunnilingus?"

"Neh, didn't work out. You know me. Miss Two Dates and you're blocked on Facebook."

"Seriously? What happened?"

"Sorry, don't want to go there. Probably, you know my usual shtick - my fault - getting too serious - let's stay friends but sex is off the agenda. Have you been there?"

"Yes, but to be honest, I've been celibate for two months. College work's getting tough."

"Hey, sorry about that. I feel really guilty. I slope off to do my sex work and still get third-class honours in my first-year prelims. Miss Goody-two-shoes, never misses a lecture and struggles to get a, what, what was it again - forgot sorry ...."

I jumped on Dixie and started to tickle her and wouldn't stop.

"Get off ... OK ... OK... a first."

"Oh, yes, that was it, a fucking first class honours. No wonder you find it tough. You actually bother to learn that shit."

"So, how's the sex work going, anyway. I had to lie for you again about your lecture attendance."

Dixie and I always referred to our part-time jobs as sex work, while, to everyone else, or rather to those who we actually confided in, Dixie was an occasional high-class escort, accompanying mostly visiting academics on dinner dates. I would describe myself as a part-time sports masseuse, with a client list of premier league footballers. I don't think we were kidding anyone. But we'd take umbrage if anyone else dared to downgrade our income supplement to the level of sex work.

"Thought I'd take a week off. Fi went mad. Said I would cost her money. But I thought - *Sod it!* You've got me four days a week now. A week off now and again isn't asking too much. Hey, Dixie, I was talking about cunny, did you deliberately change the subject?"

"What is this with you, Rache? I've never heard you talk like this."

"No, sorry, it's like this guy, the one that really pressed my button, sort of, after we agreed to end it, half-jokingly, I said I'd miss his tongue because most guys couldn't find their way up the garden path. He said I should try a woman because women know what pleases other women."

"OK... And?"

"And nothing. I was just saying?"

"Christ, Rache, I've just told you I haven't had sex for two months and the next thing out of your mouth is let's get lezzie."

"Whoops, sorry, I wasn't suggesting... Er, would you?"

"I'm straight!"

"So am I! I haven't had so much as a crush on a girl, even at school."

"Sorry, Rache. Ask me again when I've had a few glasses of wine."

"Ooh, that reminds me. I've invited a friend for dinner on Thursday."

"OK, do you want me to make myself scarce?"

"No, no. I actually want you to meet him."

"Well, that would be a first!"

"No, he's not a boyfriend. He's like a family friend. An old man. Well, not old. Anyway, he's a nice guy. You'll like him."

"What are you saying?"

"No, I'm just trying to explain who he is. He's like an uncle. I trust him."

"What do you mean, trust him?"

"I'm just trying to explain our relationship. Didn't you have someone, when you were a kid, you could tell things to, stuff that you couldn't tell your parents? Like boyfriends dumping you or puking after a night out and all that shit."

"Yes, my elder brother."

"Well, I didn't have an elder brother. But I had Vish."

"Who's Vish?"

"That's his name. Well, it's actually Vishti, but our family calls him Vish. He's my parents' age, and knows my parents well, but if I tell him stuff in confidence, I know he won't tell them."

"OK, fine. No problem. I'm still not sure why you're sharing all this family stuff."

"Vish is why we're here. I mean in the flat. He found it in the first place, but, more than that. He was the guy I told you about. He helped me after I failed the credit check."

I then went on to explain that I needed to tell him about my job and so on, so he could bail me out, guaranteeing the lease.

"Oh, now I understand. Why didn't you just say, instead of telling me I'll like him, trust him and shit. It's fine, I'm really cool, what are you planning to cook?"

*********

*I was looking forward to seeing the flat. I actually got quite a kick out of helping Rachel put the deal on the flat together. Although we had been in a sexual relationship, our age gap meant I still had a feeling of parental protection for this young woman starting out in life.*

*Once during our sessions at the massage parlour, we were chatting and she told me she'd be off the following week. I asked if she was going anywhere nice, and she told me that she had to have some tests. I was concerned about her health, and then she confided that the tests were because she was planning to have a tubal ligation. When I looked puzzled, she told me she wanted to be sterilised. I was quite shocked. She explained that she needed to be checked out physically but also have some kind of psych evaluation. That was the first time I suspected there had been some childhood trauma or abuse. I didn't want to pry. I suggested she think deeply about it because, to my knowledge, it was an irreversible procedure. She wiped her finger across her nose, in a gesture that told me it was none of my business. It did lead me to thinking about her future. If she carried out her plan. I had this vivid image of how her life was going to pan out.*

*Next session, I blurted out, not sure why, but I said I saw her having an affair with a married man. I wasn't talking about me. I even described him. Banker type, probably late forties, early fifties, with a couple of young kids. International traveller. He would take her on business trips. He wouldn't set her up in an apartment because she wouldn't want to be beholden to him. She'd pay her own way. Let him pay for the business trips, let him buy her expensive gifts. She'd be his mistress, his lover, but he'd never control her life. I'm not sure why I intuited that, but her response was:* You've really planned my life, haven't you? Don't know about the banker, but you're spot on about everything else. You're absolutely right, I'd never be a kept woman, but, yes, I'd be delighted to be flown around and shown nice places.

*This was in the early days of our acquaintance. If it had been later on, she probably would have added:* His tongue would have to be in the right place, of course.

*When she first mentioned moving flats, I suggested somewhere with a pool and a gym. She mentioned she was at Greenwich College. I suggested Upper Riverside, because it wouldn't be far from the College, and it was close to Canary Wharf. It was part one of the game plan. That's where she was going to meet Mr Wonderful. Actually, I constructed a whole scenario. A married family man wouldn't be in that building. She'd first have to meet a young banker in the residents' gym. She'd go out with him; it would have to be more than her usual two dates. Then she'd be his plus one at his boss's summer house party. That was where she would meet her future lover or sugar-daddy. It was all silly nonsense, but I could tell Cindy was taking it all in. Whether Rachel was still up for that was another matter. I never followed up on whether she'd had the sterilisation procedure. After the epiphany, would Rachel still want to avoid starting a family? A subject for another time, maybe, but now I pressed the buzzer for flat 69. Really! I had a chuckle when she sent me the address. She'd proudly told me:* It's the sixth floor, can't wait to show you the view.

*She opened the door and she welcomed me with a friendly kiss on both cheeks. Continental, she'd remarked.*

"Come in. I'll show you the place. Can't see the bedrooms, though. Dixie's getting changed and mine's a bloody mess. Cleaner won't be in till Saturday."

"You're kidding me."

*Rachel smiled her* trademark smile.

"Neh! No cleaner yet. Still not posh enough for that."

*There was just an open plan kitchen and living area to see, but it was quite spacious with a double aspect as it was a corner flat.*

"Reminds me of your place, different end of town, same river though, and same built-in coffee machine. What is it about these developers, that they think everyone needs a built-in coffee machine? You know sometimes I sit here on my own, of an evening, with a glass of wine, looking out at my very own *River View*. I imagine getting up and walking to the bedroom, and, there you are, silk scarf in hand, ready to blindfold me and gently guide me onto the bed, undress me slowly, lie me down, put on the cuffs, tease me, tantalise me, gently spread my legs, start using your tongue, twirling, licking my labia, gently pulling my lips apart, rotating your tongue, licking, sucking, taking me to the point of ecstasy. The other night, I'd probably had a couple of glasses, I closed my eyes, and jerked myself off while sitting in the chair, just thinking of that evening, your tongue, my orgasm."

*There was a stirring in my loins while she was talking.*

"You missed the bit about how I fumbled with the labial clamps. You yelled in pain. I apologised and threw them on the floor. It took me ten minutes to get you back into a relaxed state."

*Rachel burst into a belly laugh:*

"Yes, do you know I'd completely forgotten about those silly things? I remember looking at those clamps afterwards, picking up one of the dildos that you had laid out for me on the dressing table in case of need, shoving it in your face and telling you that if you ever tried those clamps on my pussy lips again, I'd take that dildo and shove it so far up your arse that you wouldn't be sitting down for a week."

*We shared a laugh and a cuddle, and just at that moment, Dixie came out of her bedroom.*

"Sorry, Lovebirds, didn't mean to spoil the party."

"That's OK, Vish, Vishti and I were just reminiscing about old times. Er…"

*I helped her out:*

"Yes, when you called me at midnight to pick you up outside a pub because you were so drunk, the taxi driver wouldn't take you. He was worried you'd puke in his car. When I got there, you were sitting on the pavement laughing. You said you thought you'd peed yourself."

"And you said?" …. *and in unison we looked at each other and giggled:*

"Don't worry, I brought a towel for the car seat."

*Dixie joined in the fun. I don't know where the story came from. I was just extemporising on some similar incident Rachel had probably told me about, but it fitted in perfectly with our trusting uncle persona.*

"I was 17, and I said if you told my parents I'd slit my wrists, and you said…"

"Better not, since I'd be the one driving you to the hospital and didn't want blood on my seats."

*The laughter persisted and Dixie smiled:*

"Ooh, you're gruesome, you two!"

*The intercom rang.*

"Oh, that will be the Deliveroo. 'Fraid I left the lamb in the oven too long and it shrivelled up to nothing. There was cold tongue in the fridge, but I thought better of it."

*Rachel and I shared a private moment.*

"Just for Vishti, Deliveroo's best Chicken Vindaloo. Sorry, I really did want to make you a home-cooked meal."

*I put on a sympathetic face:*

"The best-laid plans of mice and men…!"

# 14

## Dixie Cups

Canary Wharf comes alive on a warm early summer's day. It's not really my neck of the woods, but that doesn't stop me from appreciating the foresight of the Reichman Brothers.

The Brothers, successful Canadian real estate developers, modelled this huge project based on the needs of Torontonians, who would not wish to venture out of their heated offices in the sub-zero frost-encrusted winters. So office complexes were joined by a latticework of subterranean strips of kiosks, market stalls and more conventional stores so that worker-bee secretaries could enjoy a bit of retail therapy as they scurried along to collect double macchiatos for their over-caffeinated bosses.

Of course, London Docklands is not as cold as Toronto, so perhaps the worker-bee secretaries were quite content to spend their lunch hour and coffee breaks above ground. The added attraction of breathing fresh air instead of the re-cycled and re-sanitised variety, chilled with ozone-destroying CFCs may in part explain why this ambitious project bankrupted the billionaire Reichman Brothers.

Canary Wharf comes alive on a warm early summer's day.

The worker-bee secretaries have abandoned the coochie tunnels, lined with offers from Zara, Starbucks, Toni & Guy et al. In their quest to keep their over-caffeinated bosses supplied with their next hit, they can now be found sashaying across the pedestrianised sidewalks displaying floral patterns imprinted on mini-tunics revealing bare flesh with the occasional discrete tattoo.

Interspersed along these sidewalks, were small squares adorned with coffee stalls and sandwich displays waiting to entice the next passer-by.

In front of the food & beverage outlets, there was a mosaic of benches, tables, and small sculptures. The sculptures had been purposefully designed as temporary seating, to accommodate the posteriors of the floral patterned mini-tunic-attired worker-bee secretaries.

Dixie was perched on one of those sculptures. I nodded towards a bench to indicate my preference for something marginally more comfortable.

"What's your poison?"

"Soya latte, with sprinkles, if they've got them."

I brought the coffee.

"Thanks for doing this. Rache said you had a friendly ear. And I felt we hit it off at dinner."

"Not a problem, happy to be a shoulder to cry on if that's what this is. The attack. Rache told me. It must have been dreadful."

"No, it's not that. I haven't told anyone. Please don't tell Rache. I promised her I'd be careful after the other incident I'm worried she'd kick me out of the flat if she knew how stupid I'd been. I'm actually fine. I just wanted to tell someone."

"A date gone wrong?"

"You could say that. Rache told you about the Agency and that problem I had when I went freelance. Well, like the stupid bitch I am, I got another call. He said we'd met before. Used the same name as that of a previous client, but it didn't sound right. Anyway, he said he wanted me for the evening and to bring his wife to watch, for £500. I knew there was something odd, but the money was good. We met in a hotel. He said we'd had dinner there before. I realised that he'd talked to this other client because I had been there before, but not with him. We went straight up to the room. He said I could have a drink upstairs. But there was no, you know, foreplay. Normally, we'd at least sit for a chat and a drink in the bar, if they don't want dinner. When I got to the room, there was another guy waiting. The client said, sarcastically, that he was sorry his wife couldn't make it because their kid was ill, so his mate would have to do. The two of them just laughed. It was getting ugly. The irony was that they were both good-looking. Either one of them could probably have seduced me without too much effort, but they weren't into that. They just wanted to humiliate me. I had a choice. Try and resist and probably get a black eye for my troubles. Definitely get raped and likely sodomised, just for good measure. Rache actually came to my rescue."

"She was downstairs?"

Dixie smiled. "Very funny. No, Rache told me some of the techniques she uses when she's with clients, to stay in control. She told me that, if you tell them what you're going to do, and be very professional about it, then you set the agenda and stay in control."

"Rache said that?"

"Yes, you know how she's got street smarts. Well, that's what I did. I thought: *Get your act together, kid. You're not going to come out well from this either way, but you're not going to let those buggers win.* So I went up to the client, stood close up to his face, looked him in the eye and said: *First, give me the £500. Then tell lover boy to lock the door and get me two gins from the fridge and pour me a drink. Hope they've got tonic. Open the drinks in front of me. I'm not going to let you tossers roofie me up. Him, I want on the bed with his trousers down. He can toss himself off if he wants, while he watches me give you the best blow job of your life.*

"They were dumbstruck. But his mate did as I said. Brought me the drinks. Unopened as requested. I knocked back the gin. Didn't bother diluting it with the tonic. Undid the client's trousers to give him his £500-worth.

"I now had to work out how I was going to face doing the dirty deed. His member was staring straight up at me. I couldn't do it if it was ugly. There was this guy once that I fancied so much that I'd spent the night seducing him. I was desperate to bed him. When I saw his dingus, it turned me right off. So I just let him fuck me and tried to think of anything but his dick.

"This time it was different. I was about to suck off an obnoxious creep, but when I looked down, I thought: *I could ignore the man and just concentrate on this little fella.* It was the size that was appealing. I mean not just the size. The length was about right. Too long can be uncomfortable, but it was straight as a die. I supposed I'm a bit of a perfectionist, so I don't like the bendy ones.

"Circumcised, that's always my choice. Inside down there, it doesn't really matter, but in your mouth the foreskin gets in the way. And when I say I'm a perfectionist, that also applies to the snip. Obviously, they don't snip the glans, well, at least, for their sake I'd hope they don't. But, depending on exactly how it's been done, the skin around the glans can be a bit messy. But my cock for the evening couldn't have been more symmetrical. It wasn't really the time or the place to talk religion, but, if I had to guess, I'd say not Jewish. Rache had told me that they do it at 8 days old when the size makes it more difficult to be artistic. But a little bit older, under a proper anaesthetic, then the surgeon can use his dexterity to end up with a result as neat as a Vidal Sassoon bob. I was tempted to ask him who had done it in case I ever was contemplating a labiaplasty. But, like religion, not really the time or place to swap notes on plastic surgeons.

"So, the ultimate irony: this slob, this misogynist, this potential rapist, had the straightest, most symmetrical, most appealing, most succulent cock I could ever have wished for.

"Well, I suppose that's some consolation for the shitshow that I'd got myself into.

"I could have made him come straightaway, he was so horny, but I thought: *What would Rache do?* Well, not what would she do, because she'd never be so damn stupid as to be in this position. No, how would Rache think to get out of this, with as little downside as possible?

"She'd suss that if I made Wanker Number 1 come too soon, Wanker Number 2 would want more and might get funny with me. So, I took it slow and listened to the guy on the bed tossing himself off. I stopped momentarily to give him some encouragement. *Come on, Big Boy, I want to hear you squirt for me!*

"Mouth back around the client's cock, tongue circling. Guys can be rough when they're standing forcing their cock down your throat. Stay in control. Lick, suck, but hold onto his hips so you're pushing him away as he's trying to thrust. Another tip from Rache. As soon as I heard the wanker on the bed come, I speeded up, sucking harder, avoiding the glans because that can slow things down. Took his sperm in my mouth. What is the deal men have with that? Spat it out as soon as he'd come. Then, without even going to the bathroom, I tidied my skirt and took my handbag off the stool. I stood at the door, turned around, looking at their stupid grins and said: *Thanks, Lads. Hope the kid gets better soon.*

"I got into the lift and found the loo in the lobby area. I locked the stall door, knelt over the toilet seat, and puked out my guts."

She finished speaking. She had said it all.

I was holding Dixie's hands. She was looking at me with a tilted head and screwed-up lips as if to say: *Shit happens!*

So, I mouthed those words for her and she smiled.

We sat there in silence for maybe a couple of minutes. Then she said: "Thank you so, so much. I really am alright, but I just had to get it out. I'm not proud of myself… "

I cut her off: "Well, I think you should be. You did really well to come out of that as you did. I think I'd call that a score draw."

Dixie looked puzzled.

"Sorry, football metaphor. Sort of better than a draw. More points on the football pools."

I was losing her in my rambling.

"Sorry, go on."

"Well, nothing really. I'd learnt a lesson. I don't think there's any long-term damage. You know, mental health and all that stuff. I'm glad it's you I've told because I think Rache helped me and I know you and her go back a long time."

"You should tell her. I think she'd be proud of you as well."

"Maybe one day. It's just that I feel I let her down because I promised

I'd be careful."

With that, we parted company. I'd gotten used to this elder statesman role with Rachel and I didn't mind being a sponge for her friend, but I told myself not to make a habit of it.

*******

"Thanks. You were right about Vishti. He's a good listener."

Dixie and I were sharing a bottle of wine. I'd had a long day at work and she'd been stressing as usual to get an essay finished.

"Yes, I knew it would help. Did you tell him about the slap you got?"

"Mmm, let's not go into it. But you were right. A bit like talking to an elder wiser brother. You know, non-judgemental."

"Exactly." I could tell she wasn't interested in sharing, so I changed the subject. "I had a really weird day at work."

"Don't tell me, not the guy with the limp dick, who asks you to mock him about the size of his penis."

"No, haven't seen that client again. Hope he's OK though."

"It amuses me how you are so respectful and caring about these weirdo clients."

"I'm just practising for when we do our psych consults."

"Really, are you going to do that? I thought you were thinking of dropping out."

"Yeah, I don't know. Sometimes I think psychotherapy sounds really interesting, but then I don't think I'm disciplined enough and want to just go off and travel the world. You though, you're going to be great, Dorothy Freud, so you're the one that should start referring to my weird fucked up wankers as clients."

We shared a giggle.

"So, who was he, a new client?"

"No, you remember the dirty guy."

Dixie gave out a nervous laugh: "Ooh, what, the shitty one who liked you to wipe it on his face? I don't know how you could do it. Really, Rache, there are limits."

"Yes, I know. I wondered that myself. But to be honest, I like to try new stuff. I don't mean I enjoyed it. It was pretty disgusting, but I am genuinely interested in seeing what these guys want. Testing their limits. Funnily enough, I found it easier with the shit than what he wanted today."

"Go on. The shit stuff really turns me off, but I've got a feeling that what you're going to tell me will make me horny."

"Not sure it will. It didn't turn me on. It's the BDSM stuff."

"Yes, I knew it! I'm getting wet already."

"Dixie, I'm not telling you this for prurience. It's strictly academic, for the course, you know. Case studies."

"Yeah, yeah. I know."

We shared another giggle.

"So today, first he asked if I remembered last time. Then he asked me to remind him of what I did to him. It's quite odd, I found it easier to wipe shit over his face than to talk to him about what I did, but, *hey ho*, you pay the piper ..."

"Come on - the BDSM?"

"So, then he said he'd brought a cock ring and wanted me to put it on him. Actually, we had a laugh doing that because he already had an erection, which made it quite tricky, so I said he needed to lose the erection and we talked about the best ways. I said I could suck him off, but I knew he wasn't into that or I wouldn't have offered. Next option, use a spoon on his bell-end. He said he wanted to try that."

"Did you do that?"

"Yes, it's supposed to work. But I think he enjoyed it too much. So, we settled for a cold shower. We upsell an assisted shower for £25, but I really didn't fancy freezing my tits off, so I went next door - the room has an en suite - and got the shower ready for him."

"Did it work?"

"Yes. You see, I've got an hour unless they book longer. The game is to time things so they don't feel rushed. Normally, you've got to get the timing of the happy ending right. Too soon and there's too much time to fill in. Too late and it's a quick wank and you'll probably lose the client. Get the timing right and they keep coming back for more. Well, that's how I've built up my client book. Quite a lot of skill is required actually. Anyway, with this guy, it's not about ejaculation, so the timing is much easier. He comes out of the shower, nice and soft, I slip the cock ring on him. I hadn't seen one like this before. It was made of rubber and adjustable. Sort of a tie with beads that you pulled along the rubber to tighten it. His erection returned immediately. He kept asking me to pull it tighter. I could see the veins on his penis. I was worried they were going to burst, but he just kept saying *tighter*. His face was squirming. He wasn't acting. He was in quite a lot of pain. You know, I said I like to explore the limits, but it was quite uncomfortable for me. I wasn't enjoying making him suffer, but, and I know you're going to tease me over this, but it's true, I kept saying to myself. *Be professional, Cindy. Client satisfaction is all that matters."*

"Cindy?"

"Yes, when I am in treatment, as I like to say, I wear my Cindy persona, even in my head. It makes it a lot easier.

Then he said: "Now my throat."

"What! He wanted you to choke him. What did you do? Client satisfaction and all that."

"I said, don't be a bloody fool. Times up."

"You didn't? Risk losing a client?"

"I bloody did. I said it's all about exploring boundaries. I'm happy to go to the limit. But I'm really testing *my* limits. How far will *I* go? I really don't mind the clients pushing me or asking me to do the weirdest things. They can't embarrass me anymore, whatever they say. But the bottom line is, I'm always in control. So, I will tell them when they've crossed the line."

"That's what I like about you. How you keep control. You know, you taught me that, and it might just have saved my life."

"What are you talking about?"

Dixie then told me about the reason she wanted to meet Vish. How she wasn't ready to tell me before because I'd ball her out for not taking care of herself. And how she'd used my techniques for taking control of the situation, turning what could have been a rape or worse, into the humiliation of the two creeps, albeit at the cost of a mouthful of spunk.

By this time, we'd finished the bottle of wine and were both a little woozy.

"Hey, come here, girlfriend, you should have told me. I wouldn't have been angry. I knew you're a daft fuck and that you'd go freelance again. You're such a waste of space. Come here, give me a hug."

We embraced and looked each other in the eye.

"Remember what you asked me the other day?" Dixie asked.

"Uh-huh."

"I'm ready."

"Are you drunk? I won't take advantage of you if you're drunk."

"I'm only going to do it to you when I'm drunk, so make the most of it, girlfriend. Kiss me first. Properly. Then get on the floor and open your legs. I'm going to suck you off till you come."

********

It had been a long time since I'd had a woman's tongue between my legs and that was an episode best forgotten… I was so ready, so ready for her to take me. Up until then, it had only been in my mind. I hadn't let on to

Dixie that she'd been the subject of my fantasies for some time. I'd pictured her between my legs. We could be sitting in the flat. Dixie would be studying. I had my earbuds in, so as not to disturb her. But I'd be watching her and wondering what her tongue would be like, pleasuring me. Then I might excuse myself, tell her it was time for bed, get out my *Lovehoney* special, and bring myself to orgasm while picturing her getting down and dirty with my pussy.

But now it was for real.

It's like watching a movie that you haven't seen before. It takes me no more than 5 minutes to know whether I'm going to enjoy it or not. Well, with tongue it takes about 5 seconds. It wasn't just that I fancied her. It was simply that her tongue knew its way around. First, she touched the clit, just to say *hello*. Obviously, being there herself, knowing what she liked and offering the same to me.

This was pure Vishti. I don't believe she had had a session with him, after coffee the other day, but I had to wonder. All the things he'd done to me with his tongue. His tongue would say hello to my clit, but he would take it a bit further. His tongue would first circle my clit, as if to say, *don't worry I'll be back*. I have to suggest that to Dixie for next time, but you're doing well, girlfriend. From clit to labia, she starts sucking my lips, and yes, yes, I let out a shriek, as she sucks hard so the lips are rubbing against my clit. Dixie momentarily backs off.

"No, keep doing that, keep sucking, Dixie, you're bringing me up there."

Now the slight hesitation, that I used to have with Vishti. Don't make me come too soon. But he never let me down. He always knew to slow down when necessary and build me up again and keep going until he knew I couldn't take anymore. I felt I needed to guide Dixie:

"Dix, you're amazing, keep doing that, ease off if you feel I'm coming. It's so nice, I don't want you to stop."

She dutifully obliged, and now she was in a rhythm, the tongue circling my button, then moving from side to side to just slow me down. Then circling again, then sucking as if she gauged my clit was too sensitive. Just once I had to wriggle, when she lost position. Pretty good for a beginner.

Now leave me alone, I want to lie back and enjoy it, privately, if you don't mind.

So, here I go, into fantasyland. I know I'm ready to come, and my fantasy gives me scope to have two lovers. It's Dixie's tongue, but Vishti's on top fucking me. I want you inside me again, like the first time. I don't need the orgasm from your cock. Dixie's taking care of business in that department. Her tongue is not yours, my lover, but she's good enough and I'm starting to climax. But it's you I want, always and only you. I can picture you inside me. I can feel you inside me. I'm starting to spasm, keep riding me, keep riding me. I'm watching him from above, he's fucking Dixie. I'm watching him from below, he's fucking me.

"Don't stop, Dixie!"

I had to tell her, just in case, and I'm pushing her away from my engorged over-sensitive clit. As I spasm, and arch my back, I push her away whilst, at the same time, telling her not to stop. Drunk or not drunk, she gets the message. She carries on sucking my lips, just enough so that my contractions continue, and my orgasm will last the full 30 seconds I need to finish off the quivering until I pass out.

*******

The next day, I'd just got back from the gym. It was 7 am and Dixie was in her jams, fridge door open, swigging orange juice out of the bottle, as usual. She looked like shit.

I was waiting for her to come up with the *Boy, was I drunk last night* line, but instead she said: "Bit of a hangover. Next time I think I want to be sober when I suck you off."

"Are you serious?"

"Yes. Was I alright? I really don't even know if you came."

"God, you were perfect. Almost as good as Vi… Victor."

Christ, I nearly said Vish, but just stopped myself.

"You know the guy I said had a good tongue."

"Only *almost* as good as him?"

"Well, you were drunk. Just imagine what you could do if you were sober."

We giggled again. We both seemed to be on the same page. It was just sex; we weren't about to start a relationship. At least, I thought we were on the same page.

Then she said: "When's my turn?"

# 15
## RIP Belinda

The takeaway Chicken Vindaloo at Rachel's reminded me that they were still kids. Rache, Dixie, young students. I sort of got a kick out of being with these youngsters. It reminded me of what might have been. What we had planned.

It could have been Lyn at that flat. Lyn at that College. Could have been, would have been, should have been…

Belinda, but we called her Lyn. We had waited many years. We'd almost given up. Sex with Daphne had always been difficult. She was of a different era, where sex was a woman's duty, which she wasn't supposed to enjoy.

I don't know whether it was that or perhaps her physiology, or our destiny. Her gynaecologist had explained that he had seen the phenomenon before. As the woman enters peri-menopause, she becomes less fertile. She gets to a stage where she and her partner decide it was not to be.

Suddenly the pressure is off. There is no expectation that she will ever conceive. The stress is gone. The body relaxes. Whatever the blockage, psychosomatic or physiological, it is removed, and conception follows.

At the age of 44, it was a difficult birth. However much Daphne disliked sex before, following Lyn's birth, it was almost completely off the table.

Yet we doted on Lyn. Daphne for all her coldness in bed, was a warm-hearted compassionate woman, and a devoted loving mother. We were protective, late parents often are, but not overly protective.

That day, the day of *the incident*, Lyn was walking back from school, a journey she took every day.

On that fateful day, she happened to be crossing the road at the pedestrian crossing. A boy was crossing alongside her, bouncing a ball. The boy lost control of the ball which bounced along the road. The man who destroyed our life was distracted, momentarily. He swerved. He hit Lyn and her life was extinguished in that moment.

Initially, it appeared to be a tragic accident. The driver was routinely breathalysed. He turned out to be way over the limit. At his trial, the prosecution's expert evidence was accepted by the jury.

A sober driver, travelling within the speed limit, would have been able to break in time.

A sober driver, travelling within the speed limit, would have been able to recognise that driving over a football would have been preferable to driving over our precious girl.

A sober driver would have…

He was convicted of causing death by dangerous driving. The prosecution told me that they were expecting a 10-year sentence. It was the middle of the afternoon, broad daylight. Lyn was at a pedestrian crossing. Those factors would ordinarily increase the tariff. Somehow, driving drunk at night, on a poorly lit road, would have been deemed a less heinous crime.

He ended up serving four years.

His previous unblemished record, character witnesses testifying to his contribution to the community, and his guilty plea, all played in his favour.

It was not enough!

I'm not a vindictive person. I should say, I'm not *normally* a vindictive person. But I was going to make him pay. Our solicitor said we could sue him through the civil courts. The death of a child has its own formula, but the quantum is affected because we didn't suffer financially. Maybe £10,000 net of legals, assuming he'd pay our costs. It wasn't the money. It could have been £100,000. I didn't care.

No, I was going to play the long game.

I decided that, pillar of the community or not, he had to pay. Pay for taking away the love of our lives.

I spent the time, while he was incarcerated, researching. He was married, and ironically had a daughter himself, not far off Lyn's age. He was also a model citizen and successful businessman. What was he doing drunk in the middle of the day? He had just been presented with some ridiculous award by the local Chamber of Commerce. This model of the community had had a few glasses of champagne to celebrate during the Chamber lunch meeting. A few glasses too many.

When he was eventually released, you would have thought that he'd have slunk back into his shell after what he had done, but none of that. He'd been rehabilitated. His time in prison had been inspirational, I read in the local paper. He was now a trustee of some charity for helping offenders get back into the community. He was even up for Treasurer of his local chapter of the Chamber.

I had a new mission in life. He took my daughter. I was going to take his. Sorry, but it's an eye for an eye. Caroline, that was her name. I started stalking her after school. Well, not actually stalking, more surveillance. I wanted to know everything I could about her, because, although I knew I was going to damage her, I had to make sure I was doing the right thing.

I had developed my plan, but first I had some surfing to do. The lack of sex at home had forced me onto porn channels. The problem with porn is that you get de-sensitised. So, you go deeper and darker. But I knew I had to go right down to the gutter. The dark web. I knew that I was going to see things no one should ever have to watch. Torture scenes weren't enough. Bizarrely, that's not even illegal. Unless it's kids. That's the stuff they'll bang you up for. That's the stuff that'll put you on the register for life. That's the stuff that would separate you from your kid. That's the stuff that would mean no rehabilitation into the Community.

It was quite easy actually. The worse of it was having to watch some of the vile videos, to make sure that it was in the right category. For the other bit, I needed help. My tech guy showed me how to hack someone's broadband router. Couldn't believe it. Sit in a car outside their house and tune in. The password is on the back of the router. That needed someone to pose as a phone technician and blag their way into the house to check the wiring. Once I had the password, I could log in to his personal computer. Taking control of his computer was a little more difficult. I didn't know enough about viruses, but there's some simple software that all IT administrators use to deal with glitches in the systems they run. However, the user has to consent to hand over control to the administrator.

I was getting out of my depth. I also couldn't work out how to get the credit card details. The child porn had to be paid for with his credit card before being downloaded onto his laptop.

While things were running to plan, I hadn't stopped to think about the morality of what I was doing. He was going to lose Caroline, that's what I wanted. But, of course, it meant that she was going to lose her father. Was I really prepared to let the innocent suffer?

So, I scrapped the plan or rather went to plan B. More research. Was this guy a model dad? Apart from being a child killer, I mean. If he was a good father, I might cut him some slack. But if he was a liar and a cheat? Then all bets were off and we'd go for the jugular. So, I had to put him to the test. But I was far outside my comfort zone.

There was only one person I could think of who might have the right connections. His name was Arthur. He had been a commercial tenant of mine in an office building I owned. I got along well with him. I tried to get on with all my tenants. It made life easier. But then I found out what he was really doing. One of the other tenants complained. They said he had young women in and out all day, and they were lowering the tone of the building. It was an office, not a knocking shop, so I had to see for myself. I spent a day keeping an eye on the comings and goings. They weren't hookers, but I understood why my other tenant was having problems. Although I'd had no experience of it, I think they would be described as high-class escorts. So, Arthur wasn't using the place as a brothel, but he seemed to be running an escort agency from there. I assumed, that the girls were in and out collecting their fees or paying Arthur his cut.

I wasn't sure if the lease would let me kick him out. I couldn't prove he was doing anything illegal.

I had to confront him, but I didn't want a protracted legal dispute. I simply told him I needed the office. Asked him how much he would take for breaking the lease. He asked for £50k, and I offered him £10k. We settled on £20k and parted as friends.

"Hello, Arthur… Yes, long time… I've got a job for you… I need a girl…. no, not for me! They need to be savvy and don't mind getting a guy drunk… I don't know… what's the normal rate? How much? Jesus… does that include your cut?"

By the end of the conversation, I'd worked out that the adventure would cost me around two thousand pounds, including the hotel room, the girl's fee, Arthur's cut, and a bit extra for the shenanigans. I agreed to the deal but didn't even know if my target would bite.

I was now tracking the target's movements. He needed to be liked in the community so used social media to let his *friends* know what he was doing. He posted something about some conference he planned to attend at a hotel in Birmingham. He even thought his *friends* would like to know that he'd be staying overnight. I booked a room at the same hotel. I'd already prepped Arthur's escort. We had met briefly. She seemed up for it. She was going to clear fifteen hundred pounds for a night's work. Although I couldn't speak from first-hand knowledge, my guess was that she would have got him drunk and incapable before she had to take off her clothes.

*******

I was waiting in the hotel room when I got the call. She opened the bedroom door. He was completely out of it. I rifled his jacket and took his wallet. His laptop was on the bed.

"Did you get the password?"

"Caroline1997."

Shit! That was the same year as Lyn was born. I hesitated momentarily. But picturing Lyn redoubled my motivation.

"Here's the extra £500 that I promised you for the password. Give me ten minutes and I'll be out of here."

I opened the laptop, launched Tor, the browser you use to access the dark web, typed in the URL for the porn site, purchased the dirt and downloaded it onto his hard drive.

Asking my shill to get the password was a gamble. It was worth the £500. My backup was some password-cracking software but I didn't know how long that would take, nor if it would even work.

My shill looked at me and said: "Well, that was fun. You said your room's down the corridor. Shame to waste it. Don't worry - it's on the house."

She led me to my room. I handed her the key card so she could open the door. She took my hand and pulled me in, then pushed me onto the bed.

"I don't even know your real name."

I was trying to be polite. I honestly didn't know the etiquette in these situations. Arthur had just said: *Call her Marie, that's not her real name.*

"Does it matter?" She implied Marie was fine.

"I can be whoever you want me to be. You just lie back and think about your favourite girlfriend."

Then she explained her offer.

"I said *on the house*. That's a blow job, not a fuck. But I still want to make it interesting for you. So, think of the best blow job you've ever had. Then lie back and picture her."

I hesitated.

"Oh, sorry, or him."

"No, it was a young lady."

I settled back ready to use my imagination. It didn't take me long to recall the young lady. There had only been one. A student, yet skilled in the art of providing oral pleasure.

Marie was now down on me and starting to suck me hard. I wanted her to slow down, but thought it a little churlish, given that this was *on the house*.

She suddenly stopped, and took her mouth away, as though she didn't want me to come too quickly.

"Now lie back. Eyes closed. Picture your lady. Give me some clues. When I get down on you again, just tell me how you like it. Call out her name."

As she went back down, she was sucking too hard.

"Slow down. Please. Just lick, circle your tongue, and then suck. That's it. Just keep doing that. That's it.

"I'm coming. I'm coming. Cindy. I'm coming. Cindy! Cindy!"

She withdrew her mouth.

"Not so quick, Lover, now I know her name, I've got something to work on. I'm Cindy for tonight, I'm Cindy's tongue, I'm Cindy's mouth. Did I say a blow job not a fuck? Well, tonight's your lucky night. Cindy's here with you now. Close your eyes lover, she's going to fuck you.

Now I felt her on top. I could picture Cindy with her *trademark smile*. We didn't fuck often; it was normally oral. She didn't come when we fucked, but it was always at her request. Times when she wanted to give herself to me, just for my pleasure. Now she was on top. She was riding me, taking me to places where we'd been together. She rode me hard and, as I was coming, she forced a finger up my backside, which caused me to jerk, but gave me a more intense orgasm as she hit my prostate.

She seemed to know how to make a man come. Well, I suppose she was a professional.

She lay down next to me and started to stroke my cheeks, then she just hugged me. I closed my eyes and pictured my former lover.

"Cindy's here for you now. Just lie still."

She started to suck on my ear lobe. I wriggled away.

"Sorry, just tell me what you like."

I kept my eyes closed.

"Tell me what she'd do for you."

I kept my eyes closed.

"Just smile for me, Cindy, I just want to see your smile, your *trademark smile*."

"I'm smiling for you, lover. Just open your eyes. Cindy's here smiling for you. Look at my smile."

I kept my eyes tightly closed.

*******

An anonymous tip led to his arrest. Well, he wanted to be high profile in the community, so it made a good story for the local paper. Daphne handed the paper over to me.

"Can you believe what that bastard was doing? It says he has a daughter, poor child. You wonder how safe she was with him. Hope he rots in jail."

"Don't be so harsh, Daphne. Everyone has their demons."

# 16

## Returning the Favour

In my world, a favour done, a favour returned. I'm not one for faking orgasms. If a guy didn't pleasure me, why should I give him the satisfaction of thinking he'd made me come? But if they had made me come. Well, that was a different story.

Back in the day, when Vishti was a paying client, we had an unwritten agreement. Actually, it was an unspoken agreement, but I didn't need to tell him because he sussed me out. The first time he sucked me off, I was surprised at how good he was. It just seemed natural to return the compliment.

I give good blow jobs, but not to clients. Unless! Actually, unless I fancy them. For most clients, it's off-limits and I make that very clear if they start to hint that that's what they want. But if I fancy them, well! I have to be honest; a lot does depend on the size and shape of their cock. It's pure Goldilocks. When I give them a Lingham massage, I look at their erection and picture how far down it will go. If it's too thin, I won't enjoy it. If it's too long, I might gag. But if it's just about right and he's a good-looking guy… Actually, he doesn't need to be too good-looking, if his cock's right. But I have to relate to him.

Don't think I'm daft, but the way I justify not calling myself a prostitute is that I pick and choose. The client comes in for a massage. Anything else is up to me. The menu is the menu. Tantric, Body to Body, Lingham etc. But a blow job? I choose if I want to do it, then I put the feelers out to see if the client will bite (excuse the pun). Then I negotiate the rate. To begin with, I started at £50, but then I decided that I didn't really need the money, and there were only a few clients who I was really prepared to offer the service to. So, I upped it to £75.

I had a new client, who really rocked my boat. Why the fuck he was paying for it bewildered me. He could snatch any snatch he wanted, if you get my drift. His excuse was that he only came into town (American, maybe that explains it) for a few days at a time. He's tied up in meetings all day. Don't know if that was true or BS, but it didn't really matter. I was going to give him my number but he said this was his last trip before he was reassigned to Asia.

Story of my life!

"I just feel I should give you a fond farewell."

"That's nice. What did you have in mind?"

"What's your pleasure? You know that hand relief is included in the price."

"Right, er, I wasn't sure. That sounds fine."

"Fi, the boss, would sack me if she knew, but I had a client... You won't tell her, will you...?"

"Of course not."

"I had a client the other day who said I gave the best blow job he'd ever had. I made him last 9 minutes. I actually looked at the clock. That was 9 minutes just in my mouth, not including the foreplay when I was playing with his dick and licking his balls."

He giggled nervously.

"Bringing him up then slowing him down. I could have gone on longer but he begged me to let him come."

Bang, that sold him.

"Er, how much?"

"Normally £200, but I really like your face. To you £150. And 50% refund if you come in less than 5 minutes."

That last bit was just for me. It's more exciting if I can make a game of it. Now I had a financial incentive to make sure he didn't shoot his load prematurely. Believe me, that takes some skill on my part.

I have a routine, not for all my clients, just for those who will be enjoying my tongue: I always inspect it first. Remember, I won't have decided whether to or not until they've turned over, so I've already seen the goods. But I need a closer inspection. They never seem to mind. I run my finger along the shaft. He passes that test. I could feel his veins, but I don't like it if a vein protrudes too much. Call me daft, but I worry it might burst in my mouth.

The rest of the inspection is more about squeezing. I don't mean hard, just to feel the texture. This client was almost spongy. I don't suck the balls normally. I don't mind. It's just that some don't like it so I wait till they ask. But the testicles still get inspected as part of my routine. Here I had a lot of skin and asymmetric balls. It's funny how the guys don't know. I mean they think they're odd if their balls don't match. I guess they're shy to ask their buddies. Obviously, they can see each other's dicks in the locker room, but they can't exactly measure each other's balls. So he was really glad when I reassured him how many of my clients have mismatched testicles. Routine inspection over, I started to play with his cock. As promised, the time starts after the foreplay. So now I'm stroking him gently, just a little oil. Not too much, I don't like the taste of the oil, so we'll rub most of it off before I start to blow him.

I start to lick his balls. A bit of advice, ladies: as I said, not everyone likes it. I follow Vishti's rules. Not that he ever licked anyone's balls. At least I don't think so. No, he taught me to sense, to feel what your partner likes, and what he doesn't. So, if you're into ball-sucking, take it gently. Some men won't want you near the sack. Not because it's not pleasurable, but the testicles are pretty sensitive, and they're so shit scared you're going to bite them or something that they can't relax. It's more about trust than technique. But once they trust you, you can lick, suck, and nibble their ball sack. I keep rubbing their cock though, to keep it ready.

So, now I look at the clock and take him deep into my mouth, sucking hard. I slow the pace, licking up and down. I can feel some tension. I look up at the clock again. I keep it strategically placed so I can see it without moving away. I am worried it is going to cost me the £75 refund. So, I use a technique I'd developed, circling my tongue over the glans. Most guys like that but it doesn't lead to an orgasm (or, at any rate, not so far). The clock hit five minutes, bingo, but I was enjoying it too much. Past nine minutes, he thought I was joking about the other client. Round the glans again. Slow it down. I could tell he was getting desperate. *Not until you beg*, I thought.

Then: "Cindy, Cindy, please I want to come!"

He exploded into my mouth. I usually spit it straight out, don't like the saltiness. Never quite got into oysters. But his spunk tasted almost sweet. Pineapples? Was that a real thing? I swallowed his whole load. I was so horny I wanted to take him there and then.

"Would you excuse me? I'll get a warm towel."

I spread it over him.

"Just lie there still for me, while I take a quick shower."

I moved to the en-suite, closed the sliding door, stepped into the shower, turned on the tap so he wouldn't hear me and finger-fucked myself. I was rubbing my clit with one hand and using my fingers on my vag with the other. I can't come standing up, so I lie down, with my legs half in and half out of the shower. Now I'm working harder, my clit is responding, and two fingers are working my G. The water from the shower is hitting my head. But it's not water I can feel, it's his spunk. I can still taste the sweetness. I'm jerking myself off, and just imagining him coming all over my face.

I start to cry out.

"I'm coming. I'm coming. I want your cum all over me."

I'm shuddering. It's so uncomfortable lying on the floor, but, while my orgasmic contractions continue, I don't care. I'm also bouncing on the shower tray as I keep coming until I finish. Then I get up quickly, with sore arse cheeks. I was so carried away that I hadn't noticed that the edge of the shower tray was cutting into my bum.

Sorry, I distracted myself. Gone quite dizzy at the memory. My point was that my blow jobs are worth a lot, I don't give them away, so when Vishti sucked me to orgasm, I reciprocated the favour. He'd always pleasure me first, then it was his turn. Occasionally, he booked a short session, which meant no time for my pleasure.

Sometimes it took me twenty minutes. No reflection on Vishti. No, of course, it *was* a reflection on Vishti. He didn't care how long I took. In fact, he got a great kick out of it. His skill was his sensitivity. He kind of read my clitoris so well. He just knew when to lick and when to suck. But he was very fair, he knew that an hour's appointment wasn't long enough for both of us. He was paying, after all, so he was entitled to a proper massage on top of everything else. So, he has his massage and he has his climax.

Sometimes, if I came quickly, he'd caress me for a few minutes, then get back down there for my second go around. I always felt that was a bit of a cheat on my part. He was of a certain age where Felicity's double pleasure tended to be *off-piste*, if you get my drift. I mean we'd go through the motions, but he'd confided that he needed 24-48 hours recovery time to be sure that he'd have another ejaculation.

But on a short session, one hour, there just wasn't enough time for both of us. So, he knew that no cunny for Cindy meant no blow job for Vishti. Unspoken, but I'd just massage him, work his lingham, and then we'd share a moment to decide: *your turn or mine?*

There was only one real conflict in our sessions – I liked to watch and see his ejaculation. He used to prefer that I look at him with my *trademark smile* when he was on the point of coming. Sometimes we'd have a mock argument over whose turn it was. Sometimes just a nod from him or a nod from me would indicate: *Your turn today. You to watch my face smiling at you when you come; or my turn when I get to watch you come.*

But if we were both going to enjoy our pleasure, he had to book at least a 90-minute session, or even 2 hours if we wanted to chat. But I was now getting so many clients that Fi wanted to keep my bookings to 60 mins. I mean that was enough for a massage but not enough for the other, if you know what I mean. For Vishti and me, well we didn't like to rush.

I think that was one of the reasons he started switching to a hotel for one of my days off. More time together meant cunny for Cindy, which meant reciprocity for Vishti.

So, Vishti knew there's a *quid pro quo*, in my world. That was the expression he taught me. And I knew that Dixie was waiting for me to return the favour.

My *quid pro quo* with Dixie was playing on my mind. Not the actual act. I hadn't ever sucked off a woman, well not properly, not meaningfully. And, if you know me by now, you'd know I'm all about testing my boundaries. So, at the level of a new experience, I was up for it. The issue was similar to my issue with Vishti, though I never admitted it to him or even to myself. If I let myself, I might have fallen in love with him. Who am I kidding? I was already in love with him, desperately, which was why I had to end it.

The way it's turned out, I have sublimated my feelings into platonic, non-sexual love. I know he's fond of me, he might even say he loves me, like a daughter. For me, I do love him in the same way as I love my parents, a kind of unconditional love. Believe that or not. Actually, don't believe it. It's BS! I'll never stop loving him, and if I loved him like my parents, how come I wank while fantasising that he's sucking me off. That would just be sick.

Now, I love Dixie in the same way as I love my sister, I mean my step-sister. Of course, I wouldn't suck off my step-sister. (Note to Ed. Is that allowed? I mean if I put in the chapter about how we nearly got it on and might well have consummated the act if mum hadn't knocked on the bedroom door to see what the noise was about. Does that get clipped by the lawyers because it's incest? I mean step-sisters is not really incest, and anyway, we were just having a bit of a laugh.)

So, here's my problem. Once I got intimate, would my feelings change? Dixie handled it by getting drunk. But I wanted to enjoy the experience and pleasure her. I'd probably have a few drinks to loosen up, but I wanted to be in complete control. This wasn't about a drunken grope. But how would I know if I was going to be good at it? I'd had no practice. I hadn't really talked to anyone about the ins and outs of cunnilingus. Well, not with anyone who I thought knew what they were talking about. There was only one person who could instruct me, of course…

"Hi, Vish. I've got an odd request. Buy me lunch."

We met in Canary Wharf.

I liked Canary Wharf. Vish had predicted my future. He had told me how I was going to meet a young banker, who I'd have an affair with, and use him as my stepping stone towards ensnaring some megabucks hedge fund sugar-daddy. Ever since he'd mapped out my life, I'd roam around

Canary Wharf to get a flavour of what it would be like to be part of the world of finance. I'd watch the secretaries scurrying by in their figure-hugging blouses and skirts. I'd stare at the guys, young executives, ogling them. but I got no stares back.

In the treatment room, I'd captivate them, or, at least, captivate their cocks, but here, amidst the melee of secretaries and executives, I was anonymous. I was invisible. But I had to believe in Vish's vision for me. One day, rich pickings.

But in the meantime, I could rely on osmosis to absorb some of the nervous energy and trust that a little of the gold dust would fall on me.

Vish was in for a treat.

I told him he was buying me lunch, but I was choosing the venue. He didn't know that he was going to buy me a salt beef sandwich from a mobile van that visited every Wednesday. Vish thought it was quite funny.

"The sandwiches here are great, and it reminds me of the food my mother used to cook before she got divorced."

My relationship with Vish was so open that I had no qualms, so I just went straight into it.

"You've met Dixie. Well, the other night she sucked me off. I'd sort of hinted that I wanted to try it, and, in a drunken moment, she obliged."

"Soixante-neuf?"

"No!"

"That's right, I remember, you wouldn't come like that."

We shared a smile.

"OK, what's the question?"

"You know you're the best."

"Don't flatter me."

"Seriously, that's why I want you to teach me."

"Rache, you know I would do anything for you, but I don't really know what you want. I don't believe you want a demonstration."

I smiled what he would call my *trademark smile*.

"You told me you learned it all from the Kama Sutra and other texts. I'm not a bookworm. Dixie has to help me with most of my coursework, so I don't have to read it. Watching porn won't help. Porn isn't real, and YouTube demonstrations are too clinical. I'd like you to tell me, in your own words, how you do it."

Bless him! He didn't hesitate. He took me back to our first meeting, when he hesitated about ringing the doorbell, outside that *anonymous blue door in that anonymous back street* (was how he so eloquently described his first day at Felicity's) and then he told me something I never realised.

"I was nervous not because I was going to have my first erotic massage. I was nervous because I went in there wanting to ask if I could perform cunnilingus, and I didn't know what you'd say."

He blew me away with that admission, but it didn't stop me from answering:

"I would have told you to fuck off, and then I'd probably have told Fi to kick you out."

"So, I was right to be nervous, then!"

"You know you could have bought it. You go online and look up escorts and they list the services that they'd provide."

"Yes, I know, but it didn't feel right. Too mechanical, and I couldn't trust their reactions, fake orgasms and so on. Remember, I learnt from the ancient sutras, tantra is the spiritual side of that, so a tantric masseuse made perfect sense."

I burst out laughing. I couldn't stop. I was almost hysterical and Vish look concerned.

"Are you ok, what did I say? Really, what's so funny?"

I kept laughing, and a piece of bread got caught. I was choking and Vish grabbed me. I didn't know what was going on, but I should have realised that if you're choking on a piece of food, you need to be sitting next to someone trained in the Heimlich Manoeuvre, or, at least, someone who's read a book on it. So, now, Vish could add lifesaver to everything else he'd done for me.

It took me about 20 minutes before I'd really settled down again. When he could see I was OK, he asked again:

"What did I say?"

"I am so sorry, but you really are a daft bugger. You wanted to share a tantric experience so you could fulfil some spiritual destiny while performing cunnilingus, and you end up at Felicity's Massage and an appointment with me."

"Yes, but I still don't see what was funny. I'd booked a tantric massage with you."

"Yes, and I'd spent the week before in basic training …."

"And?"

"Which comprised being the passive two hands in a four-handed massage while I watched the other two hands give the client a hand… job."

I could barely get the words out without bursting into hysterical laughter, but at least this time Vish was sharing the joke. We were literally falling about like kids. I was so glad that Vish wasn't insulted. When I had calmed down a bit, I giggled:

"I think you should ask Fi for a refund for our first session."

Before we left the seats by the mobile food stall, Vish gave me some hints that were broadly about being aware of the partner's reaction. I knew the anatomy, but every woman is different, so he explained how you try different places and move the tongue around the clit circling and then up and down, learning what is working as you go along, gauging the speed, listening to the breath, which will tell you how close your partner is getting. It's almost like when you fall asleep and your breathing changes. Of course, you don't know that because you're asleep. You'll know if you sleep with a partner, you'll hear how their breathing changes.

So, best advice, Ladies or Gentlemen, if you're going to get down to give a little oral pleasure, listen for subtle changes in your partner's breathing and you'll be more sensitive to where they're at, on their path to orgasmic bliss.

For clarity, this is about cunny; if you're blowing a man or tossing him off, listening for the breath is a little too, how can I put it, tantric. The breathing is more like *frantic* than *vibrational* when he's about to shoot his load.

When it comes to men and blow jobs, you have to be ready for different signs. The more Vish talked, the more I realised that my experience with blow jobs *would* come in handy. The anatomy is not the same, but I know how my performance is very different when I just want the guy to come, compared to when I want to give him pleasure. Then, I am sensitive to his reactions. I do take care to feel what he likes, what gets him going and what slows him down. It's not the breath, but you're feeling, man or woman, you're feeling how they're feeling. I suppose you could say it's *empathy. You* could say that. Not a word I use, but when I looked it up, it seemed to capture the message I'm trying to get across.

"Vish, you old rogue. I knew you'd come through for me, if you'll excuse the pun. I think Dixie's in for a treat, and, by the way, thanks for saving my life."

"Well, I had to really. I don't think I could live if never again I was to see your *trademark smile.*"

Then he hit me with his real intuition:

"But seriously, Rache, you know I'd never preach, but I've met Dixie. Don't mess with her feelings."

And there I was back to square one. Dixie would have her orgasm, but was it going to ruin a good friendship?

*********

*It hadn't been long since my little escapade in Birmingham. I hadn't really given it much thought, but then I got a strange call:*

"Vishti, it's Arthur."

"Hi, Arthur, nice to hear from you. How's life…?"

"Sorry. Vishti, cut the small talk; it's dues time."

*It shows how naïve I am. I had no idea what 'dues time' meant. Arthur explained that, in his world, if you do a favour, you're entitled to one in return. Doesn't matter that you paid for the transaction, the nature of the business meant it was a favour. He also made it clear that, in his world, favours not returned could lead to repercussions, which neither of us wanted.*

*It seemed that* quid pro quo *was alive and well in the underworld that Arthur inhabited.*

*Sensing my discomfort, he also reassured me that, in his world, favours, once returned, were cancelled forever. Quits, even, nothing more would be asked.*

"Genuinely, we're in different circles. I'm not in that sort of business. I don't understand how I can help."

"Can't talk over the phone. Where can we meet?"

*It turned out that the favour involved a matter of £250,000 in cash. Once again, he reassured me that it was a one-off. Then he explained that, as I owned a property management company looking after a couple of hundred properties for several different clients, I could slip that amount of cash through the books without raising any suspicions. (He'd obviously done his homework because the size of our property portfolio wasn't public knowledge.) He even explained how the process worked and what was a reasonable amount to put through the books for each transaction. He offered to send me templates of the paperwork I could use. He'd clearly done it before. He said, though I wasn't sure whether to believe him, that he used different places all the time for security. I wondered whether his last launderer had been caught, which made me shudder. Although he seemed to have covered all bases, I knew it was a calculated risk and a possible jail sentence. But I also couldn't ignore the veiled threat of physical violence.*

"I'll pay you 10% for your trouble, if you think that's fair, for being my partner in crime."

*I challenged him to go into more detail about the process. While still illegal, the method that he was proposing appeared to minimise the risks. The fee, which would earn me £25,000, seemed rather generous. I tried to justify it on the basis that maybe one day I could put to good use what I had learnt from my one-time foray into the world of money laundering.*

*We shook on the deal and I thought that was that. Until a week later. I was at a business meeting in Brighton. I could have gone straight back to London, but I was going to be drinking and didn't fancy a late-night train journey, so I drove down and booked a room at a Premier Inn. Cheap and cheerful.*

*After dinner, I went back to my room. I'd taken my jacket and trousers off, so as not to crease them, but hadn't got completely undressed. There was a knock on the door and I heard a women's voice announce:* Room service. *I'd had a few drinks and was a bit confused, as I hadn't ordered anything. But I opened the door anyway. Standing in front of me was a quite stunning woman in a long fur coat and high heels. She opened her coat to reveal that underneath she was completely naked apart from a placard hanging around her neck with a message written on it:* Present from Arthur.

*******

*It would have been churlish to refuse.*

*I had the further excuse that it might be considered an insult by Arthur, who, while not a friend, was someone not to be crossed.*

*After my experience with Marie, there was a risk that this would become a habit.*

*She didn't waste any time. She was obviously on the clock. I didn't want to disrespect her. I let her control the pace. However, I was a little surprised. Her technique, for fellatio, was a cut above Marie. I wasn't sure whether this was potluck, or whether Arthur had some kind of pecking order. (Sorry, that didn't sound right!)*

*My lady of the night was called Charlene. Whether that was Charlene for the night, or Charlene for always seemed a little academic.*

*Her perfume was pleasant, not over the top, not tart-like, really a quite sophisticated aroma. She took me in her mouth, still wearing her fur coat over her naked body. She was just licking along the length of my erect member. No sucking, but just gently and rhythmically masturbating me with her lips.*

*For a moment, I was unsure whether this was just a tease. Perhaps some kind of in-joke with Arthur.* I'm only giving you half your normal rate so just play with the guy, *that sort of thing.*

*But I should have realised Arthur was a straight shooter (another unintentional pun), not one for games.*

*She moved her body and now her mouth was close to mine. Her lips were on my lips, and she paused slightly, then whispered:* "I'm going to kiss you, Sweetheart, tell me if that's OK."

*I didn't understand immediately, so nodded awkwardly. It was only afterwards that I realised her kissing me after she'd been licking my penis might be a turn-off for some clients. Funnily enough, Cindy and I never kissed after a blow job. But after I had pleasured her with my tongue, usually some minutes later, after her orgasm had subsided, and she was perfectly relaxed, she would look at me with her* trademark smile *and make a simple request:* Kiss me now, I want to taste my juices.

*I never found out whether that was for her pleasure, or she sensed that it was an incredible turn-on for me. Like much in our relationship, there were so many things left unsaid, because we shared so many unspoken thoughts.*

*Charlene was kissing me passionately. I was content with Cindy in my dreams. Charlene added another question:* OK with me on top? *Another nod. This time without hesitation. She was now riding me, forcing my member deep inside her. Cindy never faked. Cindy never had to fake. Our lovemaking was passionate, was sincere, was spiritual, was divine.*

*Charlene was moaning, reaching her crescendo just as she was using her pelvic muscles to pump and squeeze me, draining every ounce of semen as I came.*

*Her body was shaking, she kept on moaning:*

"I'm coming, Sweetheart. I've just exploded. We came together, you wonderful lover."

*I had to smile.*

*Charlene was a professional. She had one of those damp towels wrapped in cellophane that you get for your hands in a Chinese restaurant. She opened it and used the damp towel to clean me up. Then leant over to give my flaccid penis just one last kiss.*

*As she was buttoning up her fur coat, about to leave, she asked:*

"There was a moment, you know, when we were both coming together, that I detected a smile. Tell me, Sweetheart, was that just a moment of ecstasy or a joke we can share?"

"Truth? Or just part of this evening's fantasy?"

"Your choice, Sweetheart."

"I was just thinking, probably a resting actress waiting for her next role."

*She smiled:*

"Don't underestimate yourself, Sweetheart. It's not every client that can tickle my fancy the way you just did!"

# 17

# Vade Mecum

I'd just come up from the gym. Dixie was still in her jams, swigging juice from the carton. One of her annoying habits. I kept telling her to use a glass.

"You're such a sloppy cow."

"If you're going to be mean to me, I won't give you the prezzie I've got for you."

"Oh, no, sorry, spill the sodding juice, I don't care, I like prezzies!"

"Well, you're probably not going to like this one. It's a *Vade Mecum.*"

"A what?"

"*Vade Mecum.*"

"I'm hearing the words, but it sounds gibberish."

"It's not gibberish. It's Latin. It means: *Carry with me*. It's sort of a handbook of school notes that you carry with you. What school did you go to? I thought everybody..."

"I went to the local comprehensive near the Old Kent Road. When I come across out-of-towners, clients who don't know London, never heard of the Old Kent Road, I tell them to buy a Monopoly set. It's right there, Old Kent Road, £60 and it's yours. Mind you, at the comp, the girls would only want a packet of fags for a blow job. I dunno. Inflation?

"Your point being?"

"No fucking Latin, no fucking *Vardy Me Come*. Sounds like a tweet from the Wagatha diaries."

Dixie laughed: "Seriously, now you're doing four days a week at Felicity's you're missing so much coursework and lectures. What I've done is put together..."

I interrupted: "A *Vade Mecum!*"

"Exactly, in a ring binder, a handy compendium. Can I say that: *compendium?*"

"Piss off, I know what a bloody *compendium* is."

I smiled.

"Synopses of all my lecture notes, all in one place, to make it easy for you. You know for that downtime. You said sometimes you're kicking your heels between clients, or, as you quaintly put it, for when *the stupid arseholes cancel on me*. The *Vade Mecum*..."

"Yes, I get it, I can carry it with me... to work, have a quick read in between, before the next client comes..."

I suddenly burst into laughter. The laughter got worse, sort of like a guffaw. It became uncontrollable. I was becoming hysterical. Dixie was looking at me, asking if I was okay. It was all I could do to keep nodding, to indicate that I wasn't having a fit or anything. But I just couldn't stop laughing.

It went on for several minutes until Dixie interceded: "If you don't stop, I'm calling an ambulance. Get hold of yourself, girl."

I started to breathe deeply to try to regain my composure I gradually calmed down:

"I'm sorry, Dixie, I didn't want to worry you. I'm going to try to say this with a straight face. I don't know if I can do it. It was when you said these notes, the *Vade Mecum*, would come in handy in between clients..."

I was struggling not to break up again, but I carried on bravely:

"My day's work is evading their cum."

Dixie looked at me blankly. She hadn't got it yet so I continued:

"I spend time with a client – 'vading *their* cum, then it's time for the *Vade Mecum!*"

She finally got it and within seconds we were rolling all over the floor, legs akimbo, hands over our crotch imitating a man wanking and shouting, "Evade my cum! *Vade Mecum!*"

It took about 10 minutes for us both to calm down. Dixie on the sofa, me handing her a glass of wine, which she preceded to knock back in one.

Ditto.

We were physically exhausted and emotionally drained from the laughter session. But now she had a straight face and I was sitting next to her on the sofa. We were gazing into each other's eyes. She gave me a slightly puzzled look. I started to pull down her jams. She knew what was coming. She'd been waiting. Her *quid pro quo*.

She wriggled out of the pyjama bottoms, shuffled along the sofa, lay back and spread her legs. Now was the moment. I thought I was ready. She hadn't shaved, but her pubes were short and wispy, about a couple of weeks' growth. I got down to action. Her snatch was pungent. She hadn't showered yet. I wasn't used to the smell. I knew my own, I'd licked my fingers, during moments of self-gratification, but I'd never really smelt a vagina so close up. Quite different to cock. I just lay there breathing deeply through my nose drawing in the heavy scent.

"You haven't showered!"

"Sorry, do I smell? Shall I go shower?"

"Don't move. It's turning me on. I'm going to breathe in your fragrancy and then suck your cunt."

"Say it again, I like dirty talk."

I sucked her labia hard, took my mouth away and gave her my best shot: "I'm going to suck your cunt until you squirm. I'm going to bury my tongue deep into your pussy and drink your quim. I'm going to lick and suck until you beg me for more. I going to make you my whore bitch."

I took her and sucked her clit through her labia, and she started to spasm and screamed: "God, fuck! I'm coming!"

Did she need 30 seconds? It seemed not. She wriggled away as soon as she'd come. We were now sitting up on the sofa. I looked at her, and she pulled me close and kissed me passionately.

"What was that?"

"I came. It was great."

"If you were a client, I'd have to give you a refund."

"What do you mean? You were perfect."

"You came too soon. I was like an amateur. I'd thought about it. I'd prepared. I'd even asked…"

"Asked?"

"Never mind, I'm glad you enjoyed it. But Dixie, I can do better than that, really, you've got to let me try again."

"I told you I hadn't had sex for months. I think that's why I came so quickly. But honestly, I did enjoy it. If you're serious, I wouldn't mind another go, but not just yet. I feel tapped out."

"Can you tell me just one thing: afterwards, you kissed me. Why did you do that?"

"I don't know. I wanted to see what it was like. You know, the other night. We kissed. It seemed like the right thing to do. I've never really kissed a girl. Actually, that's not true. I've kissed girls, just never anyone I cared about."

"Thank you for your honesty. That's my issue here. I really like you. We're good friends. And I know I owed you the orgasm. I was ready for that, but I'm also worried, in case you think we're getting involved."

"Would that be so bad?"

"No, not at all. As long as we're both in the same space, which I think we are now. But what if these sessions become regular, and one of us falls for the other, but the other doesn't? It could be either way. I could fall for you. Either way, if that happened, it would start to get awkward. We share the flat; what if one of us is a roommate and one of us is a lover? One wanted to share a bed and the other wanted to sleep alone?"

"I've thought the same thing."

"And?"

"And I thought: *Sod it. Let's give it a try!* If we both fall in love, it's OK. If we both treat it as a bit of fun, when we're horny, it's OK. If one of us falls in love and the other doesn't, then I reckon you'd be the loser."

"Me? Why?"

"Because then I'd have to move out of the flat and you would fail your course."

"You silly sod. I'm being serious here."

"Seriously, I think we'd both miss cock too much."

"I'm not so sure. I like cock. It's the boyfriends I can't stand."

"Strap-ons?"

"Now, there's a thought. Let's see what *Lovehoney* has got to offer. Do you want a drink? I know it's early, but I feel we should celebrate."

The carton of orange juice was still on the coffee table. Dixie looked at it.

"Buck's Fizz?"

I got up to get a bottle of champagne. I always made sure there was an unopened bottle in the fridge. I brought it back with two tumblers. I poured the champagne. Dixie topped our glasses up with the orange juice.

"Cheers!" I toasted.

"To Orgasms!" Dixie responded.

"To Orgasms!" As I raised my glass again.

Dixie took a swig. She looked at me with a crumpled face.

"Not sure."

My face questioned: *Not sure about what?*

"Tastes better from the carton."

I topped up the glasses with more champagne.

"I'm going to miss my class. It's alright for you with your midday start."

"Finish your drink and bugger the lecture. I'm talking about us. It's important to finish the conversation."

"I thought we'd finished. I want to give this a try. I think you do too. We'll see how it goes. I know there are risks. I know that, if we fall in love, it could spoil a beautiful relationship, but what's that stupid saying: *Better to have loved and lost...*"

"Than spending your nights wanking in the bedroom."

"Talking of wanking..."

Dixie got up and led me into her bedroom.

She stood by the side of her bed and took off her pyjama top, then her trousers.

I pushed her onto the bed.

"Is my bitch whore ready for some more tongue on her filthy cunt?"

I grabbed her legs. Dixie clenched them in mock resistance. So, I pulled them again. She sandwiched my hands between her legs, I forced them apart.

"No, please, don't take me."

But now she was spreading her legs inviting me in.

I started to lick her labia. It was still moist and pungent from before. Then I opened the lips to reveal her clit. I could see it was swollen, engorged. Larger than I thought it would be. I hadn't looked before. It had all happened so quickly. I started with my tongue. Just flicking at it, at first. Then licking then sucking. At each moment, sensing her reaction. Each time I sucked, she quivered. When I circled around, she tensed. But when I moved my tongue up and down, I didn't sense her pleasure, so I just focused on the circling and the sucking. I could hear her breathing change. It was getting deeper. My tongue movements gathered pace. Her breathing got faster. I could feel her tense again. I thought she would come too soon. *Not this time, Dixie*, I thought. *This time I'll be in control.* I kept circling. Circling my tongue seemed to keep her going, while the sucking seemed to bring her to the brink. I knew how to keep her going and slow her down, while each time bringing her closer. I kept bringing her back up, but not letting her go too far. I kept going until I heard her say:

"Now, please, now. I'm going to come, going to come."

With that, she arched her back.

"Don't stop, don't stop."

I kept licking and licking until she forcefully pushed my head away from her mons.

I crept up to the bed, exhausted, and we fell asleep in each other's arms.

*******

*I got up and led her into my bedroom.*

*I stood by the side of her bed and took off my pyjama top and then my trousers.*

*She pushed me onto the bed:*

*"Is my bitch whore ready for some more tongue on her filthy cunt?"*

*She knows that her dirty talk turns me on. I'll be her bitch whore. That's who I want to be. This is a safe place. I've had men try it on and I've been scared shitless, but this is fantasy. OK...*

*She knows how to play. She grabs my legs. I'm going to resist, clenching her hands between my legs. She pulls my legs apart. I keep playing the game.*

*"No, please, don't take me."*

*I finally open my legs wide in submission. She starts to lick my labia. I'm wet there. But I still haven't showered. Will this turn her on or put her off?*

*She's using her tongue. I know you're going to pleasure me. You're going to do it right this time. She's licking me now. God that's good.*

*My guilty secret. I never wanted you to know. I couldn't tell you in case you rejected me. I think I loved you the minute we met. But first I had to admit to myself that I could love a woman.*

*God! Why did I wait? This is real. Every time I frigged myself, knowing you were in the bedroom next door. It was as much as I could do not to jump you.*

*But always the doubt. Would you want me? But now this is real. Hell! The feeling, my button so sensitive. You know what you're doing. But the real pleasure is that it's you. I'm coming again. I'm ready. She's not going to let me come this time. That's just heightened my feeling, I'm sort of quivering as she brings me towards orgasm again. The anticipation: will she let me this time? I'm completely in her power. I let her decide. She's keeping me dangling. I can't stand it any longer.*

*"Now please, now. I'm going to come, going to come."*

*Yes, she's licking, faster.*

*"Don't stop! Don't stop!"*

*More, more, now enough, I push her away, and then draw her back into my arms, and drift off to sleep.*

********

It took about two days for us to admit it. Dixie and I were now an item, but given we no longer lived in College Halls of Residence, neither of us saw the need to inform our college friends. We didn't change our relationship status on Facebook, although I don't think we would have bothered even if we'd got married.

We sat down at the breakfast bar in the flat, sipping our morning hit of coffee and I opened with:

"Can we agree some house rules?"

"What, for the flat?"

"No, us."

"Us?"

"You know - the relationship."

"Like what?"

"Well, for a start, are we exclusive?"

"You mean can you fuck another chick?"

"Not exactly what I meant. I was really talking about boys."

"Great. I have been celibate for months. You're the closest I've come to a fuck, which we've done once…"

"Twice."

"Well, one each. And you, two dates and a shag and it's over."

"Well, I guess that's what I was asking. If I see a boy and I fancy him, can I go there?"

"Face it, Rache. If you see a boy and you fancy him, wild horses wouldn't keep you away!"

"Can we be serious for just one moment?"

"I don't know. Ask me when it happens. I think it depends. I study 24/7, so I probably wouldn't notice, but, yes, if you started bringing your dates back, yes, I would be pissed."

"Anything else?"

"Can we sort of do a probation?"

"Look. Fuck off! What do you want from me? Suck your cunt once a month and do your ironing. Is this a relationship or not?"

"Sorry, I'm no good at relationships, so I don't know how to do it. Boys or girls."

"Just don't over-think it. Let's play it by ear. If we're both in the mood, we'll have sex. Sometimes we'll wake up in the other's bed, sometimes in our own. We'll have fun. We'll quarrel. Just like an old married couple. Perhaps one day we'll have kids."

"Don't even go there!"

"Sorry, only kidding, but do you get it? We'll take it as it comes. See how it goes. I doubt we'll be together for life; maybe till we graduate. Maybe we'll split before. Maybe just a two-date wonder, like your boyfriends."

"I've never lived with anyone before, you know, like a partner."

"Neither have I. Well, that's not true. I had a boyfriend in my gap year. We planned to go travelling together for six months. Lasted a month."

"What happened?"

"He kept using my toothbrush, so we went our separate ways."

I decided I'd pushed it enough. This was all new to both of us, so I thought we should move on.

"OK, can we talk about more serious stuff?"

"More serious. I thought that was heavy enough. What can be more serious?"

"*Lovehoney.com* does a strap-on for thirty quid."

Dixie laughed. "Sounds like a bargain. Could we buy two?"

"Two?"

"Yes, I want my own. Don't fancy being fucked by you after it's been up your pussy."

We both started laughing. I grabbed Dixie off the stool. She darted off. I pulled at her and we both ended up on the sofa, snogging.

# 18
# Jimmy

Fridays, I usually see Jimmy. He's a City type. He gives me all these stock tips, but I don't know what to do with them. I think he just says it to impress me. About how this company is about to get taken over, buy the shares, but don't tell anyone, or we could both go to jail for insider dealing.

Maybe one day I'll take up Vishti's advice and go find a banker as a sugar-daddy.

I just feel I'm not ready yet. In the treatment room I'm so confident. That's my turf. That's why I keep going back to Canary Wharf. I want to feel at home on their turf. I'm not ready yet. I don't speak their language.

Do I need a stockbroker first to understand the lingo, to understand what to do with the tips I get from the banker clients?

The world of high finance was alien to me. But it gave me a kick that these guys were talking to me about it, even if it was just because they thought it would turn me on.

Jimmy turned up on time. He knocks off early on Friday which is good because mid-afternoon can be quiet and I like to stay busy. He's what I call an easy client. Never tries anything on. He likes Body to Body, which involves my naked body rubbing against his. Some of the girls will lie to one side so that there's no chance of their vagina straying close to the client's erect penis. I think that's a cop-out. My legs are apart straddling the erection and I rely on accurate positioning to avoid the penis actually touching the labia. I'm actually quite proud of the technique I've developed. It's simulating sex, everything you do when you fuck without actual penetration. It needs to be a regular client that I can trust because I have a fairly slight frame and they could probably force the issue if they chose. The regulars know that that would be their last visit, so I've never had a real problem. Climax is their choice: we always refer to it as Lingham massage to fit with the Tantric shtick. For Body to Body, they might come when I'm on top of them. If they want a breast massage that can be accommodated. In the staff room, it goes under the moniker of *tit wank*, very tantric. But, out of respect for our clients, those words would never be uttered in the treatment room. I don't have very full breasts, so I wouldn't say that *tit wank* is my forte. For some inexplicable reason, a number of my clients will remove my hand during my sensual Lingham massage and toss themselves off, with me standing, bending towards them,  so that they can come over my tits. There's no accounting for taste.

Back to Jimmy. As I said, he likes Body to Body, and he'll usually come while I'm doing the simulated sex position on top of him. We sort of share a moment after he's come, where I'm rubbing the spunk against our bodies. I sort of jiggle my body so he can feel me spreading it over him. It only goes on for, I don't know, 30 seconds. Not long, but long enough for it to be a thing. I don't know how it started. I think, one session, after he'd come, he just held me there, and I kind of improvised. I don't do it with my other B2B clients. When they come, I usually get off them immediately.

My worst experience, well more like my most embarrassing moment in the treatment room, was when I hadn't noticed. The client was new. I usually pay more attention to a first timer, because, obviously, I want to convert them to a regular. For some reason, I wasn't paying attention. I always pride myself on being professional, but he was the last client after a long day, and I was daydreaming. Inside my head, I was in my bathtub, pouring a few drops of Ylang Ylang into the steaming water. Candles surrounding the bath. I saw it in a film once. Can't remember what film, but she was lying there, I remember seeing all those candles, and she was masturbating in the bath. I mean you couldn't see her fingers or anything. It wasn't a porn film; it was proper Hollywood. It was just the suggestion, the implication, which, in itself, was quite a turn-on. So, I'm in my bath, and there's, I don't know, maybe fifty candles. This is a daydream, so it doesn't matter that I would never be arsed to light fifty candles, nor that there's no shelf around my bath, so I couldn't actually put any candles there. So, as I'm sliding up and down on the client, I'm picturing myself, in the bath, masturbating. The whole scene, the sensuous setting of the candles, the aroma of the Ylang Ylang, is turning me on. I shift my position, so I can feel my clit rubbing against his leg and continue to pleasure myself. I was getting so carried away and then I was broken out of my daydream with:

"Er, I'm sorry, but I've come already, would you mind getting off me."

I could have died. He wasn't angry. But clients are paying for this experience, and I felt like giving him a refund.

*Think on your feet, Cindy. If you apologise for not noticing, he'll think you're a dork and never come back.*

This was early on, when I gave a shit about building my client base. Now, I'm so fully booked with regulars, I barely see any new clients.

*Don't apologise, make him think it's normal.*

So, all I could think of was how to convert this guy into a regular, after making such a fool of myself. Then I got a flash of inspiration.

"Ooh, that's so good that you've come, would you mind my cleaning you up?"

And with that, I slid my body off his, pressed my face onto his torso, and starting at his belly button, working downwards, proceeded to lick his spunk, sucking it off his body.

I don't like the taste of spunk, it's usually too salty. I wasn't doing blow jobs in the treatment room then, but whenever I was the recipient of a mouthful, I'd always told my boyfriends before: *You can come in my mouth, but don't expect me to swallow it.* So, they were ready for me to spit it out immediately.

But needs must, and there I was, licking and sucking the spunk off his body like I was enjoying it. When I gathered up a mouthful, I looked at the client and kind of gargled before swallowing it down.

After he got dressed, I escorted him back to reception. Fi would always be ready, as she would do a quick de-brief:

"How was it today? I said you'd be amazed by Cindy. Shall we say same time next week?"

The client concurred. It seemed I was on the way to converting him to a regular. Just as he was booking his next appointment, I suddenly had a thought. I wanted him to come back, but not under false pretences. I pulled him away from the reception desk, and whispered in his ear:

"I can't promise a repeat of the aftercare; usually, I just use tissues. It's just that I'd been so busy, I'd missed my afternoon cuppa, and I was really thirsty."

He didn't know which way to turn, went back to the reception desk to finish the booking. As he walked towards the exit, he turned his head, and shouted to Fi:

"Cindy says to make sure there's cow's milk in the fridge in future, she doesn't like the taste of these milk substitutes."

Fi looked puzzled. The client gave me a wink, as he walked out.

Back to Jimmy. He was getting dressed. Normally, I leave the room when the client is getting undressed and then again when they are getting dressed afterwards. But for a few regulars who are happy for me to stay, it saves me time cleaning the room in between clients. Where we've got a good relationship it's always nice to have a bit of a chinwag.

So, he was just zipping up his trousers when he sprang something new on me. I was tidying the room and he asked casually:

"Would you be up for a threesome?"

"Technically, we do do couples massages, but the rooms are too small and that's more of a spa treatment, with side-by-side beds."

"No, what I meant was, would you come over to my place and perform, in front of me, with my wife?"

It came as a bit of a shock. I have some weird clients who like very odd things, but I'd always thought of Jimmy as pretty conventional.

"You mean I do a lesbian show with your wife, while you watch?"

"Well, sort of."

"Jimmy, we know each other well enough. There's no *sort of*. Tell me exactly what you have in mind. I'd hate to get there and find that you were expecting something different to what was on the menu."

"OK, but, obviously, if you're not up for it, that's fine. I was thinking you and my wife caress. The Body-to-Body massage, you know all over."

"And, come on spit it out, Jimmy, I know there's more."

"Well, you know 69. Licking each other. My wife loves oral but says I'm lousy at it."

After my sessions with Dixie, I was confident I could deliver. The 69 doesn't work for me but, if the object of the exercise was to give his wife an orgasm, I knew I could do that, even if her tongue wasn't triggering anything for me while I was stimulating her.

"What are you going to be doing while the girls are having fun? Watch porn on TV?"

Jimmy laughed:

"Well, I suppose I'd be playing with myself, while I watch."

"OK, serious question. Does your wife like to watch? What I mean, and forgive me for being crude, but am I being set up for you to fuck me? I'm not saying no, but I don't like surprises."

Jimmy sat up and looked a little shocked. I think the *Not-Saying-No* bit was a mistake because it could easily have been taken as a *Yes*.

"No, no. I'd be making love to her after the two of you did your thing. Maybe you'd be caressing me or her when we were making love. We'd play that by ear, but, no, definitely no full sex between you and I."

I just had to cost this out. The two-hour rate here for B2B was £280, the lezzie show had to be extra. I didn't want to undersell myself. Worse case he'd say no, and I wasn't desperate for the money.

"£500 plus taxi fare."

"Oh, I thought around £350."

"Jimmy, don't insult me. We're not in a souk!"

Jimmy didn't respond. I'd learnt the silence rule from Vishti:

*Whoever opens his mouth next loses.*

When he ran this Estate Agency, he'd give the junior negotiators these sales tips. I talked to him about how I'd been making good money by upselling more expensive menu items or suggesting a longer session next time. I think it gave him a kick to suggest ways I could *close* the deal, as he put it.

Jimmy was quiet.

He'd obviously budgeted to pay less than £500. I knew he'd pay £400. He was waiting for me to go down to £450 so that he could settle for £400, or, if he spoke first, his next offer might be £400 where we settle on £450. So, whoever opened their mouth first, it would cost them £50. But I thought, sod it, I wasn't budging.

"Why don't we say…"

I cut him off.

"Don't, Jimmy. I like you as a client, but I'm not on an auction block. Let's just forget it and stay friends."

"OK, £500."

"Plus the taxi fare."

"Yes, OK, plus the taxi fare."

I knew I was smiling, my *trademark smile*. But I had to turn my back, he might think I was gloating. I was pleased with myself, out-smarting Mr City Heavy-hitter. Kind of got a kick out of it.

We set the date and time and I gave him my phone number, so he could text me his address.

His parting shot was:

"You should be in the City. You're a brilliant negotiator."

"And you should think about brushing up on your negotiating skills because, for the £500, I would have thrown in a blow job!"

He didn't know if I was really kidding.

I didn't know what he really had in mind. I was in for a real surprise.

# 19
# Graduation day

Greenwich College didn't have sororities in the way that US colleges did, but they did have a lot of social clubs, College Societies, usually open to anyone who shared that interest. These Societies would promote their activities to attract new members. Like other colleges or universities throughout the U.K., Freshers Week was an opportunity for each Society to display its wares to new students. Fresh fish could explore the variety of activities in which they could participate, to make their life at college more rewarding.

There was one very exclusive Society. Exclusive in the sense of keeping its membership list secret and not wishing to promote its activities. The Society, known to its members as *The Extras* was not dissimilar to Alcoholics Anonymous, in so far as AA would perhaps wish its *raison d'être* would cease. So it was with *The Extras*. The one thing we had in common was the entry requirement. We were all in the sex trade. It's a sad state of affairs that so many young women in the U.K. today feel forced to use their bodies to pay their way through college.

Our name, *The Extras,* is a sort of in-joke because that's what we often offer to clients.

We include high-class escorts, sugar-babes, even those who, unashamedly, call themselves prostitutes, lap dancers, strippers, and my own profession: purveyors of the art of erotic massage.

We get together regularly for a drink and a chat and a laugh. When we have one of our meetings, we use our stage names. None of our clients know our real names, so, at our meetings, we sort of wear the persona of our alter egos. Our particular shared interest means that the meetings and the activities we get up to are perhaps a little more raunchy or risqué, than your average student social club.

We have 30 active members, and about the same number who we see from time to time. Not a large number in a college, spread over three campuses, that boasts 20,000 students, but I don't believe we comprise the whole cadre of girls here who work, on the side, in our trade. At a guess, I'd put the number at 200, which is 1% of the student numbers here, putting the whole thing in perspective. If that figure is at all representative of colleges throughout the U.K., it is an indictment of the broken funding model for students in this country. I saw one survey that put the figure nationwide as high as 3% of the female student population, which they said meant 214,000 women selling their bodies in some shape or form to cover college fees.

Once you've started in the trade, you remain eligible to stay a member. It's not just the social activity. We provide support, emotional support, to our members, referrals to counsellors and other guidance. A girl might just have had one trick as an escort but been left damaged for life. We like to have fun, but that doesn't mean we don't take the consequences of our trade seriously.

Schools out soon, and there's an end-of-term feel, which means party, party, party. All the College Societies do their own thing and we're no exception. Half a dozen of us have formed a sub-committee to decide whether we can make this year's party more outrageous than last year's St Trinian's theme. We had such a giggle, dressed in black stockings and mini-skirted school uniforms. We prowled the corridors of the Residential Halls armed with life-sized blow-up dolls, inviting male students to pleasure themselves with the dolls at £20 a time. We were raising money for *Her Centre*, a local charity for women looking for protection from domestic abuse. We raised £1,000 from the boys and had pledged to match what we raised out of our own pockets.

June piped up:

"Can we do something really off the wall this year which will make some of the male student wankers stand up and think?"

"Do you have an idea?"

I asked June, knowing full well she wouldn't have opened her mouth if she hadn't had something in mind. What she was about to mention was a shock to even the normally un-shockable Cindy.

"*Bukkake!*"

There was an urban myth floating around the College that, a few years ago, a group of male students made a *bukkake* video, paying a local prostitute to be the subject of humiliation. The story was that the video circulated around College and the students were expelled. There's a *bukkake* video on swingers-247.co.uk that purports to be the actual video but with faces pixelated. There's no proof that anything untoward ever took place on College grounds.

In case you haven't seen *bukkake* porn, I wouldn't recommend it. It is the most disgusting misogynistic type of porn that you can ever expect to see. None of us could understand where June was coming from with this idea. You definitely wouldn't want to be part of it in real life. Briefly, though there are variations, these obnoxious videos comprise a naked woman kneeling on the floor or lying on a bed, either hands-free to imply they're enjoying it or hands tied to make them suffer. I find it difficult to describe it. Next to child porn, it is the lowest of the low. The men are in a circle. They're standing there, masturbating. The whole object of the session is to spurt spunk all over the poor woman's body. Usually, the trajectory is towards the woman's face. The most extreme examples are from Japan, where the final frame of the video often shows the woman's face virtually obliterated by the mountain of spunk. As I say, there are variations. Americans tend to like to include fellatio. For the true misogynist, there's nothing like seeing a huge cock rammed down a woman's throat until she's just gagging, choking. The other favourite, although this tends to be European, specifically German, is exchanging spunk for urine - men pissing on the lady. Technically that's not *bukkake*, but there's no need to be pedantic.

*******

*Trigger - unless you're a history buff, you can skip the next paragraph. It doesn't add anything to the story, but it does suggest some imagery of the Duchess of Sussex that might offend Meghan fans.*

### *A brief history lesson*

*The Japanese, who invented the genre, tend to keep more strictly to the traditional format. My research revealed, though I can't attest to the accuracy, that the practice goes way back to ancient times in Japan when, as punishment for committing adultery, the errant villager would be publicly humiliated by being paraded naked in the village square where the local men would ceremoniously perform the act of* splashing, *which is the literal translation of the Japanese word* bukkake. *My historical research didn't reveal the punishment accorded to the male participant of the adultery; he probably had to stand the Japanese equivalent of a round of pints at the local pub. The public humiliation has shades of Game of Thrones, but even Jeremy Clarkson did not wish this fate on the Duchess of Sussex.*

*The historical explanation may or may not be accurate, but the modern practice, or rather its use in porn, can be traced back to the 1960s. At that time, it was illegal in Japan to show an erect penis on videotape. You will still see Japanese videos, perhaps of the more vintage variety, where the penis is pixelated. So, some clever porn film director had a great idea. He couldn't show the penis, but the actual ejaculate was not considered illegal or obscene.*

Sounds very bizarre but, *hey ho*, we are talking about Japan. If you have overheard any locker room banter in your local rugby club, this disgusting misogynistic practice appears to have become a staple of the U.K. porn industry.

(Note to Ed. You may think I'm stretching the incredulity of my dear readers, who may be wondering how I could have known that this is a subject of discussion throughout the locker rooms of rugby clubs in the U.K. Well, of course that is total bollocks. I've never been asked, as a dare, for example, to walk through a changing room of a local rugby club inspecting the guys' naked cocks. What on earth would you think of me! Obviously not rugby, I'm a soccer girl, and it was only *one* Boxing Day, and I was a bit drunk, and the boyfriend, at the time, was captain of the sixth form soccer team.)

So, why the fuck is June thinking of *bukkake*? I mentioned the urban myth around College. Urban myths usually have a foundation in fact and it's not surprising that this rumour spread. I know it has spread outside to other colleges. One of my younger clients once told me that, at his *alma mater*, there was an expression *doing a Greenwich*. I'd asked him to explain. His story was a prelude to asking me if I would oblige. He was cute, a baby really, and I politely told him that, for an extra tenner, I would happily give him my best dirty talk describing the sordid practice while pleasuring him with my hand if that would turn him on: *But, sorry, Sunshine, I won't let your cum spoil my make-up today.*

By the time June had finished explaining the details of what she had in mind, we were all *onside* (Ed. That was a football pun, but I think it works here) and couldn't wait to get the party started.

*******

The evening of the party arrived. Some of the girls went down the corridors of the Residential Halls looking for potential targets. Male students who'd had a bit to drink, but not so much that they had lost control. Too-drunk-to-come wasn't going to cut it.

The pitch was easy: *A fellow student, female, of course, would be in her room lying naked on a massage table with her hands bound.* The target was told that this was part of an initiation ceremony for a college girls' club. *The student being hazed might resist a little, but that was the cost of becoming a member of the club*. These gullible men were assured that entrance to the sorority was so exclusive that, however much she doth protest, she was really gagging for it.

Pitch perfect, it took less than 20 minutes to find 6 willing and eager marks ready to take an active role in the proceedings. They were led into the room blindfolded. Each unwitting participant was then guided to the massage table where I was lying on my back, naked. My hands were folded underneath the table and bound. It was a little uncomfortable but I had volunteered for the task. All in a day's work, I thought, and ready to promote the common cause. There was some thrill in the anticipation, knowing what was to follow. The blindfolded targets were told to unzip their trousers and let them and their pants drop to their knees. Then they were instructed to shuffle forward.

There were about 30 girls squeezed into the double dorm room. Sitting on the two beds or squatting on the floor. June, who was directing the proceedings, tried to stop the girls from giggling. Someone shouted out: *Come on show us your dicks!* June looked across, angrily, putting her finger to her lips, telling them *Shsh!*

But it was comical to watch the boys shuffling forward almost tripping over their trousers. As they approached the massage table, their hands were guided towards the underside of the table so they could feel that my hands were tightly bound.

One of the girls asked the boys: *Go on, ask her if she's up for it* but, instead, one of the stupid idiots chirped up: *You asked for this, to be initiated into this stupid club, didn't you, bitch?*

This wasn't part of June's script, so I wasn't sure how to respond. I took a chance: *No, no, please, they're making me do it.* June piped up: *Go on, now, we told you she'd resist. It's all part of the initiation ceremony, the hazing.*

This bit was rehearsed, I tried to sound distressed: *Please, please, don't do it. I've changed my mind.*

June continued with the direction: *Go on, boys, get yourself hard, willies out and start tossing yourselves off. We want to see you spunk all over her face.*

There was a moment when I thought these drunken slobs will do the right thing, put their cocks away and leave the room. The irony was that my clients at Felicity's would never disrespect me and they were paying for the privilege, but here, in this environment, anything seemed on the table, if you'll excuse the pun.

"Have you got any lube?" one of them called out as he started to masturbate.

"Use your own spit, you stupid fucker," one of the girls shouted.

He duly complied. We didn't have to wait long before there came the knock on the door. The door opened. The boys stopped wanking when they heard the very recognisable Scottish accent of whom they believed to be our very own Miss Brodie.

"What do we have here?" Lily called out. Lily was Miss Brodie's secretary, a former student who retained her membership rights when she graduated and took on her admin. assistant role. She spent her working hours outside Miss Brodie's office, listening to her on the phone, and had got her mimicry pitch perfect. Lily continued:

"We had a complaint about noise in this room. What on earth are you gentleman doing? Keep those blindfolds on!"

They were, of course, scrambling to zip up their flies.

"If it is anything like it appears, you are in serious trouble."

One of the boys started to say something, but she cut him off.

"I don't want to hear any excuses. I've seen enough. You boys will report to me in my office tomorrow morning. 9 am sharp. You bring with you an envelope in which I expect to find the words: *I will always respect women*, written 100 times."

One of the boys chirped up:

"You mean 100 lines like in the Billy Bunter Books. We don't do that at school anymore, Miss."

"I haven't finished. And one more word out of you, Sonny Jim, and your task will be upped to 200 lines. Gentlemen, your sanction will be determined tomorrow. Anything up to immediate expulsion. You have some choices now, boys, and here are your options. Five minutes late and expect this to be your last day at the College. Has anyone heard of *Her Centre*?"

One of the boys piped up:

"Yes, Miss, it's a local Shelter for battered wives."

Miss Brodie/Lily continued:

"It's a local charity that provides support for women who have been the subject of domestic abuse. Please choose your words carefully and with more compassion when referring to these unfortunate souls."

"Sorry, Miss, I didn't mean to …"

"Google their website, have a look at the work they actually do. If you want to soften me up and perhaps appeal to my better nature, place some money with your 100 lines in a sealed envelope and hand it to Lily, my secretary, and I might, just might, leave the matter there."

One of the boys asked sheepishly:

"How much should we donate, Miss?"

"It's up to you. You know your financial position. I'm not going to tell you how much to give. I would, however, say it's an extremely worthy cause. Your generosity will not go unnoticed when it comes time for me to give you a reference for your future employment. These things do get recorded in your personnel file. Now don't be late. Keep your blindfolds on until you leave the room and don't think that I don't recognise each of you behind your masks."

With that, they were each escorted to the door and we heard them running down the corridor.

As soon as they were out of earshot, the belly laughs began and Lily assured us: "Don't worry, I'll be there at 9 to collect the envelopes. Brodie never gets to the office before 9:30."

"How much do you think we'll raise?"

June looks around at the girls.

"From that motley crew at least a ton," someone piped up.

"Come on, girls, there's more work to do. Our target for this evening is £1,000 and we can all chip in £20 for a sweepstake for the closest guess, to raise more for the charity.

With that, some of the group got up from the floor and returned to the corridors to find more unsuspecting targets.

# 20

## Sandy

I got to his place at 7.25 pm. I waited in the cab for five minutes, looking at the house. It was a typical terraced townhouse but in a very fashionable suburb. I had checked on Rightmove; prices started at three mill. I walked up the few steps to the front door. There was this old-fashioned bell thing where you didn't know whether to pull or press. I looked at it but then noticed a small buzzer next to it, which I pressed. I looked up to see the CCTV and movement sensor, which had triggered the outside light as soon as I'd stepped onto the first tread. I thought to myself: *Exactly the sort of security that you'd expect for a place like this.*

The door opened and a strange man was standing there. I had a terrible premonition: *Fucking hell!* I wondered if I had misjudged Jimmy and I was about to be the victim of gang rape. Then I noticed the man was dressed in some weird garb that I think I'd seen on TV at the last royal wedding.

"Miss Cindy, I presume. Mr James is expecting you."

He stepped back to allow me in.

"May I take your…"

He paused. I was wearing this long nylon anorakky thing, a cross between a coat and a jacket. He was obviously struggling to find a name for it.

"No, it's fine. Ta very much."

Beneath I was wearing the LBD that Vishti had bought me for our first non-date. It had two ties at the bottom so you could adjust the length and was in a clingy material, so it shaped the contours of my body. No bra and panties. They were in my clutch bag for afterwards. I'd built up this whole image in my mind of walking in, in my coat, and taking it off to reveal my sexy dress. But the butler gave me such a dirty look when I suggested I'd keep the coat, that I had to concede.

"Oh, OK!"

He then helped me off with it and literally took it between his thumb and forefinger before draping it over the hall stand. I had this vivid picture of him taking it downstairs as soon as I was out of view, and either dumping it in the scullery or putting it straight out with the trash.

"Just be careful with it, it's irreplaceable. Primark was out of stock last time I checked."

His face didn't change. Not even a glimmer.

He guided me to the back of the hall, opened the double doors, and *announced*, I think that's the right word, or maybe *presented* me:

"Miss Cindy, sir."

It was like a scene out of Bridgerton.

Sitting in a wing-backed leather chair, sort of an almost burgundy, with those bobbly things dotted all over, making it uncomfortable to sit on, was this stunning beauty. I called Jimmy posh, but this was... sophisticated, yes, sophisticated. Sort of Salma Hayek on steroids. She looked me up and down, rather disapprovingly. Me in my cute LBD mini-dress, her in her, I don't know, Versace. I was feeling uncomfortable. She seemed to be doing her best to diss me.

"So, this is the Cindy I've heard so much about, James."

She had a vague Spanish accent to complete the Salma Hayek mimicry.

I turned to see Jimmy, standing at the bar. Yes, they had a fucking bar, in the living room – sorry, drawing room.

"God, I'm sorry, how rude." Jimmy apologised, as he sidled over and pecked me on each cheek.

"Cindy, this is Cassandra, but I call her Sandra. Sandra, this is my lovely Cindy."

Who were these people? I'm not your *lovely* anything. I'd perched on a low stool. I think it was a footstool. In later life, I learned the word *Ottoman* to more accurately describe this piece of furniture. I was shrinking smaller and smaller and just wanted to get out of there. Then I thought: *What would Vish think if he saw me now? What would he say?*

He always seemed to have an answer for everything. When he was a client, he never treated me like the hired help. He always said he admired the way I was able to take control.

That was it. Thanks, Vish. *Get a grip, Cindy. Take control!*

With that, I got off my stool and sat in the other wing-backed chair, a hideous thing, but it was right opposite Cassandra. I stared at her:

"So, Sandy, what have you got in store for me tonight?" As I spoke, I uncrossed my legs and revealed just enough to make her wonder, as she looked at my crotch. She couldn't see anything, but the imagery was clear.

"The answer's *No*, by the way, Sandy. I left them in my bag."

I shook my bag to indicate where I'd put my underwear.

I wasn't sure if it was a growl or a smile, but Jimmy intervened.

"Er, it's Sandra, by the way, not Sandy."

I ignored the comment but looked at her:

"I call him Jimmy, is that alright? Or do you want me to call him James this evening?"

"Cindy, my dear, this is your evening. We want you to be relaxed. Feel free to call him however you're comfortable."

"Thanks, Sandy, I'll stick with Jimmy."

Jimmy was about to say *Sandra*, but he couldn't finish the word, as she cut him off with a glare and:

"That's alright, James, just a game Cindy and I are playing. You're not part of this, James."

She knew the rules. He was clueless. Battle lines were drawn. Who dares wins!

"Sorry, drinks. What's your poison, Cindy?"

They'd started before me, so I couldn't just say that I'll have the same.

"Anything with gin in it is fine."

"Dry Martini, G&T?"

"Something easy, so we won't need trouble the butler."

James didn't get it: "No, Cindy, I think I can make you a drink on my own."

"OK, a dirty martini. You know me, nice and dirty."

I looked directly at Cassandra. She smiled. She was quite enjoying this. James was in *La La Land*.

I saw him rummaging around the bar, there were plenty of olives but he needed the brine from the olive jar for the dirty martini. I saw him fiddle with something under the bar counter, and, on cue, the butler appeared.

"Do we have a jar of olives in the kitchen? I need the brine."

"Of course, sir."

"Oh, Jimmy, I said don't trouble the butler."

And the three of us shared a laugh.

There was a bit more banter. Cassandra and I were just getting the feel for each other. I needed her to know that I was no pushover. I demanded respect. She needed to know that if I couldn't come up to her level, I'd drag her down to mine. Cats fighting in the street.

Cassandra was not giving up: "I hope you like the music, Cindy."

It was classical stuff, listenable but I didn't know the tunes until the next piece came on. "Yes, I recognise this one."

"Oh, yes, we saw Simon Rattle conduct Prokofiev's Dance of the Knights at the Albert Hall. Were you there?" Another put down.

Advantage Miss Cassa-snob.

"No, must have missed that, but I do hear it every week on telly when I watch The Apprentice."

Back to deuce. "Personally, I prefer Adele."

We were having our drinks when the doorbell went.

"That will be Rafe," Cassandra said to Jimmy.

"We have a nice surprise for you. Rafe will take you to places you've never been. Get ready for your journey to ecstasy. Rafe has the hands of an angel, which can send any woman into orgasmic delight."

Oh fuck, I was just getting more relaxed and now we're back to a foursome with me being ridden both ends. I was thinking of getting up to leave when I realised that I hadn't been paid. I started fidgeting on my seat, then the door opened and the butler announced: "Mr Raphael!"

Cassandra got up to greet him. I noted that she'd stayed in her chair when *I* came through the door.

"Rafe, darling, this is Cindy, your client for this evening."

Give me a break. I couldn't believe they had employed a male escort for me for the evening or was this some kind of weird swapping thing they do in the suburbs? Car keys at dawn. I suddenly felt like a participant in a *Killing Kittens* house party. But *Raphael*, oh please, as he minced across the floor, my parents would have called him effeminate, nowadays we just say gender fluid or non-binary. I was about to ask *them* what pronoun *they* prefer, but, given that I wasn't yet ready to call Sandra by her preferred name, I thought better of it.

Cassandra turned to me:

"Cindy, when you've finished your drink, he's all yours for the next thirty minutes, just don't let him release all your tensions, we need you a little edgy don't we, James? You do like reflexology, I hope."

"Yes. One of the girls at work is a trained reflexologist, so she practices on us during our downtime."

"Cindy does massage, don't you, my Dear? Rafe's reflexologist to the stars, aren't you, Luvvie? Don't spread it around, but he used to do Gwynnie before she moved out of St John's Wood and went all goopy. Rafe will take you upstairs and, when he's had his evil way with you, I'll come up and run your bath."

This was sounding better. It seemed that Rafe's role was to give me a foot massage rather than be my sex slave.

"Bath or shower? Entirely up to you. Your special evening. I hope you'll say bath because I've got some lovely oil I bought just for the evening."

I thought to myself: *These people are trying to be nice. This might turn out to be quite pleasant after all. Not quite happy with you yet though, Cassandra!*

"Bath sounds good, Sandy."

She gave me a look that said: *What more do I have to do? I'm trying to be nice, you ungrateful S.O.B.*

I knocked back my drink and took Rafe's arm: "Come on, Raffy boy, show me the way."

The *way* was up a winding staircase with an ornate balustrade in some dark wood, to match the dark wood panelling in the hallway. Yuk!

I was led into a small anteroom where a cushioned velvet-covered chair, with a towel draped over it, was waiting for me. Next to the chair was a foot bath. I don't mean a bowl full of water, I mean a fucking foot jacuzzi like you'd get in a spa.

I was now convinced that my earlier apprehension was because I was so far out of my comfort zone. They were just being their normal, snot up their backsides, arrogant selves. Jimmy behaved very differently with me at Felicity's than James did in front of Cassandra.

First the foot spa, then the reflexology. The pampering went on. I was drifting off to sleep. I sort of heard Rafe bid me farewell but didn't open my eyes until I heard Cassandra whispering softly in my ear:

"Bath's ready."

She was sensitive to my dozing off, so she helped me gently up from the chair. She unzipped my dress and delicately let it drop to the floor. She had already run the bath. It was one of those roll-tops plonked in the centre of the room. The bath sat on a plinth which made it too high for someone my height, so you had to perch on the edge of the bath and then throw one leg over. I guess you reversed the process to get out. I probably could have manoeuvred myself into the bath but was quite appreciative of Cassandra's help. As she guided my naked body into the bath, she brushed the nape of my neck and ran her finger down my spine, sending a sensual chill that made me tighten my muscles and pelvic floor. Reminded me of a yoga class. In the bath, I picked up a pungent odour.

"Ylang-ylang?" I inquired.

"Yes, I said I'd bought some special oil, just for this evening."

Cassandra then soaped a sponge and proceeded to sponge my shoulders while I was sitting up. It wasn't nylon. It was the real McCoy. She told me to lay back while she sponged my breasts and asked me to raise my knees so she could sponge my legs. She looked at me quizzically, holding the sponge close to my crotch, as if to say: *May I?*

I arched my back, raising my butt slightly so that she could sponge inside my thighs more easily. She was playing with me, seducing me, tormenting me. OK, Cassandra, you win, game, set and match. So I looked her in the eyes and, for the first time this evening, awarded her with my *trademark smile* and then the big concession:

"Thank you. That was really lovely, *Cassandra*."

Everything was paced. Nothing rushed. I didn't remember being treated like this, ever. Even Vish. Always a gentleman. Always respectful, even when he blindfolded me, bound me in bondage tape and cuffed my hands and feet, he was always gentle and kind to me. Even with Dixie, girlfriend, now girlfriend and lover, we would explore each other's bodies with delight.

But this was pure seduction.

This was: *Come into my spider's web, I'm going to devour you!*

This was: *Lambs to the slaughter!*

This was: *Putty in your hands!*

Bath time over, Cassandra's hand guided me up. She wrapped a bath towel around my body. It was warm and soft. She patted me dry all over, gently, a little more firmly over my breasts and crotch, just to remind me of pleasures still to come.

"The towel's so soft. Egyptian cotton?"

Cassandra smiled. I wanted to say: *Take me now. I'm ready*. Then, suddenly, I got this image of Cassandra standing over me at the top of the bed holding me while Jimmy was thrusting into me *Handmaid's Tale*-style. I drew away, and Cassandra looked confused. She was wearing a gorgeous silk robe, sort of cream, with some kind of velvety piping. It looked like it would cost thousands. Then, as I pulled away and she saw me standing their full height, butt naked, she yelped:

"I thought you'd be taller. You can't wear this."

I realised she had draped an identical robe on the chair by the bath.

She started to go a bit doolally.

"No, no, James. Why didn't you give me her measurements? This evening was supposed to be perfect."

She grabbed the gown and went to the dressing room which I'd passed on the way in. It was like a huge walk-in wardrobe. I heard what sounded like her rummaging through the drawers. She came out with a pair of scissors and started cutting up the gown. I thought she'd gone bonkers. But then she held up the gown and explained:

"There, that should fit now."

The daft cow had only cut the bottom of a thousand-pound silk bathrobe so that it wouldn't be too long for me.

As quickly as she had flipped into doolally mode, her demeanour switched back to seductive Cassandra.

"Come, follow me into the boudoir."

She half turned towards me and held out her hand, her eyes looking straight at mine. I hadn't noticed her piercing eyes before. Her lips were glistening, her body captivating.

I hesitated while I was picturing her nakedness under her silk gown.

Back to her eyes, I couldn't avoid her piercing stare.

"Cindy, we're waiting!"

I held out my hand sheepishly, so she could lead me in.

I was back under her spell.

# 21

# The Boudoir

Of course, the boudoir included a four-poster bed. No Jimmy, however. So maybe I was going to be spared a Handmaid's Tale rape fantasy.

"Where's Jimmy, er, James?"

"Not sure, probably on some important business call. Don't worry, he'll join us later."

I was glad to have a private moment with Cassandra before we started, because I had a concern.

"Sandra, James told me what he had in mind, but I thought I'd run it by you, to make sure there were no crossed wires."

She had a puzzled look:

"I thought you were ready for this. This has to be consensual."

"No, no, I'm up for it, but he mentioned 69."

"*Soixante-neuf*. Is that a problem?"

"Not at all, I said I'm up for it."

So far Cassandra and I had just danced. I enjoyed the game, but that's what it was: a game. Just like college exams, we sat the prelims before the finals. The finals were at the *business end* of term.

That's where I was now, the *business end*. Jimmy and I were open and direct, talking about sex. Now I had to face Cassandra. She was the client. I just had to stay professional and tell her like it is.

"I just wanted you to know that I won't come like that. I'm sure I'd be able to pleasure you, and I'd enjoy it. So if that's what you want, it's fine. But, you see, I don't know what you want to get out of this evening. You keep saying it's my evening. Is my orgasm integral to the deal?"

"Absolutely. I'd be devastated if I came and you didn't."

"Well, do you mind, and I don't want to spoil the mood by being so clinical, but would you mind if I lie back now while you pleasure me first and then I'll take over? I'll know you'll enjoy me."

She gave me a devilish glint with those piercing eyes. She almost manhandled me up the bed, opened my robe violently, spread my legs roughly and got down to work. She was lying on top of me, riding me like one of my Body-to-Body sessions with Jimmy. Did she know what we got up to? Now was not a good time to ask.

Then, without warning, she pressed her mouth onto mine. She started kissing me and it took me a few seconds to respond.

My initial shock caused her to pull away, so I pulled her towards me and we started to kiss again. Her mouth tasted sweet, slightly of alcohol, but she'd used something to take away any hint of malodour. It wasn't mouthwash. I found mouthwash just masked any food taste, but this was different. My mind is a bit weird. If I couldn't work it out, it was going to ruin the moment, because that was all I could think about. What was that taste? Luckily, it hit me. She'd eaten an apple to freshen her breath.

Her taste pleasant, her smell, how did I miss that? Fucking hell! She's using my scent. There wasn't any in my handbag. I couldn't believe she used the same as me: Versace's Red Jeans. It's got a fruity fragrance, but it's for girls my age, not sophisticats like Cassandra. Did I even tell Jimmy? I probably mentioned it and they went out and bought it for me.

Taste, smell, ticking the box. Sound? What a character, after all the banter downstairs and all the jockeying for position over the Apprentice theme, she's only gone and put on Adele's *Someone Like You*, just for me.

I wanted to make sure she knew I was comfortable with the kissing, so as I pulled her towards me, I opened my mouth wide and withdrew my tongue to indicate I wanted her to take the dominant role. I was glad I took that initiative. It made sense to both of us that the girl on top, who was about to perform cunnilingus, should insert her tongue into the receiver. It just seemed to make sense to us and felt right. I don't know if it's a general rule, but we were deep kissing not just tickling the tips of the tongue, so one partner had to dominate. Cassandra understood my message. She thrust her tongue deep into my mouth. There was no twirling, I was sucking hard and she withdrew before re-inserting her tongue. It was like she was fucking my mouth.

I pushed her away gently but firmly: "Sandra, I'm ready, I want your tongue on my clit."

As she moved down, I grabbed her head and positioned her between my thighs.

It took me about ten seconds to realise she knew what she was doing. Her tongue knew its way around.

She was following Vishti's guide to cunnilingus. The manual he'd written and was kind enough to share with me before my session with Dixie.

*Rule One - Sense the reaction to different movements to understand what works and what doesn't.*

You can tell the reaction by the body movement of your partner. Arching of the back, tensing the pelvic floor muscles. A negative reaction is revealed by a slight fidget of the body as if to say: *Move somewhere else, please.* The first few seconds, with a new partner, are all about learning what she likes. First Cassandra licked my labia to make sure it was moist, then she parted the lips. Her tongue was delicate. First circling. Waiting, observing my reaction. Keeping circling, using the tongue to feel if the clitoris is fully erect. If not, suck a little.

*Rule Two - Always start the sucking gently, not too harsh. And alternate the licking and sucking.*

Begin slowly, to gauge my reaction. Speed up, when you know what works. Try licking up and down. Nothing happening there. Go back to that motion later to see if anything has changed.

*Rule Three - Keep a mental note of what speeds her up, what slows her down. Use that knowledge when you want to stop your partner from coming too soon.*

All there in Vishti's box of tricks. But Cassandra was good. I was getting excited.

*Rule Four - Listen for the breath.*

Actually, that was Vishti's first rule. But remember he was all Kama Sutra and spiritual. I'm just an ordinary gal from dahn the Old Kent Road, so I move the rules around to keep it chronological. Easier for a simple girl to understand.

Sorry, back to *the breath* श्वसन

*Be aware!* जागरूकता

*Be in the moment* क्षणे

The breath will tell you their level of excitement. The breath will change. Again everyone is different. So don't just assume. Vishti even warned me about the no breathers, or silent breathers. For them you just have to *sense*, to use your intuition. *Shit!* What happens if Cassandra turns out to be a silent breather? Then I'll be fucked, in a manner of speaking.

Back to the breath. It should change when your partner is coming. If you've done your job properly, you should know when this moment arrives. You need to know the point of no return. *Was that a Rule?* You need to decide whether you will let her come immediately, or slow her back down, so she can have more pleasure, and build up to a more explosive climax.

Was that in Vishti's rules or one of my improvisations? I'd started to write it all down in my Vade Mecum, what was Dixie's phrase for cunny - *Tipping the Velvet* - What was that in f-ing Sanskrit!

Can't remember whose rules were which…. doesn't seem to matter. Cassandra knew what she was doing.

She is going to string this out for me. I am breathing harder, harder. I could be coming as she circles, circles, sucks, nibbles. She knows I am ready, then she switches to an up-and-down motion. Cheeky bitch, she is going to make me beg. She brings me down just enough but immediately goes back to circling. She keeps sucking gently. She doesn't have to. She knows my clit is still throbbing. Here I go again, breathing harder, nearly ready. But I haven't crossed the point of no return. Back to the up and down motion to slow me down, but no fidgeting on my part. She never loses her position. God, she is good. Sorry, Dixie, I love you, but she's just overtaken you at the top of my cunny league.

Christ! This is hitting Vishti level. Thoughts stream through those moments of ecstasy with him. Never my lover, but always there for me. The only man, yes, the *only* man, that really knows how to pleasure me there. I had to leave you, Vishti, you know that, don't you? I had to leave you because I was falling in love. You are still my soulmate. You're still the man I dream of, whoever I'm with. Whoever is pleasuring me, it's you who's there. Even now, it's Cassandra's tongue. She's the best I've had, the best since you. Even Cassandra's tongue is your tongue. I can't betray you. I will never betray you.

And faster and faster, and then a touch, a finger inside. I pull away. I'm not expecting that. Vishti never went there. Suddenly, the moment could have passed, and I was back with Cassandra. But her tongue has moved away, and I hear her gentle voice: "Sorry, just relax."

Her tongue is back again on my clit, but she is careful, aware that she'd stopped the flow. I start to relax again. She is too good at this for me to stop. She wants to explore inside. I want to know where she is going. So I reach down to her hand and hold it close to my pussy, gently guiding her finger in.

"Now, now, I'm ready, please I want you."

She starts to use her finger, two fingers. She is exploring for my G-spot.

Vishti, I'm not forsaking you, but she's taking me to a new level. I know you won't mind. I'm sure you're watching, caring as you always do, but I have to go now, just while Casandra takes full possession of me. Her two fingers are rubbing against my G-spot. My clit throbbing, my body arched, but she draws me back again because she knows that my clit isn't ready 'though my pussy is.

I suddenly realised where she is taking me, where I'd never been before. Rubbing inside more vigorously. The feeling in my clit is ecstatic, but the feeling in my pussy is slightly sore, but I know where she is going. I know I have to take some discomfort. I know ....

My clit is ready. Is she going to let me come this time? Is my pussy ready?

I realise that I don't know. Cassandra knows. I am reaching the point of no return. I am ready for Cassandra to slow me down again. She is edging me. Vishti hadn't gone there. She doesn't slow me down; I pass the point of no return: *I'm going to come. I'm going to come.* The edging means my climax is more explosive. I arch my back and start to spasm. She stops licking as I come but carries on sucking. She senses that my orgasms last longer, but that my clit would be too sensitive, so she just keeps sucking. And, as I am still in a state of spasm, still experiencing a clitoral orgasm, it happened, as she knew it would. My pussy explodes as I squirt my juices. My pussy is coming at the same time as my clit. I am completely overwhelmed. I am totally exhausted. It seems that the orgasm, the two combined orgasms, and the squirting, have all conspired to take me to a new dimension.

And then… I must have lost consciousness because the next thing I knew was that Cassandra's body was next to mine. Her lips on my cheek, my forehead, her delicate hands stroking my body. She started to nibble at my ear. I normally hate that, but I was still in this woman's spell. I started to get up, and she whispered in my ear: "Lie still, Cindy, just relax."

# 22

# Cassandra's Turn

I thought, why's she calling me Cindy? Then I remembered where I was, and thought *Shit, I'm on a job, fucking hell, how unprofessional. Get your act together. Focus!*

So I turned and faced Cassandra, smiled my *trademark smile*, and mouthed the words: *Your turn.*

She was ready and waiting. At my prompting, she turned over, and I moved down her body. I suddenly wondered where the bit player was in this threesome, and I finally realised.

This whole evening is a present for Cassandra.

My first panic: she didn't shave! Probably a continental thing. This wasn't a Brazilian landing strip or even a neat triangle tidied around the edges. This was a bloody jungle.

I was just getting over that shock when I noticed a pungency. It wasn't urine. I hadn't smelt many snatches. Dixie was almost sterile, even though she hadn't showered when I'd had her the first time, her smell was mild by comparison. I'd smelt my own, of course, and I was trying to tell if I'd ever smelt like that. I had thrush once, that was a yeasty smell, which wasn't what I could smell now. I'd had an STI, with a pretty disgusting smelly discharge. It wasn't that. Maybe she just hadn't washed. The pubic hair is going to retain the sweat. That's probably what hairy pussies smell like. So I thought: *just get on with it, girl.*

Then, there was the squirting. This was my first real experience of squirting. Everything before just seemed like an excessively moist pussy with surplus fluid dribbling out. This was a complete ejaculation or evacuation, which I'd only seen in porn videos. I was quite self-conscious that I didn't have the skills to bring her off like that.

I started to play with her labial lips, using thumb and fingers to bring blood to her clit. But I needed help on how to deal with the hair, the smell and how to make her squirt.

I thought Vishti had taught me everything, but I realised there were still questions to ask and answers to hear. For a moment I was lost. For a moment, I could feel Cindy disappearing back into her shell. Rachel was re-emerging. Dear sweet Rachel. What? To come to Cindy's aid? Give me a break! Rachel doesn't have a fucking clue!

There's only one person who can help me now. Cindy comes back to the fore. And, while in Cindy mode, anything is possible. So I pick up the phone (not the one lying by the bedside table, I'm not that daft):

*"Hi, Vish, got a bit of a problem."*

*"Hi, Rache. Hope you haven't broken up with Dixie already."*

*"No, that's fine. This is a client issue."*

*"Oh, sorry, Cindy. Can't think why you'd need help with a client?"*

*"Can you just hang on a moment; I've got the client with me."*

I couldn't keep Cassandra waiting, so I started to lick her clit. But then I hit a new problem. I couldn't find it. It was definitely there when I rubbed her lips I could feel it, but it seemed to be hidden under the hood. My tongue didn't seem to be connecting with it.

*"Sorry, Vish. It's a female client that's why I'm having a problem. Actually more than one problem."*

The nice thing about a fantasy phone call is that I didn't have to repeat myself, Vish already knew my problems, and, of course, he had the answers ready:

*"The small clit is the easiest to deal with. You just need to keep thumb and forefinger ready to make sure it stays erect, but, once it gets started, you'll get used to the size and adjust your circling accordingly. You'll find you'll be doing smaller movements but the technique is the same. Honestly, nothing to worry about on that front. The hair, well sorry, you'll just have to get used to it. It shouldn't get in the way. Use it. You know suck it, bite it, and give it a little tug. You'll be surprised how, if you let the pubes join in, they will be your friend. The smell's a bit tricky. Have you asked her to shower?"*

*"Can't really do that."*

Then I explained the situation.

*"Oh, I see. Is the smell putting you off?"*

*"Not really, but it's not turning me on either."*

*"OK, here's the best I can do. Smell is a really important sense for humans, but we're not that good at training ourselves to sense the smells around us. There are probably other smells in the room but this one is dominating."*

*"Yes, they've sprayed my favourite perfume all over the room."*

*"There you go. Just train your nose to pick up that smell. It's there somewhere. Then, get your mind to hold onto the perfume smell so that it blocks the smell of her pubes."*

*"Sorry, got to go back to her, but can you think about the last problem?"*

*"Can't help you with that. My advice is to focus on the cunnilingus. Get that right and she shouldn't complain. Don't stress over the squirting. For all you know, she may*

*not be a squirter. As for the G-spot stimulation, I'd go with the flow. There are a lot of non-verbal cues going on down there. If she's as good as you said she is, you'll find she'll guide you where she wants to go."*

"Thanks for that, Vish. You've been a great help, as usual."

"Always a pleasure, Cindy. Must have lunch sometime."

"Sorry, Vish, far too busy, but please call Rache. She'd love to see you."

Back to Cassandra: I was getting used to the small clit. I was gradually gauging what she liked, what was turning her on. I knew she'd have a great orgasm but wasn't sure about the edging. I was concerned that if I stepped her down too much, she might lose it altogether. Can't disturb Vish again, he'd probably tell me to go with the flow, but her breathing has changed, getting deeper. I need to concentrate. She might be close to coming. Not too soon. Just realised I haven't been paid. I've got £500 riding on this. Slow her down, I know, bite at her pubes, pull at them. Cassandra reacts, she wants some more. Don't overdo it. I've tapped into my perfume smell, so that's OK.

Things are heating up, getting the clit going. I'm going to pull at the hair a little with my fingers to see if she likes that. She brushes my fingers away, but she's holding on to them. She's moving them towards her pussy. She wants me to finger her. I insert one finger and then realise I need the second for the G-spot stimulation. Don't lose the clit. The tongue does little circles. There seems to be so much room inside her vagina. Dixie's was nowhere near this size. She's spreading her legs. She wants another finger. What? What did she say? *Fist.* I'd never done fisting. I know it's a thing with gays, but even my weird clients and the prostate lovers have never asked for that. But I've got small hands. Was she sizing me up before? When I was in the bath, she was looking at my hands. OK, here goes. No need for lube, she's so moist. Don't lose the clit, she's coming, slow her down, bite at the pubes, that worked. I've got to coordinate the fist with the clit. I need all my ingenuity. She's arching her back breathing harder, but the fist doesn't seem to be doing anything. Then I hear her yell. "Deep, deeper, deeper!" I have no idea what's going on inside, but it seems to be working:

"Je viens! Je viens."

I thought she was Spanish? These continentals are so linguistic. I know what I'm doing with my tongue, but the only thing I can think of with my wrist is to turn it back and forth.

"Now, now, now!" She obviously doesn't trust my language skills, as she's switched to English.

Now she's in an orgasmic spasm, her body shuddering. She touches my hand. I slowly remove my fingers. Taking them out carefully, but she's still in spasm. I'm not licking any more, just sucking through her labia, and I continue until I feel her body go limp.

I mimic her after-play. Move my head close to hers. I suddenly realise there's a body on the other side of her. I'd been so focused on the lady garden that I hadn't noticed Jimmy had been playing with her nipples the whole time.

I move my hand across to his, just to let him know that I am aware of his presence. The three of us lie there for probably ten minutes. Jimmy is the first to stir. I feel him get up from the bed. I looked up and saw him leave the room, probably adjourning to the bathroom. Cassandra is alert now and I seize on Jimmy's absence to tell Cassandra what was on my mind.

"When I negotiated the deal, we had a bit of bartering."

"Yes, James said you were a great negotiator."

"And I said he sucked because I would have thrown in a blow job for the £500."

Cassandra laughed at the pun.

"Sorry, that came out all wrong."

"Don't be silly, good choice of words."

"I was joking. But I don't know if he knew."

"Yes, I'm sure he knew."

"Well, I'd like to - now. I mean with your permission. I mean I'd like to suck him off, in front of you, if, and only if, it will turn you on."

"Really?"

"Yes, but only on your terms."

"Is that what you do when he comes to you for massage?"

"Hell, no! I'd get the sack. Please understand, I'd only do it in front of you. James is very respectful. He'd never try it on at Felicity's just because I did it here."

"Who?"

I realised she didn't know the name of my place of work. Shit! Did this mean she'd google the website and see the menu? Doubt if she'd care, after what I've seen tonight. She'd probably book an appointment for herself.

"Sorry, the massage place."

"Oh yes, I think James has mentioned the name."

Cassandra looked at me quizzically. She'd obviously not included that in tonight's agenda.

"It just seems to me it's either the blow job or he's going to come inside you, with me sucking your nipples. And, after all you've been through, if I'd been through that, I'd probably take up my suggestion."

"What do you mean after all I've been through? What has James told you? How do you know what I've been through?"

She was looking at me, visibly angry.

I didn't know what I'd said wrong.

"James has said nothing, I don't understand. I meant been through tonight. I know how I'd feel. If I had a man inside me now, I'd just be going through the motions. I'm totally satiated, so I'd end up faking an orgasm. If you're anything like me, that's what you're going to do when he comes out of the bathroom. Or you could caress your man while you watch me giving head. I don't want to brag, but I give great head. But, as I said, only if it will turn you on, and if you're not looking forward to another fuck tonight."

Cassandra smiled. "I can see why James keeps going back to you. You've got great instincts. Let's go for it."

We waited for Jimmy to come out of the bathroom. I was lying on the bed, with the gown half-covering me. One tit exposed. I didn't know whether to leave it or cover it. My nipples were hard in anticipation of what was to come. I'd never sucked Jimmy off, of course, but I knew his penis intimately. Every wrinkle. I knew it flaccid. I knew it erect. I knew what it liked, what it didn't like. In short, although my mouth had never been near his penis, I knew how to give him the best blow job he'd ever experienced.

"James, we have a little surprise for you."

Cassandra's first misstep of the evening. Saying *we*. If she'd said *I've got a surprise* there'd be less chance of his guessing. Mind you, Jimmy's been so clueless all evening, he probably hasn't twigged.

She told him to close his eyes. He was standing there in his robe, which she eased off him. Keep your eyes closed or you won't get your treat. He was sporting a semi. Cassandra used her hand until he was hard. I was standing close to him, now ready to kneel.

I didn't like the position. Blow jobs with the man standing up never work well. The angle's all a-cock (excuse the pun). But needs must. I got to work. I was licking his shaft, sucking hard. I held his hips. That's a trick you learn early on. Men like to thrust deep, and you'd gag if you're not careful. Watch any porn film if you don't believe me. Most directors of porn films are men, or at least the misogynistic films - with the women gagging - could only be made by male directors. A woman director would understand that the man could get more pleasure if he'd let the woman do her thing, so the film would be more erotic. (I'm making a note to myself here to check out more porn to see if I can tell the difference where there is a female director.

I'm pretty sure I'll know, but if not, *hey ho*, I'll have a lotta fun trying to prove my theory.)

Anyway, you grip the hips and that lets you control the thrusting. You can still go deep but you won't gag. Jimmy was enjoying it, but I wasn't. I had to half stand and sort of bend over. I saw a chair in the room and motioned to Cassandra to bring it over. She complied. She drew it up behind Jimmy and forcefully thrust him down in it. It took him by surprise. Cassandra and I shared a laugh, and I got back on the job. I knew him so well, how to draw him out, slow him down, get him ready, and make him come. My only hesitation was where to spit his cum. I hadn't any tissues close by, and I didn't want to spoil their thick pile carpet. I looked around for a solution. Too late! He shot his load and what a load it was.

But he gave me one surprise. It wasn't salty. Quite sweet. Does he drink pineapple juice as well? Is that really a thing? What the hell! *Hey ho!* Sod it! You've gone this far, Cindy. I swallowed it in one gulp. Then, suddenly thought I might have made a mistake. I'd withdrawn and was standing up. Jimmy was slumped in the chair, with a stupid look of contentment on his face. I look directly at Cassandra and apologised.

"Sandra, I'm really sorry, I wasn't thinking. I swallowed it all up. Should I have saved some to dribble into your mouth? She looked at me and laughed:

"You are kidding, right?"

We showered. There were enough showers for everyone. More than at my fucking gym. Mine had so many buttons. I think I pressed the wrong one, because suddenly it was almost like hail stones, as large drops of water were pummelling my head in some kind of pulsating rhythm. I pressed another, and I was in the rainforest with fine mist surrounding me. Of course, I'd never been in a fucking rainforest, I must have read that somewhere. I walked out of the shower. Actually, I'd learnt that *wet room* was the correct terminology. No shower tray to trip over, or fiddly door to fumble with. I made a mental note: *Tell Fi to convert all our en-suite showers into wet rooms.* Oh yeah, really. Like she'd spend that kind of money.

Then I stepped back to try another button on the side of the shower. Now I'm getting water-pounding at all angles. I heard a voice asking if I was alright. I realise it was Cassandra. I was getting carried away:

"Sorry. Just enjoying my spa experience."

I heard her giggle.

"Don't worry. Take your time. Make your way downstairs when you're ready."

Fresh towels laid out. My dress draped over a chair, but on a hanger, and looking as though it had been ironed. Was there some invisible maid scurrying around the house, or did the butler do those chores as well? I never found out.

When I went downstairs, tea and coffee were waiting in silver jugs. Jimmy was serving and asked what I preferred. Then offered me a brandy, which I declined.

"Liqueur?"

"No, look I just want to thank you for this evening. I didn't know what to expect, but you're incredible hosts. Don't let me spoil the party. You have a drink, but I need to order my taxi."

Cassandra stepped in:

"Already ordered. James said the bewitching hour was midnight. Hope that was right." She looked at the clock on the mantle shelf. "That's twenty minutes. Are you OK with that, or shall we bring that forward?"

I really don't think she was reminding me of the contractual arrangement. I had said midnight, and she'd been fastidious all night.

"No, of course, that's perfect. It's not the time, but just coffee is fine."

"Then, James, if we're not drinking, we have to play the cocktail game."

Cassandra explained the rules. One person picks a cocktail, then the next person has to say the ingredients. If they get it wrong, the next person has a go. As long as they get it right, the game continues until two people get it wrong. I know nothing about cocktails, apart from the ones I drink. They had some encyclopaedia of cocktails, so you could check, to make sure that the person naming the cocktail knew what was in it. Then the game would continue. It sounded like it could go on all night. And I wanted to leave, so I kept guessing wrong. But each time I got it wrong, Cassandra knew the ingredients and on we went. I was getting fed up. This could have spoiled an otherwise lovely evening. Then, I remembered sitting in a bar once listening to some stupid loudmouth yank ordering a cocktail, then berating the bartender because he didn't know the ingredients. Could that obnoxious yank save my skin?

"My turn - Sazerac!"

Cassandra looked blank.

"Pass!"

Jimmy piped up.

"I know this. It's a southern cocktail, so it's going to be rye whisky, and let me see, brandy."

Shit! He knows this.

"And?"

154

I'm still hoping this will finish the sodding game.

"We don't count garnish, peel or mint do we, Sandra?"

"No."

Sandra was supporting her man, intent on prolonging the agony for me.

Fucking rules. They make it up as they go along. I suddenly felt I was in a class war. The Aristos always had an answer. They knew how to win, against the Plebs. I knew which side I was on.

"Not the garnish. There's more."

"I know. I know. There's something unusual. Very old-fashioned. Weird drink. The French Impressionists used to drink it. Hallucinogenic."

"Absinthe!" Cassandra chimed.

"Hey! Is she allowed to do that? No helping. Anyway, you still haven't finished."

"Well, Angostura Bitters is always a good standby for this game."

"One more?"

"Yes, one more round. It's nearly twelve. Cindy must go."

"No, I meant one more ingredient," I interjected.

"Really?" Jimmy challenged.

"Go look it up!" I countered.

Jimmy started looking in the Encyclopaedia.

"But you have to know it." Cassandra reminded me of the rules.

"Peychaud's Bitters," I declared in triumph.

"Never heard of it?" questioned Cassandra.

"She's right. Look, it's right here."

Jimmy had the page open.

The two of them clapped. Cassandra said:

"Cindy's won the prize."

Just as she said that the bell rang. Jimmy said:

"Taxi's outside, I'll go answer the door."

"James, tell him five minutes, and make yourself scarce. I want a private word with Cindy."

James dutifully left the room. I was wondering what she wanted to say in private. Telling me I was the best fuck she'd had? She could probably say that in front of Jimmy. I half expected her to book me for a private session. But what she had to say blew me away.

"Come here, get your present."

I readied myself for a goodbye kiss with tongues. Instead, she took out a small box and opened it:

"Come here - back to me."

I could feel something around my neck and she was fiddling with the clasp. I looked down and could see a rose gold chain. I held it in my hand. It had the letter 'C' as a pendant. Also in rose gold. Jimmy'd remarked after one of our sessions that he found my belly bar sexy. It was rose gold, and I mentioned that that was my preferred metal, as I thought it suited my skin colour. I couldn't believe he even remembered.

Then Cassandra began to tell me why she wanted a private five minutes. She was still fiddling with the clasp, so I stayed with my back to her while she spoke:

"I know we can be stuck up our own backsides, arrogant S.O.B.'s. It's inbred. We can't actually help it. We've been brought up to believe we're better than the *hoi polloi*. I'm not going to apologise for how I behaved at the beginning. I think you enjoyed the banter, and to be honest, if you'd caved, you might not have gained my respect. That was so important for tonight. We weren't going to be lovers, but I couldn't have done what we did, couldn't have been where we've been, couldn't have come like I came, if you were just someone like Rafe. Lovely guy, but not real. I did come to respect you. I suppose I could have said I did *come* because I respect you. The *Sandy* touch was very clever by the way. I loved the way you used it to show me when I'd won you over. You weren't to know, but my close friends call me Sandy when they want to tease me because they know I hate it. I'd like to think we've got, if not a friendship, then a bond."

She paused. I still had my back to her. She was still fumbling with that bloody clasp, then she hit me with:

"I had a miscarriage two months ago."

I gasped. I wanted to turn around, but her fiddling with the clasp prevented me.

"I am so sorry. I had no idea."

"I know, but that's why I freaked, upstairs, when you said *after all you've been through…*."

"James never…"

"No, I know. For a split second… but I know he wouldn't have."

Finally, she'd done the bloody clasp. So I could turn around and face her.

"I'm so, so sorry, I don't know what to say."

"It's OK. We're adjusting. It's my second miscarriage. My gynae says there's something wrong with me down there. We can keep trying, but it may be we go down the adoption or surrogacy route. The miscarriages are so emotionally draining. I'm not sure I could take another. That's what this evening was about. Sex has been awful ever since this last one. You don't know how close to the knuckle you were upstairs when you suggested I might prefer you give James a blow job instead of him just pounding an empty shell."

"I didn't quite put it like that."

"No, but that's what it's been. James knew I wasn't enjoying the sex. He was going through the motions. I was faking and he knew."

Shit! It made sense to me now. Jimmy had been coming to me more often, recently. Think I'll keep that to myself.

"We discussed it and he suggested an evening with you to re-awaken my libido. I went along with it but wasn't sure it would work. Maybe that's why I was a bitch earlier on."

Tears began to well in her eyes. I started to hug her back.

I wanted to ask about the fisting. I was really curious whether that had something to do with it. I don't mean causing her miscarriages. I mean a sort of punishment, a symbolic punishment. She really wanted to feel me literally screw her, turning my fist like a screw. I wanted to know whether it was pleasure or pain. But now was not the time for a post-mortem. Wrong choice of words. Not the time for an inquisition.

"I am so, so grateful. You will never know how you've taken a damaged soul and cured me of that trauma."

All I could think of was Vish, helping me to open up and accept my own trauma.

She was in tears. I wanted her to lighten up. She needed to smile, so I looked at her and said:

"I realise that if you'd won the cocktail game, the 'C' would have worked for Cassandra, but did you have another one with a 'J' on it?"

It worked, her face broke into a smile, then a giggle, then a laugh.

"That daft bugger nearly had you with the Sazerac. Normally he's drunk when we play the game, and he never gets one right."

Jimmy walked in and we burst into girlie giggles.

"What are you two giggling about? Taxi's been waiting ten minutes and I'm paying."

"Sorry, we got carried away."

As she said that, she handed me an envelope. I could feel a card inside.

"It's just a thank you message. You can read it in the taxi."

James went red:

"Oh shit! I completely forgot."

With that, he took an envelope out of his pocket.

"I've had this in my pocket all evening. What a tosser. How embarrassing."

I walked past Jimmy, took the envelope, without ceremony, gave him my *trademark smile*, and, with what turned out to be a penultimate parting shot:

"No more than I'd expect from you, Jimmy. You're always forgetting to pay me."

He looked bemused. They followed me out into the hall and were standing at the front door. I skipped down the steps and without turning around shouted:

"Bye, guys. Must do this again sometime."

I opened the door to the taxi, then checked myself and said to the taxi driver:

"Sorry, just a mo. Forgot something."

I turned around, They were both still standing in the open doorway waiting for the taxi to drive off.

I skipped up the steps, put my arms around Cassandra, and hugged her tightly with all my strength. I didn't let go for two minutes. Then without looking at her again, turned back and got in the cab.

*******

I can't really relate my reflections on the way home. I know I was totally drained physically and emotionally. I made a mental note to call Vish and thank him for the fictitious phone call. I think he'd be pleasantly amused. I opened Jimmy's envelope. Ten crisp (I know the plastic ones aren't crisp like the old paper notes, but this was when they were still using paper), ten crisp notes, which I put in my bag.

I opened Cassandra's envelope. I took out the card. It was edged in gold, like they used to do for wedding invites (mum had shown me hers).

She had written in perfect copperplate script in navy blue ink, proper ink. (Who uses a fountain pen nowadays? Probably a family heirloom.)

The message read:

"Thank you again for a wonderful evening and for helping me through my issues. Look after Jimmy for me. Alongside was a little sketch, which I had to look at twice before I realised it was mimicking the emoji of a woman kneeling. I smiled, and as I turned over the card, to put it back in the envelope, there was another message on the back and also a folded piece of paper in the envelope.

The message read:

*I don't know what the etiquette is in your profession, so, if it is not appropriate for you to receive a tip, please forgive my crassness, and make the cheque out to your favourite charity.*

I took the folded piece of paper out of the envelope. It was a cheque, issued by Coutts, of course, bankers to royalty. The payee was left blank. It was drawn on the account of Countess Cassandra Mariola Montessiori to the sum of five hundred pounds.

# PART III

# 23
# Abandonată și traficată

After Fi offered me the override, that extra commission if I introduced her to a new girl to work at the salon, it set my mind thinking whether I knew anyone. The idea of earning more money appealed to me, so I thought I'd keep my eye out.

I happened to be visiting *Her Centre*, with three bin bags of our castoffs. We did regular collections of the fast fashion that we were ready to discard, clothes barely worn, which might make a little bit of difference to the lives of some of those unfortunate clients that the Centre assisted.

Eileen, one of the volunteers there, told me the background of one of the girls she was trying to help:

"Mihaela hails from Romania, originally. Before we left the EU, Romanians were allowed to live and work here quite legally. Then after Brexit, they were able to acquire settled status, so Mihaela could stay here as long as she wanted. She was the victim of trafficking. As a 16-year-old, she arrived with her *uncle*. It's quite sickening how the authorities seemed to turn a blind eye. Her paperwork was fine. Her *uncle* seemed to have documentation that both proved his ID as well as his family connection to Mihaela. But it should have been obvious to anyone but the densest of jobsworths that this nervous 16-year-old child was going to be forced into prostitution. She is now 21, but, in terms of her life experience, going on 40."

"Eileen, I'm ready to help, but is it really a good idea to take a girl who's been forced into prostitution and offer her a job in a massage parlour? As I explained, my boss runs the business very professionally. But I think you know, I've already mentioned to you, some of the things that go on in our treatment rooms. It is described as erotic massage. The girls are treated with respect. No-one is forced to do anything against their will. There is nothing like full sex or blow jobs, but our lingham massage does involve what the uninitiated would call a hand job."

Eileen smiled a nervous giggle: "Yes, you did mention. But it's crucial to get her out of the clutches of these evil men. They've offered her a buyout. She needs to make £20,000, and they've given her three months to come up with it."

"Can't you go to the police?"

"It really doesn't work like that. We could go to the police, but they won't protect her. We've seen it before. Some of these brutes. We had two guys come to the shelter once. They said they wanted to see one of our clients, one of the girls who they knew. They said they wouldn't leave until they'd seen her. They made veiled threats to come back and torch the place if we refused. I was asked to sit with her for the whole time that these evil men were talking to her. I could see the look on her face. She was petrified. All the men said was that they'd just come back from her home village. She was also Romanian. They wanted to tell her that they had a message from her five-year-old daughter who was being looked after by the girl's mother. They simply said how much she was looking forward to joining her mummy. They then said that they could bring her over if she wanted. They were happy to bring her over to join her mummy. That was enough to put the fear of God into her."

I could see tears welling in Eileen's eyes. I touched her hand in sympathy.

"After the meeting, she told us that she had to leave. We can't keep our clients here against their will. I didn't really understand what they meant, until she explained. When they said they were ready to bring her daughter over, one of the men had whispered to her in Romanian: *and work with you in the brothel*. We couldn't do anything to help. It's dreadful."

I touched Eileen's hand again. She was quite distraught, and then she carried on:

"It's the same with Mihaela. She has an 8-year-old daughter. That means she was raped when she was 12. It doesn't bear thinking about. Perhaps you can now understand. If there is any way she can get out of this dreadful mess and make a new life for herself, away from these horrible people, she will take it. A few months working with you would seem like a holiday."

"If you ask me directly, could Mihaela make £20,000 in cash over the next couple of months, it would depend how many days a week she was prepared to work. But, yes, that would be doable. I could take her under my wing. I'd be happy to meet her, to tell her exactly what's involved, so that she could make her own decision."

*******

Over coffee, I explained the services to Mihaela. I was looking at this young woman sitting opposite me. About the same age as me, but she had a faint look in her eyes that added about 20 years. Thin, but not like me. People say I'm *petite*, but that's meant as a compliment. The young women that was staring at me, with that gaunt look in her eyes, was stick thin. Almost anorexic. Malnourished is what I'd say.

I think she could have been beautiful. Perhaps in another world. I mean her features, Romanian, is that Slavic? Probably some Slav blood there. But it was as though someone had taken those stunning high cheekbones, those hazel eyes, those quite full lips, and photo-shopped the beauty out of her face. This person had suffered pain.

"Before I start, I just want you to know that this is your decision. But when I've finished, please let me know, when I describe what we do, whether you think you can handle it."

I then went on to describe, in general terms, what we do and then went into more detail.

"We have extras on the menu at Felicity's. Then we have the *off-label* extras, which you won't find on the website, nor on the treatment list at reception.

On the menu extras include:

Assisted shower - £25

Prostate - £25

Double Pleasure - £25

Actually, I'd never even noticed before but all the extras on the menu come in at a standard price."

Her English was good, actually very good. She explained that her *uncle* had arranged for English lessons as soon as she arrived. Although the abuse had started immediately on her arrival, so had the lessons. They were her only respite. The teacher was a really kind lady whose day job was TEFL, Teaching English as a Foreign Language. One day the lady let slip that she also had been trafficked. *So you see, Dear, there is a way out for you* she had confided.

I continued with my description. Mihaela was listening to me attentively.

"The price of *off-label* extras is up to the therapist, negotiated directly with the client. You keep all that money yourself. For the menu items, you keep 40%."

When I said that, when I mentioned the 40%, I felt a pang of guilt. I had already renegotiated my deal with Fi. She had originally offered me the 10% so-called *override* for just 12 months. I told her that to make it worth my while, especially as I would be doing the training and giving the girl the benefit of my sales tips, I'd need that 10% to continue for as long as the girl worked with us.

Was it really fair, would I not be exploiting Mihaela? For a moment, I wavered, but then I justified it to myself on the basis that I'd be offering her a way out. After all, I told myself, her only other option appeared to be to sit and wait it out until the day when her *uncle* would take her away, force her back to the brothel, and probably give her a few slaps for running away. If Eileen thought that I could help Mihaela, then it had to be okay. Because of me, the £20,000 was within her grasp if she worked four or five days a week. I was offering her a lifeline, as long as she could get her act together.

Fi had made it very clear at the outset that anything off-label was up to us, but we shouldn't think there was any obligation to do anything the client asked just because they were prepared to pay. I tried to explain this all to Mihaela, who had been used to having to succumb to whatever perverted acts her *clients* had demanded of her.

"Fi had her red lines. No full sex, by which she meant intercourse with penetration, no blow jobs. Cross Fi's red lines and she would dispense with your services without notice, and we shouldn't expect to receive any outstanding commission."

"I'm not clear on the Mutual Massage" Mihaela seemed to be absorbing everything.

"It says on the website that Mutual Massage is a premium menu item, an extra £75 higher than the price of a standard Tantric. It boasted that the clients would be able *to explore your beautiful therapist's own body, as she would instruct you in the art of tantric massage techniques that would enhance your love life at home.*"

"Yes, that's the spiel on the website. What don't you understand?"

"How far?"

"How far you want to go is up to you. Breasts are par for the course. If they're going to suck your nipples, make sure you tell them that one bite and the session is over. They will expect to massage the inside of your thighs, so be prepared for that, but if they stray too close, well normally a wriggle is enough to keep them at bay. If you fancy them and are prepared to let their fingers stray all the way, that's up to you, but you'd be a fool if you gave that away for nothing. You didn't hear that from me. If you decide to let them explore your intimates don't come crying to me after, but, as long as you have clearly defined your own red lines, if they cross them, Fi, our boss, will be the first in the treatment room with a bucket of cold water to teach the buggers a lesson."

Mihaela smiled at my coarseness. I had decided deliberately not to pull any punches. There was no point in mollycoddling. This was actually a job interview. I was testing her. I wanted to gauge her reactions. It sounded as though she had been through so much. I needed to know how damaged she was. Would she be able to take it? After what she'd been through, working at Felicity's could be a walk in the park. The issue I had is whether she would be able to control the clients and not let them take advantage of her vulnerability.

"From what you say, fingering seems to be a bit of a grey area, I mean sometimes it can hurt, but I have had men, and I know this makes me sound so cheap, but not all of the men had foul breath or were ugly. There was one man who was quite kind to me and, when he fingered me, it was quite pleasant. He said he would pay me cash directly. You see I never saw any of the money. It went straight to my minders. He was ready to give me twenty pounds if I let him finger me until I came. I don't think I had had a proper orgasm before."

So I explained to Mihaela my fundamental philosophy. Stay professional and always be in control. You can't let yourself get turned on in the treatment room, even if you fancy the client, because you may let him take control, which is a *no-no*. If you're not going to allow yourself to get turned on by it, why let the guy play with your clit or go inside. On the other hand, if you think that you can do it without losing control, and you can negotiate a fee that you think makes it worthwhile, no-one's any the wiser.

I kept talking in the same vein. I was glad she was coming out with questions. It made it easier for me to judge whether she was going to be able to handle the kind of situations I knew she'd have to face. From the off, I'd never had any real problems, but to put it simply, there were always risks for the very simple reason that all of our clients are... What's an easy way to put this? Yes, all of our clients are... *men*.

I'd spent more than half an hour with Mihaela. I'd already decided to invite her for the second interview. After all, ultimately, it was up to Fi.

"We need to think up a *nom de plume* for you. Your stage name so to speak."

"I like to be called Mickey."

"I think that's quite nice, but when you're working, not just with clients, but also with the other girls, we all use a completely different unconnected name. If Mickey is your actual name, you want to use something completely different. Just to keep your two lives apart."

"What do you use, Rachel?"

"Cindy. When I'm with a client, I'm Cindy. Cindy does things that Rachel would never do. It just helps separate business from pleasure."

My thoughts wandered. When I said *separate business from pleasure*, I was thinking of my Vish. Vishti, when he became my client, and then Vish later on.

Cindy, you did such a brilliant job at keeping those two separate. Fell in love with a client. Didn't admit that you were in love. Continued to insist that he paid you when you would have gladly paid him for the oral satisfaction he gave you. Dumped the man, the only man, who had really pleased you, sexually. Oh yes, Cindy was so good at separating business from pleasure. So good that, sometimes, I feel there are two of me in this body. Cindy is constantly fighting Rachel, constantly struggling to get out. Or is it Rachel, the sub in this relationship, who is being held captive? Cindy is dominant, strong, and always in control. Cindy in thigh-length, patent leather boots with stripper heels. Cindy in tight black leather corset, tits exposed. Cindy with whip in hand, flagellating Vishti, until his skin was broken and the weals on his back were bleeding. Listening to Vishti's screams, not for mercy, but for more, more pain. How many times, in my fantasy, had I wanted to make Vish suffer for all the pain that he had caused me? And then, in my fantasy, for me to lick the blood from his back. For me to ask, to beg, his forgiveness. To beg him to take me, for him now to abuse me. *I only caused you pain, so that you would return the favour. Come on Vish, the* quid pro quo. *I can't be happy unless I feel pain. But it has to be you. I need you to hurt me. I need you to punish me.* And then, as always, always, in this repeated fantasy, while I'm lying there, at night, in my loneliness, hands between my legs, pinching myself, abusing myself. Always in my fantasy, Vish, Christ-like in his suffering, picks me up and cradles this child, as I whimper: *Forgive me, forgive me Vish, I didn't mean to hurt you.* He lays me down gently on my bed, a soft gentle kiss on my forehead, as I close my eyes and fall asleep.

I'm jarred back into the present.

"I think I understand."

I look at Mickey puzzled.

"I mean the *not mixing business and pleasure.* I think I could do that. I think I would be able to, how did you put it, stay in control. I speak to the other girls, you know, the ones in my position. We talk, I listen to some of them and they are suicidal. They lock our windows. Recently, they left a window unlocked, one girl climbed out. She was not trying to escape, well, yes, of course, it was a means to escape. She said that she wanted to end it. It was a second-floor window. She survived with a broken leg. Her punishment was what we call the concentration camp. They show it to all of us when we arrive. It's supposed to scare us into compliance. It's just an ordinary room, completely bare, except for a double bed and a table in the corner. There are chains on the wall, blood stains. I don't know if it's real blood or just for effect. On the table, there is some kind of electrical equipment, and what they described as a cattle prod. Each of us is given a turn. Just a touch to let us know. I mean just a touch. Really, it's just a tingle. But they show us the machine and show us the dial. And, when they think we've got the message, they lead us away. The girl with the broken leg was there for days. We had seen men go in and then go out. A constant stream, and we heard screams, and sometimes the screams would stop. We feared the worst, and then someone would go in with a bucket of water. We didn't understand. It was simply to revive her after she passed out. Afterwards, they had this ridiculous ceremony. It wasn't just the physical pain, the abuse, they delighted in the humiliation. After enduring her suffering, in front of us, they all congratulated her upon her *graduation*. They rewarded her with a meal, a proper meal, a feast compared to the meagre scraps that we were fed."

I was fighting back tears, but I owed it to Mihaela to listen calmly, unemotionally.

"Alongside the bowl, filled with meat and potatoes, there was a bottle of wine and a cup on the table. Her instruction, and remember, she had not eaten for a couple of days, was to finish it all up and consume the whole bottle of wine. We were made to watch as she was gagging. They just laughed. Finally, the ordeal was over. One of the beasts told her to go to the kitchen and wash up her dishes. She meekly complied. Ten minutes later, she was lying on the kitchen floor having convulsions, like an epileptic fit. It was only later, after she was carried away, somebody noticed an empty bottle, a plastic bottle lying on the floor, a few drops still spilling out. She'd swallowed the contents. Drain cleaner. We don't know, but assumed the body would have been dumped somewhere, or possibly buried or maybe burned."

I couldn't hold back any longer. I was in tears and I wanted to hug her. But she was calm. Amazingly calm.

"Yes!" she said.

"Yes, what?"

"You asked me, you know about the clients. Not mixing business with pleasure. I think I can handle that."

I tried to regain my composure.

"There's just one thing, just one thing that you said you girls do, that I'm really not comfortable with."

"You really don't have to do anything that you're not comfortable with."

"No, you said all the girls do it. I think you meant that I would have to do it as well, if I want the job. You seemed to suggest it was a deal breaker. But I don't think I can go along with it."

"Just tell me, I'll ask Fi, our boss, Fi, and see what she says. What are you not comfortable about?"

"I want to be called Mickey."

# 24
## Garden View

Dixie and I had been an item for over a year. We were coming up to Graduation Day. Dixie had achieved her first-class honours and was interviewing for jobs. She already had one offer. She was also considering staying on instead and reading for an MA. Her tutor said he'd put her up for a bursary. Dixie had options.

I had to start thinking about what to do with *my* life. I'd come out with a degree, just. Unclassified, because I never submitted my final thesis, but I'd still get my BSc. My options were centred around how many days a week I felt like working for Fi, and whether I should take 4 or 6 weeks off over Christmas to go to Bali.

I remembered Vish's plan for me. Find the guy from the gym first, then move on to his boss. I started getting up early and studying the other gym bunnies. Chatting to them in the changing room, getting to know the language. Mostly, they were in FX, foreign exchange, or wealth management. FX sounded fun, so I started looking at the financial press.

To get into the role, and to play my part, I'd even catch the tube, one stop to Canary Wharf, like I was commuting, going there for work. I'd sit outside sipping a mid-morning macchiato, the ones that the worker bee secretaries would buy for their over caffeinated bosses. I'd sit there with a copy of the Financial Times glancing through the pink pages as though I understood a word of what I was reading.

If I was going to BS my way into the magic circle of the gym bunnies, I needed a cover story but if I said I worked for a bank, it would be too easy for them to discover I was a fraud. I decided I'd pose as a financial journalist. Freelance. I knew enough to know that freelancers, especially a junior like I would be, don't always get a by-line. So I could be anonymous in the financial press, yet still sound credible. My new gym buddies would be thinking: *She can afford to live in Upper Riverside, so she must be selling some of her articles.*

I set up a Linked-in profile. I hadn't used it before, so there was no history. I decided that my BSc was in Journalism instead of Psychology. They could check, but probably wouldn't.

My Facebook profile could be a problem, so I started to put up some posts telling people about how excited I was with my new career and getting my first article placed in the Investors Chronicle. I even attached a link to the magazine. Let them try and find the article.

Dixie thought I was nuts, but she didn't really care. I didn't tell her that the only reason for the charade was to catch a banker. She'd probably freak out if I had told her that. I wanted to reassure her that shagging the banker wouldn't affect our relationship, because he was only a stepping stone to his boss and my sugar-daddy-to-be. If I had told her that she'd probably have had me certified insane.

Once I'd decided on the plan, finding the guy was fairly easy. It was also fun. I started putting myself about a bit in the gym. Guys are so predictable. My sweaty tits and arse were a hit round the water cooler. If I wasn't getting enough attention from the lads, I'd pop into the loo, work my nipples till they were nice and hard. That usually did the trick. Most days there were two or three of them chatting me up. It was only a matter of time.

"Would you fancy coming up to my flat for a drink one evening? We're virtually neighbours. I'm on the 7th floor."

"Front or back?"

"Sorry?"

"River or Garden View?"

"Garden."

"No thanks. Prefer my *River View*. But you can buy me lunch sometime."

"Dinner?"

"Don't think you can afford me. Let's take it slow. There's a salt beef stand every Wednesday outside Canary Wharf Station."

"You're joking, aren't you? I think I can stretch to buying you a proper lunch."

"I thought you hedge fund guys didn't have time for a proper lunch."

"You're confusing us with FX traders. *We're* the ones who do three-hour liquid lunches."

I called across to one of the traders I had been chatting with the other morning:

"Hey, Bill, buy me a sandwich outside the station next Wednesday."

"Sure, Rachel!"

My target took the bait: "She's kidding, Bill. Rachel's my sandwich date for Wednesday."

I looked across and gave him my *trademark smile*.

"OK, Wednesday, er, oh, sorry, forgotten your name."

Gee, was I having fun! My target, who I'd just bagged, was Lawrence August (Gus) Cheney the Third, a distant cousin of the former US Vice President, over here on a two-year assignment with the second largest bank in America.

I'd done my homework. His boss, early fifties, was also a Yank. Unfortunately, so Gus had mentioned to one of his sidekicks in the gym the other day, his boss's wife and family had stayed in New York, at least until they could sort out schools for them over here.

That should give me enough time, I thought.

Lawrence August (Gus) Cheney the Third, distant cousin of the former US Vice President, didn't know it yet, but he was about to become my partner as I ascended the ski-lift up the social mountain, climbing to the peak, where my sugar-daddy awaited.

*******

On the exercise bike, I normally go into a trance. I don't do hills or anything, just set a steady pace, and cycle. My earphones are plugged in. I used to listen to music while cycling, but, since I decided that my *faux* career was to be in financial journalism, I started listening to Bloomberg, daily bulletins on the stock and currency markets. With the music, depending on whether chilled or disco, it might take me 5 to 10 minutes of cycling before settling into my trance. Bloomberg did it in about 90 seconds. I was awoken by the bunny cycling next to me. I hadn't actually noticed her.

"Lindsay, you're Rachel, Rache, isn't it?"

"Yes, pleased to meet you, can't shake hands, gotta keep riding, you understand."

Lindsay seemed oblivious to the fact that I really didn't want to engage.

"I overheard you're a journo, freelance. I could hook you up with a gig."

I'm not sure whether it was because she had interrupted me, or that she seemed oblivious to the fact that I didn't want to engage, or that I thought her language was ridiculous, but I knew Lindsay was not about to become my NBFF.

"My boyfriend works at Zopa."

She said it like I was supposed to know. Perhaps, if I really was a financial journalist the name might have been familiar. I thought better to play along. I could always look them up later.

"What does he do there?"

"He's in risk management. He only mentioned the other day that their PR was suggesting a magazine article to drum up some business."

I didn't know how the thing worked, but it seemed to me that, if they employed a PR, the PR would be able to arrange that kind of thing. Anyway, obviously I wasn't looking for a *gig*, so I politely declined. But she said that Vince, Vinnie, wanted to set something up on the side, unofficially, so to speak. He was ready to pay for it himself. The idea was to demonstrate to his boss that he could show initiative. Apparently, the boss was complaining that they were spending £5,000 a month on this PR girl and he thought she was a waste of space. Vinnie thought it would be a *wheeze* if he were able to get the article done.

"But you know I'm freelance. The article would still need to get placed."

"I'm not sure if they thought that through. Vinnie told me that if he could just do an interview, get the article written and present it to his boss, it would give the boss an excuse to sack the PR. Can I be honest, Rache. Can I call you Rache?"

I'd stopped cycling. My neck, turning looking at her, was starting to hurt and I couldn't cycle and concentrate on her inanity at the same time.

"To be honest, you'd be doing me a favour. I sort of want to prove myself to Vinnie. You know, just show him that I'm not just good for a fuck."

Well, girlfriend, now you're talking my language.

"How about this, Lindsay? You know I'm just starting out. Actually, it would be good for my portfolio. So here's the deal. I won't charge a fee. If you want to make some money, let Vinnie pay you and you keep it for yourself."

"No, I wouldn't dream of doing that. I think we would have to pay you."

I told her I wouldn't accept any payment. I managed to persuade her that adding to my portfolio would help when I was pitching for business. I told her that it would be a favour but I was honest so I said she would owe me. She flippantly agreed and said that she would be in my debt. I think she thought I was joking. I had no idea what favour I would be asking in return. All I knew was that, one day, I would call it in.

I don't know why but, instinctively, I thought that the interview would not be at his office. Lindsay suggested that I come up to hers for a drink one evening, so she could introduce me to Vinnie and take it from there. They weren't living together but he came round frequently and often stayed the night.

We set a date.

*******

I left my apartment. Got in the lift. Pressed G. Walked out into the corridor, across the entrance lobby, to the other lift bank. I walked to the Garden View side, towards the other bank of elevators, musing about the two sides of the building.

All the people I knew from the gym seemed to live on the Garden View side. I wondered why. Perhaps they were more aspirational, you know, *fake it till you make it*, until they could upgrade to the *River View*.

I remembered, when I was looking at the apartment, asking Vish. I told him I could get a Garden View for £500 and save £100 a week. He asked me if I could afford the £600.

"Of course, with the cheddar from Felicity's, it's really not a problem. It's more about whether I deserve it."

"Don't ever say that again!" He actually sounded angry, never heard him like that on the phone.

"I never want to hear you tell yourself that you don't deserve something. You work damn hard. I know you say that you enjoy your job, but let's face it, there must be times when you get back from work after massaging all those sweaty bodies and wonder what life's all about. That's why you take the *River View*. So that when you do come back from work, you can sit there with your glass of wine and look out at your view of the river and say F to all of them!"

He didn't usually swear, I think he just wanted to emphasise the point. I took the *River View*.

So my neighbours aren't the gym bunnies and the young Turks like Gus. They are the more elderly Chinese who leave the apartments empty, except for the two months in the summer that they spend in London. Or, like my landlord, also Chinese, who elect to rent the apartment to defray the exorbitant cost of the service charge which covers the 24/7 Concierge, the gym, the swimming pool, the snooker room, which I have yet to see, and the mini-viewing cinema which I tried to reserve once, but couldn't work out how to do it via my phone app.

I arrive at their apartment. Both waiting for me. Wine bottle already open on the coffee table. Lindsay made the introductions. Poured me a glass of wine. Some small talk. Second glass of wine. I wasn't quite sure whether I was going to actually do the interview there and then, or whether this was just a warm-up meeting. He was eyeing me up and down, I imagined to suss out whether he thought this junior reporter was competent or capable enough. The scene was awkward and uncomfortable.

I didn't really know Lindsay. She seemed OK. And Vinnie was alright, but, really, what was I doing there? Sod it! Third glass of wine. After he'd opened the second bottle, we were all feeling far more relaxed so I thought it was now or never:

"Do you know, Lindsay, I've been sitting here all evening and there's been something bugging me that I really have to say."

Lindsay wondered what was coming and I didn't want to keep her in suspense.

"How on earth do you put up with that shitty Garden View? I think I'd die!"

Lindsay burst into giggles, explaining to Vinnie that I lived on the posh side. Vinnie joined in the fun. We had all loosened up and, from then on, it was all soppy banter. Lindsay telling me that I was just jealous of her tits, then Vinnie joining in to say that Lindsay had told him that I had a boney ass.

Suddenly, it was all laughs, nothing was off the table and then Lindsay hit me right off left field with:

"Confession time, there is no article, I told Vinnie about you, how I thought you were sexy, he said: *What about a threesome?* We set you up!"

I stared at them, momentarily in a state of shock, trying to shake myself out of my inebriated state. I stood up and turned around and marched towards the door. I was about to open it and then I half-turned and quipped:

"Oh, this apartment has a different layout to mine, where's the bedroom door again?"

And, with that, turned around towards the bedroom, taking my top off and walking inside.

Seconds later, they had followed me in to see me lying there in bra and pants, legs slightly apart in a suggestive pose. They started to undress and then I spoke:

"I think we need some house rules."

Lindsay responded. "Yes, of course, silly of me. Vinnie will be wearing a condom."

"I beg your pardon!"

"Err, you said house rules, I wasn't sure what you meant."

I didn't know what I meant either. All I knew was that I was flying blind here. They'd taken me by surprise. Up until now, Cindy had been sleeping which wasn't surprising; she would have been bored by the earlier proceedings, with the expectation of talking about financial journalism all evening. But now she had woken up. Now she was ready.

"What I meant was: *Who's in charge? Who's directing this scene?*"

I had realised that, while I'd been set up, they were fucking clueless. I'm not sure if they'd done this before. Come to think of it neither had I. Well, of course, just the once with Cassandra, who was a very capable director of the scene as it unfolded.

Since Cassandra, there'd been no more threesomes. There hadn't been any before Cassandra. So really that was all I had to go on.

I had fucked in all sorts of places: behind the school bike sheds, in the back seat of a car, well several cars, in a swimming pool. (Don't do that, Ladies. You lose all the natural lubrication which somehow gets washed away from both you and your partner and the friction is actually quite uncomfortable.)

I haven't joined the Mile High club, but I have sucked somebody off in a loo. I feel I've been everywhere and done everything in that neck of the woods, so to speak, but Cassandra was a one-off and I didn't see how this would be able to compare. There was only one way that I was going to be able to go through with this. I mean to go through with this and come out the other side, on top and satisfied with myself.

So, I got off the bed. I looked at them, in their half-nakedness, and said:

"OK, guys! I'm in charge. Do as I say."

Their faces implied that they were ready to go along with me, so I thought: *Hey ho, here we go!*

"Does Vinnie keep clothes here?"

"A few things. Why?"

"I need two neckties."

She went to the wardrobe and held up a few ties. I told her to bring them to me. I took two of them.

"Are these silk?"

"Yes, Hermes, I bought…"

I had previously sussed the scene and luckily the headboard was one of those metal railing types.

"Vinnie! Take the rest of your clothes off and get on the bed on your back. Lindsay! You just watch me and do what I do."

I used one of the ties to strap one of his hands to a rail on the headboard, nodding to Lindsay to do the same with the tie in her hand.

"How tight?"

"Just so that he can't easily wriggle free, but if he's a naughty boy, we will go and tighten them till it hurts. You don't use an eye shade to sleep with, do you?"

"No, but I do have, you know, the ones they give you when you fly first class."

"Perfect!"

I used my eyes to indicate that she should get the blindfold. She rummaged in some drawers, took it out and waved it at me as if to ask if she should put it on Vinnie. I nodded.

Next up, the oil. She didn't have baby oil. I suggested olive oil from the kitchen although I hadn't used it before for massage.

"What's the oil for?" a blindfolded Vinnie piped up.

"None of your business. Keep quiet! Or we'll have to tighten those neckties."

We went to the kitchen to get the olive oil and then I explained to Lindsay the intricate art of body-to-body massage. We went back to the bedroom.

I started to wipe the olive oil onto Lindsay, across her breasts, around her belly button, down her legs and the inside of her thighs, spreading her lips just to make sure that she was ready for action.

"From now on, no talking. One giggle from either of you and I'm out of here!"

As Lindsay commenced the massage, I was guiding her body until she got the hang of it. For a first-timer, she was doing well, managing the sideways shift, always difficult even for a professional, to wipe oily tits in the client's face while still keeping the body close.

I watched Vinnie sucking at Lindsay's erect nipples. Now it was my turn. I gently adjusted Lindsay's body, so she remained above Vinnie's waist, while I was down on the lower half, starting with his ankles, my well-oiled hands gliding up his legs smoothly. I hadn't really paid much attention. Now I noticed his legs were quite hairy. I wondered what was in store for me.

Not my favourite, as I started to lick his ball sack. The hair was getting in the way. In my irritation, I pinched at a clump and tugged. He gave a little squeal. Now is the time! I took his erection in my mouth. I had already decided not to prolong this, beyond what I needed to do. But, nevertheless, I wanted to remain professional, so I knew I was going to give him an incredible orgasm. I stroked my tongue along his shaft. I circled the glans. I sucked hard. But there was to be no edging. I sensed the moment. I knew he was ready. I wanted to get my timing right and just as I could feel, just as I could almost picture the sperm from his testicles mixing with the seminal fluid from his prostate, I knew this was the moment. I inserted two fingers quite forcefully deep inside his anus, just as he was coming. I managed to withdraw my mouth but he spurted so far that I caught some on my face.

I got up off the bed. Lindsay was now on top of him, riding him. They were kissing. She was grinding against his penis trying to keep it hard.

*Good luck with that!* I thought.

*******

*It was Lindsay's idea. I think she realised that I was getting bored with our sex life. She'd mentioned this sexy chic at the gym, always putting it out for the guys. Sweaty tits and arse.*

*She told me she'd spotted her in the loo, rubbing her nipples, to get them erect and then, when she went back to the water cooler, she more or less planted her tits in their faces.*

*I didn't know if Lindsay was just trying to get me horny, but I couldn't have expected our game would play so well.*

*I'd always thought of lying down, submitting to a woman. The restraints, the blindfold all heightening my senses. I thought I knew Lindsay's body, but she'd never massaged me like that before, with her body. Then the sexy chic, Rachel, or Rache. Her tongue. Lyndsay had blown me, but not like this. I'd paid professionals, but they just wanted to finish me off as soon as possible. This was an altogether different experience. I could tell that she was enjoying it. Actually getting pleasure from pleasuring me. I'm in another place. Come on Rachel, make me come. Now she's sucking, now her tongue is circling. Fuck me, I'm coming, she can tell I'm coming because the sucking is harder. Her fingers up me now. That's new for me, as is the sensation as I explode and the finger fucking which seems to increase the amount of spunk, so my orgasm lasts longer as I spurt it out. That was, just … wow! I feel totally satisfied. I can feel Lyndsay on top of me. Rachel's saying something, but I'm not really listening. I think she's leaving, but Lyndsay wants to ride me, to snog me, but I just want to relax. If she thought this would bring us closer together, I don't think that's how it's turned out. All I can think of is Rachel's sexy body, her erotic, sensuous, tantalising tongue, and how it's now Rachel that I want to fuck.*

*******

They were still snogging, I thought I should just depart, silently, and leave them to it. I paused at the bedroom door. I couldn't let it go.

I had a picture in my mind for the article:

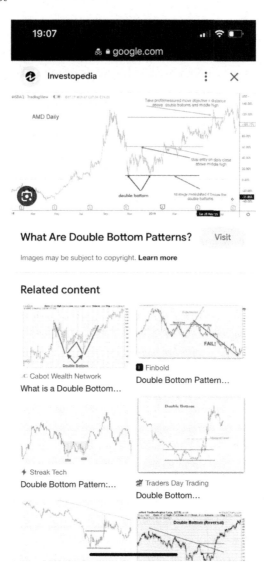

"Thanks, guys, that was fun. I'll get that article to you by Monday. 500 words on how a Zopa Risk Manager describes the regulatory problems *restraining* him in today's turbulent markets.

I don't think they were listening.

"Headline, I don't know, I thought: *Zopa analyst faces double bottom with his hands tied*. I'll drop my invoice across by e-mail."

Still no reaction from either of them. Shame, I thought it was a good headline.

They were too engrossed in each other's arms. Lyndsay snogging passionately, though Vinnie looked totally out of it.

I left the third-floor Garden View apartment, walked down the three flights of stairs, walked across the corridor, through the entrance lobby, to the other lift bank, and up to my apartment, sixth floor, *River View*.

Now I am sitting on my sofa, cranberry juice in hand, admiring the panoramic view across the Thames estuary.

I reflected on the evening, and what had just happened and thought to myself:

Garden View *residents, they're all the fucking same!*

********

Note to Ed. The only time we really fell out is over the next bit. You told me I can't write for shit, and I said you could edit my worst bits to make it readable. But there was no way that meant using a sodding computer. So I am OK with the compromise. I agreed that the readers should know what it was like to see the *River View* that I prattle on about so much. You know to paint a picture. I had to admit that the *Chat GPT* bot says it better than me. So, as long as you tell the readers that the description below is not my voice, but the voice of an emotionless machine that's never been near my Greenwich flat, never seen the *River View* and, more importantly, couldn't tell the difference between an orgasm and a silicon chip, then I'm OK with adding the bot's charming way with words, so here goes:

You've got to go back to my bit up the page where I say:

"Now I am sitting on my sofa, cranberry juice in hand, admiring the panoramic view across the Thames estuary."

And here is the bot's version:

*"The River View from an apartment at Upper Riverside, in Greenwich's Cutters Way, is simply breathtaking. As you step into the apartment and make your way to the balcony, you are greeted by a stunning panoramic view of the River Thames.*

*The river glistens in the sunlight, reflecting the blue sky and the clouds that drift lazily overhead. Boats of all shapes and sizes can be seen cruising up and down the river, their wakes leaving shimmering trails in the water. The sound of the water lapping against the riverbank and the distant hum of traffic and people going about their day create a peaceful atmosphere.*

*On the opposite bank, the city skyline rises up, with the iconic O2 Arena dominating the view. As the day turns into evening, the city comes to life and the buildings light up, creating a glittering spectacle that stretches as far as the eye can see. The colours of the sunset paint the sky in shades of orange, pink, and purple, casting a warm glow over the river and the city.*

*As the night falls, the view becomes even more magical. The lights of the city reflect on the water, creating a shimmering dance that is both hypnotic and enchanting. The boats that were once visible in the daylight now appear as twinkling dots, moving rhythmically up and down the river.*

*This view is not just a sight to behold, it's a sensory experience that transports you to another world. It's a place where you can lose yourself in the beauty of nature and the majesty of the city. It's a place where you can relax and unwind and simply bask in the glory of one of the most beautiful views in London.*

*From the apartment's River View, you have a front-row seat to the stunning beauty of the River Thames and the city that surrounds it. It's a view that will stay with you long after you leave, a memory that will be etched in your mind forever."*

You gotta admit though, my version is far more succinct.

# 25
## Potted Smashes

It had been a long time, too long in fact. I'd been meaning to catch up, but the moment never seemed right. Now I had an excuse. I needed a favour. A very small favour but she was the only person who could do this for me.

"Sandra, it's me, Cindy. I know it's been a long time. I'm a selfish sod. You're gonna hate me. I'm phoning for a favour."

"Cindy, it's nice to hear from you. I always admire your directness. You could have given me all the usual BS. You know - been too busy, rushed off my feet, had a hysterectomy, yadi yadi yadda."

"You didn't! Oh, I'm so sorry, I really didn't know. Jimmy, I mean James is no longer a client, so I... I don't know what..."

"No, it's OK, really it is, things turned out wonderfully well. We went for surrogacy. We opted for IVF, with the egg implanted into the surrogate. To be honest we went through hell. The hormone treatment, during our IVF, made me really cranky. In the end, we needed an egg donor. Jimmy's sperm, so no Montessiori genes. Could have cost the marriage. But how do you say it: *Hey ho!* Then the surrogacy thing is very difficult over here. It's legal and so on, but they make it quite difficult. So we spent 12 months in the USA. That's why you haven't seen James. It wasn't personal. He misses you like crazy. But anyway, half a million dollars later, we have the most beautiful girl we could possibly have wished for."

"You must send me photos. What's the gorgeous girl's name?"

"Well, you know our set, we don't have much choice. We have to follow family tradition. In the Montessiori clan, after a Cassandra, there's always an Anastasia. James' family has this thing with girls, taking the father's name using the feminine version, so that's Jemima.

"How lovely, Anastasia Jemima."

"Yes, that's just the middle names where we have no choice. The first name is one we choose together. The one that she will use."

There was a pregnant pause and I was waiting.

"Well, aren't you going to tell me?"

"Yes, of course: Cindy."

Another pregnant pause

"Well, come on. Stop keeping me in suspense. Tell me!"

"I just did, Cindy. Well actually it's Cynthia, but I'm sure we'll always call her Cindy."

I was dumbstruck. Didn't know what to say, but, after a brief period of silence:

"Unbe-fucking-lievable. You name her after me and couldn't even make me her Godmother!"

Cassandra laughed. It was nice to hear. We hadn't spoken for ages, but the banter was still there. She had a great comeback line with:

"We seriously thought about it, but then realised that in our set, the God-parents pay towards education, and you're too fucking poor!"

"Too right, if it was up to me, she'd be down the local comprehensive and pregnant by sixteen."

The banter went on, and then, Cassandra asked:

"Cindy, you wanted a favour?"

"Yes, I'd completely forgotten. Caught up in the moment. It's a very small thing, trivial really. On the other hand, it's so, so important for me. It literally won't take up more than five minutes of your time. But you're the only person I know who could do it. By good fortune, you happen to be one of the few people that I would want to share it with, in any case."

"You know I like these games, we both like playing them, it is such fun. I would have been disappointed if you had simply told me what in heaven you wanted me to do. Normally we're on the same wavelength, so explanations are not necessary. But, Cindy, you have to help me out here. I haven't got a clue what you're talking about and you are talking in riddles."

"Yes, I know. I like the games as well, but I wanted to ask you face-to-face. Maybe over a drink. Believe me, I do mean a drink, that's not a euphemism for passionate, explosive climactic sex. Make it lunch or tea, because I think both of us know what dinner would turn into."

"It's so, so lovely to hear from you. I'm dying to catch up. Of course, the favour, whatever you ask. Where do you want to meet?"

"How about Harvey Nicks, tea or lunch?"

"Sounds OK."

Then I thought, I didn't want to bump into Cassandra's friends who probably lunch there all the time.

"No, actually, why don't you suggest somewhere, somewhere discreet where I'm not likely to bump into, I don't know, the gossipy crowd."

"I know a fabulous little Greek restaurant in Notting Hill, the food's great. The place is tiny. You're practically stepping on the feet of your neighbouring diners. On second thoughts, you can't have a conversation there without everybody overhearing you."

"Have you got time, I mean, like with your daughter and such."

"Why, what do you mean?"

"I don't know, somewhere out of town: the Fat Duck, the Compleat Angler. One of those fancy Michelin places, where only stuck-up snobs like you are allowed to cross the threshold. Or better still, come down to my level: fish and chips dahn the Old Kent Road."

"Cindy's not a problem. Oh, this is going to be confusing. Cynthia will not be a problem. We have a nanny."

"Of course you do!"

I was going to say: *She cost you $500,000 and you can't look after her yourself.* But I thought that wouldn't land well.

"Out of town, what a brilliant idea. I know exactly where we shall go, but you have to let me surprise you."

"Deal done, but how will I find it, if you don't tell me?"

"Let me worry about that. Oh *merde!*"

"What's the matter?"

"I'm going to need your real name. If that's a problem, I could choose somewhere else."

"Why do you need… Oh, never mind, of course, it's not a problem, Rachel Levinson. Do you need me to spell that?"

"Oh, really?"

"You sound surprised."

"No, not really. It's just, I didn't picture you as a Rachel."

What did she mean: *Picture me as a Rachel.* I was slightly taken aback. I wasn't sure if that was an anti-Semitic jibe or a throw-away line. She's a European aristo. They hate Jews and what, I'm a Rachel. What's next: *Did you have a nose job to get rid of the hook, Becky?*

I was seething, but I thought I'd let it pass.

"My friends call me Rache."

"I can live with that, Rache. Give me a day when you can clear your calendar, and I will arrange everything."

I looked at my phone. Flicked through my days off. I found a day with just the personal trainer and my hairdresser. I could cancel both. We agreed on the date. She told me to expect something in the post and asked for my mailing address. I don't know what it was but, by now, I was wet with anticipation. It was only going to be lunch, but there was something about Cassandra that turns me on something terrible.

\*\*\*\*\*\*\*

A few days later, the bell on the control panel rang. It was the Concierge to tell me there was a parcel waiting downstairs. I could come down now, or, if it wasn't urgent, someone would deliver it to my apartment later in the day. I said, if it wasn't heavy, I'd come down. The only parcels I normally get are from Amazon. I didn't recall ordering anything recently. They're usually the next day. Sometimes, if the product is on long delivery, I might have forgotten. I checked my app, but nothing was due.

I went down to the reception on the ground floor to pick up the parcel. It wasn't Amazon. It was in Harrods packaging. I thought: *It couldn't be from her? What have you done now, Cassandra? You daffy cow!*

I collected the parcel. Almost ran back upstairs in excitement. Actually, alright, I wasn't going to run upstairs. It's six flights. It's a metaphor. I got in the lift and started ripping the packaging open. I couldn't wait to see what she'd bought me.

It was a small Prada evening clutch bag, decorated with sort of diamantés. Probably a couple of thou. What had I done to deserve that? I opened the bag and inside there was a thin card. I took it out. It was a ticket. A Eurostar ticket. That's why she needed my name! You're travelling across a border; the tickets have your name on them. It had the day that we'd agreed, the seat number. Of course, first class. The other ticket was an open return. I wondered whether Cassandra was telling me that I could stay on for a few days' holiday if I chose, or was there more significance to that? I wouldn't have time to spend more than the day. I had work commitments. Although it did seem a shame. A ticket to Paris, all paid. I was tempted to have a look for an AirBnB. In the end, I decided I'd just pack an overnight. You never know your luck!

Cassandra had written something on the ticket, just two words: PUFFED. SMASHES. Her copperplate handwriting was so distinctive. Although she didn't realise, that handwriting was crucial to the favour that I'd be asking.

I didn't know what the words meant. They were obviously clues to the location. The end point of our rendezvous. Well, I suppose I had a couple of days to work it out, but, at this point, it seemed to be quite meaningless. All I could think of over and over again was how could those words tell me the location. The more I thought about it, the wetter I got. Memories flashed back of the sensational evening we had together. I was back there at Jimmy's. Fuck, no, I was on the sofa, playing with myself, turning myself on. Feeling my wetness through my slacks. Imagining Cassandra's tongue. I snapped out of it. *Get a grip, girl. You can't be lying around masturbating. There are chores to do.*

Then…

Sod it! I'm now in my bedroom, stripped below the waist. I reach across for my friendly rabbit, which I always keep handily bedside. I'm back with Cassandra. But now, I'm between her legs, and she's between mine. That's the beauty of a daydream fantasy. There's no way I can come with sixty-nine, but, in my fantasy, I can be concentrating on sucking her off while lying back and letting her pleasure me at the same time. I was in the boudoir. I could picture the four-poster bed. We were in raptures. Even the picture of their butler didn't put me off. He was in his morning suit uniform, carrying a silver platter and bending slightly towards me. On the silver tray, my vibrating rabbit: *Your orgasm, Madam.*

Of course, Jimmy was standing over us wanking. Then I was kneeling, sucking him off. This is a fantasy, I can be on the bed with Cassandra's tongue on my clit, while she is finger fucking me. At the same time, I can be kneeling taking in Jimmy's erection. I can be feeling his spunk spurting in my mouth, while Cassandra is in rapturous orgasm. Everything we had done together in real life. Well, except for the fisting. For some reason, the censors had cut that scene. Both my partners were having simultaneous orgasms. I was arching my back, starting to spasm. Then…

The picture started flickering, like the old movies, like the film had snapped and I saw the reel going round and round with the torn celluloid flapping, making a whirring sound, which was just getting louder. Jimmy, Cassandra, they had long gone and so had any chance of my orgasm. The noise was deafening. What the fuck was going on? I ran out of my bedroom still naked from the waist down. I followed the sound into the hall. I opened the cupboard door and yelled.

In front of me, like something out of The Sorcerer's Apprentice, was my stacked tumble dryer. I'd put it on earlier, the usual cycle, but it had taken on a life of its own, kerchunking and bouncing. It had moved a few feet and was hammering against the cupboard door.

I pressed the off switch. It took me a few seconds before I came to my senses. I phoned down to the Concierge to send up the handyman, Derek:

"It seems to have come off its hinges, well, not the hinges, exactly, the, you know, sort of bracketty thingy, to hold it on top of the washing machine."

"I know exactly what you mean, Miss Levinson. Funnily enough, we had something similar in another flat the other day. I think we should send an email around to all residents. It's over-filling the tumble dryer that's causing it. No lasting damage. Derek can be up there in five minutes if that's okay with you."

Problem solved, but I'm all in a tizzy. I'd been interrupted before I came. It felt like all those idiot boys, the young men who thought a quick lick would be sufficient. They were sexy enough to get me going, maybe I'd even started to come. I was enjoying their tongue even though they were amateurs. Then they'd sense the moment, but instead of finishing me off, would decide that the best thing was a fuck. As soon as their cock was inside me, they'd lost the clit. The moment had passed, leaving me hornier than before I started.

Derek is at the door. He's sweet. Obliging. I wonder how obliging? Derek was staring at me with a look of amazement.

I was still naked from the waist down.

"You've got a problem with the tumble dryer," He stuttered.

"Fuck the tumble dryer, Derek, I've got a more serious problem in the bedroom. Can we deal with that first!"

I was left so frustrated after being shaken out of my fantasy by the noise from the tumble dryer that I was so, so ready. But, nevertheless, I had my pride. So, once his trousers were down and I took off his underpants, I had to take a closer look. A bit shorter than I expected and a steep upward curve, like when you make a hand sign to show a plane taking off. Foreskin intact. No problem, it's not going in my mouth. Thinner than I like. On another day that would have been enough to put me off. But I was so horny, and beggars can't be choosers.

I came as soon as I felt Derek inside me. Shit! That's a first. Never heard of premature ejaculation by the woman before. This was my first time with Derek, and my last.

Dixie and I used to joke about and tease him, but he was never close to my playlist. Nevertheless, I couldn't disappoint the boy. He still had the tumble dryer to repair. So I lay there after I'd come and let him bang away.

Fake orgasms are not my forte, but it was either that or tip him a fiver for a few screws in the tumble dryer. I started to laugh, giggling at the stupid pun. A screw in the tumble dryer and a screw for the tenant.

Derek stopped: "What's the matter, why are you giggling? Aren't you enjoying it?"

"No, no, Derek, please carry on. I always giggle when I'm coming. Go on, fuck me! This is the best fuck I've ever had. Shout something dirty at me."

Normally works, but not for Derek.

"I can't think of anything to say."

"Never mind. Please just keep fucking me. Quicker, I'm coming. Oh! Oh! Oh!"

*Oh!* *Oh?* You're such a bad actress. I could feel him going limp. I was worried about him not finishing the job. No, silly, not on me. The tumble dryer!

I wriggled free, quickly before he was completely flaccid. I had to resort to my failsafe default option. So I took him in my mouth foreskin an' all. I was so far behind with my household chores; this was going to be a quickie. I gave him the worst blow job that I'd ever delivered, but the best experience for Derek in his young life.

"You can use the guest loo to clean up. I'll put the coffee on, for when you've done the dryer. Milk and sugar?"

He declined the coffee. Paid a quick visit to the loo. Held up the hand towel, with a sheepish:

"You might want to wash this."

He finished re-attaching the tumble-dryer brackety thingy in a few minutes.

"Just a little screw. I slotted it right back in."

I laughed out loud, but he was back in maintenance man mode and hadn't realised the *double entendre*.

As he left without even a kiss on the cheek from me, I mouthed: *Our secret!* And I slipped him the fiver.

# 26
## Dixie Split

Dixie wanted to sit down for a serious talk. I knew what was coming.

She had been offered a bursary for reading an MA, which meant two more years at Greenwich. I hadn't got a job, by which she'd meant a proper job. So, if I was carrying on at Felicity's, we could stay together. The bursary would mean she could pay a proper share of the rent. I wouldn't have to worry about catching up on missed lectures. She wouldn't have to worry about writing my essays. I'd have more time on my hands, so could cook us dinners instead of Deliveroo every night. Life's a charm.

Dixie's life was mapped out for the next two years. How was I going to tell her? We said right at the beginning: *It works as long as we are both in love.* If not, she'd move out. She said that before we became an item. I knew that if I asked her to move out, she'd be heartbroken. But we couldn't go back to roommates. Shit! Shit! And gobshite! That's why I never wanted to do relationships. The break-up is too painful. I really didn't want to hurt Dixie, but I'd grown out of the relationship. I certainly wasn't ready to be a housewife.

"Rache, I spoke to my tutor today about the bursary, but I wanted to talk to you first, about *your* plans. It's not fair that my decision should affect our future. I've decided to take the bursary so I can stay with you."

"What do you mean, *so you can stay with me?*"

"Well, I've been offered a job at First Psychology Edinburgh. It's a fantastic opportunity. Entry level, but a stepping stone to a fast track up the ladder. Northumbria does a part-time MSc, so I wouldn't be giving up on my Masters. It's really a win-win. But I can't expect you to move to Edinburgh, just for me. So I'm going to take the bursary here.

I lost my cool:

"Are you fucking crazy? You got your dream job offer. Your *win-win* but you'll give that up to stay with me. Can you hear yourself? On what planet am I worth you ruining your life?"

I could see tears in her eyes.

"Why are you shouting at me?"

"Because I'm not worth it. Sorry, I didn't want to upset you but…"

"But I love you. I want to stay with you. You're the most important thing in my life."

Tears were streaming down her face. I had to hug her to console her. She calmed down a bit.

"Have you accepted the bursary?"

"No, I said that I was going to talk to you first."

"And the job?"

"I've got till the end of next week. They said the offer's open till then."

"And Northern - what?"

"Northumbria, that's nothing, it's an open application. Any time before term starts."

I knew then that the way to bring this to a head was to tell her that I was already shagging Gus. It was just a little white lie. I'd had two dates already, and the normal pattern is that the third is a fuck before we break it off, so it's just a time warp of a few days.

"Dixie, look at me and listen. This is going to be hard for you to take in. So hear me out. I love you. Maybe not as much as you love me, but I do love you and care for you. But I shagged Gus last night."

"Who's Gus?"

"A Yank. Lives on the seventh floor. On the other side of the building. Garden View. Different lift so you wouldn't have bumped into him. Met him in the gym. We've been on a few dates…"

"When were you going to tell me?"

"I only shagged him last night."

"But two dates?"

"Yea, I know. That's my normal limit, but l haven't met his boss yet."

"What's his boss got to do with it?"

"Gus isn't important. He's just the conduit to get to his boss. I've decided he'll be my sugar daddy."

"I don't know what the fuck you're talking about!"

"I'm saying take the job in Edinburgh. I'm no good for you. If you like, I'll come up and see you for the odd weekend and we can have some fun. It's got to be fun, Dix. I can't do the drama. I do love you. I really do. But I wank guys for a living and I fuck guys for fun. If I play my cards right, I'm going to get myself a sugar daddy to take me round the world. It's who I am. I can't be your fucking housewife, Dixie. I won't change. If you can live with that, I'm happy for a long-distance relationship with you in Edinburgh. But I can't live with you here quizzing me every night about my choice of lifestyle."

Dixie stared at me with a scowl:

"June always said you'd let me down. She said you were just playing with me. You're such a bitch. Go fuck your Gus, go fuck your sugar daddy and, while you're about it, go fuck yourself and rot in hell. I'll pack my things and move out tomorrow."

"Don't be like that and don't be daft. You'll stay here till you move to Edinburgh."

"Alright, I'll stay, but don't you dare come on to me. If you try anything, I'll scream rape."

"OK promise, no snogging, no sex, but you need to do one thing though, before you leave."

She looked at me with a curious gaze.

"Give me back that strap-on dildo; you never paid me for it."

I think I detected a smile as she turned around and walked back to her bedroom, slamming the door behind her.

# 27
# Shagging Gus

A call from Rache was always a pleasure. Less frequent now, than before, so I treasure the moments with her. Since our relationship had ceased to have any sexual element, she took on the role of my surrogate for Lyn. Of course, not in any normal sense. The things Rache talks to me about are not the subject for father and daughter, so I accept my role of mentor, elder statesman, whatever she wants really. I can never expect her to have the feeling for me that I have for her, but if I can help her to achieve her goals, then I'm content.

As these meetings were becoming few and far between, I wanted to treat her to something different. As she only phoned me, now, when she wanted to pick my brains, the venue needed to have an element of privacy. I chose the Ritz Hotel, afternoon tea, corner table. For Sunday, you need to book weeks in advance, so I opted for mid-week.

The Ritz occupies a prominent spot along one of London's most celebrated thoroughfares. It sits right in the middle of Piccadilly, a pre-eminent highway, boasting iconic retail brands along its sidewalk, and connecting Hyde Park corner, a stone's throw from Buckingham Palace, to Piccadilly Circus home to the world famous Eros fountain, which has enjoyed many a naked drunken reveller on New Year's Eve.

The hotel itself is an icon, built over a century ago in what is described as neo-classical Louis XVI style, the influence of the French architect, who designed it, persists today. The name of the hotel and the eponymous Swiss hotelier, who developed it even spawned a phrase, no longer in popular use *putting on the Ritz* or in the vernacular *ritzy* to describe the ultimate in sophistication. In an era when we are supposed to be a classless society, the Ritz has retained an elegance, and, if no longer the exclusive reserve of the aristocracy, nevertheless still a place where the aspirational will still pay over the odds for a cup of tea as long as it's served in an EPNS teapot.

Tea is served in the Palm Court Restaurant, another icon amongst the icons. Unsurprisingly, real potted palms frame the entrance. No space for the plastic variety within this upmarket café that has served royalty.

Cindy, with in her usual succinct way with words, would simply have described the place as: *real posh*.

I was sitting at the table. She's rarely late, which I take as a mark of respect. I spotted her as she walked through the entrance. She was wearing - what else but shredded jeans and a long nylon anorak. The anorak, a favourite of hers, which, previously, she had proudly described as: *twenty quid at Primark, a real metsieh*, her mum's Yiddish word for *bargain*. Rachel was still my Cindy, so out of place amidst the splendour, and, yet, she carried it off so well. Completely care-free. That's what I loved so much about her. That's what I still love about her.

She looked around and saw me in the corner and approached me. I stood up, greeted her with a friendly kiss, and offered to take her coat, the long anorak, which I draped over the spare chair.

As she took off her coat, I noticed, on top of the shredded jeans, she was wearing that LBD. The one I bought for her on our first non-date. The one with the pull strings at the bottom, so you could adjust the length from mini to knee length. I'm quite embarrassed at how little I spent on it, and what good use she'd got out of this versatile number. Today, it was drawn up to micro-level, so it was more or less just a long blouse on top to her jeans.

"Where's the loo. I've gotta change. It was so bloody cold out, so I put my jeans underneath."

I pointed in the direction of the entrance to the tea room where she'd just come in and explained that the ladies was virtually opposite, across the corridor leading to the hotel lobby.

She was gone a mere few minutes. When she returned the jeans were no longer to be seen, screwed up, I assumed, into the small rucksack she was carrying.

Now the Little Black Dress had been pulled down to the knees, deliberately smart, not sexy but, remarkably, showing her VPL (*Visible Panty Line* – an abbreviation she had taught me). I couldn't stop myself from commenting:

"Is it my imagination or are you deliberately wearing granny pants underneath to make a point, just in case I booked a room?"

She smiled her *trademark smile*.

"*Au contraire*, sweetheart. They are pure silk. I love the feel of them against my skin. Commando works well for the evening, but, at tea time, it's French knickers any day of the week."

We shared a smile.

We ordered cream tea and started with a glass of champagne. We were halfway through and I was wondering when she was going to raise the matter she wanted to discuss when she suddenly blurted out: "Puffed. Smashes."

"Sorry?"

"Puffed. Smashes. Do those words mean anything to you?"

"Could you give me some context here? It sounds like an advert for a breakfast cereal."

"Context?"

"The words mean nothing to me, but if you can tell me what it's all about maybe that will trigger something."

She then told me about Cassandra. How she played games with her. Well, actually, they both played these kinds of games. Sort of *double entendres* or teasing each other. When they first met, Rache kept calling her Sandy instead of Sandra, not just because she knew she hated being called that, but to make a point. Like Cassandra had to prove herself before Rachel would concede and call her Sandra. It all seemed very juvenile, but I could see that the women had formed some sort of bond. Rachel had huge respect for Cassandra.

So, written on the back of a Eurostar ticket, you think that the words are a place in Paris. "Here, google translate: *éclats soufflé.*"

"You're so, so clever, where is that?"

"I don't know, it's not a place. I just thought, you know, Cassandra might be giving you some cryptic clue."

"Yes, yes, like a crossword puzzle. Go on, tell me."

"I think you overestimate my knowledge sometimes. I'm just coming up with random ideas to see if it triggers anything. You're sure it was only two words, not three?"

"Quite sure. They were written on the back of the rail ticket. Why?"

"Well, there's something called What3Words. I don't suppose you've heard of it."

"Funnily enough, I have. I used to go out with this tech nerd. *Go out* is a bit of an exaggeration. I went through an intellectual phase when I first went to College. It was all new to me, so I started to hang out with these nerds, thinking some of it would rub off on me. Then, I discovered that the rubbing off or rather rubbing up was all they wanted from me, so I ditched that crowd and took up with the sex slaves instead. Far more my scene."

We shared a laugh. She flashed me her *trademark smile*. Cindy was alive and well and still living inside Rache's head.

"Anyway, this techie nerd told me about this 3 Word company. It took some time to catch on, but now it's everywhere. Venues use it, printing their three-word location on their marketing literature and so forth. I think it's one of those things that no-one ever used then suddenly one day people wonder how they ever managed without it."

I then explained that, even if Cassandra was using that as part of the treasure hunt, having two words was no good, because the words are completely random, so the property next door wouldn't have the same first two words. It wasn't like a map reference where the neighbouring locations would have close-by numbers. I could see I was losing her.

"OK, I'll park that. But, if I mysteriously find a third word, between now and Paris, what do I do with it?"

"You just download the app and put in the words and it gives you the address. It's very easy. Actually, I wonder if the inventors had realised how it would be a great computer game treasure hunt. Like that Pokemon thing, a few years ago. Talking of Pokemon. How's Dixie? She told me she used to be a gamer until she met you and discovered sex."

Another shared laugh. Another *trademark smile*.

"Difficult. Sticky ending. Actually, let's not go there. It's a guy I wanted to talk to you about. Gus. He's a yank. For an American, he's very posh. Not posh like you, but he's almost American royalty. Lawrence August Cheney the Third. Distant cousin to some Vice President."

"Dick Cheney?

"Something like that. I felt a bit of an oik. I was supposed to know who that was."

"Sounds just the ticket."

She then proceeded to explain that she'd had two dates already, so it was decision time, and she'd decided it was time to *fuck*. I was still fascinated by her directness. Her problem, what she wanted to discuss with me, the reason for the call and why it had to be face-to-face, was to ask me whether or not she should fake an orgasm. She's always told me that the men she goes out with are basically boys. They never know how to pleasure a woman. How she needed oral to come.

"How do you know Gus won't be able to pleasure you through conventional sexual intercourse? Love can do strange things."

She let out a belly laugh.

"That's a joke, right? It's a fuck not a marriage. Plus he's the route to the sugar-daddy."

She then explained the grand plan. To use her relationship with Gus to meet his boss.

"Do you think that's a good idea?"

"What do you mean? It's your fucking idea. I'm following your game plan."

"How's that?"

"You laid out my life for me. You can't have forgotten. First, the flat, with the gym, where I meet the right guy, form the relationship, then use his connection to meet the boss."

"You amaze me! Oh, Rache, I do love you!"

I leant across the table and just held her cheeks between my thumb and finger and gave her a big smile. Belinda's face flashed before me. I used to do that with her cheeks when she'd done something really silly, just a father and daughter thing.

Rache pulled away.

"Sorry, you just reminded me of someone. I didn't mean to startle you."

"No, it's OK, it's just that you've never done that before. Someone else used to pinch my cheek. I had a flashback."

"You mean…?"

"Let's not go there, sorry I didn't mean to interrupt."

"Oh, I'm sorry. I didn't realise."

"Stop it. You weren't to know. Seriously, I'm alright. I don't sweat the small stuff."

"If you're sure."

She nodded.

"When I said that about the banker and the sugar-daddy et cetera, I was just laying out a possible scenario. I never expected you to follow it, word for word. You could have chosen another path."

"What do you mean?"

"Your life! Your choice! Make your own decisions. Don't do it just because I said so."

"Fuck off, Vish. Sometimes you say things that make me think you don't understand me at all. I actually listen to your advice. I consider it carefully, weigh up the options, develop a risk assessment model…"

I smiled. She was teasing me.

"And then… I do exactly what you told me to do in the first place!"

We shared a laugh.

"OK, but tell me why this Gus is going to lead you to Mr. Wonderful."

"His boss. Another yank. He will want me, don't you see? I only have to meet him and bat my eyelids. His wife, they have two kids. He's ripe for the picking. It's obvious."

"Of course, batting the eyelids never fails."

"Don't mock me!"

"Well you have to be honest, just because he has a wife and kids, doesn't actually mean he'll immediately jump into bed with you. I still feel I'm missing something."

"Oh Vish, how can you be so clever yet so stupid? You set it out perfectly. He's fifty. That's what you said."

"If I recall, I gave you an age range."

"Well, he's bang in the middle of that age range. He travels extensively, so he'll definitely take me on business trips. Gus told me he's on a million dollars a year."

"Tell me about the wife."

"She's staying in New York until she sorts out the kids' schooling. But Gus says that'll never happen. He's met her and she loves her life in New York too much."

"You don't think mentioning that earlier might have helped me to understand."

The penny finally dropped.

"Duh! OK, sorry if my presentation skills aren't up to your standard."

"Alright, let's assume he might easily fall into your clutches, what's the deal with Gus?"

"Well, that's what I wanted to talk to you about. I'm using him. Now I don't normally fake an orgasm. If they haven't actually pleasured *me*, why should I give them the satisfaction of thinking they've satisfied me?"

"Yes, I think you've described your general philosophy before. The *quid pro quo*. They suck you off and you come, they get a blow job. No cunny for Cindy, no fellation for the client."

"Precisely, is *fellation* a word? I thought it was *fellatio*."

"I believe fellatio is the noun, describing the act of giving the blow job, whereas fellation is a gerund to be used in the conditional tense, which is more appropriate here."

"You daft bugger. You realise I haven't a clue what you're talking about."

"Sorry, but you did ask. So where does faking the orgasm come in?"

"Well, initially, I thought, as I'm going to dump him as soon as I meet his boss, at least he's going to get a few fucks out of it. But then I thought, if he knows I wasn't enjoying it they'd be miserable fucks, so is that fair? A one-night stand is one thing. Who cares? But I could be fucking him for months. He might even end up getting fed up with me before I met his boss. But I'd stay faithful because I'd be really motivated."

I started to laugh.

"What's so funny?"

"It's not funny. More endearing. You're ready to stay faithful to this guy, while you jockey for position to dump him."

"Of course. Doesn't everybody think like that?"

"Oh, I love you so much. No, everybody does not think like that - on the conscious level - but on the subconscious level - I think I'd agree that all relationships are contractual. What makes you unique is that you're ready to admit it."

"I'm not sure if that's a compliment or not. Anyway, I thought that if I fake the orgasm, Gus would have better fucks, so that would be fairer all around."

"I see a hitch. What if he realises you're faking?"

"Don't insult me. First, he's a guy. They're clueless. Second, I'm good. It's not that I can't fake, it's just it rarely makes sense."

"Is that what you did with me?"

"Don't be so offensive! You never put me in that position. You were always numero uno. You're still the best I've had. Well, apart from Cassandra. Still the best of the male species. Plus, you'd spot me in a minute. You know Vishti's first rule: Listen to the breath. If you heard me panting, I think you'd just crack up with laughter."

"We should try it sometime. You know a sort of challenge. Improve your faking skills."

"Seriously, what do you think?"

"I think you're barking! Just let him give you an orgasm."

"How?"

"Seriously, you want *me* to tell *you*."

"Yes. If you really need me to say it, I will. I value your opinion. There! I've said it. No shit! You're the smartest man I know. I really respect and listen to the things you tell me…"

"OK, enough of the compliments. I was really in fact referring to the fact that you have had much more experience than I have, despite my age. Shall we say a lot more of a varied experience in these matters?

"Whatever, so come on, read me the Kama Sutra, how do I get this Yank to give me an orgasm."

"You sit the man down. You're going to seduce him, right? Once you have him in the mood and he's thinking you're up for it, you come clean. Let me give you the script.

*Gus, I'm really very fond of you. I'd like to take this to the next level. I'm ready for you to make love to me, but I have a terrible confession. I can't come with penetration. I enjoy it and I can make sure you enjoy it, but I won't have an orgasm. It's just the way I'm made.*

Then you pause while he mumbles some confused garbage, continuing with the script.

*I can come, but I need your tongue. Would you do that for me?*

Pause five seconds while he thinks about the proposition, but you need to get in quickly because he may doubt his ability.

*But I need to guide you, show you how I like it. I'll show you how to make me come with your tongue. And after I've come, I'm going to get on top of you and fuck your brains out.*

Rache was thinking about what I said. She was silent for several minutes, then:

"I think it's brilliant. I think you're brilliant. But do you think I'd be able to teach him?"

"Of course, well you might need to brush up on Vishti's rules of cunnilingus, but you've got them in your head. Remember, you can always make an imaginary phone call."

"Why are you so, so brilliant? Every time you come up trumps!"

With that, she stood across the table, held my head towards hers and gave me a great big sloppy kiss on the lips. Then she squeezed my cheeks, like I did earlier, with her thumb and finger, as if to say: *See I'm over it. I'm not going to let my abuser define my life.*

"Let's finish our tea. I think I should pay the bill for the advice."

"No, thanks, but no. I invited you."

"You only invited me, because I asked you to."

"I think I'm going to insist."

I gave in. Rache was growing up. She was earning good money. She could afford to pay. She views every relationship as contractual. I relented and nodded to indicate that I'd let her pay.

We carried on chatting for a bit. I asked her what happened with Dixie, but then I went to a different place. A place I wanted to go before, but I was waiting for a moment when I thought Rache was open to it, sure she trusted me.

"Do you mind if I ask you a personal question? If you don't want to answer, you can tell me to mind my own business."

"Go on."

"You mentioned some time ago that you were thinking about tubal ligation. Did you go ahead?"

"Why?"

"Sorry, it's none of my business."

"No, I'll tell you. But you tell me why you want to know."

"To be honest, it's been playing on my mind, ever since you told me. When you mentioned Gus, I misunderstood, but it triggered the thought.

What if you did meet someone, and you wanted to start a family."

"Oh, what you're asking is whether, after my epiphany, now that I can face up to my abuser and my abuse, would I be happy to bring a child into this world, and risk that they'd be abused? No, I haven't changed my mind."

"Sorry, I was being obtuse."

"Stop using words I don't understand."

"Sorry."

"And stop saying sorry. The answer is *No*. I got fed up with the NHS. They had a ridiculous waiting list. I'm now going private. I can have the procedure any time I want. £5,000. Any other questions?"

"Can we talk about it sometime?"

"Not really, not if you're going to try to persuade me to change my mind?"

"No, I wouldn't tell you what to do, but I'd like to lay out a scenario for you to consider. Take it away. Think about it. Then make up your mind."

"A scenario?"

"Yes, like the banker and the sugar-daddy."

"Go on."

"Well, you're going to do that. I have every confidence. You'll meet the boss. You'll travel the world. You'll keep your independence. You'll make money. In 10 years, you'll have, I don't know, your own your apartment, maybe another property. Wealth, I don't know, maybe a few million. You'll have achieved everything you've wanted. You'll have enjoyed the jet-set life. You'll have enjoyed the sex with whoever you choose, men, women. Life will be great. Then you'll wake up one day, and realise you've got everything you wanted to have, done everything you wanted to do, and think: *What now? What am I going to do with the rest of my life?*"

"Is that it? I wake up one day and say: *I'm going to look for a sperm donor and have IVF and magic up a family.*"

"No. Forget the family, for a moment. Let me tell you, just my intuition, but what I see for you in that next phase of your development. You'll find your soulmate and with him, or her, contentment."

"Soulmate, what the fuck!"

"I can picture you, just taking off by yourself and going on a walking tour, I don't know, joining a book club, something that you'd stay a million miles from now. But we're talking ten years hence. There, you meet someone and find you are content in their company. You're ready to live modestly because you've lived the high life. You're ready to have calm gentle sex because you've had the other, the passion, the frenzy, the ecstatic orgasms. I don't expect you to understand. You're still young. Not the youngster I first met at Felicity's. You've developed into a mature woman, but in the next decade your tastes may change. They may not, but my money is on you finding a companion, a soulmate, someone with whom you want to spend the rest of your life."

"Will you please stop saying that word."

"What word?"

"Soulmate!"

I could see that Rache was getting upset, but I wanted to finish, so I suggested maybe she'd want kids with that person, maybe not, but why not keep her options open?

"Because that person doesn't exist. That other soulmate."

"How do you know?"

Tears were starting to stream down her face.

"Because you can't have two soulmates!"

"What do you mean? You've already found your soulmate? Who?"

"You, you idiot. You're my soulmate. I knew from the moment you walked into the massage parlour that first time. I fell in love with you when you walked through that door. I was in love with you when you were my client and you paid me for sex. I was in love with you when I dumped you and said I never wanted to see you again. I was in love with you when I saw you. I was in love with you when I stopped seeing you. You're my soulmate. I don't want anyone else. You were, are, and always will be. I love you. I need you. I... I dream of you every night. I... I am... one with you."

She was struggling to get the words out. She was swallowing the tears. She was an emotional wreck. She ran out of the tea room, leaving her coat behind. I was confused and momentarily froze. I had no idea she had those feelings. I was so fond of Rache, and, foolishly, thought that she just tolerated me for my advice. Respected me, liked me, but beyond that... I never realised.

I didn't know where she'd gone, but I couldn't leave her alone in that state.

# 28

# Reconciliation

I ran straight out of the front door of the hotel and jumped in a taxi which was waiting outside. I had the presence of mind to remember my address but everything else was a blur. When the car stopped at a set of lights, the taxi driver sort of turned his head.

"Are you alright, love? Only it seems you're upset."

"I'm OK. Fuck off and mind your own business. I've just made a complete arse of myself."

The journey was going to take about an hour. Probably £80 fare. The driver was likely wondering if he'd get paid. He stopped the cab, not sure where, but he turned around and said:

"There's a copper there, love. I can ask him to help you if you've been attacked."

I tried to regain my composure:

"No, no, it's nothing like that. Bad bust up with my boyfriend. I'll be OK by the time I get home."

"Look, I don't want to be unkind but this will be at least £75. Are you ok with that?"

I fumbled around in my pockets, then I saw my rucksack on the seat. I had no recollection of picking it up when I ran out of the hotel.

"Yes, I've got my bag and credit card. I'll be OK, honestly."

He continued the journey. Next I knew, I heard the driver again.

"We're here, love. Is this the right entrance?"

"Yes, how much is that?" I saw £83 on the clock.

"Have you got cash?"

"Should have."

"Give me £50 and we'll call it quits."

"Are you sure?"

"Just take care of yourself."

I took out a note and handed it to him. I managed to get upstairs to the flat and lay on the bed and crashed.

*******

I'm not sure how long I was out for, but I heard a shrill sound which stirred me. I was in a daze. The buzzer kept ringing but it wasn't the door. I realised it was the intercom which went straight down to the Concierge at reception. I walked to the panel by the front door and pressed for the mic.

"I'm sorry to disturb you, Miss Levinson, but I have an urgent message from your former flat mate, Dixie. She said it was really important and you weren't answering your phone. She was worried you might have lost your phone or been in some accident. If you don't have your phone, or don't have her number, you can call from down at reception. She left a land line number in Edinburgh."

I hadn't heard from Dixie since she stormed out of the flat. She owed me the last month's rent, but I really didn't care.

I checked my phone. Battery completely dead.

I plugged it in to charge and went down to reception.

"Hi, Dixie. What the matter? Have you been in an accident?"

"Me? No. What are you talking about? I got a call from Vishti, hours ago. I'd never heard him like that before. He was as close to panic as Mr Calm & Collected could be. He said you had some kind of breakdown."

"I'm actually OK now, but my phone is dead. How's Edinburgh?"

"Fine, but do me a favour and call Vishti, will you? We can catch up later. I'm over the break-up now, so don't be a stranger. I'd be happy to have a long call, just not now. Please call Vishti. He's really worried about you."

"I don't have his number. It's in my phone. What's the time?"

"About half eight."

"Morning or evening?"

"Evening! What's the matter with you?"

"Can you do me a favour and call him. Can you give him this message. Tell him… Can you write this down? Please, word for word.

"OK, wait. Better, I'll take down the message on my phone and then text him."

"Yes good, this is the message: *I will be at the Ritz at* … you said 8:30, 90 minutes, that's 10 pm… *I will be at the Ritz at 10 pm. I need to pick up my coat. Also I've also got the bill to settle. If it's not convenient, I'll understand.* Got that? Read it back."

She read it back.

"Oh, can you sign it from… "

"Rache?"

"No. Say *Love from your hysterical idiot.*"

"Are you sure?"

"No, scrub that."

"Just sign it *Soulmate*."

"Soulmate?"

"Yes, private joke, just that. Press send. Thanks Dixie. I really appreciate that and we will catch up. I'd better run. Bye."

I was just about to put the phone down when I heard Dixie scream:

"Wait!"

And then:

"He's just replied: *OK!*"

*******

I got to the Ritz at 5 to 10. Vish was already there waiting. He'd managed to get the same corner table somehow. Maybe he had a permanent reservation. I approached the table. My anorak was over the chair, of course. We looked at each other. I couldn't read his face. My expression said: *Sorry for being a bloody idiot.*

I led with:

"I think I have some explaining to do."

"When you're good and ready. It doesn't have to be now. I'm just glad you're OK."

"No, let me get it off my chest."

He stood up to adjust the seat for me.

"OK, look, I'm not going to say *Sorry*. It's not that I'm not sorry. Of course, I am, but I wanted to explain. So much of what I said was complete bullshit."

"Really, you sounded spot on to me."

"No, I mean that crap about love at first sight. Don't kid yourself. You weren't that good."

*Trademark smile.*

He got the humour.

"The issue, the main issue: I was falling in love with you. It happened gradually, but that's why I made up those silly rules, non-date dates, keeping it on a professional level. Client to therapist, so you had to pay, when I would have been prepared to pay you. I was desperate to see you but had to wait for your call. I was driving myself crazy. I wanted to tell you how I felt, how I really felt. You made it clear. You weren't going to leave your wife. And, in any case, the age gap. I was a bundle of nerves, with very confused feelings. So I had to end it. I don't trust myself with those feelings. You know how I like to be in control. But it was true, I did dream of you for weeks. I dreamt that we were lovers. I never got suicidal, but I did think I was pre-suicidal, if that's a thing."

"I don't know. You're the Psychology graduate."

"Yes, but I kept skipping classes for my day job, remember?"

A shared smile.

"Anyway, the way I survived was to tell myself that we were soulmates. Even if I couldn't make love to you, we were soulmates. Even if I never saw you again, we were soulmates. Please don't laugh, but I kept a photo of you on my phone and I used to cry myself to sleep, crying: *Soulmate.* Gradually, I got my act together and decided that I could live with an avuncular platonic relationship. Seeing you occasionally, asking for advice, with just the occasional erotic fantasy during particular lonely moments. I'd adjusted, learning to live with the new relationship between us that, without your knowledge or consent, I had conjured up. Then I came here this afternoon, and you brought it all back up. I know you didn't mean it. You weren't to know but, by your suggesting I'd find a soulmate, I took it as a complete rejection of everything we had, everything we have and everything we will have, together."

I paused for breath.

Vish stepped in with:

"Well, can I say sorry, then, because I *am* sorry. I had no business putting that on you. You're about to embark on a new adventure, and I've already ticked that off and started picturing your next adventure. A decade, for me, is a short time. I've just arrived at my seventh. For you, ten years is half your life so far. How dare I disrespect your next adventure so much that I'm talking to you about stuff that you're not ready to hear? It's just that I won't be here for ever."

"Please don't say that."

"Well, it's true. Anyway, I don't buy that you can't have two soulmates at the same time, especially if one has dementia."

"What do you mean?"

"Well, if I had dementia, I'd still expect you to push me around in my wheelchair, even if I didn't know who you were."

"Kidding, right? If you had dementia, I'd drop you like a stone. I only come to you for the free advice. Why would I want to bother coming to see some old fucker with a drooling mouth who couldn't even remember his own name!"

And, to my amazement, I was able to get that sentence out without a tear, without another meltdown. Vish looked at me and gave me a characteristic grin. The grin he gave when I'd give him my, in his words, *trademark smile.* I knew we were back on track when he shuffled in his pocket and withdrew a crumpled piece of paper, which he slid across the table:

"£190, you owe me."

"£150. I checked before I came to make sure I had enough cash."

"You forgot the champagne, but, seriously, if you're short, I'll cover the cost of the bubbly."

I sheepishly moved one hand to my bag to start to unclip it and pull out my wallet, while my other hand was on the table pulling on the crumbled bill which Vish was still holding onto.

Vish's grin turned into that more determined avuncular look that he gave me when he wanted me to know he was serious.

"Don't even think about it!"

We spent the next 15 seconds in a mock tug of war over the restaurant bill until it finally tore in two.

I took the scrap of paper, folded it carefully, and put it in my handbag.

Vish looked a little bemused until I explained.

"A small memento which I'm going to keep as a reminder of what a daft fuck I am, and what an impossibly kind and generous man you are."

"You're so sentimental, that's what I love about you."

"Oh, Vish, you misunderstood. I'm not keeping it for me. It's to put in your sensory room when you've finally lost the plot. I read it helps to have familiar objects around you."

Vish looked puzzled. He usually gets my sick humour without me having to explain.

"Sensory room for a dribbling dement, get it?"

Vish smiled. I stood up, grabbed my anorak from the chair, and turned abruptly. I had to leave with dignity this time. But I could feel the tears beginning to well. So I turned my back, but, in as calm and unfaltering voice as I could muster, to give the impression that I was completely OK, I bade him farewell:

"Got to run to catch my night bus." I walked away from the table. I couldn't look back, I kept telling myself: *Hold it together, Cindy, at least till you walk out of the door. Don't waver, Rachel.* But I had to quicken my pace. I left the room and turned to walk down the corridor. I was now crouching and sobbing. Stop being such a bloody fool. Get your act together, girl. I managed to get back to my feet, I was wiping the tears with my sleeve. I was walking out of the side door of the hotel, but realised I needed a taxi, so I turned left and left again onto Piccadilly, back towards the hotel's main entrance. There was a taxi waiting and the doorman saw me approach and moved towards the cab, holding the door open for me.

"Your taxi, madam."

I thanked him, then hesitated.

"Would you mind holding that for a minute or two?"

"Of course, madam. I'll make sure he's still here for you."

I turned and walked through the main entrance of the hotel, my pace quickening. Would he still be…? But I didn't have to worry. He was still sitting at the table, fiddling with his phone. He hadn't seen me, so I walked up to the table carefully. He was about to get up when he saw me, but I motioned for him to stay sitting down. I put my fingers on my lips to indicate for him not to say a word. A memory flashed. That's what he did back at Felicity's.

After he'd become a regular, and we'd got to know each other well, he'd told me to expect a surprise for my next visit. I remember it clearly. I was waiting for him at the reception when he rang the bell. Our sessions had been pretty conventional but we'd talked about doing more. Banter, about what I would let him do and what I wouldn't. Vishti had opened up a little during our previous sessions and we had joked about the things he could do to me but - ever the gentleman - his hands had never strayed. As I opened the door to the treatment room, he had held his finger to his lips, the same as I was doing now. He was telling me not to say anything.

We entered the treatment room. He faced me. Again, finger to his lips. He motioned for me to take my clothes off. I was standing there naked. He was looking at me, admiring my body. His eyes looked down towards my breasts. I was getting excited at the anticipation. I didn't know what was in store. My nipples were hard. His gaze lingered while he looked, before raising his eyes and looking at me again. Those moments were incredibly seductive. Vishti, the innocent, who couldn't face the *blue door* on that first visit, had metamorphosed into my Romeo. Again the finger to his lips. His eyes dropped down until he was looking at my shaved mound. Christ! I was moist already. I wondered whether my juices were dribbling down my leg, as his eyes moved down to look at my feet. The moment nearly passed.

I have always hated my feet and I made a nervous fidget. Vishti seemed to sense my discomfort, so immediately looked up. I couldn't read his look then, but now I realise his eyes were actually saying sorry, sorry about looking at my feet, and appealing for me to relax. I gave him my *trademark smile*. He motioned for me to turn around. A shiver went down my spine as I felt soft satin over my eyes. I felt him tie the scarf gently at the back. The blindfold now heightened my senses. He was running his fingers down my back. I couldn't believe what was happening. I'd been around the block a few times, but, pre-Cassandra, no-one had ever seduced me like this.

I quickly flashed back, out of my daydream, to see Vish sitting staring at me and I wondered whether the finger over my lips was triggering the same memory for him as for me. Of course it was. Soulmates, remember? We are one, our souls merging with each other. He was giving me the same look as then. He was sitting there, eyeing me up and down, just as he did then. He was picturing me nude, admiring my glistening naked skin.

My mind returned to the treatment room. Blindfolded, his fingers, the touch so light, were now lingering on the erogenous zone at the base of my spine. If I hadn't been standing up, I might have come there and then. I wanted to scream. *Take me. Fuck me. I want you inside me.* But Vishti had other plans. He was now holding my shoulders. His hands were a little cold. Again a nervous shimmer. He was pushing me. Not hard, just a little shove. Not aggressive, but just enough to say he's in charge, I'm his sub. Fuck, fuck, my fantasy to be tied down, restrained while… fuck, what's next…?

I knew my room blindfolded, so I edged forward until my foot touched the mattress. I wanted to tell him I could manage this myself, but I had to keep the silence. I was now on my back. Again, the blindfold heightened my senses. I could hear the faintest sound, even the shuffling as he removed his trousers. Vishti was now lying naked next to me. He turned me so that I was on my side. I could feel his erection rubbing against me. It was now moving inside the cheeks of my butt. He was easing the cheeks apart. I was tensing. My worst nightmare was anal rape, but also my deepest guilty fantasy. But, in my fantasy, those many times of solo pleasure, it was always another girl being abused. The times I came, my orgasm more intense, when my mind was imagining a struggling woman, with a throbbing cock pounding inside a tight anus. But that was fantasy. Was Vishti about to abuse me?

That was but a fleeting second. Vishti, or rather his penis, wasn't going there. He was simply saying: *I'm in control. You're mine. I can do whatever I want to you now.*

It was that feeling of being totally dominated that was so arousing. That feeling of anticipation, of not knowing what was coming next. He turned me onto my side. Shit, shit, how does he do it? His touch aggressive enough to excite, but still just gentle enough to seduce. Now on my back, he was spreading my legs again, aggressive and calm, not violent, not sheepish, but just about right. Vishti, my Goldilocks lover.

I remember thinking, without a word, but with my vulva doing the talking, screaming in my head: *Take me! Take me now! I want you deep inside me!*

But it wasn't his penis I could feel.

I flipped back to reality. Vish still sitting there. My finger still over my lips. I swear anyone else would have gone back to looking at his phone. Not Vish. Vish was saying with his eyes, with his face, Vish was saying, finish, finish yourself off, you know how excited I get when I watch you come.

So, back to the mattress I didn't feel his penis, I felt his fingers parting my lips but not penetrating. Again, it was the not knowing that was so exciting, so stimulating. A finger fuck or just foreplay, I didn't care. A tease to get me in the mood, no. I was ready, use your fingers, if you must, fingers, or cock, I don't care. I just want to feel you inside. But I didn't, the finger went up to my labia. Now he was rubbing my lips over the hood. I could feel my clit throbbing. I was about to come, but he stopped. Not long enough to bring me down, not short enough to make me come. Just about right. Fucking Goldilocks again.

And then it happened. With an imperceptible adjustment, the fingers had gone and in their place a tongue. The first time I felt it. And, of course, I don't need to tell you. The touch of his tongue, the pressure, not too hard, not too soft, just about right. Fucking Goldilocks!

My lovers, well, boys really, had sucked me off before. But that is exactly what it was, sucking me off. They didn't have a fucking clue. It was as though their maths teacher had said: *Girls like your tongue between their legs before you fuck them, so remember the square on the hypotenuse was…* They just didn't have a fucking clue. But more to the point, they didn't care.

No-one, until Vishti. His tongue was asking me: *Is this ok? Faster? Slower? Clockwise? You seem to like that. Up and down, no, sorry. I'll save that for later, when I want to bring you down before sending you back up. A nibble on your lips, not a bite, but just enough to let you know I'm in charge, you know, Goldilocks. The sucking now, don't worry, I know. Sucking is fine, but don't lose the clit.*

This man had written the textbook. He went on. I could have come so quickly but he wasn't going to let me. He was going to decide when I was ready, he was going to let me beg. And beg I did, not with my voice but with my body, until my back was arching, the spasm was starting, and, in spite of the vow of silence, I couldn't stop myself from crying out. *I'm gonna come, I'm gonna come. I'm coming. I'm coming!* And then, for just the fleeting nano-second. *Will he know? Will he know not to stop.* I need a full 30 seconds. After I've come, I need to continue not too long till it's over-sensitive but just long enough for a second convulsion, a third or fourth, to complete my orgasm. But, of course, he already knew. 30 seconds. Not too long, not too short, fucking Goldilocks!

*******

Back to the Ritz. I'm not sure how long I'd been standing there, while I was fantasising about my first real experience of the delights of cunnilingus. Better than a fuck, but *only if the tongue knows its way around.*

Time to get back to reality:

"Vish, does that thing have a timer?"

I pointed to his phone.

"I think so. No, of course, it does."

"Can you set it for five minutes?"

I watched him do it.

"Now press start."

I pressed my finger to my lips again. Talking's over, and I beckon to him to stand up. I moved towards his body and held him tight around the waist.

He wrapped his arms around my shoulders, an avuncular hug. I could hear his heart beating. I knew he could sense my breath.

Can two people really hug in silence for five minutes? I was going to find out.

*******

The phone buzzer sounded. I didn't look up, but pushed him gently away:

"Sorry, got to dash. Taxi metre's running."

I looked at Vish.

*Trademark smile*, as I turned around and walked away with my head held high.

Of course, it was purely in my imagination, but as I was brushing past the tables of the other customers, I saw them putting down their cocktails, and putting their hands together, some standing up to pat me on the back, as I walked by, and chanting in unison as I made my exit:

*Well done, girl. We're proud of you!*

# 29
# Informed Consent

"Did you read the consent form?"

"It was 5 pages. Why did I have to initial each page?"

"So we know you read it."

I looked up and smiled:

"I initialled it, I didn't say I read it!"

He looked up at me, with a deadpan face:

"Please take this seriously."

"I was serious, Doc. I skipped over most of it until I got to the juicy bits, you know, the bit where it said I might bleed to death, but don't worry, George Clooney will be waiting for me in ER."

"Wasn't that before your time?"

"There are re-runs you know."

He didn't crack his face.

What did I have to do to get him to smile? He was quite good-looking, and I thought: *Another time. Another place. Yes, maybe.*

Then he got up:

"Can I listen to your chest?"

"Sorry, did you just ask to listen to my breast?"

Still deadpan. No reaction.

But as he put on his stethoscope, I deliberately looked down at his crotch and was going to tell him there and then: *You don't know me, Doc, but if you don't lighten up, I'll just keep trying to embarrass you.*

Still looking at his dick. Did I detect a slight bulge? No, nothing. He moved back to his seat.

"Do you mind if I ask you a few questions, so I can take down contemporaneous notes?"

"Yes, I do actually."

"I beg your pardon?"

He was quite taken aback.

"You asked if I minded and the answer was Yes, I do mind - if you're going to use words I don't understand. Contembulatory what?"

"My bad."

Oh, Doc, I thought, you're trying to speak my tongue - *my bad* indeed - does anyone use that expression anymore? I played dumb.

"You're bad at what? Not surgery I hope."

"Sorry, I was apologising for my mistake. It's my job to make sure my patients understand me. You're not supposed to sit there with google translate."

I detected a slight change in his facial expression and thought: *You're getting there, but I've still got work to do to humanise you.*

"*Contemporaneous notes.* It means… actually, let me tell you a story. A colleague of mine, quite a brilliant surgeon, was doing a complicated procedure, nothing like yours, so please don't worry. It required general anaesthesia. There's always more risk with GA, sorry, general anaesthetic, that's why I recommended local for your procedure. Epidural, we call it. You'll be numb from the waist down so you won't feel anything, but you'll be wide awake.

"So, to continue, my colleague performed the operation perfectly, but, and this sometimes happens with GA, the patient's breathing changed. The anaesthetist made an adjustment, but her vitals - you know, things like the heartbeat - went crazy. To truncate this missive, sorry, cutting a long story short, for some reason, for a short time while she was under the anaesthetic her brain had been starved of oxygen."

"Did she die?"

"No, but she had had a mini-stroke and when she came around one side of her face had dropped and her speech was slurred. She had physiotherapy for several months and was 90% back to normal, but her speech was still a little bit slurred and that made all the difference."

"Why?"

"I'll get on to that."

"You do spin a good yarn. I've got the attention span of a gnat, but I'm enjoying this story."

"Well, she sued the surgeon. The insurance company - we all have insurance, medical negligence insurance to cover this type of thing…."

"So he *was* negligent."

"No, that was the point. The insurance company looked though the medical records, they interviewed the anaesthetist and the surgery nurse, looked at the equipment, everything, and concluded that the surgeon had done nothing wrong, so there was no need to settle."

"Sorry – settle?"

"Yes, quite often, the insurer will look at a case and think it's not worth the trouble and settle with the patient for, say, £25,000."

"What, £25,000 to shut her up?"

"Yes, we call it a nuisance suit. Hazard of the trade, I suppose."

"Can you help me out here? If, after the op, I go all spaz," I start demonstrating, shaking my hands, "and threaten to sue you, I could get 25 large!"

Almost, almost. In spite of my non-PC rhetoric, his lip curled, I will crack that face before I leave, if it kills me.

"No, Rachel, it's not that easy. Would you let me continue?"

"Sorry, Doc, no more jokes. Please go on."

"As I was saying, the insurers wouldn't settle and it went to trial, which was quite unusual, but they were so confident of winning the case. My colleague, the surgeon, gave evidence. He was confident, crisp, and clear. Then it was the turn of the patient's brief."

"Brief what?"

"Sorry, the patient's barrister, his turn to cross-examine. We did a post-mortem afterwards…"

"I thought you said she didn't die."

He gave me a deadpan look.

"Sorry, Doc, I did say no more jokes, but I couldn't resist that one. I thought that was quite good. Sorry, sorry, please go on, I didn't mean to interrupt the flow."

"Thank you. The reason I mentioned the post mortem, the analysis we did afterwards. We agreed that the barrister saw that the surgeon was a good witness. The barrister wasn't going to get him on the facts, so he was going to break him."

"I don't understand."

"He kept him on the witness stand for five hours. That's quite a feat. You see he can't keep asking the same questions, so he had to build up slowly. You know first reading a bit, then speeding up the questions. If he found a soft spot, he'd slow down, jumping across to another area, probing and probing, before he went straight back to the soft spot, then speeding up again, circling around before hitting that spot again."

My mind was wondering, I started thinking of Vish, and smiled. Obviously Doc wouldn't know, but he was describing Vish's tongue, probing, and circling.

"Yes, you paint such a good picture, Doc, probing, circling, nibbling …"

"Sorry…?"

Whoops, I was still with Vish.

"Nibbling, er, nibbling away at the truth."

"Yes, well put!"

"This went on for hours, and my colleague was getting tired."

"I know what you're going to say next. When he saw he was ready, he built up to the climax."

"Exactly, you do have a way with words."

He couldn't have known that I was picturing Vish and how he would sense when I was ready. I was feeling moist down there and I suddenly jumped out of my daydream. Shit! He's going to be looking at my pussy soon for the procedure. I can't be whiffing of snail trail.

"You're absolutely spot on. My colleague was tired and started to get a bit irritable, here's how the final dialogue went:

Barrister: *You said that the patient had given her consent.*

Surgeon: *I've already said that hours ago. You're repeating the same questions. How much longer?*

Barrister: *The way this works is that I ask the questions. Can you just give brief answers?*

Surgeon: *Sorry, yes, she gave her consent.*

Barrister: *Yes, she signed the consent form.*

Surgeon. *Yes, you know she did, it's been submitted in the evidence file.*

Barrister: *A simple yes or no will suffice. How long was the consent form?*

Surgeon: *Oh, really,* (turning to the judge) *do I have to answer that?*

And then the barrister took out some paper and started waving it in front of the jury.

Barrister: *No, you don't. Look I have it here.*

He walks past the jury flicking through the pages.

Barrister: *It's seven pages of closely typed print, barely legible. You just shoved it under her nose and said: "Sign here!"*

Surgeon: *What do you mean?*

Barrister: *I mean, you led us to believe that my client knew the risks she was taking, because she has a piece of paper thrust into her hand and made to sign. You call that consent?*

"My colleague was tired, but visibly angry at having his integrity impugned."

I looked puzzled.

"Sorry - his reputation sullied."

Try again, Doc.

"Being disrespected."

OK, stick to English, I thought, and we might get through this more quickly.

"Continuing....

Surgeon: *Don't be so stupid. I spent about fifteen or twenty minutes, after she signed, making sure she understood what she was signing, going over the risk factors. Don't be an idiot, man. I explained everything…*

Barrister: *But we have only your word on that, don't we?*

Surgeon: *What?*

"And the barrister turned his back on my colleague and *sotto voce*, sorry, in a soft voice, with his back to him said: *Where are your contemporaneous notes?*

My colleague couldn't hear what the barrister had said so turned to the judge and asked if he could repeat the question. Whereupon the barrister turned and looked straight at the jury and bellowed:

*Your contemporaneous notes. Shall I explain to the jury. The notes you make, at the same time, that's what* contemporaneous *means, doesn't it?*

And then he started waving this folder theatrically in front of the jury. *There we are, members of the jury. Here's the file, you expect this jury to believe that you spent fifteen, no twenty minutes, explaining everything to my client, but no notes.*

Surgeon: *I really object to this line of questioning. Of course, there were my medical notes.*

Barrister: *No, not your medical notes, your contemporaneous notes, confirming that you spent time explaining things to my client. You didn't write that in your file because you never did do that explaining, did you?*

Surgeon: *What do you mean. She sh-sh-she signed.*

Barrister: *Yes, we know. She signed your form, job done!*

And then he turned around with a flurry and at the top of his voice shouted: *No more questions, no more questions. Witnessed excused.*

My colleague's barrister was entitled to re-examine, to ask some questions to give him a chance to explain to the jury. But my colleague was so tired, mentally, after the hours of barracking. The damage had been done. There was no turning back. But I learnt the lesson."

"Contemporaneous notes."

"Exactly, Rachel, contemporaneous notes."

"So what happened to him?"

"Well, he lost the case. Of course, he had explained everything to the patient but the jury was persuaded that he hadn't done his job properly. The patient's barrister had done a brilliant job of destroying a brilliant surgeon."

"And £25,000."

"Sorry?"

"You said it would cost £25.000, what, for the settlement."

"No, no, Rachel. Twenty-five if they'd settled. The damages are assessed separately, in a hearing after the trial. That was why I mentioned that she was a speech therapist. Loss of earnings."

"I'm sorry, Doc, you must think I'm so stupid."

"No, not all. No reason for you to know. You see, there is a scale of damages, so much for a loss of an eye, loss of a limb, loss of life even. It's very ghoulish, my colleague would have been better off if she had died. You see, the disfigurement to her face on the scale would have come in at around £10,000, but then loss of earnings comes into play. How much money did she lose because she couldn't work? Now, if she was secretary, perhaps, she would have been off work for a few weeks, a few months, it wouldn't really matter, another £10,000, chicken feed. However, the patient was a renowned - a well-known - speech therapist, pulling in over £200,000 a year. She was only in her forties with at least twenty more years working life left. The loss of earnings came in at one five."

"Wow, one hundred and fifty thousand pounds!"

"No, one million five hundred thousand."

"Fucking hell and shag a monkey. Oh sorry, Doc…"

It was just an involuntary comment. We use *shag monkey* to describe someone who is so drunk they will suck the booze out of a shag carpet. I felt a bit embarrassed, but my inadvertent comment had done the trick. He burst into a kind of a hiccupping giggle. At last, I managed to break the ice.

The consultation went a lot easier after that. More questions and *contemporaneous* notes. But there really was only one important question that he needed an answer to.

"It's the irreversibility that I need to ensure you understand. No going back."

"Yes, I do understand. I know I piss around a lot, but you have to believe I've thought this through, very carefully."

"Yes, I'm sure you have. But you're only twenty-one, and we wouldn't normally entertain this procedure for someone so young."

"I'm nearly twenty-two. Do you know, it wasn't until the seventies that the age of consent, in New York, you know, for sex, was lowered to 18. Here, it was lowered to 18 for gay sex in 1994. That's for boys. Girls were old enough at 16 for gay sex, but boys, before 1994, not until 21. I made a study."

"What is your point, Rachel?"

"My point is, Doc, that when I was 16 the law thought I was old enough to shag who I wanted, even though I didn't have fucking clue. I think I'm old enough, Doc."

"Rachel, I've read your psychiatric evaluation. It's pretty clear that the doctor believed you were competent."

"Competent? I was bloody amazing. Twisted that shrink around my finger."

"Rachel, that's not funny. If I thought for one moment that you had fooled your psychiatrist, this consultation would be over."

"What do you want me to say? Do you have any idea what it's like for an eleven-year-old girl to have a cock rammed down her throat until she was choking on his spunk. Of course, you don't. Do you know what my worst nightmare is, Doc? Not that I'd have a daughter and she'd be abused by her grandfather. No, I know my dad, no chance of that. It's not abusing a child I worry about. I looked it up. It's more common than you think, but still you've got to be unlucky to be a victim. My nightmare is that she would grow up like me. I know what I was like as a teenager. Got drunk until I was legless. No, my worst nightmare is that my teenage daughter would go out one night and end up getting gang raped by some drunken stupid fucking students. I've heard the guys at college, the way they talk. I know a lot of it is banter, but I hear them talk about schoolgirls. Perhaps they would, perhaps they wouldn't. If that happened to my girl, I'd slice off their testicles and then slash my wrists. You see, I would love my daughter, so I wouldn't let that happen. I would protect her. I would lock her in the bedroom and never let her out. That shrink had it spot on. Did you read it? Read the fucking thing out loud, before you do your barrister thing and interrogate me. Read out the bit about attachment. Go on read it out aloud."

"I've read it."

"Read it to me. Read it, go on!"

He was hesitant but could see I was serious, and he knew exactly the paragraph I meant.

"Rachel has difficulty forming attachments, directly as a result of the deep-seated trauma. There is no question that she would be at all physically abusive to her child, but abuse can be mental as well as physical. In my opinion, if Rachel had a daughter, there is a strong likelihood that she would be mentally abusive to the child by being over-protective. Studies have been conducted that demonstrate that pathological over-protectiveness can affect the emotional development of the child, leading to alcoholism or substance abuse in later life. In spite of Rachel's tender years, she has a clear understanding of the potential challenges she may face as a parent and the damage she may cause to her child…"

"That's enough, Doc. Would you mind if we just stop there? Could you just write in your contemporaneous notes, here, I'll dictate it: *Rachel knows she's a nutter and would make a lousy mother. Go on scribble that down.*"

"I couldn't possibly."

"No, I mean in your medical gibberish, put down those medical terms like in the shrink report."

"I can't!"

"Do it, or I'll go find another doctor who will."

"No, Rachel, you don't understand. My job is to make sure you are competent to understand the risks involved in the procedure, and to review the psychological assessment to ensure all the correct protocols have been followed. I am not qualified to make a psychological assessment myself. Or, to put it in your parlance, as long as your shrink says you're a nutter, then I can tick the box."

He was actually smiling when he said that. I think he finally realised that if he was going to get through to me, if I was going to let him stick a pair of scissors up my pussy and cut my tubes, he was going to have to gain my trust. And that meant coming down to my level.

We carried on for another thirty minutes or so. He had lightened up. He began to realise how to talk to me, take in my silly humour, give me a bit of banter back, but always staying professional, and making his own assessment until he was ready, then he opened up a bit.

"OK, Rachel. I think you are a remarkable person, truly. I've enjoyed this consultation. I don't expect you to understand this, but we're taught that we have to relate to the patient. But that's just in the books. I confess I never understood what that meant until today. You've taught me not just to pay lip service to that dictum but to respect my patients and ensure that I relate to them. Please don't think I'm talking down to you, I now understand that means relate to them at their level."

I looked at him. He actually had rather dishy eyes. Maybe, if he weren't my Doc, maybe. I thought about that young George Clooney in ER.

"OK, Rachel. We're all set to go."

I looked around for my bag which I'd left lying around the room somewhere. I got up and grabbed it, shuffled around in my bag. Got out my credit card and handed it across his desk.

"No, er, we don't do it like that. Please pay Emily."

He was totally embarrassed.

"Just kidding. I know you doctors don't like to get your hands dirty."

He lightened up and came back with:

"Yes, have to keep my hands sterile for the op. Never know where credit cards have been."

As he said that, he brushed his fingers over each nostril sniffing. I couldn't believe he actually used nose candy, but it was a good riposte.

"Touché!"

I picked up my card and gave him my *trademark smile*. I thought he deserved the smile for the crack about the White Lady.

Emily was at the reception.

"Doc said to pay you."

"Yes, I'll take your card and then I'll show you down to the pre-op."

"Sorry?"

"Downstairs, there's an ante room for you to get undressed. There's a shower and a loo there if you want. Sometimes patients like to freshen up first."

"You mean we're doing it now?"

"Yes, sorry, we've booked a two-hour appointment."

"Yes, yes, of course. I don't know what I was thinking."

But I did know what I was thinking. I was thinking of Vish, talking about my future, not the now future but the future future. The one Vish knew about which was too soon for me to contemplate. Thinking how Vish didn't want me to have the op. What did he know about my future that I didn't?

"Sorry, £5,000, that's right, isn't it?"

"It's actually £4,800. You've already paid £200 for today's consultation, and that comes off the £5,000 for the op."

"Not sure if that makes the operation cheap, or the consultation expensive."

"Er, that's just how we do it."

Lighten up, girlfriend. Does no-one have a sense of humour around here? I gave her the card which she put in the machine. But Vish was in my head again. What was he saying about me going on a walking holiday, meeting some guy? What was he saying? I think I told him to fuck off and mind his own business. But the guy on the walking holiday. What were you talking about Vish? Then I was suddenly woken out of my day-dreaming by Emily.

"Rachel, Rachel, are you ok, we need your PIN?"

"Yes, sorry, PIN."

"Don't worry, everyone's a little nervous beforehand, but it'll all be over in 30 minutes, then you can relax with a cup of tea in recovery for as long as you need before you go home."

Emily escorted me downstairs. I took her advice and showered. I guessed Doc had seen a lot of snatches, but I wanted to make sure that mine was fresh and clean for him.

I was sitting down wearing one of those funny gowns which leaves your arse hanging out. Wonder why they make them like that?

It was probably only five minutes but seemed like an age. Then the nurse came in. She showed me into the surgery and explained about the epidural which was going to be injected into my back. As I walked into the room, I saw those awful stirruppy things. I'd only been subjected to that ignominy once before, when I had an STI and the doctor wanted to have a good look inside.

Now I'm up on the stirrups, legs akimbo. I'm lying back waiting. Haven't had the injection yet. Apparently, Doc will do that.

As I lay there, waiting, Vish came back. It was as though he was hovering over me. I'd read about those people in hospital who die, and when they're dead their soul is looking down on them. Only I wasn't dead and it wasn't me but my soulmate who was looking down on me. And the vision of the walking holiday came back and I'm walking hand-in-hand with my faceless companion. Who is he? His face is pixelated, I can only see his mouth, a funny moustache, but not a moustache. I look up at Vish. Help me out here. Is he really my future future? Or are you just pissing me around?

Just then, in came Doc. He walked across until he was facing me. He was glancing down at my wide-open vagina. He glanced up at me. He was wearing a surgical mask. I could only see his eyes. Dreamboat eyes. I really could have fancied him if he hadn't been my Doc. I started to fantasise about the Doc, then I snapped out of it. I kept reminding myself that he was about to shove a pair of scissors up my snatch. I was so concerned about that, that it was difficult to think of him as a lover.

He then explained that he was going to give me the epidural injection, but he wanted me to relax. He asked if it was OK to put some music on and suggested that I close my eyes if I wanted.

I closed my eyes and I was back on the walking holiday, holding hands with… who is he, Vish? I look up at Vish, imploring. Is he my future future? Is he why you didn't want me to be here? What's special about him? There he was. We were still holding hands. I still couldn't see his face, apart from that non-moustache moustache. Then I heard a sound, and there behind us, skipping along the path… I started shaking. They were holding hands, they looked like twins, two young girls. The shaking was getting worse. The girls were laughing and shouting. What were they saying? I looked at Vish and, in my mind, asked him again: *My future future?* And the girls were skipping. What were they calling? I couldn't hear, and then I heard the word *Mummy*. And I let out a yell at the top of my voice, as the shaking became uncontrollable:

**"Get me the fuck out of here!!!"**

I was hysterical. And I heard panic around me. It was full ER and George Clooney again.

"Did she have the anaesthetic?"

"No."

"Shall we sedate her?"

I heard Doc respond: "No, not yet. Give it five minutes. The shaking has stopped, let me see if I can calm her down."

Next thing I knew, I was alone in the room with Doc. He was stroking my hair.

"Really, Doc is that part of the protocols?"

I looked up and smiled.

"Are you OK?"

"Yes, I'm really so, so sorry. I don't know what came over me."

"Look, Rachel, you're not leaving here till I know you're OK."

"I think that's kidnap, Doc."

"So be it. But I'd least I'd have you alone for a while longer."

"Are you flirting with me?"

"Rachel, you know I could be struck off for just thinking about you in that way."

"Don't tempt me." I started looking at his crotch.

"By the way, do I get a refund?"

"Sorry, you read the form. What part of *no refunds* don't you understand?"

"Oh! Sorry. I thought I'd ask. I understand. It was my fault."

He smiled.

"Well done, you got me there, Doc."

"We'll go upstairs, and Emily will process the refund."

"£4,800, I've got to pay you for the consultation."

"OK, that's a deal, but on one condition: you let me buy you dinner."

He smiled.

And for that, he earned my …

*trademark smile.*

*******

On the taxi ride home, I was thinking of that man and me, walking together along the path, with the twins walking behind. Why was his face pixelated? Then I remembered what the Doc said. Not my Doc, Doc Brown from the film *Back to the Future*, when he said: *Your future hasn't been written yet.* Vish is no fortune teller. He's just a wise man, my guru, and he was using a metaphor. Because he knows I'm just a stupid kid. He was trying to make me understand that, however I feel now, I can't possibly know how I'll feel in 10 years' time. They might have found a cure for nutters by then. A pill that I could swallow, that would allow me to have a normal relationship, like normal people. Not a relationship like I've got with Gus, where I'll fuck him and fuck him until I meet his boss, then drop him like a stone.

So, until they invent that pill, I'll be Rachel when I'm nice and Cindy when I'm a horny whore. And talking of Cindy, what am I going to do with Doc and those dreamboat eyes? I couldn't believe that, after all the shit I put him through, he wanted to take me out for dinner. Next, I'm picturing him, and I'm starting to get moist between my legs. I can see him now. I'm straddled on the stirrups, my legs wide apart.

Now I'm reaching down my pants. I shuffle across the seat to make sure the taxi driver can't see me in his mirror. I start to play with myself, I can feel my juices flowing. I can see Doc there, in his surgical mask, looking at my pussy. He's got some metal instrument in his hand. Now he's wiping the steel tool over my pussy lips. It's cold, but it's making me hot. My fingers are working harder and harder. Suddenly I hear the taxi driver ask if I'm OK.

Shit! I didn't realise I was moaning so loud. Sod it! I'm not stopping now. Come on, Doc. Eat me, eat me out. Doc, holding my legs, pushing them against the stirrups, wants me to feel some pain, just to let me know he's in charge. Then he eases the pressure on my legs and buries his head deep in my pussy, he's biting, he's sucking. Shit, I pull my trousers and pants down so I can use two fingers on one hand to fuck myself, and thumb and finger vigorously rubbing my clit, and then I come, I'm jerking, I spasm, and settle back across the seat of the cab.

I must have passed out because I suddenly hear the taxi driver calling me. Sometimes after Vish had made me come, I was completely out of it. He would drain me of so much energy when I came that I needed time to recover. But I don't remember that happening before when I fingered myself. At home, I've got a rabbit, which gives me adequate orgasms but I surprised myself just now. I've had plenty of shags in a car before but never came. And with my fingers? Was it just dreaming of Doc, or was it that I'd been building up tension during the last week, anticipating the op, and maybe the relief that I wasn't going ahead with it, maybe that relaxed me enough to just let myself go?

"We're here at your building, but there are two entrances, Riverside or Garden side."

"Riverside please."

I got out of the taxi and asked:

"What's the damage?"

"Well, the back seat of the cab for a start, Dear, but the fare is £35."

"I took out a £50 note, and said: "Will this cover it?"

"You are kidding me, darling. I was going to comp you for the fare. That was the biggest turn-on I've had since my wedding night. In fact, tell you what, I will comp you, no charge. Here's your fifty back."

I looked at him and smiled.

"Don't be silly, I'm happy for you to have the money. Just one favour, though. Please don't dine out on the story; I'd be a little embarrassed if I was met with giggles each time I gave a cabbie my address."

He drove off, leaving me with the fifty in my hand.

Obviously, he wasn't prepared to grant me the favour.

# 30
## Meet the Boss

I was getting ready for the pool party. I took out my swimsuit. It was the bikini, the sexy one that I had described to Vish, when he was Vishti, and sex was still on the table. I was telling him about my trip to Bali. How I was looking forward to getting blasted with the girls on the beach. He made some lame comment about how I should be good and not let any boys near my pussy. I remember telling him to fuck off. I said we weren't exclusive. He said he was just joking, but I wondered.

I had told him the bikini was sexy, but not too sexy. Enough to show my butt cheeks, but nowhere near a thong. The bra was showing my tits, but not slutty. I remember him saying that I was making him drool. He asked me to send a photo, a selfie, when I was in Bali, so he could admire my body. I clearly remember nodding in approval and giving him my *trademark smile*. I never sent him the photo. I took the photo, well, actually, I asked someone there to take it for me, with my back to the phone camera, showing my butt cheeks. And turning my face towards the camera giving my *trademark smile*. I remember lying there on the beach bed looking at the photo, pondering whether to send it. *No, no girl, he's a paying client why the fuck should I provide him with wank candy free of charge?* That was Cindy talking, she's such a bitch. It would have cost me nothing and would have given him a little bit of pleasure. I called up the photo on my phone. I looked at it and said out loud:

"Cindy, you're the bitch, but, Rachel, you've got a kind heart."

I tapped the photo on my phone, opened Vish's last chat. Wrote a message: *Off to the pool party. Thought you'd like to see what I'm wearing. Finally going to meet the boss. He doesn't know what's in store for him.*

I was putting my things in my bag, when I heard my phone ping and opened his reply: *Lovely photo. Good luck with the boss. Have a good time. V.*

Then I thought, he needs to know. I hadn't even bothered to call. I actually hated texting and used abbreviations though some were my own invention, but I thought he'd understand so I typed: *btw the op was CX.*

He instantly responded: *I'm so so glad.* And he signed off with a heart. I pondered for a moment. As I said, I hate texting. I'm not really any good at it. I'm not sure if my weird SOH comes across at all. But *hey ho*, I'll give it a whirl.

*I think you misunderstood. Doc was ill. Rescheduled for next week.*

I pressed send, then thought better of it. Panicked a bit. Tried to delete it. The blue tick meant he'd already opened it. The phone showed he was typing a reply. God, I hoped I hadn't freaked him out. He replied with a rolling on the floor laughing emoji. I needn't have worried. We're like two peas from the same pod. *God, how I love you. If only I could mouth those words.* I put the phone in my bag, opened the door and skipped down the corridor. I had to go to the ground floor to the other bank of elevators and then go back up to the 7th where Gus would be waiting for me, my unsuspecting accomplice in my plan to seduce his boss and become his sugar-babe. Put on your Cindy mask. Rachel could never be such a conniving cow.

*******

I'm upstairs now with Gus. I greet him with a passionate kiss.

"Do we have to go? Can't we just stay here and fuck?

I started to unbuckle his trousers.

"Don't! Come on we've got to go."

"Ooh lover, just a little lick."

I was teasing him. I knew we didn't have time, but I also knew my motive. How I was using Gus to meet his boss. I didn't want to give him any impression that I was anything other than totally devoted to him. He wriggled away.

"OK, but just let me have a look. You know that seeing you hard just turns me on so."

I looked down to see his erection. I wasn't joking. Gus's was perhaps one of the most beautiful members I'd seen. It curved a bit, not too much, and it leaned to the left. But it was the colour that always fascinated me. It was darker than I expected. If I didn't know that he was American royalty going all the way back to the Mayflower, I would have said there had been some hanky panky going on between the sheets over the past generations. Apart from the colour, it had a lot of loose skin even when erect, as though someone had been expecting a larger tool in the toolbox.

He started to zip up his trousers.

"Really, we have to go."

"But I get a bit nervous with these parties."

"Don't be silly. You'll be wonderful. You'll be the success of the party. Jack is going to love you. You might want to stay away from his wife. I know she worries about what he gets up to when she's back in New York."

"Eh! She won't have to worry about me. Didn't you say he was fifty? Can't stand old men - they all have droopy cocks."

Gus just laughed.

"You're probably right. Just be yourself and everyone will love you."

We got an Uber because Gus knew he'd be drinking. I had to decide. If I was going to pull this off, I needed to have my wits about me. A few drinks would loosen me up, and make the flirting much easier, but this was serious. This was business and I couldn't risk making a mess. I thought to myself that I had one shot at this. If I didn't get it dead right, I'd have to dump Gus and look for someone else. Poor Gus gets dumped either way. But I remembered what Vish had said: he will come out of this an accomplished lover, a confident cunny merchant (my phrasing, not his), able to please any woman he chooses. He doesn't know it yet, but what I've taught him is probably the best gift I could provide, however pissed off he might be when I dump him. I looked across at Gus as the taxi drew up outside his boss's house and gave him a lengthy snog.

*******

I'm in the house. I have a glass of champagne in my hand. I'm sipping it slowly.

I put it down when the waiter (you just know there would be a waiter) hands out sparkling water in champagne flutes, obviously for the designated drivers amongst the guests. I decide that's the ploy, should anybody be looking, to pose as a lush, so that no one will take me seriously.

Eating is a potential problem. Didn't want fishy breath from the smoked salmon and crab sticks. Why does finger food have to stink? I need to understand the lay of the land. I make my excuses to Gus, saying that I have to circulate. He seems to think that is a good idea and is happy to let me roam, while he chats to his workmates. I spot Jack, the boss. I watch him carefully. I reckon I have, at most, 15 minutes to study his demeanour, monitor his body language, and overhear his conversation, if I can get close enough. Then I can work out my moves.

Gus had already described him to me, but as he is standing chatting to some of his junior staff, he appears shorter than I expected. The young Turks gathered around him may stand at 6 foot 3" or 4", while Jack is just hovering at maybe 5' 11". But it isn't his physical presence that counts. He holds their attention. OK, they are his juniors, absorbing his every word. But he holds the room. He is talking to them, but aware of what's going on around him. His eyes settle on another guest nodding across at him. He reciprocates with a nod. And OK, he's in home territory, but even so, this is a man in total control. How had Gus described him? A Master of the Universe.

Could I fancy this bespectacled, slightly balding, almost rosy-cheeked middle-aged man? Ever heard of Henry Kissinger? Right-hand man to that President they kicked out of the White House? Kissinger was ugly as sin and spoke with a very thick German accent. People wanted to know how he managed to always be in the company of beautiful women. *It's the power that attracts them,* he used to say.

Can I fancy Jack? Sorry, wrong question. Can I wrap this Master of the Universe around my finger and lead him into the bear pit that is waiting to swallow him up?

I also had to find his wife. If anything, she was the most important person here. I had to square with her. I had to leave her feeling comfortable that I was no threat. I decided in my own mind that Jack would be a pushover. *Men* are my territory; I knew how to play them. Women, on the other hand, were a completely different matter. I was quite nervous. I saw her over the other side of the room. It's now or never, girlfriend. Take off your Cindy mask, sober up and here we go:

"Mrs Chalmers? May I introduce myself to you? I'm here with Gus, Gus Cheney. I'm Rachel, Gus's plus one."

"Please call me Ellie Mae."

If Jack was J R Ewing, Ellie Mae was no Sue Ellen. And if *Dallas* never rocked your boat, think Bill and Melinda Gates. Ellie Mae wasn't a trophy wife. She was as American as Apple Pie. I read Ellie Mae as a dutiful, devoted wife, willing to sacrifice her independence for her hubby and their two kids. I read Jack as a *bastard* with a capital C.

We chatted, mostly small talk. I got her started on her kids because I knew I could just listen with the occasional: *interesting, amazing* etc. I was going to ask her when she planned to move over to London but thought better of it. In any case, I had something far more important to disclose to her.

"Ellie Mae, we don't really know each other, but I have to tell someone, but please, please, keep this to yourself. No one else knows, not even Jack, sorry, his boss, Mr. Chalmers."

"Rachel, don't be silly. Everyone calls him Jack. We're Americans."

"Well, in that case, you'd better call me Rache."

She smiled.

"Gus is a bit shy when it comes to these personal things."

Ellie Mae looked at me, intrigued, flattered that I would confide in her.

"He just proposed to me today, although he wouldn't let me wear the ring."

She put her arms around me and kissed me.

"That's wonderful, dear. I thought for a moment you were going to tell me you were pregnant. No, that's wonderful news, and, yes, I promise my lips are sealed. I won't even tell Jack."

"And no mention to Gus. He'd be mortified. He hasn't even told his parents yet."

More small talk. Job done. Now it's time to bag the elephant.

I went back to see how Gus was getting on. My new fiancé. If only he knew. He was a bit tipsy, but quite happy for me to carry on circulating. I spotted Jack. He was chatting, but I needed him alone.

Someone shouted: *Pool time!* and, as if in unison, people started to disrobe, running to the garden and jumping in the pool. It looked like something out of the Playboy mansion that I'd seen on TV, with the difference that none of the girls had removed their tops. I looked around for somewhere to get changed. I didn't realise that you were supposed to come to these things with your bathing suit already underneath your clothes.

I quickly found the loo and put on my bikini. I looked in the mirror and smeared some mascara on the side of my left eye. I marched out into the garden to observe the proceedings. I hit pay-dirt. Jack was watching the shenanigans, laughing at the idiots jumping in the pool, but clearly bored with their juvenile pranks. I waited and waited. I started to worry that the moment might pass and all my preparations would be for nought. But then I spotted Jack walking back into an empty living room. *Carpe diem!* as Vish would say. I quickly followed him in to the living room. He was sitting on the sofa. I sat beside him and introduced myself.

Hi, my name is Rachel, I'm Gus's plus one. He's told me so much about you. Thank you so much for allowing me to come. This has been so great. I also met Ellie Mae. She seems such a wonderful person and told me about your super kids. He looked at me and smiled sweetly.

*Come on, Jack,* I thought. *You're not gonna let me down are you?*

No, not at all. Here it comes.

"Sorry, Rachel, you seem to have something on your eye. Maybe your makeup smeared in the pool."

"Oh, yes, maybe a lash. I was wiping my eye. It's only mascara, but would you mind wiping it off for me?"

He did the deed. He held my face. He looked at me while he wiped the mascara off. *Trademark smile*. That was enough. Cindy, you're so predictable. Vish, you would have been so proud of me. Now there's just one thing left to do. Arrange to see him again and then we're off to the races.

"Jack, I can call you Jack, can't I?"

"Of course."

"Can I ask an enormous favour?"

He looked puzzled and noncommittal and with a slight reluctance:

"What is that?"

"I've got a surprise for Gus. I need to give it to him in the office. I don't want him to know I'm coming, but I don't know how to pass security. If it's convenient, would you mind awfully telling security that I have a meeting with you on Tuesday at, what, say 3:00 pm, so that I can come upstairs. Look, I know it's an imposition, so you pick the time and date that suits you. If that doesn't work, here's my phone number, just text me either way to let me know."

I noticed a pen on the coffee table and reached across to grab it. I took his hand rested it on the inside of my naked thigh, palm up, and wrote my number on his palm. (Not sure why, but men find the *writing-of-the-phone-number-on-the-palm* thing quite intimate.) I quickly looked around to make sure that the room was still empty. I left his hand on my leg for a few seconds, moving it very gently so he could feel my naked skin on his knuckles. I got up. *Trademark smile*. Bent over slightly just to give him a quick view of my tits. A kiss on the cheek, not passionate but more than a peck. *Trademark smile*.

"Jack, you're a doll. Can't thank you enough."

Did I say: *Job done*? Well, it is now!

I had had enough. It was time for me to go and find the drunken boyfriend and take him home. Don't tell me what you're thinking because I already know. Don't worry, of course he gets a fuck when we get home, as a gift for his unknowing part in my grand plan.

I wanted to debrief Vish, to tell him how I got on, but I reserved my meetings with him for when I needed his help. So far, I'd been flying solo and I believed I could land this plane on my own.

In case you think I'm a total cunt, you should know Gus had confided in me. The rumours were that Jack played away, so he wasn't exactly an extra-marital virgin. OK, Cindy's looking after number one, but on this day, at this party, Rachel made the commitment to herself that, if ever she had the opportunity, she'd see Ellie May right for any damage done.

Although I thought things had gone perfectly to plan at the pool party, I was a little concerned when, the following day, Jack hadn't confirmed. I chose Tuesday because I had already checked his wife's schedule. She was flying home Monday. I thought I'd give him till then before I'd call Vish for advice.

Spot on, the text arrived: Monday at 6 pm. What's this? No go for Tuesday, he's in meetings all day. Shit!

His initial message was immediately followed by a second text: *Would Wednesday work for you? I'll be in the office. Thought that would be better, in case Security tried to contact me. I can leave your name, sorry didn't get your full name, and didn't want to ask Gus. Hope Wednesday works. How about 2 pm? J"*

Think Rachel! Do I respond immediately or make him wait? No, this is a favour to me. No point in playing hard to get. So I send him a reply confirming my full name and the 2 pm time. How to sign off? Smiley face, no keep it professional. He signed off with a single letter, J, so an R will do it.

Now I had to get Gus out of the office on Wednesday. Phoning him was impossible during the day. He was constantly tied up on the phone or in meetings during working hours. I hate texting as it doesn't have room for nuance. Face-to-face in the gym - 6 am. Shit! Needs must!

*******

"What brings you here so early? You usually arrive towards the end of my workout."

"I wanted to catch you for a quick chat. I'm in the City, Wednesday. Are you OK for a quick lunch?"

"Sure, but it will need to be quick."

"Let's make it 1:45, we'll grab a sandwich."

"That's a date. Wednesday, the salt beef guy will be outside the station. I'll get the sandwiches and see you on the seat by the lawn where we normally sit."

Deal done. Next step, wrap the present. I'd already got my script prepared for Jack. This was going to be fun.

*******

Wednesday arrived. I was a bit nervous, but not about meeting Jack or bumping into Gus. I knew the route he would take from the office to our rendezvous. I was only worried about the security downstairs. There shouldn't be a problem as long as I didn't stand out in a crowd. That means LBD knee length or just below, medium heels, and my secretary-style horn-rimmed glasses.

Needn't have worried. Security didn't pay any attention when I put the nicely wrapped present through the scanner.

A quick text to Gus: *Sorry, running late. Keep my sandwich warm. Heart emoji* *No prob. Sitting. Waiting. See you soon.*

Great, that's confirmation that the office is safe.

Now up to the floor where Gus worked. Jack was in the corner office, just as Gus had described. I barged straight in. No time for formalities. Peck on the cheek. Nice touch. Awkward peck back from Jack. I sort of jiggled Gus's present in front of him, indicating that this was what I'd planned to give him. Jack gave me a knowing nod. I turned to leave Jack's room.

I looked back as I was holding the door:

"Do you want me to close it?"

Jack smiled. "No, that's fine."

I walked back towards him but not too close.

"Jack, you must think me so rude, I really appreciate this favour, let me repay you somehow."

"Don't be silly, it was nothing."

"Let me buy you a drink next time I'm in the City."

"It's really not necessary."

"No, I insist. I've got a reason."

He looked puzzled.

"*Quid pro quo*"

"Sorry?"

"It's Latin, it means…"

"I know what *quid pro quo* means."

He was smiling, that was good.

"No, what I mean is, I like to square off my debts. Suppose next month, I've got another present for Gus. I'm not saying I will have, but you'd think I was just taking the piss, sorry, taking the Mickey …."

"*Piss* is fine," he smiled.

*Getting there* I thought.

"But if you let me buy you a drink…"

"*Quid pro quo.*"

"Exactly."

His face said: *Dotty girl, but she's quite sweet.*

*Trademark smile.*

"Go on, why not? But I warn you, a pretty lady buying *me* a drink, that would be a first."

"I only said I'd buy you one drink. The second one's on you."

*Trademark smile.*

He smiled back.

"I'll look forward to hearing from you."

*Putty in my hands.*

"I'll text you when I'm going to be in the City to see if you can fit me into your busy schedule."

"Don't worry, I'll clear my calendar." He joked, then a little more seriously: "Don't leave it too long. I've got a series of business trips planned."

I pretended not to hear that remark as I turned to leave, with a parting: "Thanks again, Jack."

But I was thinking: *business trips.* I wonder if he knows I'll be joining him.

# 31

# Drinks with Jack

Things were moving rather quickly and I didn't want to lose control of the pace. I waited a week before I sent a text to Jack suggesting the drink. Got an immediate response proposing a time and place. He seemed a little too eager, and I was concerned in case he was thinking I was a quick shag and that's that. I was playing the long game. That's why I needed to control the pace. He mentioned a wine bar close by the office which I knew well. A bit busy, a lot of his team might be there. I wanted an intimate venue but it would have to do for our first meeting. Then he sent me another text the following day.

*Can we do the ME Strand instead? Only, I have a conference there on the day we fixed.*

I couldn't reply immediately. It might look too keen, but the implications? I had to understand the implications.

On the face of it, the venue seemed OK. Far enough away from his office, so he wouldn't bump into any colleagues of his. I knew the hotel from one of the daytime sessions with Vish. The bedroom, *River View*, naturally.

Vish knew the history of the site, which used to house the massive Gaiety Theatre, a famous place for old-fashioned music hall before it was pulled down in the 1960s. He was like a walking Encyclopaedia, or maybe he just used Google. Why should I have cared? Because of Eliza Doolittle! Because I always call myself *the flower girl from dahn the Old Kent Road.* Doolittle was the original cockney flower girl made posh by some dude named 'Enry 'Iggins. I saw the film, which was a stage musical first, just the kind of thing I could imagine being performed at The Gaiety. Should I care? Only if you believe in fate and believe that Vish is the 'Enry 'Iggins dude who wants to make me posh.

Back to *drinks with Jack.* Rooftop Bar, sort of indoor/outdoor, should be OK. Do I need to check it out?

There was a slight problem, though. I didn't buy the BS about a conference. These bigwigs had their diaries booked weeks in advance. Did he want me in a hotel setting - more intimate? Or was his intention just to

234

bed me? I could read him like a Kindle, but only face to face, for this, I was going to need someone cannier.

Although I prefer a sit down when I'm picking Vish's brain, I really didn't have time. I was already trying to fit in Felicity's while running Gus as a full-time boyfriend. That meant weekly date nights, early morning gym sessions, a couple of home-cooked meals with me doing the cooking and, of course, two fucks a week.

"Vish, I have something to ask, but first an apology. I'm not taking the piss, but it is urgent and I don't have time to see you."

"Hey, Rache. Please don't feel guilty. We know each other well enough. You'll see me when you have the time. Now, tell me what's the problem?"

I explained where I'd got to with Jack. Judging by his reaction on the phone, Vish was quite impressed that I had gotten so far, so quickly. Then I told him what my concern was. Maybe the pace was too quick. Then I mentioned the switched venue to the hotel and the bogus conference. Well, at least, my reason for thinking it was bogus.

"That's fine, but what's your real issue?"

"Has he booked a room at the hotel, for a quickie?"

"Well, there's one way to find out."

"How?"

"Just phone the hotel. If he's booked the room, it will be in his name. Remember, these guys always charge it on the company card."

"I have my script planned, based on a simple drink. I was going to gentle him in by explaining that things were getting awkward with Gus. But that does not fit with the hotel room scenario."

"You never cease to amaze me. When I first mentioned this whole plan, I was semi-serious. I had no conception that you would be able to implement it so faultlessly. In this whole game, you rarely mention morality. I have long accepted that all your actions are contractual. I will always be non-judgmental, and, unless I think there is a serious risk of you being hurt, I won't interfere with the path you've chosen."

"That's very nice of you, Vish, but as you realise, that doesn't exactly help me."

"No, of course, but I just wanted to get that out, because someone, not me, might say you're being callous and cold."

"OK, I think I understand. You're talking to Cindy now, not Rachel, so give this your best shot."

"If he hasn't booked a room, then Plan A, exactly as you describe. If he has booked the room, you have to move to Plan B."

"Which is?"

"You're not slowing down with Gus, as in Plan A. You've had a bust-up. You told me about the unofficial engagement you mentioned to Ellie Mae at the Pool party. I can't believe that Ellie Mae hasn't spilt the beans to Jack yet. Well, Plan B is that it's all over, engagement off, unofficial or otherwise. You break down in front of him. He consoles you."

"Think I'm with you. Just trying to understand those pesky implications."

"If he has a shred of decency, he will not take advantage of you in that state. You could then go home to regroup and work out how to deal with the Gus situation. If he does try to bed you, then he'll get what he deserves. You don't need my advice on how to play out that act. But just one word of advice, if you do end up having sex with him on that evening, under the scenario that I have just described…"

He paused.

"We're not on the speaker, are we? There's no one listening?"

"Of course not! Don't be a bloody fool. Go on, what were you going to say?"

"I was saying if you ended up having sex on this occasion make sure he just fucks you. No blow job and, definitely, no cunnilingus."

"Er, okaaay, I'm listening, but why?"

"You were so right to worry about this going too quickly. A quick shag and then that's the end of a beautiful relationship. This is all about him feeling guilty afterwards. Then, you can start to build the relationship from a position of control."

I paused for a few seconds, maybe a minute, reflecting on Vish's wisdom. Of course, as usual, he was right. I bade him farewell, promised we would get together soon and thanked him for his customary sound advice.

Next stop, a phone call to *ME London*, confirming that the conference was a BS excuse and checking to see if he'd booked the room.

So Plan B it was. I had to do my homework. While the rooftop bar would have a spectacular view, it probably wasn't going to suit my purpose. So I said I'd meet Jack in the lobby bar.

*******

I walked into the lobby and I could see him sitting at a table in the bar area. I caught a glimpse of him before he saw me. Cool and calm. He'd done this before. He wasn't knocking back his drink in nervous anticipation. Could he really be that much in control? If I was going to succeed in my plan, I needed to find a chink in his armour. Either that or put on the best performance of my life.

The timing was awkward, though. If he was to believe that I had just broken up with Gus, then I'd have to be in a highly emotional state. It would make sense for me to be late. But, on the other hand, I didn't trust him. I didn't really know him. If I kept him waiting too long, he would probably phone up one of his escorts. The room was already booked, expensed on the Company's credit card. Too good an opportunity for a player like Jack to waste.

I had to get this right, so I decided to turn up on time. I also had to make the tears effective. This may have been the act of my career. If he sensed crocodile tears, the game would be over. But I had a trick up my sleeve. As ever, Vish would come to my aid. So, before reaching the hotel, I prepped myself. I went back to the time when I finished with Vish, Vishti, in those days. When I would see him and we would have sex. Great sex! Where he would take me, pleasure me, using that magic tongue. And I would give back as good as I got. We'd fuck, but it was always the oral pleasures where both he and I would have the most ecstatic climaxes. And then, I'd make him pay because he was a client and I had my stupid rules. Never a date-date always a non-date date. Contractual, paying me for sex. That way - no emotion. I think he knew, before me, that I was kidding myself, that I was falling in love with him. I just wouldn't admit it. I tried to remember the emotional state I was in at the time, the things I thought of when I had known the time was coming and I knew I had to end it, or he would completely take me over, emotionally. I just was not ready. How many times had I gone over that in my mind? How many times had I cried out in those moments of solo pleasure: *Vish, I'm sorry. I loved you then. I love you now. I will love you forever?*

When I look back to that moment in the hotel lobby in the cold light of day, I have to congratulate myself. Having deliberately reminisced about such an emotional moment in my life, by the time I got to the bar, and was in front of Jack, I was an emotional wreck. I was sobbing uncontrollably and this wasn't an act.

To give him his due, Jack responded fairly well. He managed to calm me down. At least enough to enable me to describe, as though it had really just happened, the traumatic *break up* with Gus.

We had a few drinks. I needed to make a decision. I knew that he was pondering how to get me up to the hotel room. But even Jack, so knowledgeable in business, yet so gauche when it came to dealing with women's feelings, even he realised that he could blow it if he came on too strong. I had to guide him, so I started my prepared script:

"Jack, I feel so self-conscious, is there anywhere more private we can go? I just want to, I don't know, pour my heart out to you. You've been so kind, so understanding. I don't want to embarrass you by being a soppy cry-baby in front of all these people. But I do want to stay with you a bit longer, just really not here."

Brilliant! I'd practised but hadn't really known how it would play. Bullshit! I'd practised and had known exactly how it would play!

"Do you want to see if I can get a room upstairs, where we can have some privacy? Just a few drinks and you can relax. Maybe an hour or so and when you're ready I'll make sure you get safely home."

"That would be perfect. Do you think you could get a room just like that? It doesn't have to be a room. I don't want you to spend money if there is just some private corner somewhere."

"Don't be silly. The money doesn't matter and the bar is too busy to find a private corner."

"You're such an angel. I trust you so much. Give me a second, I must freshen up. I must look a total mess with my soppy tears."

"OK, just go to the ladies room. I'll see you at reception. In the meantime, I'll pick up the bill and then book the room."

*******

He took me to the room. It was only a fucking suite. I remember thinking: *You've misjudged this, Jack. You thought the suite would impress me, but now you've got the problem of getting me from lounge to bedroom. You have to give me some time. You won't know how to do this. I'm going to have to somehow take the lead, without appearing too keen.*

Actually the problem solved itself, because I suddenly needed to relieve myself.

"Jack, Jack I'm so embarrassed. I just went to the loo to freshen up. But now I need to pee."

He smiled an innocent smile: "Don't be silly. It's in there, through the bedroom."

Job done! I came out of the loo and lay on the bed. The bedroom door was open, so Jack would be able to hear me:

"Jack I'm in here! Sorry, but I'm completely shattered. Do you mind if I lie down? Give me five minutes. I'll just close my eyes for a bit and then I'll be back out. I'm being such a fool and you're being so kind."

"Of course, Rachel. Take as much time as you need."

"Jack, please call me Rache. If it's not too much to ask, I'd really appreciate it if you could come in and give me a little cuddle. I'm still a little bit shaky."

I couldn't believe how easy this was, but I still had to stick to the script. I knew it wouldn't be all plain sailing. I was going through in my mind the things that Vish said Jack should be allowed to do and those things that were, for tonight, off-limits.

Jack started off as the gentleman that I knew he wasn't. He took his shoes off and lay next to me on the bed. At first, with my back towards him. Just very gently pressing himself against me and not trying to make his erection obvious. I waited a few minutes. I felt I should have waited longer, so as not to appear too keen. But then I really thought that if I waited too long, I was in danger of genuinely falling asleep. So I turned around and he straightened up so I could cuddle him. Again not too long, but just enough time before I executed my coup de grace. I looked at him.

*Trademark smile.*

We kissed.

I had to be in top form. My natural instinct, given that most men are clueless, is to slow them down, in case they come in their pants. But I knew, I'd listened to Vish's advice, that Jack had to take me uncontrollably. Fuck me quickly and feel guilty afterwards.

I unbuckled his trouser belt, unzipped his fly. Size and shape didn't really matter. Tonight was a fuck, pure and simple, but that didn't stop me playing my guessing game. Short and fat was what I'd pictured. Short and fat was what I got. I wondered, for a split second: was this the chink in Jack's armour? Only for a split second, mind you, until I remembered that Jack didn't need to please women. You don't fuck someone like Jack to enhance your pleasure, you fuck someone like Jack to enjoy your leisure. Jack was going to be my ticket to the lifestyle that Cindy had decided Rachael was entitled to enjoy.

Jack didn't know whether to pull down his underwear or mine. My dress was already above my waist. I couldn't go on with his fumbling, so I took off my pants, which, I suppose, in some sense, implied consent, so he knew he wasn't raping me. Then, with as straight a face as I could muster:

"Jack, please be gentle. I'm not very experienced at this."

He didn't pause. He didn't think to ask about contraception. I thought: *You planned the f-ing room but didn't think to bring a condom!*

Then he was inside me and it was all I could do to not slow him down. But this was all about lust. He wasn't violent, but it hurt because I wasn't wet. Fortunately, it didn't take long, as I had expected. To be fair to Jack, absent the condom, he used withdrawal as the next best contraceptive.

The script required that I didn't let him console me afterwards, not that I really expected him to.

"Jack would you please leave me alone for a minute. I feel I need to re-gather my composure. Just let me rest, in the bedroom. You have a drink next door. I'll come out when I'm ready. Please leave the door open. I still feel a little vulnerable."

I thought the open door was a good touch, just in case he was inclined to give me privacy and close it.

I lay on the bed and cried. Crocodile tears would do. He wasn't there to see me. The sound of my sobbing would do the trick.

The plan could not have worked better. He was true to his word and accompanied me in the taxi home. It must have been at least an hour out of his way. I lost count of his mumbling: *Are you sure you're alright?* And my mumbling: *I've been such a fool!*

********

*This kid had been coming on to me ever since the Pool Party. I wondered:* What's her game? *But did I really give a shit? Is she playing me? Can't see that it matters, as long as I fuck the bitch.*

*But I didn't expect an emotional wreck. Ellie Mae told me she was engaged to Gus, and now she's sobbing in my lap because they've broken up. I'm ready to fuck her, booked my usual suite, which should impress her, but I'm not a slob. I'm not going to fuck her because she's upset about her break-up. No sirree, I'm going to fuck her in spite of her break-up.*

*She didn't seem impressed by the suite, just for a second it was as though she did a double take, looking for the bedroom. Then the soppy bitch wanted a piss, when she'd been in the loo downstairs for 20 minutes, drying her eyes.*

"Jack I'm in here, sorry but I'm completely shattered. Do you mind if I lie down? Give me five minutes. I'll just close my eyes for a bit and then I'll be back out. I'm being such a fool and you're being so kind."

*Then, she asks me to come in to comfort her. By now I'm getting a little fed up. Either she planned the whole thing because she'd get a thrill from fucking Gus's boss, what, I don't know, some revenge thing, perhaps* he'd *dumped her. Or she really is upset and vulnerable.*

*Either way, Jack, you get to fuck the bitch, so play the gentleman, Jack, until it's time to play the* cad!

*She's inviting me into the bedroom, but be careful, Jack. You know these bitches. Easy to cry rape. So remember every detail. Remember that she unbuckled my trousers, that she pulled down her pants. I've been there before, kiddo. If you come for me after, I'll lay that on you, and expose you for the ho' you are.*

"Jack, please be gentle. I'm not very experienced at this."

*You gotta be kidding, you prick teaser, this is going to be hard and rough. I'm in control here, Kiddo. She wriggles a bit. Not resisting, but just because it's not sliding in. The bitches are usually moist and ready. Just for a split second, I wondered whether I was taking advantage here. Too late, you're inside. You're pounding. That's the way I like to take them. Master of the Universe that's me. It's a power thing.*

*The ho's love it. Not the first time I've fucked the partner of one of my juniors, or even wives. The wives are the best. They think they're doing it to help hubby get a bonus or a promotion. Best thing, after I fuck them, I tell them that their husband is shit at his job, so don't expect any favours just because you opened your legs.*

*This one's a bit different. Come on, Jack, fuck her hard. Yes, I can feel it coming. Grinding her into the ground. Here we go, Sweetheart. I'm coming now. This is how I want to feel. Nothing better than when I come, with a bitch underneath me, gagging for it. Better whip it out, don't know if she's on the pill on anything.*

*Afterwards, I was ready to cuddle her, but she didn't want me to:*

"Jack would you please leave me alone for a minute. I feel I need to re-gather my composure. Just let me rest, in the bedroom. You have a drink next door. I'll come out when I'm ready. Please leave the door open. I still feel a little vulnerable."

*Drinking a bourbon next door, I can hear her crying. Got to admit, I felt a bit guilty when I heard her sobbing. I'd better take her home. I'm not a complete cunt. Plus, in her state, she might get taken advantage of. There's a lot of pricks around who would take her for an easy fuck.*

*Taxi back, she seemed OK, but kept mumbling that she'd been a fool. For me it was a one-time fuck. Unless, unless… the bitch asks me!*

********

I was proud of my performance. I'd prepared a few different scripts for the end of the evening. While he had his arms around me in the taxi, I told him I just wanted silence, but what I really meant was: *Need to concentrate, to work out which script to use as my parting shot!*

The taxi approached my building:

"The River entrance please!"

I chose the following:

"Jack, I'm very confused. I really do like you, but I think what happened was wrong. I don't know how to say this, but I really want to get to know you better before we do *that* again. Would you mind awfully if you take me out to dinner, and, really, I do mean just dinner. I'm not saying that we would never do *that* again, but I'd like to move at my own pace. I feel that I could let you enjoy my body far more when I'm ready and prepared."

I had different endings, but I thought that one worked well, the suggestion that I would be ready and willing, but the firm statement that he needed to feel guilty. I had directed the whole evening, and I knew I had to take one more initiative: the goodnight kiss. More than a peck, lips okay, definitely no tongue!

Upstairs in my flat I wanted to send a quick text to Vish: *Plan B worked a treat. Catch up soon. Thumbs up emoji.*

Deleted

Try this: *Always grateful*

Deleted

*Smiley face emoji*

Deleted

Deleted the original message about Plan B

How about: *Just thinking of you*

Deleted

He was probably asleep by then anyway. I decided to just call him tomorrow to de-brief and thank him.

I put in a calendar reminder to call and suggest lunch.

Fuck it! I went to the bedroom, lay on the bed, reached across for my *Lovehoney* Rabbit, and just dreamed of Vishti's tongue.

# 32

# Two violins

It's 5 am. I'd set my alarm early, even though it was nearly midnight before I got home.

While the evening with Jack couldn't have gone better, it left me with a huge timing problem. As far as Jack was concerned, I had had an emotional and traumatic *break-up* with Gus. Gus, of course, knows nothing about the *break-up*. He will be in the office today. The likelihood of Gus and Jack discussing me was actually quite remote but I couldn't risk it. It could ruin everything. I had to see Gus before he went to the office and tell him the news.

The problem for me was one of preparation. The evening with Jack was easy. But it was only easy because it was so well prepared. It was the preparation that was difficult not the implementation. I had help, of course. I don't believe any project can be successful flying solo. Vish was always there, my confidant and mentor. He created Plan B. But I played my part. I had my scripts. It was me who was out in the field of battle, who had to bob and weave.

But now, for what was to come with Gus, there was no preparation. I was going to have to improvise. And I didn't know if I was going to be able to do it.

My mind went back to a famous TV interview, well, I guess a repeat from the BBC archives. Actually, it was more a conversation than an interview, with the two violinists Stéphane Grappelli and Yehudi Menuhin. They came from totally different disciplines: Grappelli was a jazz violinist and Menuhin classical. While their music was so different, they had a mutual respect for each other. They were both at the pinnacle in their respective fields. Menuhin mentioned his routine and this is how I recall the conversation between these two geniuses:

Menuhin: *I practice for six hours a day, six days a week. I have had the same routine for years. How about you Stéphane?*

Grappelli: *Practice, no, no, no. I don't practise. I'm a jazz violinist.*

Of course, he was being pedantic. The likelihood was that Grappelli would play the violin for a similar period every day. But he wouldn't call it practice. The main difference was that, for Menuhin, he had to be note-perfect. His practice was repeating and repeating the same pieces over and over, ensuring that his chords met the composer's music perfectly.

For Grappelli, it was all about the improv. When he wasn't performing, he would be playing, trying this, trying that. Seeing what worked and then trying to recall it when he performed, even then he might vary the rendition. Perhaps responding to one of the other musicians playing with him. Jazz was all about the improvisation.

Last night, it was all Menuhin. I knew I had to be note perfect. I was playing Jack with my violin. Each chord, each variation had been rehearsed. Menuhin would have been proud of me.

But today, in the next few hours, it would be all about Grappelli. I needed to think on my feet. I needed to improvise.

I was nervous. I was apprehensive. I knew that if I blew it, my whole future could be at risk. I don't think that it would be exaggerating to consider this a pivotal moment. I wasn't being a drama queen. I would recover, but it had taken me over a year to get this far. If I messed up, it might take me years to recover.

So first, I had to meet Gus, which meant 6 am at the gym at the start of his workout. This couldn't wait until he finished at 6:45. I was down there promptly. He was surprised to see me. We normally overlapped by no more than 5 minutes, if at all. 7 am start was my routine. He was surprised to see me. I had to make my play:

"Gus, we need to speak. I have to see you before you go to work. Please come up to mine after you've showered and changed. I promise you won't be late for work. The coffee will be ready. I've taken croissants out of the freezer. You can have breakfast with me for a change. Just think, the *River View* instead of the dreadful garden."

I was constantly harping on about our respective views. By now, we would alternate between our flats for our soirées. But I would always rub it in. I got a kick out of the fact that this kid, who grew up in the East End, whose mother was the daughter of an immigrant, was in the flat with the *River View*, while August... mucky muck and distant cousin of a former Vice President of the USofA had to languish in his bachelor pad looking at the crappy Garden View.

"Promise you'll knock on my door. Believe me, it can't wait."

Back to my flat. Took the croissants out of the freezer. I made sure there were fresh beans in the built-in automatic coffee machine (a feature in all the flats in the Upper Riverside development, even those with the crappy Garden View, although I believe, for them, it was an optional extra, rather than rolled into the price, as it was for the posh side).

Then I waited. Put on some music and hoped that my pitch at the gym would have been enough to get him to come up for breakfast.

The knock came at 10 after 7. Cutting it fine. The City boys live in the Upper Riverside development because they can literally get to Canary Wharf in 10 minutes, one stop from North Greenwich on the Jubilee Line.

Even so, I needed him out of here by 7:40. He still had to get to the station and then walk to the office to arrive there by 8. That gave me half an hour and I had so much to achieve in that short time.

I opened the door. He was suited and booted. It was just as well; if he needed to get changed from his gym kit, all bets were off.

He walked in with a slightly puzzled anxious look on his face:

"Great music. I like jazz."

"Stéphane Grappelli. Gus, it's over!"

"You mean the music?"

"No, us!"

"What do you mean? Why? You're going with another guy, aren't you? You've been two-timing me!"

"No, I promise, there's no one else. It's just that I've decided the time has come."

"*You've* decided!"

His face was red. He was furious. Shit! This wasn't working.

"Please don't be angry. I was hoping we could stay friends."

"Friends!" he bellowed. "I know you're fucking someone else. How can you expect to stay friends if you're lying to me."

"OK, Gus, the honest truth. There's no one else. But I know there will be. This is not about you, it's me. It's all me! I told you when we started dating that I'm a three-date gal. We've been together for more than a year. I've never done that before, but I've been faithful to you. You wanted honesty. I've always had a roving eye, and I noticed that my eye has been roving. I don't want to two-time you, but I'm worried, I fear that one day I might. I'm no good, Gus, never was, never will be. You're better off without me."

"Sorry, that's just not good enough, Rachel!"

He always called me Rachel, not dropping the L, when he was angry with me. The look on his face - he was still angry. He wasn't going to be violent, but if he walked out of the door in this state of mind, I would have burnt my bridges.

My fear with the breakup, an acrimonious breakup, wasn't just how it might upset the dynamics of my relationship with Jack. It was more about how Gus was too important a contact. He was a comer. A young financier going places, with connections across the pond, and now, in this country, which could be very useful to me in the future. I didn't know how or when, but I did know that I couldn't let this man walk out of my apartment unless we were parting company as friends.

Grappelli was still playing and I needed to improvise. Unless I could get Gus to crack his face this was going to turn into a disaster.

"I know I'm treating you badly, so all I can think of is to give you something in return."

"What could you possibly give me that would make up for how you've just treated me?"

He's still angry but I gave this a go. It was my best shot:

"I thought we could swap apartments."

"Are you out of your fucking mind? What makes you think I would want your apartment anyway?"

"To punish me, for being mean to you."

His demeanour had changed. He was now looking at me as if I was demented. I thought: *Better than being angry.* His look had changed. Without words, he was demanding an explanation.

"Just picture this, Gus. One evening you're sitting in my apartment, sorry, your new apartment. You're sitting here on this soft leather couch. You're sipping a Jack Daniels, on the rocks, looking out at this panoramic view of the Thames estuary. And you're thinking to yourself: *Yes!* You have a wry smile on your face. You're thinking of me sitting in your old apartment on that IKEA couch of yours, with the wobbly leg, with my lukewarm Perrier in my hand, looking out… over that proxy garden.

Has it worked? Bingo! His face is cracking. He's starting to laugh:

"Come here, Rache. Let me give you a hug. You're such a soppy cow, but I do love you."

He was still laughing while I needed to go for the pre-close. I wasn't sure whether he was ready yet for the finale that flashed through my mind. Still Grappelli. Nothing planned. All about the improvisation. He was still hugging me. I pushed him away slightly, just so I could look up at his face, all 6 foot 5 of him, and I thought *Here goes*:

"No hard feelings?"

I got the response that I was waiting for:

"No hard feelings, Rache."

And here it comes, I repeated: "No hard feelings? Are you sure no hard feelings?"

He was nodding.

"Well, I'll have to do something about that to firm you up."

And with that I grabbed his trousers by the belt and quite forcefully pulled him into the spare room. The door was already open. I knew this had to be quick. His trousers now dangling. Thank goodness, he'd remembered to take his shoes off when he came into the flat. My tracksuit bottoms already off. No time to loosen his tie. Legs open. He's erect.

"Take me, Gus. Fuck me, Gus. Punish me, I'm your bitch! I'm your whore. Harder, harder! Hurt me!"

It didn't take long. It was all over in a few minutes. He withdrew and looked lost for words.

"Rache, I'm so sorry. I don't know what came over me. You OK?"

"A bit sore, if I'm honest."

"That wasn't me. I'm not like that. I've always respected you."

"It's really alright, Gus. I think I wanted that. I think I wanted you to punish me because I've been so mean to you. Don't think you forced me. I led you into the room."

"But I was horrible. That wasn't making love."

Juggle this carefully. He mustn't think he raped me or that he's some fucking misogynist.

"You have to believe me. That was consensual. I said I was no good and that's how I wanted you to treat me. Just for that moment. Just to get it out of your system. Just to get it out of mine. I hope you can live with that."

He nodded, while getting himself dressed.

"Time to go. I promised you wouldn't be late for work."

As he put his shoes on, he looked up.

Now was the time for the test:

"Friends?"

"Friends!" he responded.

This time he meant it.

I held the door open for him. He was crossing the threshold into the corridor, turning to bid me goodbye. I flipped back from Grappelli to Menuhin. This was the only line I had prepared and only to be used if things went well:

"Gus, when I said friends, I meant it. I've only said this to one other ex, because I never cared so much about the others. I really care for you. Any time, any place."

He looked at me, a little confused.

"I will be there for you, and that's a lifetime thing. Bad day in the office, problems with a girlfriend. Who knows? Troublesome divorce? You pick up the phone and I'll come running, a shoulder to cry on, a sympathy fuck…"

He smiled.

"Please believe me. I'm serious. Friends for life, and I mean real friends."

I held out my hand and he held out his, as we were about to shake on it.

"Don't be so bloody stupid; you nearly crushed my fingers last time we shook. Come here. Give me a farewell kiss."

I closed the door. Now I was sitting on the couch. Mentally exhausted. Physically still sore. That rape scene or aggressive sex, whatever you want to call it was Grappelli. Improv. I couldn't have planned that. But I realised, at that moment, that I had to give him something.

And I certainly wasn't going to give up my *River View*!

I think it worked. In some peculiar way, he could walk out with his head held high. But, at the same time, knowing that we shared a secret, a bond if you like. This friends-for-life shtick was no BS. I'm not sure where I got it from. This time for once not Vish. I think it was from Mum, but it probably came from Gran.

The Gran I never really knew. Or, rather, I only knew through the stories Mum told. Gran was a refugee. No, not really. Nowadays, we'd say an economic migrant. Looking for a better life from war-torn Eastern Europe. Not a victim of the Holocaust. Well, of course, a victim. Left an orphan. The way Mum told it, she was forced to make her own way. When I think about it, it makes me feel cheap. I went into the sex trade to pay for a fucking holiday in Thailand. Gran, starving and penniless when she arrived in this country, could, I'm sure, have fucked her way up the ladder. But I have no reason to believe that she did anything other than a hard day's work. She did it through street smarts. I'd like to think I'd inherited some of that. But that's not all I'm referring to here. What Mum told me about Gran's modus operandi, although she didn't call it that, was how she would meet people and keep a record. I suppose a database. Mum showed me a handwritten scrapbook, and in it were the names of people Gran had met, with times and dates. Alongside each name - their USP. She would write in the book any favours done. She would then note down what skill set they had, whom they knew, contacts and so on.

No spreadsheet for Gran, no algorithm. Just a little black book. But in it she held the key to her life. Who she could go to for a favour returned. Whose ear she could bend when she needed help or guidance. So far, at my tender age, my black book comprised Vish. But now I could add Lawrence August Cheney the Third, distant cousin of a former Vice President of the

United States of America and friend-for-life of this grand-daughter of an immigrant, and, against his name, one day, a marker to call in.

I went to the bathroom and sat on the loo. I didn't know what to do about my throbbing pussy. The closest I'd had to the way I felt inside then, was an early fuck with some callow youth who hadn't discovered foreplay and was unable to get me moist but went ahead anyway rubbing inside my dry cunt. As usual with these kids, he ejaculated prematurely. It was over so quickly, and the discomfort was gone the following day. This was different. I thought I could grin and bear it for a day or so, and if it was still sore then, off to the quack for some pessaries.

I explained why I had to let him do it, but since meeting Vishti, I had been trained in the art of controlling the member while inside me. So I wasn't accustomed to having a man ramming and rubbing. My cunt hadn't really recovered from the dry fuck with Jack last night, and now a second uncontrolled fuck. My shtick was control, and, as Vishti would put it, Cindy's grip. That hadn't come easy. I had the Kama Sutra to thank for that.

Before meeting Vish, I thought the Kama Sutra was a dish you'd eat down the local Indian, when you wanted a change from Chicken Korma. But Vish had shown me, by way of practical demonstration that a student of the Kama Sutra could provide immense sexual satisfaction. In my case, the oral pleasure that Vishti was able to deliver, just from reading that ancient text. I wanted to give him what he gave me. Orally, I had no problem. Actually, I had developed my own technique for fellatio. Based on some years of trial and error from about the age of 14. Of course, Vishti helped me to improve that technique by guiding me. I knew how and where, but he explained about pace. I tried edging a guy way back when, but in those days, I was pretty clueless. Vishti was able to introduce me to subtlety in the process, to explain how the tongue around the glans could help to maintain arousal but delay ejaculation, for example.

But enough of fellatio, I am referring to the Tantric art used in sexual intercourse. And the skill is in the grip, and the grip requires strengthening of the pelvic floor muscles.

So I was delighted when Vish presented me with his copy of the Kama Sutra. He explained that he still had the Sanskrit version, so he was able to part with the English translation. I'm not sure whether he was kidding. Before I met Vish, I'd never heard of Sanskrit. The English translation was good enough for me. It wasn't a scrappy paperback. It was a nice leather-bound volume. I decided I was going to use the Kama Sutra to improve my techniques and, in particular, to understand the importance of the grip. So every night, I would take the book which I kept on the table beside my bed. I would open it to a random page, and hold it open at that page with my hand.

With my other hand I would reach back across at the bedside table. I'd open the table drawer and take out *Lovehoney's* most expensive remote controlled Kegel balls. I'd then rest them on the book so they kept it open at that random page.

I'd leave the Kegel balls there for a few minutes until I thought they had absorbed the ancient wisdom from whatever random sutra they were resting on.

Then very gently, very respectfully, I replaced the book on the bedside table.

The balls were controlled by an app on my phone and, quite cleverly, you could personalise the workout. For 10 minutes a day the balls vibrated inside me, causing my muscles to contract.

I was really proud of myself when Vish told me he could recognise a difference. And it was downhill after that. Well, anatomically, I suppose it was actually uphill. Once I knew that his erect member was sensing my muscles, I was in complete control. With his guidance, I could bring him up and hold him there. I could relax his movements whether slow and rhythmic or speed it up. But no rubbing, no pounding. We moved in harmony and I began to understand the meaning of Tantric sex. The irony for me was that Felicity's Tantric massage was a joke. Whatever the label, the clients - Vishti excepted - were neither expecting nor deserving of a Tantric experience. It would be unfair to them to imply that all they wanted was a happy ending. But seriously, they weren't looking for some Asian erotic massage and wouldn't recognise Tantra if the Vedic Goddess Rati had come along and hit them in the face.

Our moments of Tantric sex with Vishti inside me and me using, in his words, Cindy's grip, were pure bliss. But I have to admit, for me not orgasmic. My orgasms came via Vishti's tongue. I wasn't complaining. They were exquisite moments. He was the best. But I never have vaginal orgasms.

With one exception: Cassandra. That was not Tantra. That was but pure lust. Just the one time, at Jimmy's, I experienced an orgasm with clit and G-spot vibrating in unison.

So when Vishti and I were having full intercourse, without words, we had both decided that the session would be pure Tantra. The experience would last hours. Well that's an exaggeration. Our record was 40 minutes. I looked at the clock when we started and when we finished. I'm talking about the time his erection was inside me, maintained for the whole period, hard and throbbing. But let me define those points: the starting point was not the foreplay. The love-making may have started 30 minutes before, the gentle touching, the stroking, the tickling, the intertwining of our bodies and then, when I was moist and he was erect, the starting point, as he entered me. The 40 minutes of me grasping his member with my muscles, of easing the pressure, of listening to his penis asking me to squeeze as he moved up, and relax as he moved down, to be careful as he approached the moment of climax. I was now as much in control during intercourse as I was when taking him orally. But much more. I mentioned that I had only had a vaginal orgasm once, with Cassandra. Let me re-phrase that; in Tantra with Vishti, we would have simultaneous orgasms but it was a wholly different experience. In Tantra, the male orgasm is more prolonged, it's not climatic in the normal sense. No, at least for Vishti, I can't speak for anyone else, the orgasm would last several minutes, the seminal fluid wouldn't spurt, it would come out more slowly. It reminded me of a prostate orgasm, or, at least, the ones I'd elicited at Felicity's.

When Vishti told me he was ready, not with words, none of this *I'm coming!* with Tantra. No, he would tell me non-verbally, via the throbbing of his penis, his clenching of my buttocks with his hands, the pace of his heartbeat. I would know he was ready. My muscles pumping. I would tighten my grip as hard as I could and feel the fluid come out, yes, a ripple, not a spurt but, with the ripple, the tensing of the back. Perhaps a better description would be a series of mini orgasms, because as soon as the ripple subsided, it was back to work again. The penis softened but didn't become flaccid. What some might call, at Felicity's, a semi, referring to the guys who struggled to keep it hard, even with our best body-to-body or breast massage techniques. But calling Vishti's softening penis a semi would be a misdescription. Somehow, his penis would stay erect, but I could sense that the veins were less evident, less protruding. His member was simply saying: *A brief pause, to re-group, to replenish, now please resume Cindy's grip, keep contracting.* As I did so, I could feel the veins throbbing again and getting ready for another burst of ejaculate.

Vishti would soften and Cindy's grip would go back into action. This would go on maybe half a dozen times or more until the fluid was totally drained, and, with his orgasm, came mine, with synchronicity, but just as his was not an explosion, so neither was mine. I have no words to describe it. Well, I have the words, the experience is *spiritual* and, on completion, we were in a state of *bliss*. I am reluctant to use those words, however, for one simple reason: *I don't believe in all that crap.*

Sorry. I wanted to describe that in order to explain that my Tantra has only been with Vishti. And no more with him, after the flood. When Vishti morphed into Vish, and I had to content myself with a soulmate rather than a sexual union.

But I was left with the techniques of Cindy's grip with anyone I fuck, including Gus. That's what keeps me in control. Many of my female friends say they fucked their boyfriend or he fucked her. But they tend to be describing their position, who's on top, who's grinding away. When I say I fuck a man, I'm not talking about above or below, I am referring to Cindy's grip, that's what brings them to orgasm.

So that's why the Gus experience left me not just sore but a little bit distraught. I asked for it. It had to happen, for reasons I have explained above, but I could still regret the consequences.

I needed to shake myself out of my gloomy mood. I thought about my girlfriends describing their experiences: *Who's on top?* Then, I thought of Gus, our first fuck. I was seducing him with my oral foreplay, licking, sucking. I withdrew to take a breath. He was ready to fuck. I thought I'd be polite and ask him: *Who's on top?* He replied: *Who's on first!* And burst out into laughter, completely ruining the moment. I got off him, and, rather irritatedly, asked what was the matter with him. It took him a few minutes, as every time he calmed down, he repeated *Who's on first?* Resuming his girlie giggles. I'd finally had enough, I gave him a playful slap on the face, not hard enough to hurt but enough to make him realise I'd had enough. Finally, he explained. Well, actually to explain he googled a YouTube video, which I'd never seen before of these two comedians, Abbot and Costello, I don't know, like a hundred years ago, doing this routine about baseball with the punchline *Who's on first?*

Gus had ruined the moment, but at least, I was now able to share the joke. It became our thing. As a prelude to sex. We'd be having a drink, either of our flats. One of us would say: *Who's on first!* We'd share the joke and have a laugh. But we'd both know it was code, and we'd knock back our drinks then rush into the bedroom, ripping off each other's clothes on the way.

That memory, that silly video clip, was enough to shake me out of my gloom.

Enough of Grappelli on a loop in the background. I looked at my phone, thinking to myself that it wouldn't be on my playlist. But I knew it would be there somewhere online. I located it and tapped a key.

My jam box, a portable speaker, came to life again. And then I did something that I've never done before:

I picked up my coffee. Cold by now. I poured it into a large mug. Took it across to the trolley. Poured a generous helping of brandy into the mug. (I know it's only 8 am.)

I sat on my soft leather couch.

I looked across to the river and admired the view.

I listened to the jam box playing Brahms's Violin Concerto: First Movement, the virtuoso. Menuhin, of course.

Well, I did say I was doing something I'd never done before.

# PART IV

# 33

# Busy

I was wearing my ear buds.

When I shared with Dixie, right back in the days of the dorm at College, she used to hate them. She'd be talking to me about some lecture. Filling me in on what I missed on my *loo* day.

That was a private joke we had. We used to say, when I was at work, instead of being at college, that was my day *in lieu of* college. After I told her about my shenanigans, and the day with the guy who crapped in the shower, we just abbreviated that to my *loo* days.

Anyway, while she'd be filling me in on the lecture so that I wouldn't fall too far behind on my course work, I'd be listening to Adele on my ear buds. She wouldn't notice that I hadn't heard a word she'd said. She'd be furious. It would end up as a pillow fight. The pillow fight would end up with us staring at each other. Both feeling the urge to get down to it, but in those days, not feeling comfortable enough or confident enough to express our feelings for each other.

Now I was on the Eurostar, wearing those same ear buds.

Listening to Stéphane Grappelli. He was now my go-to violinist after he served me so well in my *Dumping Gus* playlist. So, sorry, Papa John Creech. I first met you when Mum bought me my Sony Walkman for my 10th birthday. I thought it was really grown up. I never knew, till much later, that Sony had just stopped making them and Mum got them for a knock down price down at Petticoat Lane market. She now had a DVD player which had just gone mass market, so she had slung most of her cassettes.

Papa John had survived, not particularly because of Mum's penchant for New Orleans Blues, more due to the fact that Papa John had found a resting place in the secret drawer in her bedroom. I found the cassette while rummaging through the drawer. As it was strictly out of bounds, the lock was ripe for the picking. What ten-year-old would not want to find the secrets that their mother wished to hide away? At first, I simply used the contents of the drawer as a source of batteries for my new Walkman. But it didn't take long for me to start experimenting with the other contents.

Unfortunately for Mum, it took me a few goes with the toys before I realised the purpose of the *Lovehoney* fresh biodegradable wipes.

You might wonder whether a ten-year-old would have a sophisticated enough ear to appreciate the dulcet tones of New Orleans violin, but, when I heard Papa John's instrumental version of *Over the Rainbow*, straight out of Judy Garland's playbook, I went carpool karaoke. I played it over and over again, singing at the top of my voice. I kept playing that cassette until I'd saved up enough pocket money to buy something else. But that left me with a taste for New Orleans Blues, so Papa John was my first download when I migrated to an iPhone.

I hadn't been on Eurostar for ages. COVID had more or less added a couple of years to Rachel's travel plans. But, even before, Paris hadn't figured big. Maybe there hadn't been the time or maybe the inclination, or nobody that I seriously wanted to spend a romantic weekend with.

I was sitting in a single seat, with a table in front of me. The seat opposite me was empty. I hoped no one would sit down. I can't stand engaging with people on planes and trains.

The train doors were closing. I was relieved that the seat was still empty, but then I saw this man walking along the corridor. He was quite attractive. He looked at his ticket and sat down in the empty seat.

To say he was charming is an understatement. He looked French or maybe Spanish, Italian, sort of just European. He dressed well. No, that's another understatement. He dressed immaculately. I pictured him as some kind of European aristo. You know, one of those former princes whose family was wiped out in the revolution. Oozing education, refinement, and status, but piss poor. But he couldn't be that poor. He was travelling first class. So now I adjusted the scenario. He was still impoverished, because the family estates were expropriated by an Eastern European communist government, after the war. But someone of his breeding, of his class acquires a, what's the female version of a sugar-daddy? A sugar-mummy? Some wealthy widow, in her dotage, has taken him under her wing. No sex is involved, she's beyond that, or maybe? I haven't worked that out. No, I don't think so. I think he just panders to her whims and flirts with her.

Anyway, I felt I knew him already, so no point in engaging in conversation. I start scrolling down my playlist, looking down at my phone, which for my generation means *No talking, please!*

"I hope you don't think I'm being forward, but would you mind if I introduce myself?"

I stayed looking at my phone and pretended that I hadn't heard. I looked up casually:

"Sorry, did you say something?"

"I was just saying that I hope you don't think I'm being forward, but would you mind if I introduced myself?"

I looked back at my phone. It was taking a bit of time to work out my response, but I think I had it now, so I looked up.

"I'm not being rude; it's these earbuds."

I took them out of my ears.

"Would you mind repeating that, just one more time?"

He looked slightly taken aback. He didn't know if I was serious or playing with him. Either way, he gave it one last shot, looking directly at me, maybe half a smile, very slowly, drawing out his words, as if to indicate this was my last chance:

"I… hope… you… don't… think that I am being… forward, but… would… you… mind if… I introduced myself?"

"Nah, mate, I'd be fucking annoyed if you ignored me for the whole journey!"

He looked at me, with a chuckle. He knew he was handsome. He knew I was playing.

Come on! I thought about the two-and-a-half-hour journey. This was going to be fun. I held out my hand to shake his:

"Cindy!"

He took my hand but didn't shake it. Instead, he raised it towards his lips and gave the back of my hand a soft gentle kiss, which sent tingles down my spine. *Fucking aristo,* I thought. *Euro-fucking-pean aristo!*

"Monty!"

"As in *Full?*"

And now, I'm picturing him on stage starkers, with Gazza - who was it, Robert Carlyle? - covering his cock with his hands.

"Full?"

"Sorry, you just reminded me of someone."

"Someone nice I hope?"

"Tommy Cooper."

He looked puzzled.

"Stand-up comedian, from my mum's era. Used to wear a funny hat. Claim to fame - he died on stage. Literally, shouldn't laugh, but you know comedians often talk about dying in front of the audience. But he did, literally. You should catch it on YouTube. It would be a laugh, if he wasn't actually, well, you know, having a heart attack and dying!"

"I'm really glad you told me that."

"Oh, why?"

"I had intended to spend the next two hours impressing you with some hilarious one-liners. But the thought of ending up having a heart attack, and never seeing you again is just a little too much. So, my dear Cindy, I'm awfully sorry, but you will now have to spend the rest of this journey listening to my boring conversation about our 5000 acres of woodland in Westphalia."

I wanted to say: *I love you!* Grab his face and give him a big kiss. He was extraordinarily amusing. He was able to charm me without flirting. He reminded me of, I don't know, I just felt comfortable with the banter back and forth. It reminded me of... of course, yes, the only other European aristo that I knew. The one I was travelling to Paris to have lunch with.

Suddenly, I got a flash of Vish and the silly 3-word game. No, she couldn't have, could she? Was he a plant? She'd booked the ticket so would know where I was sitting. But I dismissed the idea. Not even Cassandra could go that far in her game plan.

We got on very well. Another place another time, who knows? The waiter, or whatever you call the guy on the train who serves the meal, approached. Is he a porter because he works on a train? No trolley! A proper meal, wine and everything, right down to the cheese. I declined an after-lunch drink. The journey went like a flash. I wanted to thank him for being such good company. But I think he would have been disappointed. He could tell that was not my style. The train drew into Calais, and, as he made his excuses to depart, he stumbled while clutching his chest, mimicking a heart attack. We both shared a farewell smile.

I was surprised he was getting off at Calais. I had expected a European aristo to carry on to Paris. As he recovered from his mock heart attack, I held out the back of my hand so he would kiss it gently, like he did before. Of course, he took it, but no kiss. Instead, he gave me a very British firm handshake, and I wanted to say: *Touché. You clever bastard!* but I couldn't get the words out, so instead...

*Trademark smile.*

As he was leaving, an afterthought since he had already turned his back to leave, he turned around to face me again and handed me his name card. Then, with an almost Germanic click of his heels, turned round and walked down the corridor. I just gazed at his butt until he was out of view. As the train pulled out, he was standing on the platform and gave me a friendly wave. A few minutes later, I looked down at the name card, Count Marco Dominic Rudolph Montessiori.

There were so many similarities, but it just hadn't really sunk in. Her brother, or maybe a cousin? Now I could see the family resemblance. I was holding the name card and, as I put it down, I noticed something written on the back. In perfect copperplate, in a handwriting I recognised, just four letters spelling out 'BUSY'.

The treasure hunt! This was so much fun. Oh, Cassandra, everything you do turns me on. The thrill of the chase. I was feeling moist with anticipation. I had to get up to go to the WC. And, as I sat there having a pee, I was suddenly back in the dorm room, with Dixie, Adele, and my fucking *loo* day.

*******

Vish the Brilliant. How did you know? I now had the third word. I wonder whether these people, who invented this stupid location tool, realised how effective it was for playing a treasure hunt. I looked at the app and tapped in the three words. I might have known the location: Hotel George Cinq, off the Champs Élysées.

A flashback. My stepdad had taken Mum there. A birthday, anniversary, romantic Valentine's weekend. I don't know. I only remember it because I had to stay with my granddad and all the ice cream and lollipops that would entail. When they came back, my stepdad was giggling about George Cinq the Fifth. Some old comic had used the line, and he thought it was really funny. No one else seemed to get the joke.

Sitting in the taxi from Gare du Nord on my way to George Cinq the Fifth. No, the taxi driver didn't get it either. It's just a thing with me, but I'm uncomfortable with people unless I can make them laugh, so *hey ho*, here goes:

"*Excusez-moi, Monsieur!* The last time I was in a Paris taxi, I was starkers. "*Comment?*"

"Starkers, stark naked. *Comment dit-on cela en français ? Completement nue.*"

His English comprehension was perfect, but, like all these frogs, he was just testing my French language skills. I continued my taxi story:

"So he's staring me up and down. I think how bloody rude, me starkers an' all. So I asked him what's he staring at! He does one of those typical Gallic shrugs and says: *I was just worried about the taxi fare, and wondering where you kept your purse!*

He didn't want to laugh, but I could detect a smile. I thought I'd settle for that and lay back and thought about myself in the nude and the lady I was going to meet.

Did I say lady? Sorry, I meant the Euro-fucking-pean aristo. Oh, Cassandra! What do you have in store for me?

When I think about the favour I was going to ask of her, it seemed so trivial compared to the amount of effort, ingenuity, and inspiration she was putting into her game.

Thinking of Cassandra made me moist. I thought of her sitting in the hotel café, drinking her tea, and her hands wandering under the table between my legs. I'm playing with myself now, picturing her hands. Suddenly, I'm back at Jimmy's, on their four-poster bed. Cassandra's head is between my thighs, licking and sucking hard. Her fingers start exploring.

I flashback to my mum and stepdad at the George Cinq the Fifth, and then I'm picturing them at home, flicking through an old phone book or something. Both of them together giggling, singing some stupid jingle from an ad for the Yellow Pages: *Let your fingers do the walking!*

I'm telling Mum: *I'll let Cassandra's fingers do the walking any day of the week.*

Back to Jimmy's on the four-poster bed. Cassandra is touching me, massaging my labia, exposing my clit, now her tongue, and - and, that's it, the G-spot. Why the fuck can't you tell Lovehoney where it is? Even my rabbit can't find it. But you're right there. And now it's Jimmy's turn. But it's not Jimmy lying there. It's Monty. I'm looking at Monty's face, but it's Cassandra's fingers. Now it's Cassandra's body and Monty's face. Now they're switching. It's Cassandra's face and Monty's body. My fingers are rubbing more quickly. I'm getting confused, but I don't care. I'm moaning out loud.

I'm wondering whether the Parisian taxi driver will comp my fare like the Greenwich guy when he nearly had an accident listening to me coming in his cab.

Still confused about who's fucking me. Cassandra? Monty? Oh! Now I get it. Rachel's lying on her back completely in Cassandra's thrall. Rachel, the submissive, giving herself, being taken by Cassandra. While Cindy, dominant, is riding Monty. As I rub my slacks, I'm rubbing up and down, taking Monty's throbbing prick deep inside me. I hear him shouting: *Grip me! Grip me! Cindy's grip!*

I now I hear my voice: *Je viens! Je viens! Maintenant!*

And now I hear Cassandra screaming: *English, please! I can't stand hearing French in your stupid bloody cockney accent!*

But suddenly the voice changes. A man's voice, in French, but it's not Monty.

"Ici! Ici! Voilà! Mademoiselle!"

And I'm back in the present, as the taxi driver pulls a catch to release the back door of the taxi.

I thought it worth trying my luck: "*Tout chance d'obtenir un tour gratuit?*"

# 34

## Tea for Two

After I gathered my composure, grabbing my overnight from the seat alongside me, I was a bit miffed that no hotel porter opened the taxi door for me. I thought *I'm in Paris already, fucking… Fr…*

Then I changed my tone. Typically arrogant French, but I'm in their neck of the woods, so I shouldn't be rude. Their attention was rightly on the swanky Parisiennes, dolled up to the nines. Even the girls who worked in offices here had a certain *je ne sais quoi*. I'd been swotting up on my French, just in case. I remembered that time with Cassandra when she cried out *Je viens!* before switching back to English and screaming *Now!* leaving me convinced that she didn't think my language skills would stretch that far and was worried I might stop sucking if she'd cried out *Maintenant!* instead.

As the doormen were ignoring me, I pushed the door myself. Now, I've been in some posh hotels in London, not just with Vish. I had a boyfriend once that took me to the Savoy. OK, it was just a cuppa joe, and there weren't no honeymoon suite. But we did snog in the lift like we were real hotel guests. That was a bit of fun. So I've been around a bit, but this blew me away.

I'm going through one of those soppy roundabout things which you can get stuck in, if you're not careful. I remember once as a kid going round and round, just to annoy Mum, but not today. As the revolving door turned so that I could step into the lobby, it was like it had been designed as a mysterious portal to transport you into a different world. Like a time machine taking you back to those bygone days, when Counts and Contessas would strut on a marble carpet… And no ordinary marble for George Cinq the Fifth. There were patterns of little mosaic, delicately woven into the floor to produce a landscape worthy of Monet.

If the floor was magnificent, just tilt your head on high, and look up to a ceiling that seems to go on forever, with those paintings like in that chapel place in Rome. Then your eye settles on a crystal chandelier about 100 foot up that must've had 1000 candles.

I didn't have words for it, so I asked my Ed - *opulence*. Look it up. The dictionary says something filled with wealth and luxury... just about sums it up.

But, of course, this flower girl from dahn the Old Kent Road had a different way with words. I was now in *Cassandra-land, a fairytale castle, the home of Euro-fucking-pean Aristos*. If I closed my eyes, I could have been in some royal court with men in those soppy wigs wearing their colourful morning suits and the women with bellowing dresses and 18-inch waists, squeezed like a lemon by some godawful corset.

Except, when I did close my eyes, instead of the opulence, I pictured another Europe, another time warp to another bygone day - a bedraggled child, walking the streets of an anonymous village in a war-torn Europe. I could see Gran when she was a kid, limping through the rubble, with one shoe. The other shoe had been discarded because her swollen ankle could no longer accommodate the tiny sandal. She told me how she'd exchanged the worthless shoe for some stale bread that a kindly woman had offered.

Gran's misery was searing through my mind, a penniless waif orphaned by an evil Fascist regime propped up by... Euro-fucking-pean Aristos, the same Euro-fucking-pean Aristos now wallowing in the opulence in front of me.

I opened my eyes to refocus on the opulence and screamed out at the top of my voice:

"Get me the fucking guillotine!"

********

I was shaken out of my hallucination by:

"Comment puis-je vous aider, Mademoiselle?

"I'm looking for the Countess."

"Which one, mon petit chou, we have so many?"

I couldn't make out whether he was being nice or whether the *little cabbage* jibe was a condescending put-down. I decided to give him the benefit of the doubt, otherwise, if I had thought this porter was being an arrogant S.O.B., I would have squeezed his little cabbage, both of them.

So I ignored him and walked straight to the reception. I had one important question to ask. Of course, they weren't going to help me out. Bloody Fro... I waved my overnight at another arrogant slob, who waved his arm towards the Concierge in an *over-there-you-silly-thing* manner.

"I'll just be an hour, two at the most." Handing my overnight into the Concierge's care.

"The café, tearoom?"

I'm now making a drinking motion with my thumb and finger holding an imaginary cup. You speak perfect English, you arrogant prick, so why pretend you don't understand?

*******

Now I'm walking through the lobby into their, I don't know, the café, tea area, open-plan thingummy. It was actually the lobby but morphed seamlessly into an area with tables where they served the tea. I didn't get it at first. Then I thought how clever. They can expand or contract the area according to demand. A bus load of Yanks - lobby space is needed when they're checking in, so take away a few tables. Christmas, everyone wants tea at the George Cinq, so put some more tables in the lobby.

Cassandra was already there talking to somebody else. I was a bit surprised. I was hoping that I wasn't going to have to play gooseberry with her and some other aristo. As she saw me approach, she kissed her friend who then departed. Their kiss was on both cheeks, very European. I decided that I would follow the pattern:

"Didn't introduce me to your friend?"

"One of our breed. I don't think you would have liked her."

"I knah, you're just ashaymed of this flower girl," I mouthed in my best cockney, "but arv'd been 'aving me lessons with Professor 'Iggins."

We continued in the same vein. We were having a laugh, such fun. Tea was being served. You know, a bit like supper with Mum dahn the Old Kent Road. Everyday sort of stuff. *Amuse bouche*, caviar, finger sandwiches of smoked salmon, then onto the tray of pastries. This was France so no clotted cream, but everything else. And, because they're bloody French, they waited for you to stuff your face until you were completely full, and then brought out the most comprehensive cheese board you could imagine. Champagne with the tea, naturally. I accepted an Armagnac with my cheese.

"I told them you were English. That's why they brought the cheese last."

I wasn't sure whether she was serious and I was just about to show my ignorance of cheese etiquette when she suddenly mentioned:

"So, you met my brother?"

"Yes, very mysterious."

"He called me from Calais. He needed to get the train back to London. Said you were a lot of fun."

"I didn't know he was your brother. I thought maybe a cousin. I would have fucked him, only it seemed a little incestuous, you being a relative and all that."

Cassandra just laughed and then inquired: "The favour?"

"Yes, I should have got to it earlier. I've written a sort of journal. Handwritten, put together in what, do you remember Filofaxes?"

She looked at me blankly.

"You know before PDAs."

"PDAs?"

"Personal digital assistants. Are you joshing me?"

She smiled:

"Yes, I know what they are but I'm surprised that you do. All of that stuff went out before you were born."

Then, I explained how I sort of jotted down notes. I suppose it started when I kept a diary as a teenager and I'd score my boyfriends, not fucks, maybe a date or a snog, a comment, a score, you know out of 10.

"Anyway, when I grew up…"

Cassandra laughed. I looked hurt:

"Sorry, I didn't mean to be rude, but you are still barely in your 20s."

"What I suppose I meant was: I thought I was grown up. Anyway, the point is, I've recorded my experiences, sort of notes. When I started, I was worried that somebody might find them because I have a habit of leaving things lying around. You know, my roommate at the time. So I invented this code, which I thought rather clever: the person's name, the first letter of the first syllable of the name, and the first letter of the last syllable of the name, and then reversed.

"OK let me try, would I be DS."

"Yes, spot on San Dra. Or maybe DC. Well done, you picked it up, straightaway."

"Yes, we had a secret code at finishing school. We would take the first letter and put it at the end and add a syllable."

"Pig slang, we called it, you would be Andra-Say and I'd be Indy-Cay."

"E-Way Id-Day At-Thay Ust-Jay O-Tay Iss-Pay Ff-Oay Oys-Bay."

And she was back at finishing school, and I was back dahn the Old Kent Road Comp. Funny how our lives, so different, could come together over some stupid schoolgirl language.

"Anyway, everyone has a code letter and I've jotted down these notes. This was all about my clients at Felicity's. I thought it would be good for my psychology course, research into sex weirdos, but it became a sort of diary of all my experiences, clients or boyfriends, girlfriends, and what we did. It turned into, I don't know, I could flick through the pages, when I was on my own. Bring back memories, a bit of a turn-on.

"I'm in there?"

"Of course, but it's not for publication and its anonymised. When I first started, I just happened to have one of these old Filofax things which I was about to throw away. Then I noticed it had all these blank pages in the back. So, anyway, I've compiled this. It's not really a diary, more of a guide, perhaps a sex guide. For me it was an *aide memoire* of things I've done or had done to me. But I wrote it as a kind of textbook, you know, a small book that you could carry around and look up notes, sort of a *How To* book. Not exactly *How to get ahead* more *How to give good head*. It was silly really because I actually carry things in my mind, but, as I said, lonely nights, something to read. If it turns me on, it could be a turn-on for other people. But, I mean, it's not like something you'd publish."

"Could be a best seller. The family has a publishing house in…"

"Thanks, but no thanks. Let me keep one thing for myself…"

Cindy's desire for fame and fortune was fighting Rachel's appeal for modesty and anonymity.

"But, anyway, it's all handwritten and there's only actually a couple of people I would dream of letting see it. In fact, there are three people. I made three copies and that's the favour. Because it's all handwritten and it's like a Filofax, you know, loose leaf. So, actually, it never ends. After each experience, I can add a page. Well, I suppose one day it might get full up. Anyway, sorry I've been rambling. I've got these labels and you've got this wonderful handwriting, the copperplate. All I wanted you to do was write the title on the labels.

As I say just three copies. One for an elderly gentleman. He's very special to me. Sort of my mentor, life-guide, I don't know. I'd love for you to meet him. Maybe one day. But the special people in my life, I mean, the really special ones, I tend to keep apart. I don't know, maybe one day. Anyway, at first, I thought I would just give him the only copy. And then, I thought of my roommate, who became my girlfriend, you know my live-in girlfriend. We were an item for a while. Things broke up, not very well. I think we're sort of back on level terms. But I never see her. Anyway, we went through things together, and she was my first, you know, that kind of experience. So she gets a copy, and, of course, Dear Heart, in return for writing the labels, and with my love, so do you."

"That's actually very touching and, of course, I'd be delighted. No! I would be honoured. But you forgot the fourth label."

"Who? What James?"

"No! If you'll allow me a Cindy-ism: *You, you daft fuck!* You have the original, but I'd be really upset if you didn't allow me to personalise your edition with my copperplate."

"Funny, didn't think of my copy. Yes, of course, I've got plenty of blank labels."

"Well, go on then! Tell me what I have to write."

So I handed her a piece of paper. On it was written:

*Vade Mecum on Tipping the Velvet*

Cassandra looked up and said, "I don't understand?"

"Oh? It's Latin!"

"Don't be silly. Of course I know the Latin. We used to have Vade Mecum's at school. I think we had one on each subject, at the Lycée. It was the other words I didn't understand T*ipping the Velvet?*

"I got that from Dixie, my ex-roomy, and my ex-ex. I don't think you'll need Google translate. You'll get it soon."

And I was thinking, hoping, that she was going to get it soon.

I handed her the labels and felt it was time to go. I saw her glance at a waiter to indicate that she wanted the bill. I took that as my cue that my time was up.

"Please, you must let me."

"Don't be silly. They charge a ridiculous amount. It could be €300 or more. I chose the venue, so I pay."

"Oh, by the way, do you remember the message you wrote after we first met, for me to read in the taxi home? What you said was you weren't sure of the etiquette and you didn't want to embarrass me. Well, we do accept tips and it was very nice of you, very generous. As you suggested an alternative, I did make the cheque out to *Her Centre*, it's a charity for abused women, sort of a shelter. I spend some time there helping out. Actually, I don't spend enough time there. Anyway, that was much appreciated, it was a nice thought and I was touched by how you phrased it, you know. Not wanting to embarrass me."

The bill arrived. It was placed in front of her in one of those folding things, too posh to leave the slip of paper exposed for those to see how much we were being ripped off. The folding thing was on some kind of silver platter. Give me a break. Cassandra had her handbag out but my debit card was already on top of the silver platter. I touched her hand which was on her bag.

"Now, no arguments, please, don't embarrass me!"

I thanked her for the favour, kind of sincerely, from the bottom my heart. I really don't know how to do *sincere*, but I gave it my best shot. I was very appreciative. It meant so much to me. Although, on the face of it, the favour was perhaps so trivial.

I got up to leave. I'd already made up my mind: it would be a continental kiss on both cheeks. I turned away, walking out of the café, tea room, open space thingummy, whatever it was, where we had actually sat and eaten. As I walked away, I slowed down and I thought of that moment when I left her house to get in the taxi and I turned around to run up the steps to hug her. Well, now, I had to turn around and was she looking at me? Yes, still sitting at the table looking straight at me, as I was walking away. Was I going to? Of course I bloody was! I turned, but a controlled turn. I've grown up. I walked elegantly, yes, that's the word, not a patch on her elegance, not with her sophistication, but, in place, in keeping, with the other guests at the Georges Cinq the Fifth.

As I approached her, she was standing up.

Was she expecting a hug?

"I hoped you'd turn around, but I wasn't sure."

Then my confession. How my Plan A had failed.

"This wasn't how I planned it. I had it all worked out in my mind. I wanted to surprise you. I thought you deserved to be surprised. It was going to be a treat. *I* was going to be the treat! But those bloody arrogant French ponces at reception wouldn't tell me your room number. But, at least, they did say they'd hold onto my overnight bag!"

# 35

# 1928 Malbec

I was not disappointed. She'd booked a suite, obviously. So we were in the salon. The bedroom door was slightly ajar, just a suggestion. The seduction. I sat down. There was Champagne in the bucket. A bottle of red wine, standing on the table.

"I remember you're more of a red wine girl, but happy to open the Dom Pérignon."

On the table next to the Champagne bucket was a small nicely wrapped box.

"Go on open it!"

I was so excited, but I had to restrain myself.

"Not another C for my jewellery collection? Already got one of those."

"Go on open it. It's from our family."

"What you and Monty, or you and Jimmy?"

"No, I mean handed down. A family heirloom."

"I hope you're shitting me. I don't mind some bling, but hand-me-downs are beyond the pale."

"You're not going to let me enjoy this moment, are you?"

"OK, here's the deal. I'll tell you a little story about the last time I was looking at jewellery. And if it doesn't put you off, I'll have a look at your bangle."

She smiled and held out her hand to shake on the deal.

I could hardly hold back my excitement. The gift was part of the seduction. A family heirloom. It wasn't the value. She was showing me how much I meant to her. I couldn't just open it there and then. I had to give her something back. Something from me, if only a stupid little story, to make her laugh.

I started the monologue.

"So before Jack, my sugar-daddy, all my jewellery used to come from that shopping channel on TV, QVC, but Jack introduced me to a contact in Hatton Garden. I had no idea such places existed. I would go there with Jack, and we would choose from an array of polished gems. The guy would literally sprinkle them onto a piece of blue velvet. We'd choose a stone or two, together. Then Jack would leave me to sit there with this sales guy, for another two hours. Snobby sort, *obsequious*. Didn't even know that word until I met Jack. So we're discussing settings for a ring, bracelet, pendant, brooch, whatever I wanted. One day, once I got to know the guy better, I ventured:

*"I do have a body piercing, on my belly button. I'd also fancy a diamond and gold belly bar."*

*"Of course, madam. We have a private room back there. If you'd let me see where your current bar sits, we could certainly set one for you with one of the stones you have selected."*

I'm not sure why, well, I am sure, but would never admit it, but when he showed me into a little ante-room and said: *Let me have a look,* he turned his back, just for a few seconds to allow me some modesty while I picked up my top, to reveal my belly button. When he turned around, I thought he was going to faint. I was sitting on the chair, having dropped my slacks and panties, holding my labial lips apart:

*"I thought maybe a new piercing here, what do you think?"*

Cassandra was beside herself in hysterics:

"What did he do?"

"He wanted to leave the room immediately, but I really believe he was worried that it might upset me. He didn't want to risk losing Jack, who was such a good customer. So he just stood there, gazing at what the lawyers call *my invitation to treat!*

"He could barely stutter out the words, but the gist of it was that they didn't do the actual piercings in the shop but he could introduce me to a tattoo parlour close by.

"I zipped up my slacks casually, gave the guy a peck on the cheek and left him still gazing at where I'd been sitting. My parting shot:

*I think I'll go for the two-carat D Flawless in the rose gold setting that I've already chosen."*

Cassandra had calmed down after her hysterical laughter.

"Thank you. That was serious fun. Haven't enjoyed a moment like that since… Well, probably since our time together… "

She looked serious for a moment, reflecting, then…

"The deal. Now open the box."

I unwrapped the small parcel with the care it deserved. I carefully folded the wrapping paper.

Cassandra looked at me quizzically.

"Oh, I'm definitely keeping the paper. I might need to re-wrap it in case I want to send the…"

I was suddenly speechless as I opened the small box. It takes a lot to silence me.

"Fucking Jesus!! Sorry, you're not religious, are you? Fuck, Cassandra! You can't expect me to accept this. Please, let me wear it, let me borrow it, but no, I can't accept it…"

"It's from the Russian end of my family, some distant aunt. I didn't know her. Yes, it's nice and it is family, but not OTT really."

"Fuck off, Sandy! It's a bloody Fabergé Egg!"

I used her least favourite moniker deliberately to make a point.

"Well, technically, it's a pendant."

"Sorry, your highness, a fucking Fabergé egg pendant. Please, don't make me accept it."

"I do think you're overreacting a bit. I wanted to give you something meaningful. You always said you liked rose gold. It just so happened that Aunt Anastasia passed recently. It's been sitting around in some vault."

I looked at this mini-egg on a gold chain. There was like a mosaic of little rubies criss-crossing, against a gold background, the rubies catching the light and somehow lighting up the gold. Rose gold, of course, to blend with the rubies. A perfect match for the necklace Cassandra had awarded me when I won the cocktail game, the first time we'd met.

"A hundred fucking Sri Lankan rubies in 24 karat gold."

"Well, not exactly. If you're going to be fussy, Cindy, it's 284 invisibly-set, princess-cut Mozambican rubies set in 18-karat rose gold. They're selling replicas for $50,000 so really, darling, not over the top,"

"But it's not a fucking replica, is it? So it's not worth 50k. How much? A million?"

"Well, it doesn't really have a price. I mean it'll never be sold. Of course, it's yours to sell if you want to. So, maybe a million, maybe two or three. Depends on who wants it if you ever put it up for auction. I'd hope, if you were to sell it, you'd let the family make you an offer. Auctions are fun, but it would be a little demeaning if the family had to bid at a public auction."

I'd stopped listening. I stood up, turning my back on her. I felt like I was having a panic attack. I took a deep breath. It probably took me 30 seconds to calm down enough to give her my decision.

"One condition."

"Here we go, another game!"

"No, no game. This is mine, right? I can do what I like with it?"

"Well, I hope you won't donate it to a museum. Not just yet anyway."

"No, but I'd like to keep it in the family. I'll wear it. I'll wait until I'm about 40."

"Why 40?"

"Until Cynthia's 21st. It's up to you, of course, but I hope I'll have the chance to meet her, see her grow up and so forth. It's just that it will mean more to her if she knows me when I give her a special birthday gift. And that great aunt of yours, the one you didn't really know. Do me a favour. Check out some history and let me know. Just for the provenance."

"Provenance. But you said you're not planning to auction it."

"No! God, no. For Cindy. Kids don't really appreciate these things, but when they get a little older, and all the oldies are long gone, they regret they never paid much attention to all that stuff."

"Sounds like you've had some personal experience."

"Not really. Rotten eggs, scotch eggs, not a lot of Fabergé eggs in the family."

"No, tell me, please."

"Well, it's Gran. Never bothered much when I was a kid, but Mum used to tell me stories. She had a tough life, but I think she was quite a remarkable woman. I wish I had bothered, you know, to get to know her when she was still with us."

"You're sounding serious. You're not normally that reflective, or should I say, that open with me."

I snapped out of it.

"You know something, Sandra. I wanted to tell you that silly story about the jewellers, just to give you something in return. I get a Fabergé egg. You get a stupid story about me embarrassing my jeweller.

"And?"

"And, well, I think you got the better end of the bargain!"

Cassandra smiled.

My turn. *Trademark smile.*

And I thought: *Time for a drink!*

"What's the wine?"

"Just something I picked up from home."

"Really? What? You brought that with you from England?"

She smiled.

"It's a Malbec."

"You remembered."

"Of course!"

"Argentinian?"

"No, French."

"Really? I don't think I knew that the French had Malbec grapes, but then what do I know about…"

"I wasn't actually joking when I said *from home*. The family has a vineyard in Cahors. Not many still produce Malbec. Actually, in fact, we don't anymore."

"So how did you…?"

"From the cellars."

"I hope you chose a good year," I joked.

"But of course: 1928. It was a legendary year for Bordeaux and Cahors. The summer was unusually hot which resulted in a richer wine. As you know, Malbec has moderate tannins but the unique weather resulted in a more concentrated highly tannic vintage. Why are you laughing?"

"Sorry, didn't mean to be rude. I don't have a clue what you are talking about. I like my Malbec, but to me, it's a bottle of plonk. No sorry, go on."

"It was the best year of the decade, so we put some down."

"Like a few cases?"

"No, the whole harvest."

"You kept that all for yourself."

"Pretty much. Yes, just for the family to drink. For special occasions."

"How much, if you wanted to buy?"

"Well, you can't. We auctioned some a few years ago. They only fetched €1.000 a bottle, so we thought it wasn't worth selling, and we kept the rest."

I had no idea if she was playing with me. She was so matter-of-fact about it. But, really, no. That's who she is. That's who they are. She wasn't trying to impress. Nor was she trying to tease. I really think she was being genuine. She wanted something special, for a special moment. She wanted this to be special for her as well as me. She would, what does Sainsbury's say, *taste the difference*. She would know that she was drinking something unique. For me, it could have been Sainsbury's Malbec, £5.99.

So I knew that when the time came, I had to reciprocate with something equally unique. I had to know that she would be able to *taste my difference*.

*******

The art of a good lover, I have decided… No, let me rephrase: There's a skill set, that very few people have, of moving your partner seamlessly from lounge to bedroom, without spoiling the moment. Students have it easy. You're in a dorm room. There's only really the bed. But when you grow up a little, you know, you have a sitting room. Well, you fumble on the couch, but you both want to go up to the bedroom. By the time you get upstairs, you've both cooled off. So you think better of it and end up in an uncomfortable shag, half on, half off the sofa.

And then there are people like Cassandra. I swear it's part of their upbringing. I think they're trained from an early age to be able to guide their partner from drawing room to bedroom, navigating winding staircases and ending up on a four-poster bed. All without their lover even noticing they'd moved. So, I was on the bed, and undressed, in one blink of an eye and one *trademark smile*.

Cassandra asked me if I minded a little foreplay. I thought that was a little strange. We both knew what was about to happen and, usually, we didn't need words to convey our desires. She meant it in a slightly different way. She wanted to give me some options. At first, I thought it was just another of her games, which I was more than happy to play.

"Soixante-neuf. You told me you didn't like it?"

"No," I responded, carefully, "what I actually said is that I won't come like that. If I recall correctly, I said I was up for it but if you wanted to make me come then it wasn't going to happen like that."

"Yes, of course, but why do you think that is? Why do you think you can't come at the same time as your partner?"

"Look, Cassandra, sorry, Sandra; actually, what do you prefer?"

"Anything as long as it's not Sandy."

"It's just every time I think of you, and I really do think of you quite often, you know, in my head, I'm calling you Cassandra. I like that name, and it suits you. How can I put it? You look like a Cassandra."

That was an allusion to her Rachel crack, just a test, I wanted to see if it raised a reaction, but nothing.

"What do you mean, I look like a Cassandra?"

"Well, it's what you are. A fucking aristo!"

She broke into a belly laugh. We shared a giggle, and then I carried on.

She started laughing again: "Oh dear, now every time you call me that I'm just going to think of you saying fucking *aristo* and I'll just crack up. Sorry, I tried to control myself, it's just your quaint way of describing things."

"Let me explain my problem with 69. I give good head or eating pussy. I like to think I'm up there with the best of them."

She nodded in confirmation.

"But when I'm down there, with a man or woman, I am giving my all. It's Cindy, you see. Cindy comes out, Cindy knows no boundaries. Cindy is always in control. Cindy knows how to take a partner up to the limit and pace them. Cindy knows what pleases and what doesn't. Cindy knows when it's time to accelerate the pace. Cindy knows when the time is right. Cindy ensures her partner will climax, will explode inside her, whether in her mouth or her cunt, or even in the other place. Cindy is a professional."

Cassandra smiled.

"Yes, but professional in more ways than one. When I'm in full Cindy mode, she takes it very seriously. I have to confess I was taught by a master, some kind of Zen freak."

"Like a guru?"

"Pretty much so. Yes, I hadn't really thought of it like that. It goes much more, beyond sex. He has become like my spiritual guide. But actually there's no sex anymore, I mean with him, but he was my teacher. Does this make any sense?"

"Well, in a strange way, it does. We have a tradition; I mean in our clan."

"Clan?"

"Yes, it's the same word in English."

"Well I sort of know what a clan is, but I'm not sure who you're referring to."

"Our extended family. You know, I have cousins all over Europe. I suppose we count the clan as several hundred."

"Sorry, I was interrupting, please carry on, I think you're gonna tell me something about…No, go on, I won't guess …"

"Well, it's really about our godparents."

"Your godparents?"

"You have the same?"

"Well, yes. Yeah, I have god-parents, although I never actually see them. They're actually related to my dad, and we don't see much of each other."

"Well, within the clan, we have godparents, but they each have different functions. There will be perhaps a godfather or godmother who will be responsible for our religious upbringing. Then, another one who looks after our general education. I don't mean actually teaches us, but perhaps sponsors us through school. For example, they may give us access to their alma mater."

"Elmer who?"

"Sorry, the old school, college, university. They may have a connection there and provide us access. You understand we are all about connections."

"Yeah, I was teasing you about the Elmer thing. Yes, connections, why doesn't that surprise me? Carry on. I'm intrigued."

"Well, sometimes, we might have a godparent who actually looks after or nurtures us in sports. Perhaps, if there's a tradition. In my case it was skiing.

"Yes, definitely on the same wavelength there. Even in my neck of the woods, I've come across SKI-ing. Spending the Kids Inheritance."

*Keep quiet, kid, with the chockhmelach, Mum's Yiddish word for little wisecracks. That one didn't land well.*

"Well, one of our godparents is assigned to look after our other educational needs. Not, immediately, but when we pass through to womanhood."

"I'm beginning to feel a bit uncomfortable about this."

"Sorry, I'll stop."

"Don't you dare! I've heard about you lot. I'll tell you when it gets too disgusting for me."

"OK, stop me if you've heard enough. This special godparent isn't really involved in our upbringing at all in childhood. They take on the special assignment when you reach puberty. In my case, I was 13 when I had my first period. And my mother had prepared me."

"Yeah, my mum too. She sat me down and explained to me about the curse. She told me how enlightened she was. In her day there was nothing like that. When she first had hers, she was completely clueless and went hysterical. But her mother knew what to do."

"What was that?"

"Gave her a good slap. That shook her out of her hysteria."

"Of course, my mother explained, how you'd say, about the birds and bees. She told me that the woman's role was to please the man and, in turn, the man, some men, would return the pleasure. She explained that there were no guarantees, but on that day, which had just arrived, I had to understand my duty, as she put it. She prepared me for my initiation."

"Oh that's fucking disgusting. You're telling me that your mum ponced you with your godfather. I think I'm gonna be sick."

I realised that as she was talking I was getting wet and my hands were between my legs. Cassandra looked at me, masturbating over my clothes.

"Yes, I can see how disgusted you are," she smiled.

"Oh that's Cindy. She's enjoying this. It's Rachel that's disgusted."

"So, Cindy would like me to carry on."

I nodded, still rubbing myself, over my clothes.

"Well, there's not really much more to tell. My mother set the scene. The bedroom was all laid out. She helped me to dress. She showed me how I should undress, you know, seductively. She even told me the words

I should use to encourage the man. Of course, I knew who it was going to be. She'd already told me that and, by the time she had finished, I was damp with anticipation. She left the room when he came in.

*Thank Christ for that, I thought you're gonna be full on Handmaid's Tale.*

"So she exchanged pleasantries with my special godfather and wished him good luck. And then he proceeded to fuck me."

Cassandra finished her description and I finished myself off, still fully clothed. Not an explosive orgasm. More of a dribble. Definitely came, but it was like what I've come to call a mini orgasm. The type that wants me wanting more, leaving me horny. The experiences I used to have, with, what I politely called, the boys. The ones that I had before Vish showed me what a real orgasm was like.

"Well, Cindy seemed to like that, even if Rachel was a little miffed."

I loved the way Cassandra would ape my language.

"It takes the biscuit, even for Cindy. I mean a dirty old man with a 13-year-old kid?"

"Oh no, no, no!"

Cassandra started to laugh again.

"I didn't tell you; you see, the special godparent was assigned when you're born. I thought you realised, when I said they weren't involved in my upbringing, during my childhood. Mine, the one who took my virginity, was five years older than me. No, no, no, you didn't think .... Oh you're so precious, how funny!"

"OK, now I get it! They choose a boy, one of the clan, so it's not like ecky sex with some ageing Duke. It's like a *coming* of age for both of you. But then he's got no experience?"

"Well, you're right of course. He has limited experience. But the boy, I mean the male children, will also have had a special godparent assigned to them. It's slightly different for the boys, because, in that case, you know, when their virginity is taken, it would be by a mature woman who can introduce the lad to the pleasures of sex."

Now it was my turn for me to let out a belly laugh.

"Oh, so all the boys in your clan have their own Maggie May!"

"I'm sorry, I didn't follow."

"Maggie May, the old Rod Stewart classic."

"Well, yes, I do know the song but I don't get the reference."

"Maggie May was the bird, the older bird that took Rod's virginity."

"Seriously? I never knew that."

I started singing the opening lines of the song:

*Wake up, Maggie, I think I got somethin' to say to you.*

*It's late September and I really should be back at school.*
*I know I keep you amused, but I feel I'm being used.*

"Yes, I see it now."

"Well, that was quite a story."

"I'm sure you have an equally stimulating one about your early experiences. Perhaps not exactly the way that we do it in our family."

"Nah, you're right Cassandra. Let me try, you know, in my own words. I can't really relay it in your style. I don't really have the vocabulary but let me try to explain how I lost my cherry."

"Go on, I'm sure this will be as stimulating for me as my description was for you."

"Here goes. I wasn't sure what to expect, like any kid, well, young girl, I was hoping for a bit of romance. I knew it was coming, yes, a little bit like your story. There was a bit of preparation. No, it wasn't my mother. It was the boy himself. This is how it kind of went. He asked me if I'd suck him off, because he knew that I'd been putting it about a bit with his mates. I told him I only sucked them off because I didn't fancy them. But I told him I did fancy him. So, if he was up for it, he could fuck me behind the bike sheds. A quick grope, sore twat, and it was all over. End of."

We shared a giggle.

Then Cassandra put on a more serious face:

"Can we get back to the *soixante-neuf*? You were talking about how Cindy, the professional, would give it her all."

"Yes, let's go back to that. I don't know, maybe you're a natural, more spontaneous. I have to work at it. I really know what I'm doing but and, don't laugh, it does require concentration."

"But why does that stop you enjoying being pleasured?"

"Well, that's Rachel. Her best orgasms are when she can lie back and enjoy it. What am I talking about? I can count on one hand the number of people that have really pleasured me. I can't count the number of so-called orgasms: dozens, hundreds, I don't know. But real pleasure, a real orgasm? No. Very, very few and far between. I'm not exaggerating when I say I can count them on one hand. Three people that stand out, four maybe five, but seriously no more.

Cassandra put on a pretend miserable face.

"No, don't worry, obviously you are one of that handful. But my point is, my serious point, just as I give my all when I'm pleasuring my partner, man or woman, so I want to give my all when it's the other way round. But you know differently. I want to completely submit to them. Again, not the boys, the idiots. I mean those few who know how to please me. I want them to take complete control. But, don't you see, I can't do both at the same time. I can't be both Cindy and Rachel."

"Why not?"

"Well for one, they always argue. You know Cindy's the bitch, the slut who's up for anything. Rachel, well she's not pure, but she does have morals, scruples."

"Thank you, thank you for explaining. I think I understand, so please Rache, let me know what you prefer. Last time, you said you'd never had a vaginal orgasm before, you know, when you squirted."

"I can't remember what I said, but it was the most amazing experience, my clit and cunt exploding together in unison. Never before, never again."

"I can't promise, but I would certainly be prepared to see if I could replicate that experience."

"You'd better be quick, lover. I think I'm coming just thinking about it."

"Or, or, but it really is up to you, I will do whatever pleases you, you know how I feel about you. You know that I love you."

I had to do a double take. She'd never said that before. I was visibly shaken.

"Sorry, I shouldn't have said that. Don't flatter yourself too much, *girlfriend*."

She was using my vernacular again. She didn't do it to imitate. I think she just wanted to show me that she's not always a fucking aristo.

"What I should have said is that you have a special place in my heart. You really do. You're the best fuck I've ever had, but I don't want you to think that's all you are to me. You really are a special person, in spite of, how can I put it, our different upbringing."

"Fucking aristo. Euro-fucking-pean aristo!"

"Exactly, it can really be a struggle for us sometimes to escape from our breeding. Anyway, my point is, it really is your choice – what do you prefer?"

"You mean I have options other than the most sensational climactic simultaneous orgasmic explosion?"

"I'd like to try; I've done it before both with men and women."

"Done what?"

"Come together in *soixante-neuf*. Like you, I stay in control. I can gauge when my partner is coming, but at the same time I'm letting them pleasure me. I wait for the moment when I'm ready, when I pass the point of no return and they are poised, so I have them exactly where I need them. So as I come, I can take them to their climax.

"Fuck me sideways with a soldier. Sort of like in a porn movie, where it's all fake."

"Not fake, I promise you, but neither can I guarantee it. I can only say that I will give it my best shot and, at the same time I will try to guide you, to keep Cindy in the present, you know, in the moment, while coaxing Rachel out of her shell. But as I said, no guarantees and to be honest, the safer bet would be the squirting. I've got the technique. I'd be more confident in repeating the pleasure I gave you last time. But it does seem a shame for someone like you, who enjoys sex so much, to deny yourself at least the opportunity, the ultimate pleasure that *soixante-neuf* can provide."

"God! What a choice. Don't suppose I can have both can I?"

"Not this evening. Either experience is likely to leave you completely satiated and, I would hope, falling asleep in your lover's arms."

"Of course you're right, and I didn't mean this evening, there's not much on TV at breakfast time is there?"

Cassandra was laughing: "Come over here, lover, let's get down to it."

*******

We were on her bed, bloody Egyptian cotton, what else in the George Cinq the Fifth? We started to explore each other's bodies, caressing, kissing repeating the tongue fucking that we did before. I start to massage the inside of her thighs, feeling her moist lips, just squeezing the lips but not exposing her clit. I started fingering her. I sensed that she was content for me to continue and leave her clit out of it for the time being. I don't know why I said that I *sensed* it. She opened up her pussy, no sensing or subtlety there. It was an open invitation.

I asked her, not verbally, of course, there's no talking once we start. We just talk with our bodies. So I asked her, with my hands, whether she wanted my fist. She was open. She was taking me in. She was inviting me and she was ready. This time, so was I. Last time, I felt it was almost a violation. This time I wasn't twisting my fist, I was rubbing my knuckles against her G-spot. I wasn't sure, but I think I understood that I was supposed to save her until later. I think this was just the foreplay to precede what was to come. I didn't know how long to go on. I didn't know if I was supposed to work towards her orgasm. But I didn't need to worry. She delicately touched my hand, and I withdrew. Without any awkwardness, no fumbling around, our bodies were now intertwined.

She had turned over, so that my mouth was facing her and she was now taking me in hers. Now here's the test. Cindy was working her clit, working in the only way Cindy knew how. Cindy knew exactly what she was doing. But the challenge was, could Cassandra draw Rachel out? Cindy was on top, but I knew this was impossible. There was just no way that Rachel would allow herself to be taken in this position, so I had to roll over.

Now Rachel is there on her back as Cassandra buries her tongue deep. And now she is using her fingers, as Rachel feels the blood running to her clit, completely engorged. Rachel is ready to give herself totally to Cassandra. Rachel is beginning to feel the moment. But Cindy is underneath Cassandra. Cindy the professional, who knows exactly what she's doing. She finds it more difficult at this angle. *Concentrate, concentrate hard*. You know where Cassandra's clit hides. You know it's small, but you don't need no phone call to Vish this time.

Cindy is nibbling. Cindy is playing. Cindy is doing what she's never done before, tapping the velvet from this position, from underneath. Rachel is ready. Rachel is about to come, but Cindy knows that she has more work to do on Cassandra. Thank goodness Cassandra has taken over. She's still dominating Rachel, but she's taken her fingers out of Rachel's cunt and moved her hand down to her own. She's now pinching her lips, exposing her clit to my tongue. We're working in unison, the three of us, Cindy bringing Cassandra up to the moment, and Cassandra is holding Rachel there, holding, asking. Is she ready to come? Who knows? Rachel, Cindy, Cassandra, we all know, as we come together with our bodies shaking.

Cassandra knows that she has to continue to take me through my 30 seconds arching, spasming. But Cindy won't stop either. Cindy is sucking hard on Cassandra's labial lips. I don't know how we managed it. Both in orgasmic convulsions and yet, somehow, managing to stay in place. We continue beyond our orgasms, just gently winding down, continuing to suck our clits - too sensitive for each other's tongues, just a gentle sucking, down into that special place, that moment of bliss after the explosion.

And Cassandra was so, so wrong. We didn't fall asleep in each other's arms. We fell asleep just lying contented with each of our heads buried deep between each other's legs.

# 36
# Mimi

To say that the journey back to London was an anti-climax would be an understatement, but it did give me time to think. Two and a half hours to think about where I was, in particular, in my relationship with Jack.

On the one hand, things were going well, I kept telling myself. He'd left his old job where he was head honcho in London for a major international bank, moving into a boutique hedge fund. It seemed like a step-down but he was now CEO of a $5 billion fund that boasted as its investors some of the wealthiest people around on this side of the Pond. I'm not a maths wizard, but even my GCSE in Arithmetic meant I could work out that their 2% annual fee was worth $100 million. On top of that, their share of the profits probably doubled their take-home. Of course, he had to share that with his partners. But, even so, that was some serious cheddar. To top it all, as he proudly told me during pillow talk one night, his share options had the potential to put him in the 3 commas league one day. It took a bit more than my GCSE Arithmetic to work out that the three commas referred to 1,000,000,000 - a Bill instead of a Mill.

Put that with the fact that I was now Jack's official plus one at corporate dinners, business trips and the like, meant that Rachel's upward social mobility was on a fast track. I so, so wanted to tell Vish. I know he would have been proud of me, to see how happy I was. But I couldn't do a face-to-face with him. He would see the charade for what it was. The shallowness of my life. But it was the plan that he had outlined and it was the path that I had chosen.

I was sitting in my Chelsea *pied à terre*, paid for by Jack, alone as usual when Jack didn't have anywhere to take me. But how could life be better, when I could sit there watching the latest Netflix programme about super yachts? Jack hadn't quite got there yet, but he did own a Sunseeker 60-footer which set him back about $250,000. He kept it moored at his pad in Barbados. The place he can't stand *Over-run with ugly sodding Canadians.* The place I love *Over-run with sexy rippling Bajans.* I'm dreaming: *One day, Jack, you'll just hand over the keys of the apartment and the yacht as my going-away present when we part company.* Carry on dreaming, Rache, that's not in Jack's nature.

I had a large bowl of gourmet chips. One of the few advantages of living in Chelsea. The corner shops only sell gourmet, no Walkers in SW3. A large glass of Malbec. Not quite the 1928 from Cassandra's cellar, but *hey ho!*

Life was sweet. The things Jack gave me, the people he introduced me to, and the social events I attended, were all worth the compromise in the bedroom. Jack knew he never pleasured me in that department, but I don't think he really cared. He was too selfish a lover. I sometimes wondered if he knew what he was missing. You know the deal: no cunny for me, no blow job for you. I still wanted to please him. As he was strictly missionary position, I had to improvise, with my own version of the plough, legs wrapped around him, feet almost touching my face. It was on one such occasion, when I got a twinge in my stomach and looked at myself in the mirror afterwards. I realised that I was putting on weight. Don't worry, notwithstanding that I chickened out of the tubal ligation, I knew pregnancy was not a factor.

Chelsea was great, but unlike in Greenwich I couldn't take the lift downstairs to the gym. Coupled with the gourmet chips and the Malbec, a little spare tyre was but a small price to pay.

Did I miss my orgasms? Did I miss a tongue that knew its way around?

Sorry, I should have said: Did I miss a tongue that new its way around!!!

From the off, Jack and I had agreed that our relationship was not exclusive. He confessed that, as he was married and continued to see his wife on his, what had become, very occasional visits to New York, he could not, in fairness, expect me not to occasionally take another lover.

Of course, I knew, and he knew that I knew, it was not actually his wife that he was referring to, but rather his various escorts whom he continued to see on the side despite our relationship.

On the one hand, he offered me the opportunity to find sexual satisfaction elsewhere, but, on the other hand, he kept me on a very tight leash. He wanted to know where I was and what I was doing every minute of the day. He expected me to be at his beck and call.

Realistically, the only time I could stray was when he was away on business on those occasions when he had elected not take me with. That tended to be New York East Coast trips when he would spend time with his family.

His next scheduled trip, a flight across the Pond, was coming up in 10 days. I would have four nights of freedom. My thoughts wandered to places I thought I'd left far behind.

I was out of practice. There was a time when I could walk into a bar, choose who I wanted, and just by flashing my *trademark smile* be assured of a friendly fuck. I could probably do the same today but had no desire to do so. What I wanted, what I desperately needed was someone who knew what they were doing. Or, as I so eloquently mentioned above, *a tongue that knew its way around*.

Where could I drum that up over the next few days? It was a mystery to me. I started flicking through my contact list of men that I knew. Lest I forgot, I had my own, not very subtle code. A letter T beside their name. Depressingly, there were very few T's on the list. And even more depressing, haven't seen any of them for some time. There was still only one man whose tongue really knew it's way around, but he was off-limits in that department.

So I was searching for new blood but had no idea where I would find it. Could not see the point of just picking up some random on the off-chance he would satisfy me. I needed to have done my homework. I needed to find someone who, if not skilled in the art of cunilingus, at least had sufficient nous to bring me to orgasm orally.

*******

I do believe in *Serendipity*. I never used to, until I learnt to spell the word. But to prove a point, I just got a text from Fiona, no, not my boss. Fiona Fontescue-Smythe. No, that wasn't her real surname, but she was so stuck up her own arsehole, that even her posh Sloane friends took the piss. Fiona had just messaged me with an invitation to lunch.

I was not part of the group. I knew I was just tolerated because of my connection with Jack. I was too much of a comer for them to ignore me, so I joined the *Ladies Who Lunch* set. Tolerated for lunch, but not the evening gatherings. I still had not graduated to that level of acceptability.

Lunch was Harvey Nicks. Where else? To make it tolerable I would play my own little games with them. Today, I decided it would be my menu game. We went around the table each one ordering. Each one declaring how much, or rather how few, calories there were in their choice of the day. Ever since the Nanny State had decreed that menus should give diners the calorie count, the LWL posse were in their element, in a race to the bottom. Smashed avocado on granary, quinoa, edamame salad, baked goat's cheese, the latter I quite fancied but it didn't fit within today's game:

"And what would Madam care to have today?"

It was my turn:

"Is the chef's burger with cheese *and* bacon? That sounds good but I would like some triple baked fries. And if you're going to bring those ketchup sachets, I need about half a dozen. Must have my greens, so a side salad with mayo, of course, full fat. Again, if it has to be those post-Covid sachets, another half dozen please."

All that adds up to 950 calories, about 50 cals more than the other five ladies combined.

I knew that when I was with these women I was going to have to eat shit. I mean in terms of the snide comments that they would make, the innuendos, the implication that I was a kept woman. So I thought if I was going to have to take that crap from them, I might as well order the shit off the menu, as well.

Now it was down to business. One of their husbands must be able to fit my quite specific requirements. Just for a night or two, while Jack was away. How the fuck was I going to find out who, if any, would qualify? I had some thoughts but was going to have to rely on chance.

The one thing that I had going for me was that they were curious about my relationship with Jack:

Fiona started: "How do you two get on? I mean there is quite an age gap."

Then Mimi: "Well, Fiona, you know what they say, older men make better lovers."

The banter went on until I got fed up:

"Sorry ladies, but I'm not going to go there. Not with Jack, so no more questions please. If you want to know about my exes, I'm an open book and I'm more than happy to tell you about some of my best lovers."

I watched one of those U.S. legal dramas once, where some attorney was cross examining and the other attorney objected, to which the judge responded: *Well, you did open the door.*

These women certainly had opened my door. I was ready to give them the salacious description that they were looking for to wet their knickers. So I went on to describe one of those exes who was able to pleasure me orally. That ex was actually an amalgam of a good-looking waste of space coupled with my Vishti's tongue.

I glanced at each of them, to gauge their reactions. Would I be able to tell if any of their partners was going to meet my rather specific requirements?

As I was describing a piece of erotic fiction, tongue licking, circling and so on, explaining or describing my orgasm, I saw them each getting hornier. But that was not my goal, so when I had finished my rendition, I announced:

"So come on, Ladies, your turn. I want to know whose hubby treats you like that."

There was a deafening silence. I thought I'd blown it. They needed some more encouragement:

"Here's the deal: lunch is on me, if one of you has a story of a bit of cunny half as good as that. I'll order another bottle of champagne, on my tab, to get the party started."

I looked directly at Mimi. When I was describing how I liked to receive oral pleasure, she was the only one out of this bunch of frustrated cows who seemed to have a clue what I was talking about.

"Go on, Mimi, I know you have something you want to get out of your system."

"Well, I must say, Richard," Mimi started to open up, "was my first experience of that sort of thing, but everything you were telling us, Rachel, fitted in with what we do."

"Do you mean," interceded Fiona "that you always have an orgasm?"

"Well, pretty much, but that's because of my *quid pro quo.*"

"Your what?" It was not a request for a description, more an irritation that Mimi had stolen my line, but she continued:

"Richard likes to open," Mimi couldn't look at us in the face, "open the back door."

I looked around the table quickly to see who amongst us was into anal. From the look on their faces, it didn't appear a popular pastime.

Fiona, the leader of the group, was not going to let Mimi off the hook and urged her to continue.

"Richard badgered me for a long time to let me do that, you know. I resisted, and he said that he would never force himself on me, but, if he could open me up in a way that I had never experienced before, would I at least consider it? And then he showed me the delights of, well, Rachel has a far better way of describing it. The answer is *yes,* I will usually have an orgasm and in return, but only as long as I do, then I let Richard take me from behind."

Fiona still wouldn't give up. "But do you enjoy it?"

I'd had enough. I got what I came for. Richard was my target. So I stepped in:

"I think Mimi has been an excellent sport in sharing. Let somebody else have a turn."

Mimi looked at me with gratitude. I was pleased with the way things were going. I was going to need Mimi onside. No one else was going to share, so we moved on to the usual topics of fashion and Kim Kardashian.

Rachel was a little upset that it was Mimi. She was quite sweet. Cindy had no such qualms, although she had been hoping that Fiona's husband would have been the target. That stuck-up cow needed bringing down a peg or two.

All I needed now was to get myself alone with Mimi. I got up to go to the loo:

"Do you want to powder your nose?"

She got the message. We went back to the ladies together nattering away like old school friends.

"Thank you so much, Rachel. You saved me there. It was getting quite embarrassing. I owe you."

"Don't be silly, Mimi. What are friends for? Let's have a drink sometime."

"Yes, I'd love to, but let me pay."

"I think I have your number. Maybe something next week. I'll give you a call."

# 37

# Richard

Strike while the iron is hot. In this case I waited two days. Long enough. When we met, late afternoon, I knew I had to get her drunk enough so that I could offer to take her home.

We were in a wine bar. I had to gauge the amount I could let her drink. More than tipsy but not wasted. As she got up from the table, her knees buckled a little:

"I'm taking you home in a taxi. I can't let you go home on your own."

She objected but really put up little resistance. The taxi home was uneventful. I was rather relieved. We were outside her house. This should be easy:

"I think I'll take you to the front door. Actually, if you don't mind, I do need to use your bathroom."

The door was opened by, oh shit, the nanny! I hadn't factored in the kids.

Richard was due home at 7. I checked that beforehand. He was going to want to put the kids to bed, or, at least, see them before they went to bed. That was probably half an hour. Now I was gonna have to stay for dinner. That wasn't in the plan. I had to gather my thoughts quickly... Mimi won't be thinking clearly. I needed to decide whether to call the whole thing off.

Richard arrived. I'm introduced. He is surprised to see me. More surprised by Mimi's inebriated state. I grabbed a moment when I saw him going into the kitchen:

"Richard, I didn't mean to impose. We were just supposed to have a few drinks and got a little carried away. I feel responsible and I couldn't let Mimi come home by herself. Let me stay with her while you go and settle your kids. I'll try and sober Mimi up, then leave you to enjoy your evening."

"Don't be silly. It looks like I owe you for looking after Mimi. The least we can do is offer you dinner. I'm sure there'll be enough."

All things considered, dinner was fairly relaxed. There was one piece of information I needed in order to move this forward: "Mimi said you were something in the City, but not banking."

"Hell, no! Worse than that - insurance. Dull."

"No, no, I'd like to hear. I bet it's all big-ticket stuff, floods, and hurricanes."

"Funny you should say that, we are in reinsurance and do do a lot of weather-related claims."

Nothing funny about that at all. I'd done my homework. Even so, the re-insurance market is big corporate stuff. I didn't know if my ploy was going to work.

"I don't suppose you are involved on the claims side?"

"As it happens, yes."

I wanted to say that nothing just happens. Again, it was my homework. That was my lead-in.

"I know this will sound trivial, but you might just be able to help me. It's not mega millions, but it's a lot of money for me. I've been at loggerheads with an insurance company and it's just gone on too long. My broker is completely hopeless. I think he's out of his depth. Could you possibly help me out? I don't really mean help me, but would you just give me half an hour over coffee? Not now. I've imposed on you enough, already. Perhaps your lunch hour, just to hear me out. I'm sure you'll have some ideas that would help me to try and resolve this thing."

I sensed resistance. I was reserving it for later. I had to move quickly. So here it comes!

*Trademark smile.*

"I'd be ever so grateful. Don't suppose it could be tomorrow or Friday."

"Yes, of course, let's do Friday. My offices are in Fenchurch Street. There's a sandwich bar across the road. Give me your phone number and I'll text you the address."

I spent the rest of the evening making sure that Mimi was OK. I had to make sure she wasn't going to get balled out by Richard for drinking too much. She was very sweet and didn't deserve a ticking off.

*******

Friday came. I was waiting downstairs in the lobby of his office building. He greeted me with a friendly kiss.

I had to get the insurance thing out of the way first. I'd made up some completely random bullshit. I just hoped it didn't sound totally implausible. Richard responded with a few random thoughts which made even less sense to me. Now I had to draw it to a close:

"You've just given me an idea. Thank you so much. I know what I'm going to do now. I'll get hold of my broker."

"I don't know what I said."

"I just needed someone to talk it through. You were just a sounding board, but I'm really grateful. Please, coffee's on me. Richard, I don't know how to say this, but you're a really friendly ear. Do you mind if I bend it again?"

*Trademark smile.*

"I hope you're not gonna make me regret this," he said, smiling back.

"We don't really know each other. What I'm going to say is a little personal. I can only really ask a man, because I need someone to look at it from a man's perspective."

"Try me, but I don't know how helpful I'll be."

"I don't think you've met Jack."

"No, but I know who is."

"And our relationship?"

"Well, not exactly."

So I enlightened him. *How some would call me a sugar babe, but I didn't see it like that. I'm really in love with the guy:*

"Although, I have to confess he does supplement my income. Oh shit! There's no point in hiding it, he pays for my Chelsea *pied à terre*. That's why I'm looking for help from a man's perspective. I'm sort of a kept woman and I don't really know what the rule book is. I know that Jack and I have a great time. I'm in love with him. He's fond of me. But, and it's a big but, I don't know if you know the expression, but he *plays away.*"

"Yes, I have heard the term."

"So here's my issue. We sort of have an understanding that we are not in an exclusive relationship. He is quite open about that. He says he doesn't mind my doing it with someone else. If I'm honest, I don't want to. I'm not really experienced in that sort of thing. This is why I'm seeking your guidance. Do you think it will improve my relationship with Jack if I have, not a lover, but how can I say, a sexual experience, perhaps just on a one-off basis? I'm getting a bit embarrassed."

"I'm not sure that I'd suggest it would be a good idea."

"I'm so glad you said that. It just didn't seem right. Who would I do it with anyway?"

I told myself not to worry. I had prepared a script for all answers, so now in the space of the next three sentences I had to turn him round.

"The problem is Jack wants me to. He wants me to do it and tell him what I've done. He doesn't want to know who I've done it with. He certainly is not the jealous type. It's a little more complicated than that. He's told me that he wants me to do it and then talk about it because it will turn him on. Do you see how that changes things?"

"I suppose it does, but you have to be willing."

"That's just the point. To be honest, I've already made up my mind to do it - for Jack. Of course, I'd never tell him who it was with, but he was so insistent. He's away on a business trip, for a few days. He wanted me to do it so that I could tell him all about it as soon as he was back."

"I'm not sure if I understand if you say you've already decided?"

"That's just the point. I know I'm going to do it, but I don't know who with. I can't just do it with anyone. It has to be with someone I trust. I don't really know anyone I can ask."

Hands across the table. Mine over his. *Trademark smile*. Look down at hands. Take one hand from his. Start stroking the other. Look up. *Trademark smile*.

But I needed a *tell*, what we call, in the business, *a buying signal*.

"You said he's away?"

That was the signal. Hammer goes down: *Sold! To the gentleman with the nice face*!

"Are you gonna help me?"

*Trademark smile*. Stroke his hands.

"I'm not sure if you're serious. "

"It's strictly one time only. It's just to help me out. I do hope you'd enjoy it. I'd want to make it pleasurable for you, but you have to know it would just be physical between us. Mimi could never know and Jack would never know that it was you."

"I'm sorry, you will have to let me think about this."

"Of course! I just don't know what will happen if Jack comes back and I haven't done what he wanted me to do. Of course, he won't end the relationship. It's just that, in a very odd way, I'd feel that I would have let him down."

I've learnt that the worst response someone can make to a sales pitch is: *Let me think about this*. If the salesman, or salesperson, has done their job properly there shouldn't be anything left to think about. Or, if the target had any concerns, things to think about, and you'd paced the sale properly, they would be raising those concerns, giving you a chance to respond.

So Richard's: *Let me think about it* meant he was not yet sold, or he was getting there, but I was pushing the agenda too quickly.

I couldn't let it ride. I didn't want to open this door, but I thought it was the only way.

"Richard, it's true when I said I'm not very experienced, but I should have said I'm very open. As long as it's someone I trust, I'm open to doing anything." And I looked up at him and repeated, "I do mean anything, there are no limits. You will be satisfied!"

"You're a very persuasive young lady, and you're very attractive, but…"

Excellent, no more *I'll think about it*. Now here come the objections. I can deal with those. The good salesmen, salesperson, loves objections. I've even done the *Objection handling* module. How do I know this shit? Who else? He used to train estate agents before he set up his property management company. Bless you, Vish. You didn't think I was paying attention, but I was absorbing every word. OK, Richard, tell me the *buts*. Is one of them going to be your butt!

"… it's really just Mimi. She's your friend."

Vish gave me a list. A script for each type of objection. I flicked through the list in my head: 'Feel, felt, found'. Go for it, Cindy!"

"Richard, I know how you *feel*. When I went through this in my mind, I *felt* the same way, but I *found* myself saying that Mimi would want to help her friends. I mean she can never know, but something inside me says, she's really OK with this. I never actually mentioned it directly, but I sort of confided in her about some of the things I might have to do to please Jack. She said she understood, that when a woman loves a man, sometimes they have to make sacrifices. Do things that they didn't really want to do, you know, for the man you love. I think in an odd sort of way, she was giving us permission."

And I think in an odd sort of way, I was dropping a heavy hint that I knew about their back door activities.

"Well, if you put it like that."

Here's what Vish calls the *alternative close*. Give them a choice, only two things, three's too complicated. Then, they are thinking which of the two things. The two things can be 'Red' or 'Blue' but mustn't be 'Yes' or 'No'.

"We've…"

Nice touch, Cindy, losing the 'I'; this has to be a joint venture from now on.

"… we've only got Tuesday or Wednesday before Jack gets back. You choose, Richard. What's better for you?"

See how I did that – two choices, Richard, *Red or Blue* not *Yes or No*.

Next rule of Vish's Sales Course: Now silence, wait for him to choose. The first one to speak, loses.

Look down. Silence. Pregnant pause. Taking a bit too long. Look him in the eye. *Trademark smile*. Don't speak. He's still pondering. But he's no longer - *if*, now it's just about - *when*.

"Wednesday. Drinks first. You choose the place, near your apartment."

Feeling quite relieved. Still not 100% that he'll go through with it. I need to do a bit more work.

"Richard, let's make sure that there aren't any more *buts*."

Now I'm still picturing his butt. Now picturing my butt. Still not sure if he's getting the double entendres.

"Let's clear the air. This thing is not gonna happen unless I can answer all your questions."

"No, I've decided. I'm OK with it."

Once we'd agreed on the day, I knew it was all plain sailing from here on in. But I still had to bed it down (forgive the pun). So, when we got up and we parted company, my final shot was:

"I did mean *anything* you know. All doors are open."

*Trademark smile.*

Depart scene left.

*******

I needed to pick up some clothes from Greenwich for my date with Richard. The Chelsea pad was convenient, but it really was a postage stamp. No storage, and just one wardrobe. On the taxi ride back I was mulling over the selection of clothes I was bringing back to Chelsea. I couldn't really make up my mind. Sexy or professional? I didn't see the point of *seductive*. There was no mystery. Richard might not know the exact details of what we would be doing but he knew that, in exchange for a few cocktails, he'd be getting a quick lay.

Oh shit! Who's going to pay for drinks? According to Cindy's very strict rules, I should pay for the drinks. In essence, I had asked him for the fuck. *Quid pro quo* and all that. But it didn't seem right. I don't mean morally right. It's more, dunno, I wanted this to be as normal a date as possible, so I thought I should let him pay. That's what he'd expect if he was picking someone up in a cocktail lounge. You know, men: *I'll buy her a few drinks, then she's bound to be up for a shag.* Or am I being too - what was that word Vish used, that so annoyed me - *obtuse*?

Back to the clothes. I'm picturing the various dresses that I'd chosen. One stood out. Not a dress, a skirt, bought for me by Rob, my first boyfriend.

I call Rob my first boyfriend because he was the first, well, what I considered a man. I was 17 and had had a few fucks and a few more fumbles by then, with children. I felt I was a fucking paedophile. I mean all the boys I'd fucked or sucked by then were all older than me, but they were kids trying to understand why having sex with a woman was better than wanking themselves off while watching porn. But Rob was different. He was 22. I thought I was really grown up. Shagging someone over 21. God how the girls at school must have hated me. I lorded it over them. How mature I was. Shagging a real man. They were desperate for me to tell them what it was like. I made out it was like heaven, but Rob had sworn me to secrecy. You know, like a silly schoolgirl pact: *Cross my heart and hope to die!*

If they actually knew what Rob liked to do, they probably *would* have died, on the spot.

I was 17, he was 22, and remember I hadn't met Cindy yet. Maybe she was always there waiting to burst out, like that scary horror film where some monster burst out of someone's tummy. Was Cindy really spawned from my granddad's seed, as Vish believed?

I was 17, he was 22, which basically meant he was Mr Experience and I was a drooling schoolgirl. No, there was no abuse. I was over the age of consent and he never forced me to do anything. Anyway, to be perfectly honest, I don't think I could have put up with half of Felicity's clients if I hadn't gone through some sort of initiation with Rob. Showing me things that I didn't...

Sorry, and excuse me if this lot gives you the creeps, but it's easier if I give you the details. First the disclaimer: *If you are of a sensitive disposition, now would be a good time to sod off!*

1. He wanks over my feet. Then licks his spunk off my toes. Odd, but again, a 17-year-old in love thinks maybe that's what all men like to do.

2. He has some kind of balsa wood thingummy, with a hole cut in it, and I'm supposed to wank him through it. Sounds painful and doesn't look too pleasant. Can't understand why that's better than my pussy, but *hey ho!*

3. Here it gets a bit dodgy. He likes to give and receive. Giving means anilingus. I didn't know what the word for it was then, or even that it was a real thing. We'd run around the playground shouting *lick my arse* but it wasn't ever intended to be, as Vish would say, *an invitation to treat.* I was OK as the receiver. Can't say I enjoyed it, but I was happy to go with the flow, so to speak. When it came to giving, I told him that he'd need to flush his arsehole with Domestos before I'd get near it. As I said, Cindy was not yet ready to come out to play, but somewhere, maybe in my Jewish genes, I was ready to negotiate. So I said: *Drop the arse licking, and you can come in my mouth.* He drove a hard bargain. So I agreed to swallow it as well.

I could go on, but I think I've painted the picture. Probably a good analogy, colourful, I'd say.

A long digression, but the point is: Rob bought me that skirt. The one now draped over the back seat of the cab with the rest of my clothes.

He said he bought it on *Lovehoney.com*. That was another thing I have Rob to thank for. I'd never have seen that site otherwise.

So what's so special about this leather skirt? Firstly, it's not short. A midi that is tighter below the knee. It has a zip at the back. But its USP is that the zip goes all the way down so you can literally open it up and the back just falls apart. So, what's the big deal? Rob, who this 17-year-old kid was soon beginning to realise was basically an arse man, wanted me to wear the skirt with nothing underneath and lie on my front while I unzipped it, gradually revealing my bare tush. Of course, I fumbled with the zip and my arms weren't long enough for me to reach and pull the zip right down anyway. I'm sure it wasn't designed for this weird kind of striptease. I was thinking of putting a review on *Lovehoney.com* but couldn't find the skirt on the site. I may have been distracted by the other stuff that's kept me stimulated, so to speak.

After the abortive skirt striptease, I'd practised on my own. I realised I could unzip it a little, then use my butt to stretch the zip so that, once I'd started to unzip, it kind of opened by itself. I wasn't sure if I was doing it the way he wanted. Never got the chance to find out. I was approaching my 18th birthday, and he had just found a 16 year old to replace me.

On the one hand, Rob was just a creep, preying on young schoolgirls. On the other hand, he did teach me a few things. Last time I saw him, he was walking along with another young kid, all St Trinian's in school uniform with laddered black stockings and nose piercings. He smiled at me, from across the street. Rachel froze. She was going to ignore him and walk on by, but Cindy couldn't resist. So I crossed the road and rummaged in the pocket of my jeans. I pulled out a crumpled £20 note and put it in his hand.

"Thanks, darling, but what's this for?"

"Commission!"

He looked puzzled, so I explained:

"Your idea. I owe you."

Then looking directly at his latest squeeze:

"Sucking their cum off my toes, dear? My clients love doin' that."

On second thoughts, I'll dump the leather skirt and stick with Vish's LBD.

# 38
# What's up, Doc?

It was Wednesday. The drink session went smoothly... He was quite relaxed. A double Jack Daniels, straight up, would have got him past first base with me, even if the sex had not been pre-arranged. Can't stand cissies who fill their glass with water. For me, two dirty martinis in quick succession were ordered to send a message, but also to help build some Dutch courage. I was pretty sure he'd done this before. The only reason he had been hesitant was because I was pushing the agenda too fast. If I had been able to control the pace, this would have been a doddle.

When we got to my apartment, I needed to lay down the ground rules. This was to make sure I got my orgasm:

"Richard, can we just be open and discuss what we're going to do here? I want to make sure you get what you want out of it, but I do believe it should be a two-way street."

"I'm not sure what you mean. I thought we were going to have sex. I'm ready to do that if you are."

"I like oral. Receiving and giving. Are you up for that? Is there anything else?"

He looked at me. I knew what was coming. It was my own fault. I'd asked for this. Although I didn't want to do it, it was the only way I could get my satisfaction.

"I'm OK to pleasure you orally. I'm used to that. I don't mind if you want to reciprocate, but, if I'm perfectly honest - and you did say that you were open to anything - I do like to penetrate a tight opening. I'm not sure if you get my drift."

I was standing, facing Richard. I half turned my head to look down at my butt and looked straight back at him with a face that said: *You mean here. Oh, Richard, you're so naughty.*

He nodded.

I took him into my bedroom and within moments we were undressed. I fancied his body, all the more because he drank his whisky straight up, but I was still nervous about the anal. It is not to my taste. I don't relax. I find it painful, but *hey ho*, Richard, you're going to give me the orgasm that I've been missing so let's see how it goes.

I wouldn't put Richard anywhere near Vishti or Cassandra, but his tongue knew its way around. That was all that mattered. He brought me to orgasm. He knew not to stop until I'd run through my contractions, so I didn't have to finish myself off. That was a relief, in more ways than one.

Now it was his turn but I had to ask.

"Do you want me to take you in my mouth first?"

"Not if you're going to make me come while you blow me."

Shit, he's not stupid after all. OK, here goes. Reach for the lube.

"Please use this and please be gentle. Just let me guide you in and I will relax."

Lube on. He's on top of me. I'm parting my legs. I can feel him throbbing. I stretch out behind. I'm holding his erection. This is difficult, but I have to keep some control. I'm trying to relax my anal sphincter but it's tensing as he starts to insert his penis. *Please let this be over with quickly.* I'm breathing quite hard. I'm trying to relax my muscles. I don't know how to do this. My instinct is to keep asking him to be gentle, but I fear that just might prolong the experience. I want to get this over with, so here goes:

"Take me, Richard, I want you deep inside. Do you want me to talk dirty?"

"Yes, you bitch, tell me you want it!"

"Fuck me, Richard, fuck me hard. Fuck my arse deeper. Fuck me harder. Hurt me! Hurt me!"

I could sense he was coming from the pace. This was painful so I didn't need to play act. I was screaming and crying:

"You're hurting me, keep fucking, fuck me harder!"

He came, withdrew immediately and went straight to the bathroom, which I thought a little discourteous. Whatever happened to *Ladies first?* I was sore. I thought I was probably bleeding. I needed to get him the fuck out of my flat.

I sat down on my comfortable chair. It's moments like these that I miss my Greenwich apartment with my *River View.* Chelsea is fine. Far more fashionable, but at moments like these, I just like to look out and dream. All I know is that I needed the orgasm. I needed someone who knew what they were doing. It didn't have to be the best, but I couldn't take a random fuck. The cost to me was a sore arse, and it was sore. Not hurt pride. Not a violation. Certainly not non-consensual. Someone could say: *she asked for it,* but not in the same sense that some misogynist would say of a drunk mini-skirted teenager that he'd just banged, that *she asked for it.* No, I had literally asked Richard to have sex with me and knew all about the *quid pro quo.* Our parting was sudden, but that was at my request. The issue I really had is that I'm not a submissive. I like to be in control and I know how to stay in control. As I've described already, I can take a penis right down my throat but still retain control. The man might believe he's taking me but I'm able to decide exactly when he comes. The issue with my most recent experience was just that: making him come quickly because I wanted to get it over with. That is not what Cindy means by *controlling when he comes!*

And now, you will think I'm crazy. Because, much as I dislike anal sex, all I'm thinking of is how can I develop a technique so that I am as accomplished in that orifice as I am in the other two.

Dare I ? Dare I? Dare I?

Am I able to seek guidance from the Oracle? The only person who will give me an answer that is honest and non-judgmental.

I decided that this was beyond the pale. Vishti would be non-judgmental, morally. But I know he wouldn't want me to put myself through that. He would think that I wanted the abuse, the punishment. I'm not sure if he would understand that I wasn't looking for pain. I actually wanted to prove that I could become the complete package and please a man every which way and more importantly, so much more important to Cindy, front or back, always to stay in control.

********

My solution came when I thought that I needed to be checked out medically just to ensure that no serious harm had befallen me. So, I took myself to the clinic that I had visited before to see the doctor who had experienced an earlier meltdown by this patient. While this was not actually his area of expertise, it seemed, quite bizarrely, appropriate for me to openly discuss with him how I could begin to enjoy anal intercourse.

I basically went to see him on an entirely bogus pretext. I had no intention of letting him perform a tubal ligation, which was his area of competence. I rationalised my deception by comparing his job to mine. I had an hourly rate, or at least a rate for the particular service, and within that hour I might perform other services that were within my area of competence, albeit not necessarily my specialisation.

The man was a doctor, would respect patient-doctor confidentiality and he was being paid for a 30-minute consultation. By my reckoning, a little white lie to get the appointment could be justified but I needed to fess up as soon as I was face to face.

"I have to be honest with you, Doc. I didn't come to see you about having a tubal ligation. It was an entirely different matter. Please don't freak out. I'd like you to check me out. I don't think I could do this with anyone else. I would just be so embarrassed."

"I'm not sure what you want me to do. Please ask, but you'll have to excuse me if I decline."

"Two days ago I had anal sex. I'm not worried about STDs. I'm confident that the partner will not give me anything. But I will get tested. That's not what I'm here for."

"I'd be happier if that was what it was. In any case, you should be tested straight away. I will take bloods, but you will also need to be tested in a few weeks. So let's get that out of the way, the blood test I mean, while you discuss whatever it was that's really on your mind."

So now he was strapping up my arm, in preparation for taking blood. He was by the side of me and I was looking straight ahead as I felt that perhaps it was better not to be looking him in the eye. I proceeded to explain that I did enjoy sex, but a lot of the enjoyment for me is to be in control. I carried on to outline, and not in any prurient way, how I was able to give very competent blow jobs, controlling the penis by holding the man's hips. And, for conventional sex, by the use of Cindy's grip, my pelvic floor muscles meant that, whether I or he was on top, the timing of his ejaculation was still in my hands, so to speak.

"The problem with anal is that it bloody hurts, and because of that I can't use, sorry, Doc, I don't have the anatomy language, those muscles to exercise control. So that's the dilemma. I believe I could be more accomplished. I would like to be able to get the same kind of pleasure from satisfying a partner as I do via the other routes. But I don't know how to achieve that. Your turn, Doc!"

"I said two things when you came in here. Firstly, not my area of expertise and second, if I didn't think I could help I would tell you. To be perfectly honest I don't think you're asking for a medical opinion. Some might say, and remember I've read your file, there are deep-seated psychological issues. As I explained to you at our earlier consultation, these are outside my area of competence."

I thought he was going to decline to help, so I gave him my puppy eyes. This was definitely not a time for my trademark smile.

He went on, "I am, in a very odd sort of way, flattered that you came to see me. I do have a piece of advice, although I can't believe I'm saying this. But can I ask you first, how often have you had anal relations?"

"As little as possible. In terms of actual full penetration, I could count on the fingers of one hand. Of course, there's been lots of fumbling but that doesn't really count."

"I think that is the problem. You don't like it, so you don't do it and then you wonder why you're no good at it. If you'll forgive the vernacular, anyone else would say *I don't like it. It hurts. End of.* I'm not sure whether to admire you or certify you. Your approach is *I don't like it. It hurts. How can I get better at it?* Please, please don't think that I am suggesting that increasing the frequency of your participation in anal sex is an appropriate course of action. But, and I'm not wearing my medical hat here, if you actually want to get good at something, there's that old adage: *Practice makes perfect.* I don't think I need to tell you that the more you can relax the less it would hurt. But you know all this. Maybe you just haven't done it enough to be able to adapt those techniques at which you seem to be so adept. If you applied yourself in the way that you so obviously have with, how should I put it, the other orifices, I sincerely believe that you would be able to accomplish your goal."

"Doc, above and beyond, and you have definitely earned that £300 consulting fee."

"Miss Levinson..."

I gave him a stern look.

"Sorry - Rachel. I won't be charging you the consultation fee. It wouldn't be right. Just the normal charge for the blood tests. And while I'm not charging you, here's a few more free tips. Use liberal lubrication. I can't speak from personal experience, but I understand, from some of my gay friends, that there is a lube out there that has a mild anaesthetic to numb the area a bit, without taking away all the sensation."

My mind went straight to *Lovehoney* and a mental note to check out the anal lubes to see which had that anaesthetic.

"I have to say, you rather impressed me there, Doc. That last point."

"The anaesthetic lube?"

"No, the bit when you said *numb the area, without taking away all the sensation.* Straight out of my playbook. I need to ease the pain, but you read my mind; I need to be able to feel what's going on too if I am going to be able to tighten and release, control the moment, feel when he's ready to ejaculate, maybe edge for a while..."

"A bit too much information, Rachel."

"Sorry, Doc. Some people would pay me £5 per minute in a chat room for that description. Thought it was the least I can do, seeing as though you're comping this consult."

He smiled an awkward smile and continued, "I can't recommend your course of action for one obvious reason: you'd be exposing yourself to unnecessary risk of STIs or STDs. And, in addition, there's risk of damage to the anal lining from frequent and aggressive anal intercourse."

I don't know what I was expecting from Doc. I'm not quite sure how he did it. He kept the tone so professional and, although he ended up giving me, essentially, non-medical advice, what he said made perfect sense.

"Thank you, Doc for giving me such a candid opinion. I can't tell you how much I trust your advice."

"I can't help feeling that's because I told you what you wanted to hear. If I told you something you didn't want to hear, you'd probably tell me to mind my own business, but in the more colourful language you normally use."

"Not true, Doc. I think I would have taken your advice whatever it was."

"Are you serious? I'm not sure I believe that."

"I don't know how I could prove it to you. I genuinely trust your advice, even when you stray to areas that are not within your expertise, as you put it."

Doc had a smile on his face as if he was thinking: *Here you are. I'm going to prove my point.* He scribbled something on a piece of paper on his desk, folded it and placed it in an envelope. He handed me the envelope.

"What's this, racing tips?"

"Call it a little test of what you just said. I'm giving you some advice that you won't find so comfortable."

"I don't care what it is, but I promise I will take it."

And with that, I took the unopened envelope and pressed it against my heart. I picked it up towards my lips and gave it a kiss.

Doc smiled, "Please, Rachel! Take this seriously. That is what we call a referral letter so that you can see a specialist."

"Gee, thanks, Doc. I'll get onto this as soon as I get back."

"If you want, I can ask my secretary to make your appointment here and now."

"Not necessary. I've given you my word."

I turned to go, then turned back. Put my hand out. He took it.

"There you are, Doc. I would never go back on that.

He smiled. I left.

In the taxi home, I open the referral letter. There was a lot of gobbledegook. But, in essence, it seemed to say I'd seen him before following a psychological assessment. It then went on to say that, although I came in for elective surgery, I chose not to proceed. It says I came back to see him, today, on an unrelated matter, but it was clear from my behaviour that the psychological issues had not been resolved. Blah di blah di bloody blah!

I re-read that last bit. But it was *clear from my behaviour that, in his non-expert, outside his medical competency, shit-hole opinion, the psychological issues had not been resolved.*

Well, Doc, you're certainly telling it like it is. I went in for some advice about how to improve my anal sex. You gave me what I thought was sound advice, that I should keep doing it until I got good at it. Made sense to me, but now it turns out that you still think I'm a nutter. Thanks a million, Doc.

I then asked the taxi driver whether I could smoke in his cab. He just pointed to the sign.

"In that case, would you mind pulling over? Just put down over here. Keep the meter running. I'll just be a few minutes and then we can continue my journey."

He nodded. I got out of the cab. I lit a cigarette. I held the letter up to my cigarette lighter and watched it disappear in a few flames and a puff of smoke. The charred remains lay on the grass verge. I stepped on them and trod the ashes into the grass. *Good fertiliser,* I thought and then muttered to myself, *"Once again, thanks Doc. I'll stick to your first suggestion about improving my anal - but no one's taking me to the fucking funny farm!"*

# 39

# Training Module

"Hello, Richard? Things seemed to have ended a bit suddenly. I don't want you to think that was your fault. I take full responsibility."

"I'm glad you phoned. I just want to make sure that we are OK, you know. I mean between us."

"Yes, let's stay friends and all that garbage. But that really isn't what I wanted to say."

"OK, so just get it out."

"Well, you know I did say, I think I may have promised, just the once..."

That's how it started. Well, I suppose you could say it had already started, when I first put the proposal to him, across the road from his office.

Now, he agreed to meet me again. Same place. That's across the road from his office, not across the road from my apartment. I chose mid-afternoon, when there's no one in the sandwich place, so we could have a bit of privacy.

"I have an issue that I want to resolve. I believe you could assist me with it, and, at the same time, I think I could be of assistance to you."

"Right, can we cut out the riddles? I think we know each other well enough, so let's cut to the chase."

"OK, no riddles. Here's the skinny. What we did was wrong!"

"Well, at least we're on the same page. I'm not avoiding responsibility, but I believe you seduced me from the off. When I think back, I now believe your plan started when Mimi got drunk. I'm beginning to think that it was you who got her drunk, just so you could be at my house to meet me and pursue your plan. I'm not sure what your agenda was. Somehow, and I don't know how, because I'm sure that Mimi would not have said anything, you seemed to know about our sex play and used that information to have sex with me. Of course, it was wrong. What is wrong with you?"

"What is wrong with *me*? That's not exactly what I meant. What was wrong, and this is what I want to correct, was the technique."

"I don't believe I'm hearing what I'm hearing."

"Please hear me out because I think I'm going to be able to help you.

No, don't interrupt me. Just hear me out."

I then outlined my theory, namely that, without boasting, I provide the best oral sex around.

"When I take someone in my mouth, I have complete control. I control the pace, speed up, slow down. I control when they come. I control how they come. OK! Yes, I am boasting, but I'm bloody good at it. Then, when it comes to my pussy, well, shall we say that I have perfected the technique. My lovers even call it…"

I nearly said *Cindy's Grip.*

"… refer to it as my *grip.* I have worked hard at my pelvic floor muscles so that when I let my lover penetrate me, I can achieve the same level of control that I have for oral…"

"I think I've heard…"

"I said to let me finish. It doesn't really matter who's on top, so to speak. I can build him up, slow him down. I am holding his erection just using my muscles inside. I decide when he's ready and he can pound me. He can fuck me, but it's the grip that gives him the most explosive orgasm."

I paused for breath, but now he was silent.

"I like you, Richard. I told you I was inexperienced. Shall we just say that was a little porkie? But, and I guess you know what's coming, if you forgive the pun. When it comes to the backdoor, I am an amateur. Yes, it was wrong for me to urge you to do it - yes. Did I seduce you? Yes. And I knew it was coming, I mean I knew anal would be involved. Yes, I'd done my homework. Yes, I admit, I wanted your tongue, and the anal was the *quid pro quo.* But, and this is why I wanted to talk to you, when it came to the anal, I was a fucking amateur. And I'm embarrassed! I can do better. I know I can do better.

"Have you finished? Because I think I've heard enough."

I ignored his intervention, and continued:

"So, let me be honest and direct. I want to improve my technique. I don't want a repetition of what we did the other day. I need practice. But I can't just practise on any random guy. This needs to be a proper programme with planned exercises. And it needs to be with someone who I can speak to, who hopefully can understand. So, here's my proposal. Depending on your stamina and your marital commitments, I'm suggesting that once a week we meet to have anal sex. My task is to achieve a level of relaxation so that I can take you without too much discomfort.

"In between sessions, I will be exercising my muscles, just like I did with my pelvic floor. I'm not sure whether I can use my Kegelly thing. I need to do a bit more research, but that's my job, not yours. Your job is simple: come over once a week and fuck me in the arse. Perhaps a little feedback would be nice, but to be honest, once I get the hang of it, I will know how much you're enjoying it. I'm guessing, but I can't be sure, I can't see how I can get where I want to be in less than six sessions. So unless you want to up that to two a week, it'll be a six-week commitment on your part."

"Have you finished?" I detected a slightly angry tone in Richard's voice, but I still ignored him.

"I want to be able to take you to places you've never been. I want to be able to hold you tight while you slide in and out. I want to grip you and ease you gently, to let you slow down then, by just using my muscles, bring you back up and hard again. To continue to squeeze you. To feel you when you're coming and to hold you back for more. To keep repeating the hardening and softening to bring you back to the edge. Taking you to the point of orgasm and then taking you down just a peg, taking it back up again, repeating as many times as you can take, until I think you're ready. And then let you take me, hard and deep, until you explode into an ecstatic orgasm."

I think I was capturing his attention.

"One day a week, just the anal sex? What about the other thing? I think I gave you something you quite enjoyed," he replied.

"Before I answer that, I have just one question. Answer me, and I'll answer yours."

"OK."

"This anal thing with you. Is it a homo erotic experience? Just indulge me. I have a reason. Then I'll move on."

"I don't know, but I don't think so. I don't think I'm gay. In fact, I know I'm not gay. I don't fancy men. I think the anal thing relates to wanting tightness."

"I'm glad you said that. The answer to your question is *No*. This is strictly business. I'm not looking for you to pleasure me. But, if you are ready to accept my terms, I can explain how I will improve your life."

"This gets more interesting, intriguing, by the minute."

"We both love Mimi and I don't want to come between you. In fact, I believe I can improve your love life. I keep mentioning my pelvic floor muscles. I work very hard to keep myself tight and firm down there. I'm suggesting I assist Mimi in that direction. She starts with the disadvantage of having had a couple kids. I don't mean to be funny. It's just that having a loose vagina is very common after childbirth."

"So how are you going to get her to do the exercises?"

"I honestly don't know at the moment. Let me worry about that. What I would like you to do is to pay attention to how she is with you. The ultimate goal for you two is to move towards more conventional sex. She's not keen on anal. Maybe, you can cut it down to once in a while, for a bit of a variety. If I'm doing my job and Mimi is doing hers, you should notice the physical difference over the six weeks of our project."

"This is one of the most bizarre proposals I've ever heard, but I have to admit to some fascination. Can I just see if I've got this right? If I can't say it with a straight face, it's not because I'm not taking it seriously, it's just that you have to admit it is a bit weird."

"Go on, summarise."

"Well, the first part you've been pretty clear on. You offered me, the husband of your best friend."

"I said friends."

"Best friends, friends. Still, you invited me to have sex with you. By your own admission, that wasn't a pleasant experience for you."

"Half of it was very pleasant."

"OK, but the half that was unpleasant was actually violent and painful."

"You missed something - my initial motive."

"Yes, sorry, I omitted to mention that you somehow, I don't know, what, by bugging my house, you knew what Mimi and I got up to in the bedroom. I know you didn't bug my house. The information could only have come from Mimi. I think you are conniving. I think somehow you managed, in the same way as you seduced me, to get that out of Mimi. At the risk of your withdrawing your proposal, I have to say you strike me as a very unpleasant, scheming..."

He hesitated. I knew what was coming so I finished the sentence for him.

"Go on say it. You said it to me before when you were piercing my backside. Go on use the B word. Perhaps that's what I am. OK, I'll tell you, yes, you're right. But you know that it was at Harvey Nicks with the other Ladies Who Lunch."

"Who?"

"The Ladies Who Lunch. You know, the set led by Fiona Fontescue-Smythe."

"That's not her surname."

"No, but that's what even her friends call her. Anyway, when the girls have lunch there's usually a few glasses of champagne and a bit of tittle tattle. And I can't deny it. I wanted to find out which of their husbands would eat them out. I wanted to find that out because I was missing that part with my current partner."

"Jack?"

"Yes, I'm sure I have already said, Jack and I are not exclusive. And I miss my orgasms. I was prepared, just once, to exchange an orgasm for anal sex. I went through – well, I went through, with you, the pain and the humiliation on the off-chance that you could give me the pleasure I'd been missing.

"Off-chance?"

"No, you're right. Poor choice of words. I *am* a scheming bitch! I planned the whole thing and bugger the consequences for your marriage. Now, I'm trying to make amends because I honestly believe that if you carry on forcing yourself on Mimi…"

"That's unfair! I never force her."

"No, maybe not. I'm sorry, but what I mean is she doesn't enjoy it. Sooner or later something will snap. It seems so unnecessary, when I could help her to address what appears to be a physical issue suffered by so many women after childbirth."

"What are you, some kind of physiotherapist or sex therapist?"

"Richard, you're annoyed with me. I get that. My motives at the beginning were not pure."

He let out a belly laugh.

"Shall we get back to your analysis?"

"Yes, I'm going to finish off, don't worry. You were saying that you were prepared to put up with the pain and humiliation in exchange for one orgasm. I guess there's no accounting for taste. But there was more. In some weird, perverted way - and I'm sorry I have to describe it like this - you decided, and perhaps you're right, the reason that experience was so physically painful for you was because you haven't learned how to enjoy anal sex. A normal person might very well decide it wasn't worth it and leave it at that. But if you wanted to see me again, you could have used that technique that you are so good at."

"Sorry, what technique?"

"Deception. You probably could have got me with another BS story about insurance or some such crap."

I smiled, but he wasn't returning the smile.

"And then flatter me, tell me how wonderful I was, seduce me again. But no, you opted for that rare commodity, well, rare in your life…"

He paused for dramatic effect but let me finish the sentence.

"Telling the truth?"

"Yes, that is exactly what I was going to say."

"Well, I am going to flatter you now, Richard."

"Go on, here it comes, more BS. Go on, flatter me!"

"I was going to say you got that out without cracking your face."

"What do you mean?"

"You said that you thought the thing was so absurd that you might not be able to say it without laughing."

"So what?"

"I'm just flattering you, Richard. You're so clever that you could work all that out and then say something that you find absurd, without laughing."

He looked bemused.

"It's a compliment, Richard. Take it at face value!"

At last his frown left him, and he smiled. And I thought: *Thank God for that!*

I decided now was the time to give him:

*Trademark smile.*

"Has anybody ever told you that you have the most sexy smile?"

"I don't know what you mean. That's just my natural look. I'm sorry if you find it so beguiling. I will make sure that I frown at you in future."

He was smiling now. He was softening up.

"I don't know. There's something about you that means I can't stay angry with you for too long. I think you're weird, but I have to admit I do enjoy your company. I like the way you are so open about sex. I also like your sense of humour."

"So that's a yes?"

*Trademark smile.*

Richard was now laughing and laughing and laughing, so he can barely get the words out.

"You… you just made me an offer too good to refuse."

"Do you trust me, Richard?"

"What do you mean?"

"To keep my end of the bargain. To mentor Mimi. To guide her through those exercises, to improve your sex life, for your mutual satisfaction."

"Yes, in some weird and wonderful way, I do trust you. I trust this weird, perverted scheming bitch to carry out her side of the bargain. Shall we fix dates?"

After leaving Richard, having compared diaries, I had to reflect on that conversation. But I also wondered whether I could see Richard, have sex with him, even if the sex was, how should we say, contrived, and for Rachel not to develop feelings for him. Cindy, and it was really Cindy who took over as the scheming bitch, didn't really care. She takes life as it comes. To hell with it! Let's see!

\*\*\*\*\*\*\*\*

"Can I tell you something, in sort of confidence? I'm not looking after myself."

"What do you mean and why in confidence?"

"I've stopped going to the gym. I'm putting on weight. I don't normally confide in people. Well, I suppose it's not really confidential. Anybody looking at me will know I've put on weight."

"I hadn't noticed."

"You're being too kind."

"You seem to be in control, Rachel, that's what I like about you. You always look like you're taking care of yourself."

"Yes, you're right. I do. Here's the confidential bit. When I was a gym bunny, I was chatting to one of the girls at the gym and she told me something about Kegel balls."

"What?"

"Yes, I hadn't heard of them either. We were talking about pelvic floor exercises. You have to strengthen your muscles down there. It is supposed to help you enjoy sex. I think it works for both partners. Anyway, I did a little research. I found this device on *lovehoney.com*.

"Oh, you are saucy."

"Well, yes, but it is designed for a medical purpose. Anyway this device, it's like a couple of balls, you insert inside you. Then you have this phone app and you can control it remotely. It sort of vibrates or rather pulses so you tense your muscles. It's very clever because you can even programme your own workout."

Mimi was giggling, either in embarrassment or disbelief.

"You're kidding me. Remote control by phone app. How is that possible?"

"You use your phone for Apple Pay, or contactless, tap & go. How does that work? I'm not a techy."

"But does it work. I mean to tighten things down there?"

"I suppose you'd have to ask my lovers ..." We started to giggle. "Yes, it bloody does. I don't want to boast. And I don't want to break my rule, you know, not talking about sex with my current partner..."

"Jack?"

"Yes, Jack. This was all before Jack. I was with a guy and our sex began to take off."

"You mean just from a few sessions with the... what did you call it?"

"Kegel balls. Not a few sessions. I don't want to put you off. It's only 10 minutes a day. But you do have to keep it up. I've done a bit of research. It could take weeks or months. I also discovered, I don't know if it's relevant in your case, but it's actually quite normal, vaginal laxity, after childbirth. I don't know why the NHS doesn't include this in post-natal classes."

"Well, they do do the pelvic floor bit, but I think so many women don't take it seriously enough. I know I didn't."

"No, I mean the NHS giving women the Kegel balls for free. I bet *Lovehoney* would give them a discount!"

"Do you think this will help me with Richard?"

"What do you mean?"

"Well, do you think he has to, you know, stick it up my bottom, because he can't feel anything when he puts it in the other place?"

"I don't know Richard well enough, but he is a man!"

We share a laugh which develops into girly giggles and in the spirit of the moment...

"I'd give you my Kegel balls, only I don't think you'd want to use them after they've been up my pussy."

The laughing continues.

"That could be a turn on!"

We were falling about so much, the people in the bar were starting to look at us. We finally settled down and I looked at Mimi, who straightened up.

"I have a feeling that what you have just said could save my marriage." She said musingly.

"Why do you say that?"

"I don't know how much longer I can go on with this anal thing. I really find it unpleasant, actually worse; I find it quite painful."

I was going to say: *Tell me about it!* but thought I'd change the subject.

"I'll send you the link on the *Lovehoney* site. Let's move on. Tell me some more gossip about Fiona Fontescue-Smythe's absurd life!"

More giggles.

# 40
## Anal 101

"Can you tell me what I'm supposed to do. Be gentle or fuck you to this side of Christmas?"

"Don't suppose there's an in-between. Seriously, all I really want you to do is follow my lead. My job is to stop you getting so carried away that I end up not being able to sit down for a week.

Richard smiles.

"But at the same time, you have to enjoy the sex."

"Rachel you're so weird but I do love you. I thought women needed to be warmed up first and it was men that were constantly at the ready. But even us men take a bit of warming up."

He looked down, so I could see his limp dick, under his trousers.

"Well, if it's warming up you want..."

And then I proceeded to undress him slowly, until he was lying on the bed completely naked. I then started to undress myself, in a sexy stripper style, bumping and grinding, singing *Hey, big spender!*

Now I'm on top of him with my pussy in his face, gyrating. I start to rub my moist pussy lips up and down from his own lips to his nose. He reciprocates and starts to use his tongue. I move away.

"Do you know the clapping song? It's an old song starts off: *369 - the goose drank wine - the monkey chewed tobacco on the streetcar line.*"

"I think so, not sure."

"It's all sexual innuendo. It actually refers to 69. The goose is the man, you know drinking her nectar as he pleasures her orally. The monkey is the woman chewing at his member."

"Are you serious?"

"Well, you never know with me, do you? I was just looking for a segue."

"A segue to what?"

"Soixant-neuf, Lover!"

I knew I would enjoy that. I also knew there was no risk of my coming in this position. As for Richard, I would stay in complete control. I waited for the moment to come when I knew he was ready. I hoped that I had prepped suitably. Ever the professional, I had done my homework. For me, this wasn't a casual encounter. I was deadly serious. I took it as a mark of pride if I was to be able to add anal to my repertoire.

No, I was not going to go that far - I was not about to add *anal* to my off-label services at Felicity's. I was really doing this for me to prove to myself: Best at O. Best at V. Soon to be best at A. I didn't even know who my partner would be. I hadn't really thought about that.

********

My mind was wandering back to my solo practice sessions since the first episode with Richard.

*Thanks to Doc, I had searched anal lube on* Lovehoney.com. *I discovered Doctor Johnson's (other anal lubes are available). Funnily enough, I'm sure that June mentioned it years ago when we were chatting, half-jokingly, about how to keep a client's knob away from your backside, but I didn't pay much attention back then. It's what it says on the tin. Relaxing gel. It slightly numbs the anus. I was pretty sure it was going to work because, and this won't surprise you, I'd been practising all week.*

*Once I decided that Richard was up for it, I realised that one session a week was not going to be enough. I'd cast my mind back to the piano lessons when I was a child. I really enjoyed the lessons. I'd been taught a new tune. Then the piano teacher told me to go home and practice. Of course, we didn't have a piano, so Mum used to take me around to my aunt's. She was ready to take me there every day, bless her. But I was a stupid kid and didn't want to practice, so I told her that my uncle would come home before I finished my lesson and he creeped me out. Poor sod! He was completely innocent. But what with my granddad and all that, I knew all about dirty old men. So I stopped the piano practice. I felt sorry for the old fucker when, some time later, at a family wedding, he asked mum to dance. She gave him such a look and nearly fell off her chair.*

*Still, I'm not that stupid kid anymore. The lessons were to come once a week with Richard, but the practice I had to do daily. I had already decided that the weekly Richard sessions were more about monitoring my progress than improving my technique. So the daily practice, solo, meant back to* lovehoney.com, *to checkout their website. I spent about £200 on a variety of anal vibrators. Then the anal lube. I started with just a few beads on my finger. I tried different lubes with and without the anaesthetic. It was important that I retained sensation. I experimented, as I didn't really know how much to use. It took me a few days to get the dosage right. I started with one finger, then a second. I looked at the display of the range of toys I'd laid out on the bed. Too much choice. I settled on a simple one to start with. They were laid out in order of size. When I saw the last one, it made me shudder. But I didn't think it was going to be necessary, because I'd never seen a cock that size in real life.*

*So I'd swapped my nightly solo wanks for a bit of anal tickling. Of course, doing it myself meant I could control the speed and the pace. God gave me two hands, so my clit didn't have to feel left out. But since the whole purpose of the exercise was to teach my muscles to flex, I needed to focus on my anus. Once I got the hang of it, my fingers on my clit were getting better co-ordinated with the dildo which I was using to fuck my arse.*

*By about the third day of practice, I was using two vibrators. The rabbit at the front, to keep my clit happy, G-spot still not throbbing in unison, so I settled for turning up the speed on the vibrator in my vag while the one in my bum was on pulse. It was all a bit fiddly and wasn't doing much for me while I was adjusting speeds and modes. But once I'd settled on the right combination, I just lay back and enjoyed it. I needed to press the rabbit ears against my clit for optimum effect. The vag was set at no. 3 out of 4 speed settings while my anus preferred a medium setting for the pulsing. It was beginning to work pretty well. Just one more thing before I was ready. Who was going to join me? I could have chosen Vishti. Always a good fantasy for an explosive orgasm. But as I was feeling the pulsing in my rear, and beginning to feel a throbbing on my G, I was back at Jimmy's. I was in the suite at the George Cinq, I was holding Cassandra. Fantasy, remember: I can have both hands on the dildos and still be hugging and caressing Cassandra. Now it was happening. Now I was understanding, yes, clit, G and now the complete package,* as I heard Cassandra's seductive voice imploring me: I'm fucking your arse now, tell me you want it. *Now deeper, no longer playing around the edges, it's Cassandra fucking me with the dildo. I hear myself screaming out loud:* I'm coming, keep fucking, keep fucking my arse, deeper, deeper, now, now!

*I just collapsed and almost shat the dildo out of my arse as I took the rabbit vibrator out of my pussy. I'd just had the most rapturous solo of my life. I guess I fell asleep, as the next thing I knew I was woken by these whirring sounds. I was confused for a moment until I realised I'd forgotten to switch the dildos off. Momentarily, I wasn't sure where I was. Then I remembered:* Thank goodness I'm in Greenwich. Couldn't do this in my Chelsea pad.

*I got up, still naked, grabbing the silk gown that Cassandra had bought me. Went into my living room. Across to the drinks trolley. There's always a clean glass sitting there. No corkscrew necessary for my screw-top £5.99 Sainsbury's best Malbec. Now sitting on the couch. Looking out at the only thing that keeps me alive during solo moments like this. My very own* River View. *Sipping my wine, I laid the glass down on the coffee table. I picked up my phone to scroll through my playlist, jambox at the ready. I pressed play and started to listen to the only track that met this moment, the throbbing tones of Frankie Goes To Hollywood belting out:* Relax, don't do it, when you want to go to it. Relax, don't do it, when you want to come!

*******

Still exhausted at the thought of my practice session orgasm, I returned my thoughts and energy to the Richard session. With the 69, his member was now throbbing from my circling tongue. It was certainly ready and willing.

"Stay with me here, Lover. I want you to lie on your back. I'm going to get on top of you. I'm going to try reverse cowgirl. It's a bit of a bummer, because I can't look at you and I get turned on when I see a man really horny. But from my research to date, this may be the best position."

I might have to change position. I'm sitting on Richard but with my back to him. His penis is now positioned over my lubricated anus. I'm trying to slide it in. It's not working. Why the fuck did I think *reverse cowgirl* was the right position. I turned around. Now I'm sitting facing him. It's working, this time I could feel him. Doctor Johnson where have you been all my life? My muscles are working. I hadn't realised that the Kegel exercises for my pussy were also helping with the muscles around my anus.

I was squeezing. I could feel him throbbing. I was shouting: *Come on, Lover! Keep banging my tight hole. Who's your bitch now, then?* I saw the look on his face. He was turned on. Doctor Johnson was doing his thing. I could feel his cock. It wasn't painful this time. It still wasn't pleasurable, not compared to my solo, when I was penetrating myself from both ends.

But this was about proving that I could keep the man under control and use my grip to turn him on. I remember thinking: *You're getting good at this, Cindy*, as I slowed him down to make sure that he didn't come too soon then used my muscles to bring him back up. I did it once more before I let him explode inside me. I withdrew his penis, got off him and excused myself to go to the loo. This time I decided I'd go first.

He smiled sweetly and just lay there in post-orgasmic stupor. I sat on the loo and looked across at the rubber tube and water container – the enema I'd used earlier to thoroughly clean myself out. That was an experience I could have lived without. Sort of diarrhoea without the tummy bug.

I cast my mind back to the time in Felicity's with that obnoxious client. It was only once. The client had paid for a BDSM session. This was a menu item but not on the website. We charged £200 for half hour's treatment. I didn't really understand it because I think they could get an enema legitimately on the NHS, except they'd have to blag their way to tell the GP they suffered from dreadful constipation.

Anyway, the deal with the client was I had to dress up in a nurse's uniform. Fi had one in the staff room. I didn't mind, but I hadn't done it before and I didn't know what to expect. I set up the enema in the shower room. The client knew what he was doing, so helped me out. I really didn't like that. I was supposed to be in charge, but I didn't know how far up the rubber tube should go. I had had colonic irrigation before, at the Medispa, where you're lying on your side and the therapist inserted the tube quite high up the canal. You can feel the water flowing up. It's a very odd feeling but when it's done in the proper environment, with the right equipment, all the inside stuff flows back out through the tube, so it's really not messy. You're guided to the loo next door to get rid of anything else. It is a sterile environment. It's a proper treatment and it doesn't cost £200.

That's not what you get at Felicity's. You can't do this on the couch. There's no machine with a tube for the stuff to go into. He's standing in the shower, while I'm inserting the tube. I suggested that he sit on the loo. He said he knew what he was doing and that as soon as it was ready, he would move to the loo. Well, fuck that for a game of soldiers! Either he misjudged, or he was just an arsehole. While in the shower he just started to shit. It was all gooey and I just pushed him onto the loo. He was actually laughing, not embarrassed at all. There was shit, or rather brown water, all over the floor. It stunk. It was disgusting. He had the decency to wipe himself. Then he had the audacity to say that he was going to lie on the bed for me to do the massage. I looked at him and asked: *Who's gonna clear up that mess?* He just looked at me blankly: *Sorry, love, that's your job.* I wanted to kick him out there and then, but I thought that he was right. I did the massage. I couldn't get him out of the room quickly enough. I went to the staffroom to get the bleach and bumped into Fi on my way there. I told her to cancel my next client or, if not, to find another girl. Told her I was sorry but I had some tidying up to do. She looked at me. I think she knew. This bugger had been in before.

"Don't worry, love, no problem," she sympathised.

"Do me a favour, Fi, block that guy from my list. If it was up to me, I wouldn't let him in here again."

"I might take your advice, love. I think he's a liberty taker. We all have our demons."

*We all have our demons.* That phrase rung though me, but I couldn't place where I'd heard it before.

I cleaned the place up as best I could. It looked OK, but it still stunk and I wasn't sure whether that was just the smell in my nostrils or whether it was the room. I took a can of air freshener and sprayed and sprayed and sprayed until the can was empty.

That was then, this is now. The enema I gave myself earlier had cleaned me out well, so I had no fear of any accidents while engaging with Richard. I went back into the bedroom. He had one of those stupid grins that men wear to indicate that they have enjoyed the moment.

"Rachel, I don't think you're gonna need any more lessons. I think you now can add that third orifice to your CV."

I smiled, but actually thought he was quite right.

"That's so disappointing. I knew if I was too good you wouldn't want to come back to help me with more lessons."

"Who said anything about lessons? I'll see you back here, same time next week."

We continued to see each other. My excuse was… what did Doc say? *Practice makes perfect.* So, even though I considered myself adept at the art of anal intercourse, I felt that a few more sessions would certainly improve the technique.

*******

Richard arrived for our sixth and final session. The sex was just anal. He'd offered to pleasure me first, but, you know, Cindy's stupid rules. Keep it professional. That wasn't the only reason to keep it professional.

I was falling for Richard, and I really didn't want to go there.

The anal was pleasurable. I don't think I have the right nerve endings, so it was never pleasure in the physical sense. It was the same pleasure I got out of giving a blow job. For me, it was such a turn on. I know it's supposed to be all about my childhood abuse, me wanting to control men, but I enjoy giving them pleasure. I enjoy the look on their face as they're coming. It's the same for me with anal. Once the pain had been removed from the equation, I got the same satisfaction seeing them enjoying it, watching them come, and always knowing that I was in control. At the moment of ejaculation, with me sitting on top, pumping to squeeze every last drop as they spurt into me. Watching them squirm while spasming in ecstasy.

So, so glad that the reverse cowgirl wasn't the natural position for anal.

"How are things going with Mimi. Has the straight sex improved?"

"Yes, I should have thanked you. Apparently, you've been a wonderful teacher, or inspiration. I think I'm cured of the anal obsession, at least with Mimi. Not sure whether I'm ready to give up anal with you, though."

I ignored the last comment.

"Anything I can do save your marriage! Now you're cured."

"Well, I confessed to missing anal a bit and she said we could do it once in a while, just for a change."

*Yes,* I thought, *you can thank me for that suggestion, as well.*

"But yes, I am engaging in, as you quaintly put it, conventional sex with Mimi."

"I hope that doesn't mean you've stopped eating her out."

"No, I'm not that selfish. Something I've wanted to ask you. How do you know what you're better at: Vag or anal?"

"Run that by me again?"

This was new. Richard about to quiz me on the finer arts of sexual excitement.

"Obviously, you're good. You know you're good. You can even see from the look on my face, when you've hit the right button, how close I am to coming. You can probably rate your performance from one to ten based on the dilation of my pupils."

"Well, I wouldn't exactly go that far."

"Don't underestimate yourself..." He smiled. "But you don't know whether that's better or worse than, what you like to call, conventional sexual intercourse."

"Of course, I can tell which is better, which you enjoy more."

"But that's just my point. You've never seen me that way because we've never fucked!"

"Are you saying what I think you're saying?"

"Well, yes let's face it. What is today's session for? This is the sixth and final session. Let's not kid ourselves. However this started, we just enjoy the sessions. If you decide this is the last one, I need to say *if*, let's see whether you're tantalising me more with the big A rather than the big V. That's your challenge. I know you like a challenge."

"I'm not so sure, Richard. I'm not sure I want to go there. I'm rather concerned that it might lead us down a path that we don't want to go down."

"Well, if this is to be our last session, let's go out with a bang!"

Of course, I wanted to do it. Of course, the same thing had been on my mind. I wanted to see how far I'd come. To compare the A and the V, as he would put it.

But it was more than that. If this was to be the last time, I wanted him not as an academic exercise, but as a lover. So that required some courting, seduction, foreplay, before moving forward, when we were both warmed up and ready.

I'm sure Richard would have been quite happy for me to just grab his hand, pull him into the bedroom and go at it like rabbits. But that was not my style and, if this really was going to be the last time, it had to be memorable.

"Richard, you've made a fair point, but you know I can't let this happen. I want to part as friends. I've decided, and it is for me to decide, how our last meeting together should be played out. I'm not looking for arguments, but, at the same time, please respect my decision."

He looked at me, sort of a resigned look. Of course, there was disappointment, but really what was he expecting?

So we sat down on the sofa. I volunteered to get him a farewell drink, my favourite: Malbec. I knew he would only have one glass. I would maybe have a couple. He made some kind of mock toast and, after a couple of minutes, I poured my second. He was still halfway through his first glass. I picked up the glass again.

"Here's to us and what could have been!"

We chinked glasses and looked at each other. I put down my glass and waited for him to put down his. We stared into each other's eyes.

*Trademark smile.*

"Come here, lover boy."

I grabbed him close on the sofa, pressed my lips to his and we kissed for the first time, since all previous contacts had been the classic Cindy non-date dates. A passionate kiss. I nibbled at his lip. I sunk my tongue deep in his mouth. He wanted to push my tongue back and circle my mouth. We played a bit of a game and the kiss lingered. My thought was how to move from here to the bedroom. I knew, left to his own devices, it would end up as a fumble on the sofa. No way!

"Richard, that was perhaps the nicest farewell kiss I've ever… Would you just excuse me, please, just for 30 seconds, no more than a minute. Just wait there. Finish your drink."

*Trademark smile.*

I move to the bedroom. My clothes are now on the floor, except my robe, my silk robe that Jack had bought me, similar to the one I had worn at Cassandra's, at Jimmy's, except this one fitted. I left it loosely hanging untied, so it exposed my nudity underneath. I opened the bedroom door. Richard was still on the sofa, dutifully obeying my directions. I stood there with my finger over my lips to indicate silence and then I beckoned him into the bedroom. I slowly undressed him until he was naked from the waist up. I then carefully unzipped and removed his trousers. His shoes had already disappeared. Socks are always a nuisance, they're fiddly to get off. If you leave it to the man, he ends up half tripping over while he's trying to get them off himself, standing stalk like. But I've never mastered the technique of removing them sensually. Sod it! I left them on. Now his pants are below his knees and I am kneeling down. His member is standing up. I take him in my mouth. I don't like to interrupt the flow with useless words but Richard had to understand where we were going, so briefly: *I'm not gonna let you come like this. You're going to come inside me. Just relax and let me do my work.* I took him up. I took him down. I was edging him. I took him to places he'd never been before. I have a nice touch where I keep sucking gently while manoeuvring my partner from standing position onto the bed. It's a Cindy special, seamlessly guiding them. It takes some skill not to break the momentum. I was out of practice, so I gave it a miss. Made a mental note to get back into that.

So Plan B: the Cindy push. I hold his hips, withdraw my mouth. Then, making sure he's close enough to the bed, I firmly push him so he falls backwards onto the bed and take him back in my mouth to resume fellatio until I'm ready to slide up the bed until I'm lying on top of him. Now I guide myself into him and start to ride. He wants to thrust. I let him take control for maybe 15 seconds. I look at him and mouth softly: *Just lie back and let me…*

He's now lying there. I start to hold him using my muscles, using Cindy's grip. He's in a different place. I'm now gripping and he is thrusting from beneath me. I'm now moving more quickly, up and down, releasing the grip, tightening the grip. I'm thrusting, almost bouncing. I'm saying to myself: *This is for him, not my orgasm.* But I can feel my clit throbbing as it's rubbing against him. I don't really understand. I can usually feel something in this position but it's never brought me to orgasm. This is somehow different. I start moving more rapidly. I don't think I'd gripped him hard. I am watching his face. I am telling myself to slow down, to ease up. I don't want him to come too soon, but while I am saying slow down, I am speeding up. My clit is throbbing. But I am feeling something somewhere else. A feeling I had not experienced since my evening with Cassandra. His penis is rubbing against my G spot. I realise that we are a perfect fit. He is as accomplished in this position as he was when he sucked me the first time. I have a decision to make; I am coming but I need to be in control for him.

Think! You've done this before. George Cinq. Cassandra has shown you. I can do this now. Rachel relaxes and just breathes, feeling my clit and my G spot, while Cindy is riding Richard keeping full control over his orgasm. And then I feel him inside me, I look into his face. He is now moving quite violently as I feel his fluid spurting inside me. Cindy is pumping, and Rachel is coming. The three of us: Richard exploding inside and me - Cindy and Rachel together - just screaming out D*on't stop! Don't stop!*

I keep bouncing. He keeps thrusting. All I can think is *Stay hard! Stay hard!* I may actually have shouted the words out loud. I need 30 seconds, just the 30 seconds, as I am in rapture. I am having a clitoral orgasm while my vagina is exploding at the same time. I can't describe it. Cassandra isn't there, but she is. Then I'm looking at Richard's face. Another contraction. His spunk fully drained. Stay hard till I get to the end. Yes! Yes! I collapse onto his body. He wraps his arms around me. I am exhausted. He is still inside me, although I can feel him going soft.

"Stay, stay there. Leave it there."

I pull myself towards his mouth and give him a gentle kiss. Not the passionate kiss we shared before, just a *that-was-wonderful* type of kiss. I want to say: *We came together, that's never happened to me before.* But this is not the time for a post mortem. This isn't part of a recap for Cindy's Teaching Module Lesson 6. This is a time to fall asleep in my lover's arms.

I think we slept for an hour or so. Or, at least, I did. When I stirred, he was already dressed.

# 41

# Decision Tree

"I wanted to say something when I came here this evening, but I didn't know how to say it and I thought you'd laugh."

I looked up, sat on the side of the bed. I think I knew what was coming. I held out my hands, so that he could take them. He looked at me.

"Rachel, I'm in love with you. I've known this for a few weeks now. I've held back because I know you and Mimi are friends. But I've decided I'm leaving her. I want to be with you. I think I want to spend the rest of my life with you. I'm not proposing, but I would like to find a flat together. Or, if you'd have me, move in with you for the time being."

"I am with Jack. You know I am with Jack."

"You don't love him. You know you don't. You don't enjoy sex with him. You've never admitted it, but I can see it on your face. What we just did, that wasn't sex that was passionate love. After that, you can't tell me that you don't love me. We have to be together. I'm ready to tell Mimi now."

No-one has been able to read me like this since Vish. He was right, of course. I was in love with him. He had made me an offer that I couldn't refuse.

"Don't be silly. Don't talk like this. I can't leave Jack. He looks after me."

"He looks after you like a child. Yes, he buys you toys. No, I can't support that lifestyle. I can't buy you expensive jewellery. I can't take you on private jets. Rachel, that's not you. I can give you love. I can give you companionship. And, yes, I can give you the most ecstatic sex. We joked earlier about you reading my face to see if I was enjoying it. I read your face. But that's not what I'm proposing. I'm not proposing popping over every week for great sex. That time is over. I'm offering you my life. You cannot refuse. I won't let you refuse."

"Richard, oh, Richard! You're messing with my head. Have you told Mimi?"

"No! Not yet. Of course, I had to speak to you first."

"Promise me you won't tell Mimi until I've made up my mind. Promise me, Richard!"

"Yes, yes, I promise. But how long do I have to wait?"

"Two days, no more. I have to think this through. This is a big decision for me. I need to take it seriously. I haven't even checked the lease."

"What do you mean the lease?"

"I need to tell you the rent you have to pay. Can't really expect Jack to continue paying. Also, I need to get my last month's statement from Harrods, so you can see the bill that Jack pays for as well."

For a moment, Richard looked stunned. Then the amazed expression turned to a smile and we started laughing together.

"For a moment I thought you were serious. You told me you still had your flat in Greenwich. Of course, I'd find a place, but I thought we could start off there."

"One step at a time. We can sort out the details later. That's not the issue. Let me be serious, for a change. I need two days. I need to go through all of this, in my head. My relationship with Jack. Your relationship with Mimi. You have to let me. You have to give me time. It has to be my decision."

Those were the longest two days of my life. I was agonising. I knew I had to make a choice. That was why I limited myself to two days. I had to weigh up the lifestyle with Jack, which I'd become accustomed to. I knew there were drawbacks. The Ladies Who Lunch. I wasn't part of their team; I could probably live with being ostracised by them. But no Jack? Jack knew how to wine and dine a girl. Was I ready to give up the private jets, the flat in Barbados, the Sunseeker yacht, the fun of the charity auctions? Doesn't sound a lot, I know, but I was in a different place with Jack. A place I could never have imagined he'd have taken me to. Places, and I don't mean physical places; he'd shown me an amazing lifestyle. Was I really ready to give that up?

What was I comparing that to? A future with Richard. Well, not exactly a life of poverty. Richard was financially comfortable. Of course, I knew he would be less well off if he had to support two households. But that wasn't terribly relevant. I had more than enough to support us both. Richard was offering me real companionship. Yes, the sex was so much better. We had only just started to explore our sexual experiences together. Based on today's performance, Richard and I could look forward to more fulfilling ecstatic episodes. I never thought I'd think this, but I could actually imagine being exclusive and staying faithful to him. Why stray, when he could offer me the kind of sexual encounter that I went through today? We were, to put it simply, a fit!

Could I spend the rest of my life with him? That was too long for me to think about. But, since Vishti, he was the only one that had come close.

I started doing that decision tree piece of nonsense, where you take a blank sheet of paper and you draw a line down the middle. On one side I wrote: *Jack*. On the other side: *Richard*. Then I realised, I'd got it wrong. You're supposed to put pros on one side and cons on the other. I screwed up the paper and started again. I wrote down: *Jack*, at the top of the paper. I put *Pros* on one side, *Cons* on the other. I would do a second sheet of paper for Richard but begin with Jack.

Then, I started listing the pros:

1. The flat.
2. The jewellery, lost count, about £200,000. Okay, that's what they're insured for. Would probably only get half of that if I had to sell it.
3. The wardrobe full of designer dresses plus that couture number, which set him back about £10,000.
4. The Harrods expense account alone – £5,000 a month. Most months I couldn't even reach the limit, and often paid for lunch with the LWL's, because I thought if Jack noticed I wasn't spending enough, he might lower the limit.

The list could have gone on. The shoes. Should I put all the shoes down, what each pair of shoes cost? And then I thought, no, I couldn't just list all the items he bought me. That was stupid. I was listing the positive features of Jack. In my relationship with him he paid for everything. That wasn't 25 items or 50 or 100, that was one item on the pro category. He paid for things. OK, that was Number One, now for Number Two. What was the other pro for Jack? He took me places. Was that Number Two, or was that really still Number One, because he was paying to take me to those places? I mean, he didn't send me off on my own somewhere because I want an adventure. I tried it once. I did. I said I wanted to go to Peru, on the Machu Pichu trail. Would he pay the £3,000? I said that I'd always wanted to do that. His answer: *He didn't want to go!*

So, Number One: He paid for everything that *he* wanted me to have.

OK, next please. What else was there in my relationship with Jack? He introduced me to interesting people. Yeah, I thought, that's Number Two. That wasn't just paying for things. He introduced me to interesting people. OK, Jack, you could have that as Number Two. What else? *Come on, Jack*, I thought, *help me out here.*

Sex? Was that Number Three? No, that would be on the other side of the sheet. I was not there yet. I had to finish the pros. But I started listing the cons in my head. I realised that if I started writing down the cons, I wouldn't have enough paper. He was arrogant. He wasn't abusive, but he treated me as if he owned me. He was selfish, and not just with the sex. If I listed why I didn't like having sex with him, that would be a whole sheet of cons on their own. No, the cons far outweighed the pros. But that wasn't the point. The point was: *Were there more pros with Jack than with Richard?*

I went back to the sheet of paper. I screwed up Jack's and it went in the bin. Two lousy points in his favour. I went to Richard's.

1. I love him.
2. The sex is the best. No, not the best. Vishti and Cassandra, he hasn't usurped them, but the G-spot orgasm? Does that put him above Vishti? Maybe, but we don't have the… What should I call it? The *spiritual* connection. *I haven't forsaken you yet Vish.* I couldn't believe I had just thought *spiritual* connection. I checked the paper to make sure I hadn't written that down. *Perhaps I should be taken to the funny farm. I don't believe in all that shit, remember.*
3. Companionship. He's fun and funny. I really enjoy his company. I don't know, is that point three, or three and four?

What difference? There was no comparison! Now, in my own mind I was thinking: *How do I end this with Jack? I hope it won't end in dramas.*

I said two days. I needed to let him know my decision quickly. I sent Richard a text:

*Decision made. Meet me at the Charing Cross Library. It opens at 10:30 tomorrow morning. I'll be in the reading room. Don't be late.*

Richard's text reply was immediate:

*If you've decided, can't you just tell me. Why there? We've never been there together. I don't understand.*

Then me again:

*Please let me do this my way. I've made my decision. I don't think you'll be disappointed. The library is important to me. You're important to me. Please let me do this my way.*

But he was persistent:

*No, I'm sorry. If you've decided, tell me - either way.*

I still wasn't giving in:

*I'm sure you'll be pleased with my decision. Why won't you wait?*

Richard continued to push me:

*I still don't understand. Let me come over now.*

Then my final offer, the compromise:

*No. I want you - correction - sorry, I want to see you in the library. I have my reasons. If you're going to insist, the library closes at 7 pm. It's 5 o'clock now. I can be there by 5:40. There, I've compromised. I think this could be the start of a beautiful relationship. I've never compromised with anyone else.*

Richard agreed. The timing wasn't the issue. I wanted it to be at the library.

*******

5:35 pm. He was already there.

Now I had a bit of explaining to do.

I told him that they were planning on closing the library down and gave him a brief potted history. I was thinking of setting up a page on *gofundme.com* to launch a Save the Library Campaign. Yaddy, yaddy, yaddah. I was rambling.

I probably carried on for a few minutes more and then he said:

"Enough! Rachel, it's time to tell me. I hope it's good news!"

"Please hear me out. Please don't interrupt. I need to get this out. It's not easy for me. I thought very hard about this. I don't want you to think that this was an easy decision. I had to weigh up everything that Jack offers me. But yes you're right. It is mainly the material things, not the spiritual. That sounds silly. I'm not a spiritual person. But you know what I mean. What you offer would not be material. Physical, yes. For a start, you wouldn't be supporting me. Forget the lifestyle. I've already decided, I could live without that. Financially, I'm very comfortable. This would be a partnership of equals. We give and take, but it's more, I feel we're merged souls."

"Yes, soulmates!"

"No, please don't use that word. I'm not saying soulmates. I'm just saying, I don't know, we're so good together. We understand each other. You are everything that I could possibly look for, dream of, in a life partner. Yes, I did say a life partner. I don't think I've ever thought in those terms before. But I did write these things on the sheet of paper to persuade myself. I suppose that I had already decided. The boxes you tick. I'm not going to run through them. It would just be pandering to your conceit."

He giggled a nervous giggle.

"But we are good together. And I do love you. I couldn't tell you then, but I think I've known it for a few weeks as well. Yes, you are so right. The consummation of our love was beyond my wildest expectations. To be honest, I would have still taken you if the sex wasn't half as good, but that really was the icing on the cake, so, yes, Richard."

"You mean the answer is yes!"

His eyes looked lit up. He looked quite excited.

"I said let me finish. Please let me finish. Yes, I do love you. Yes, I want to spend the rest of my life with you. But I must ask you, I have to ask you. Mimi's a friend. You know we've become very close. I don't want to be seen as a marriage breaker."

"I've thought this through. I know it might cost you your relationship with Mimi. But you know as well as I do, and it's not selfish, well, I suppose it is selfish. We have to live for each other, don't we?"

"Yes, that's what I thought. You once referred to me as, I think it was, a callous bitch. But you're right. I can live without Mimi. I'll get over that. To be honest, she was the only one out of the Ladies Who Lunch that I had any time for at all. So, yes, Mimi will be missed. Collateral damage in the ground war of personal relationships. But, in the end, I thought about our love and what's important in my life. So let me give you the answer that you've been waiting for. And I'm sorry I kept you in suspense, but I did say that, if you gave me time, you would realise that I'd come to the right decision for us."

I paused, there was just that last question. As ever, the script was prepared. My two violins were playing in my head, but there was no room for improv in this performance. His answer would determine my future.

"Just one last question. Your kids, what will happen to them?"

"Well, obviously, Mimi will keep them. I mean she'll have custody or whatever the deal is, in any future divorce. So I haven't really thought that through but I will still see them."

"Yes, I understand. What I really meant was: How do you think this would affect your kids, your two beautiful daughters?"

"Kids? Kids they get over it!"

"You're so right, Richard. That's why I know we're so right for each other. You've got all the answers. Yes, kids are kids. Who cares about a divorce?"

"I didn't mean that. I didn't mean it like that. I know your parents went through a divorce. I know it must have been difficult for you."

"Not about me, Richard. I'm just asking you how do you think your kids will be with it?"

"They'll be fine. I'll see them at the weekends. You know, Weekend Dad. Spoil the girls. Can't see a problem there. Yes, I won't see them every day but I'm sure they'll be OK."

"See, Richard, I thought this through. Because, of course, I met them. Only briefly. I thought this through, very carefully. I agree with you, they will be OK. I said one last question so this is really the same question. Would they be better off if you stayed with Mimi and, I don't know, maybe had an affair instead of a divorce?"

"I don't know. I don't think it'll make much difference to be honest. Living a lie with Mimi won't be easy. Maybe the kids will notice. Getting divorced, they'll know exactly where we stand. I'll make the right noises, you know, to smooth things over."

"Yes, but think of it this way:

Option One - you stay a happy family, maybe not a happy family but you stay a family, a family unit.

Option Two - you become Weekend Dad, as you put it.

Which will be better for the kids, Richard?"

"I don't think it'll make a lot of difference."

"I'm not talking about *a lot of difference*. I'm talking about which option, one or two. Think forward. I don't know, 10 years, would your daughters be happier if you had stayed with Mimi or if you separated?

"I don't know. Why are you asking me that? I just said I don't think it'll make a lot of difference."

"It's a binary question, Richard. Option One or Option Two?"

"Oh, OK! If you're going to make me choose. Of course, they wouldn't want me to divorce. As I say, I think they'll get through it, alright. Go on, I admit it, they would be better off if I stayed with Mimi."

"Thank you, Richard, I appreciate your honesty." I looked across the table where he was sitting. I pulled his head towards me. I gave him a kiss on the lips. I pulled away from him. I stood up and moved my chair back:

"Richard, the children are our future!"[1]

I turned and walked towards the exit.

I knew if I turned around, how my future would change. It triggered memories:

Of when I left Jimmy's and stopped the taxi and turned round and ran back up the steps to hug Cassandra.

Of Vish, at the Ritz, where I walked out the side door and then back around through the front – that 5-minute hug, in complete silence.

I knew that, if I just glanced back, it would all be over. I'd rush into his arms and kiss him passionately.

I couldn't see, as my back was turned, but I could feel him standing up about to shout: *Rache, don't go!* But he was in a library. Perhaps that's why I chose the venue; so that there couldn't be any loud remonstrations.

I knew I had to tell him, but I didn't know how I was gonna get the words out.

---

1.　A shout out to the memory of Linda Creed. Her lyrics from the Whitney Houston classic may have subconsciously influenced Cindy. She holds onto this message to far better purpose in Volume II of the Cindy's Diaries Trilogy.

I knew my destiny.

I knew that:

*however much I loved him,*

*however much I wanted to be with him,*

*however much he turned me on,*

*however much we were made for each other,*

*however much we were a fit,*

I knew my destiny.

I was quite proud of myself. That I reached the right decision without needing to confide in Vish.

Well done, Rache, you've grown up. Had I really extinguished Cindy's demons? Only time would tell. But I knew that Cindy would never have cared about destroying Mimi's family, the impact on the kids. Cindy would only have thought about her lustful passion for Richard.

But Rachel knew that she would never achieve peace and harmony, just fleeting moments with the ones she loved. The ones she has loved. The few she's ever loved. Her destiny was to wander forever in search of her elusive happiness, a happiness she would never be allowed to find.

Make the most of those fleeting moments, I beseeched myself.

*Lifelong companionship*, Rachel, you missed that train.

I had to snap out of this. I was still thinking of Richard sitting there. I hoped, by now, he had noticed the book that I'd taken from the library shelves as I approached him when I entered the library. I hoped that he would have turned that book around by now, so he could read the title on the front cover.

It had at the top, the author's name: a German Philosopher, Immanuel Kant, and the title, which read:

*The Critique of Pure Reason.*

# PART V

# 42
# Jack's an Arsehole

Severing all ties to Richard meant distancing myself from Mimi.

Richard had phoned me to find out if the chat at the library indicated that I was proposing to have an illicit affair with him:

"No, Richard. There is no more us. We had our swan song. It's time to go back to our humdrum lives. You to enjoy your beautiful children, to watch them grow into womanhood and be proud in the knowledge that you did your best to see them right. For me, a return to the private jets, the jewellery, the second home in the Caribbean and to be proud in the knowledge that I have extinguished the memories of the poverty of my grandmother's immigrant roots. Oh and by the way, did you enjoy Kant, isn't he a blast?"

I'm not sure if those were my exact words, but I know I told him what I tell all my exes:

"I won't part bad friends. What we had was special. It will remain with me through my whole life. Know that I will always be there for you. A favour, if ever you're desperate, a shoulder to cry on if you're depressed, a sympathy fuck if you've split up with a partner. I hope I can call upon you for the same if the need arises."

Cindy's only rule for break-ups: *Never burn your bridges.*

Now I had to work out what to do with Jack!

I was trying to figure out in my own mind whether we could turn a page in our relationship. If only sex were a little bit better, I don't know, more interesting. I needed to find out what it was about his escorts. I just knew I was better than them. Actually, I didn't even know if they were a *them* or if there was just one. I kept racking my brains, thinking back to who I saw before Jack and I were an item. It was something Gus had told me, a name he'd mentioned. I was struggling to recall. Suddenly serendipity struck. The TV was on in the background. One of those MTV video clip shows. And then I saw this young singer, who I recognised from about a decade ago, some sort of disco-type music. I once did what teenagers do and tried to ape this singer. She had these highly made-up eyes, really OTT. I got into trouble at school. They couldn't stop the girls from wearing a bit of mascara, but they insisted that eye makeup was kept simple, nothing punk, nothing Winehouse. They sent me home. I bunked off school for days until I finally came off my high horse and used Mum's Pond's Cold Cream to remove the offending eye décor.

The song was called *If We Were*. I used to play it over and over. I don't know why, but I glanced up at the TV and there was a caption on the video. I'd forgotten my role model's name. It flashed up: *Belinda*. And then it hit me. I could picture Gus talking about his boss and complaining, well not complaining but more criticising: *Jack's wife, Ellie Mae, is in town. I just don't think it's right. I saw him with one of his escorts, or maybe his mistress. He's quite brazen about it, although he's a bit coy about whether he has more than one woman on the side even if we all know his favourite is called* Belinda.

I was apprehensive, but I knew I had to confront Jack.

*******

"Jack, please don't think I'm being judgmental. Your life is your own. From the outset, we had agreed that neither of us was exclusive in this relationship. But I do need to know one thing. What is it that Belinda has that I don't? Just be honest with me. I promise you I will be able to take it. I'm not going to get emotional, ranting and raving. But for my own self-confidence, my own self-esteem, I have to know."

I had no idea how he was gonna react. Was he going to be angry, going to walk out on me? Was he going to think I was spying on him? But what I got was a total surprise.

"I didn't realise you knew, or, at least, I didn't realise you knew her name. Yes, she is special to me. No, she's not like you. Yes, she's an escort. If you wanted to be a bitch you would say she was a ho' or a slut. But I've been seeing her off and on for over five years. Before I met you. Maybe I will continue to see her after we part company. You asked me what the attraction is. Is she more beautiful than you? Maybe, but that's not it. Her intellect, her mind? Well, she does have a degree. But that's not it. No, there's just one department, and it's somewhere you've made very clear you don't want to go. So if it's confession time, then I will concede, I do have a certain, I'm not sure how you would call it, some would say a *kink*. You probably don't remember, in our early days, when I tried something and you resisted. Or, at least, you wriggled away. And I didn't press. You used a phrase I did quite like. So much so that I started to use it in some of those lectures I give, even some of those after-dinner speeches. Perhaps I should credit you next time.

*"Some do. Some don't. Some will. Some won't. So what!*

"Some will open the back door and some won't. So what! So there you have it, I'm surprised I even told you. To be honest, Belinda is much more than that to me. But I cannot deny that that is part of our relationship and I have accepted that it is not part of ours."

I was speechless. It's certainly not what I had expected. I had nothing more to say. I asked. He answered. As Doc would say: *End of.*

"Jack, I do appreciate your honesty. I appreciate you sharing that with me. I won't mention Belinda again or the other thing. You have my word on that."

What Jack had just told me played on my mind. I didn't know how to handle it. Belinda before me, Belinda after me. I could accept that. I didn't even see her as a rival. My time with Jack would come to an end one day. So be it!

There was, however, just one thing that I couldn't accept. I didn't know what I was going to do, right then. But I did know I was going to do something. I just needed to wait until the right moment.

The moment didn't come for several weeks. It was one of those charity dinners and there was going to be an auction, a charity auction. I don't know why, but Jack got a huge kick out of winning these things against his rivals. It was all for charity so, what do they say: *all in a good cause?* As long as he won the auction, he came home on a high. Of course, when he lost, he was quite morose.

This evening he lost. He lost because even this Master of the Universe could not bring himself to spend more than the £10,000 limit he had set himself for the two Centre Court tickets for the Wimbledon final, which I could buy on the black market for £2,500 a seat. In the scheme of things, who really cared? Jack wasn't fussed to go to Wimbledon, but it was about being aced by a rival who took the bidding up to Jack's limit. He'd basically outsmarted Jack.

I was in the loo at Gro Ho, as my LWL chums liked to call it, better known as Grosvenor House, the Park Lane hotel where the function was being held. I overheard the wife of the donor of these tickets telling her companion that her husband had a Wimbledon debenture that entitled him, every year, to four Centre Court seats. He got a great kick out of donating two of those tickets. I thought she was a bit derogatory when she referred to her husband as Mr Big or Mr Big Shot, something to that effect. And this lady was bragging to her companion that she, of course, would be accompanying her husband with the remaining two tickets to the Wimbledon Centre Court final.

Her husband's name was Lord Fisher. He was one of those young Turks who politicians fawned over, who ended up in the House of Lords in exchange for some large donation to the party in Government.

The bidding went up in £200 slots until it got to £8,000. Jack had had plenty of bidding room before he would reach the limit he'd set himself. Then for no obvious reason, unless he knew Jack's limit, his rival suddenly bid £10,000. Jack could afford to go higher, but that wasn't his style.

I saw the look on Jack's face when the lot was knocked down to someone else. I couldn't believe that it meant anything to him. I was going to lean across and tell him that I could get those sodding tickets for £5,000 on the dark web. But, of course, this was all about pride and his proving, in front of this crowd, that he had money to burn.

I'd had a few drinks. I needed them to get through these evenings. They were fun, at first, but were growing tedious. Same old! Same old! The champagne had loosened me up. I couldn't face going home with Jack's long face. I looked at Jack and he was looking across the room at the winner of the auction who was being congratulated at the other table.

I stood up and I shouted, as loud as I could, so that people could hear me over the hubbub. The auctioneer was Grant Chester (yes really!) a former soap actor, C-lister, who seemed to have carved out a sideline, probably for a set fee, as an auctioneer at these charity events.

"Grant!" Nobody heard or if they did they weren't paying attention.

"Grant Chester! The auction is not over. Can I come up to the mic?"

Jack looked at me. A look that said: *Don't embarrass me here, kiddo, or this could be the end of us.* I ignored him and strode up to the mic. Grant didn't know what to say, but he was a professional so he played it by ear. I put my arms around him and gave him a big kiss on his cheek. The audience of half-drunk charity-wallahs cheered. They liked that, so I did a little curtsy for them.

Then I declared:

"Can I ask Lord Fisher to stand up?"

The young guy was sitting a few tables in front of us.

"Come on, please come up. We'd like to thank you for being so generous, wouldn't we, Grant?"

Grant nodded. I was milking this for all it was worth. I saw Jack about to stand up, perhaps to drag me off the stage, but he was restrained by one of our table guests.

Now Lord Fisher was up at the mic, and I gave this member of the nobility, who I'd never met before, a huge slobbery kiss on the cheek and the audience went wild, raising a huge cheer in unison.

"Your Lordship, a little birdy told me that you actually have two more tickets for Wimbledon, don't you?"

"Well not spare. My wife, Caroline, and I..."

"Yes, Caroline, thank you for your generosity. I think Caroline should stand up and get a big clap. You are both forsaking the final to donate those extra two tickets. You see Jack Chalmers was the underbidder, just now, but he's ready to take those tickets off your hands here and now for the same winning bid of £10,000. Come on Jack, get your cheque book out. It's all for charity. Stand up."

Finally, Jack was on message. He stood up waving a mock cheque book. *Grant, use your hammer again!* A round of applause for Jack, everyone.

On the taxi ride home, you'd think it had been all Jack's idea. I didn't want any credit. I just wanted to see the look on his face.

Back at the flat, I rushed to the loo. I had some prep to do. While I was in the loo, he must have been in the bedroom because I heard him shout, asking me if I wanted to have a drink. It was Jack's code, for: *Get me a drink when you've finished.* He had a thing about not pouring his own drink, if there was a woman in the house to be at his beck & call.

When I came out, he was back in the living room, still on a high. I poured out two Jack Daniels. I sat on his lap, picked up my whisky and threw it back in one gulp. He glanced at me with a smug grin on his face.

"Jack, you get a kick out of these charity things. But would you do it if there was no glamour and pomp?"

"Probably not."

"What I mean is, would you donate to my charity?"

I told him about *Her Centre* and how they were raising money for new premises. There was a drive to raise £500,000. They had a deadline or they would lose the premises. They only had £35,000 and it seemed like an impossible task.

"Sure, how much? Tell you what, use your credit card. The Harrods one I gave you."

"It would bust my limit."

"What, you've spent your £5,000 this month already?"

"No, but I'm talking about more than that."

"How much?"

"Well, so far they're short of £465,000, they might have raised a few more thousand, but £460,000 at least."

Jack didn't look amused and I had to explain my proposal - a kind of a wager.

If I won, he would donate the money. But if I lost, he didn't have to donate at all. He was intrigued, the more so when I explained what I had in mind.

I was straight up with him. I told him that I wasn't jealous of his relationship with Belinda but telling me that she was better than me at anal was, quite frankly, an insult. He could at least allow me the opportunity to have a go at demonstrating that I was superior in that arena.

After a little bit of back and forth, I'd cut the deal. He was still on a high at his kudos, being seen as the great benefactor at the charity auction. He said if I was ready for him to fuck my arse, he was certainly up for it.

Yes, he was also up for a wager, especially as I'd told him he could be the judge and jury. If he said I was better, he'd have to pay up. If not, all bets were off.

"So what are you suggesting? Let's do £10,000."

"I told you, they're about £460,000 short."

"And I said you can't be serious."

"Well, if you think about it, you only have to say you didn't enjoy it as much. You're the judge."

Deal done, I took Jack to the bedroom. It was always a bit of a struggle to get him going, and tonight was no exception.

I start working his body. I am now on top of him, I'm sliding down the bed so I can take him in my mouth. I'm not getting the response I want. Then I think to myself: *You want anal, I'll give you anal.* I insert my index finger, then my middle finger. He isn't objecting. I am looking for the prostate. I start massaging it. Now I am getting a response from his penis. I slow down. If he comes, I lose the bet. I ease right off the cock sucking to focus on the prostate. He's responding well. I think I can see some fluid running quickly out of his penis. Shit! If this was a prostate orgasm, the whole deal could be fucked. It's now or never.

Now I'm sitting on top of him. I'd prepped in the loo, with an enema and the Dr Johnson's. I am quite relaxed. That was one reason I'd gulped the whisky earlier. I am using all the experience from the Richard sessions. I am clenching. He can feel me tightening. He wants to turn over, but, by just using my body, I gave him a firm *No!*

Now he is thrusting up, while I am clenching; it's the anal version of Cindy's grip. Tense, release, tense, release. I start the bouncing, the technique I taught myself from the Richard sessions. I could see the look on his face: *Don't stop!*

"£500k for me to carry on."

"Yes, yes, keep going."

His spunk seems to keep on coming. I keep squeezing my butt cheeks. I hadn't noticed he had so much when I blew him or fucked him.

"You spray it on me now."

"Sorry?"

"My face. Sit on my face and shit out my spunk."

*Thank God for the enema!.*

I can feel the fluid dribble from my anus onto his face.

I'm thinking: *Here goes!*

I start moving my butt cheeks, smearing his cum over his face.

When he's had enough, he gently slaps my backside and says:

"Shower time!"

I am not sure whether he wants an assisted shower or not, but I think *hey ho*, I want to seal the deal.

We're soaping each other in the shower, so I go on to reconfirm the donation.

"I want to take you to *Her Centre* tomorrow and show you around. You'll meet the Director, and you'll let me close the deal."

"The deal?"

"Your half mill will earn you naming rights. The Jack Chalmers Building, the new home of *Her Centre* – a nice brass plaque. I originally thought of inviting the local mayor to the unveiling. But I think we should go for the Mayor of London. You've met him, surely?"

"No."

"Well, that will give you a good opportunity to pitch whatever you want to him."

I knew Jack wasn't going to donate much more than a few thou unless he got something in return. The building name was a start, meeting the Mayor of London *mano o mano* was the clincher.

I was pretty chuffed: *Well done, girl, done some good for a change!*

I was picturing the unveiling ceremony. I wondered whether I should invite Richard. After all, if I hadn't met him, I'd never have mastered the third orifice.

# 43

## TIA

"Just go now. Don't waste time talking. You might be too late and you'll regret it forever."

I thought I recognised the voice: "Dixie, where are you?"

"Edinburgh, it doesn't matter. It's Rache, something dreadful. She's at the Westminster, no Chelsea & Westminster, Kings Road, I think. Look it up, no don't look it up. Just go, go now!"

The phone went dead. I wasn't thinking clearly. Taxi or car? I was at the office; the car would be quicker. It was in a parking bay downstairs. Parking is impossible at the Hospital. A taxi would be better. No, I might have to wait too long to flag one down. I walk out of the office door and brush past Billy, my IT guy.

"Hey, careful, what's the rush?"

"Do you have a driving licence?"

He looks puzzled.

"I think so, no, of course, yes, but I ..."

"Come downstairs with me. You're driving."

I'm in the car, giving Billy directions. I need to speak to Dixie to find out what was going on:

"Dixie, it's Vishti. I'm in my car on the way to the hospital, what on earth has happened?"

"Are you driving?"

"Why?"

"I don't want you to have an accident."

"What are you talking about? Why? No, I'm being driven."

"We think Rache has had a stroke."

"I don't understand."

"Well, neither do I. I got a frantic call from June. Not sure if you've met her. She was at the College, but she works with Rache, at the... you know... the place."

"Felicity's?"

"Yes, I didn't know if you knew the name."

I realised, that as far as Dixie was concerned, I was the avuncular

340

family friend and not the former client.

"This is the best I've got because June wasn't making much sense. They were at work, larking around in the staff room. June gives her a friendly push. Rache stumbles, and when she got up, her face had dipped."

"What do you mean.?"

"The left side of her face was drooping. But Rache hadn't even noticed. She was fine apart from that, no slurred speech or anything, but she looked, I don't know the word, it's not PC, but like *spastic*."

"But you think it was a stroke?"

"Well I don't know, do I? June just kept repeating that daft acronym F.A.S.T. Maybe not so daft, because F is for Face, the T is for a Time, and she, or rather her boss Fi, had the presence of mind to call an ambulance."

"So do we know how she is?"

Dixie's voice was faltering. I could hear the tears, sobbing, she stuttered the words:

"No, she could be d-d-d... dead."

She recovered her composure and continued:

"As soon as you get there look for June in A&E. Better still, if you're not driving, phone the hospital. I tried but they were all *sorry-data-protection-only-family* on me. You're family, aren't you?"

"Well, not technically. I'll call and see how far I can get. I'll text you as soon as I have any news. And thank you for calling. That was very kind."

"Don't be stupid. I think you're the only person she cares, you know, properly cares about."

We rang off, and I spent a few moments contemplating Dixie's words. I wasn't seeing much of Rache nowadays. Only when she needed something, or more recently for a quick update on her latest adventure with Jack. The last text message: *Spending a few days chilling at Jack's pad in Barbados*, with an emoji of the sun.

I called the Chelsea & Westminster:

"Levinson, Rachel, my niece. I believe she was brought in perhaps half an hour ago. Suspected stroke..."

Then the usual data protection brick wall, exactly as Dixie had encountered.

"Yes, of course, I can give you her date of birth... No, I'm not her next of kin... Her parents? No, they don't live in London...Look I'm more or less outside the hospital, now just tell me where I can find her."

"She's been moved to the Trauma Ward."

"What does that mean?"

"For assessment. But it means there's nothing life-threatening at the moment."

I was now in A&E reception. Dixie had texted me June's mobile, and I'd already received a message telling me to meet her at the canteen. There was a small open plan café alongside the reception area, and I looked across and saw a young woman sitting on her own. I guessed right.

"June?"

"Vishti. It's so nice to meet you. I feel I know you. Rache never stops talking about you."

Well, I was rather relieved she didn't recognise me as a former client of Felicity's. I didn't think she would, because everyone there was fairly discrete, so clients only tended to see their individual therapist, not the other girls. But there were still people moving around, so I wasn't sure.

"Have you any news?"

"Yes, the doctor's coming over now. The nurse just came to find me and said she's out of danger."

I saw what must have been the doctor approaching. He sat and introduced himself to June.

"Are you a relative?"

"Friend."

"Uncle!" I chipped in.

He looked at me.

"Oh, sorry, I didn't mean to be rude. But I wanted to speak to June, I believe, who brought her in. But maybe you can both help. I'm interested in any changes to her lifestyle recently."

"Well, I suppose June would be… I haven't seen much of Rachel recently."

"What do you mean lifestyle?"

"Well, first the good news. Miss Levinson, Rachel, didn't have a stroke. We call it a TIA, which stands for Transient Ischemic Attack: colloquially, a mini-stroke. The only thing we've really been able to identify, although we're still doing tests, is the slight drooping that you saw on one side of her face. Actually, it's already much better than when she first came in. She'll undergo physio for the next few months and will probably be 95% back to where she was."

"So, still disfigured?"

"Well, we'll have to wait and see, but given the fact that there's been this improvement so quickly, my guess is that the change in her face will be imperceptible to all but her closest friends."

I butted in.

"Sorry, doctor, you said changes to her lifestyle?"

"Yes, sorry, when she came in her blood pressure was 170/95. At her age, it shouldn't be more than 120/80."

"Is that what caused her mini-stroke?" June inquired. I sensed with some relief that it was not her friendly shove in the staff room that triggered the crisis.

"Well, I'd say it was the main contributory factor. Frankly, unless she addresses the problem, let me put it like this; after a TIA, your chances of having a stroke are dramatically increased, so she does need to address the issue."

June seemed to get the message.

"What type of lifestyle changes?"

"Mainly, we're talking about over consumption of alcohol, drugs, food and so on."

June looked at me, and I made a face to indicate: *Go on, don't mind me.*

"Well, I'm not sure about drugs. She doesn't do drugs, except maybe an occasional pill at a party, but she's certainly not a user, or anything like that. Alcohol, not an alky. I mean, she doesn't keep a hip flask at work or anything like that, no alcohol on her breath. And again, I'd say not really a party girl. But there was an incident, recently, when she, well, I confess that I'd never seen her that drunk since the time she groped a boy in college."

The doctor intervened.

"So, would it be fair to say, and I don't want to put words into your mouth, that Miss Levinson...."

"Rachel!" Dixie and I chimed in unison.

The doctor continued, "That *Rachel* was not a stranger to over-consumption of alcohol, but this was not habitual, although recently there had been signs that she was drinking more? How about food?"

"It's funny you should say that," June explained. "I had noticed that she'd put on weight recently, and I did tell her that the clients might start complaining."

"Clients?" the doctor inquired.

I gave June a piercing glance. She looked up, her face slightly red.

"The photographers, Rachel and I do a bit of spare time modelling for fashion photographers. You know how they like size zero models."

Good save, June, I thought, but I don't think the doctor really cared either way.

"I have seen this before, a previously healthy fit young lady, although, of course, it could be young man, just that I've seen this in a young woman before. Regular gym-goer, her body is a temple, strictly Perrier water and celery for lunch. For some reason, I won't go into the detail of this particular young lady, suffice to say that she went off the rails, was drinking every night and went from celery to junk food. Her weight ballooned. She came in with a TIA. Symptoms not dissimilar to Rachel's. Her blood pressure through the roof. She got a wake-up call. Went through six months of therapy but came out the other side and was back at the gym."

"And the celery?" June needed to know.

"Not exactly, but I guess you see my drift. By the way, I was just giving an example, and not suggesting there are any mental health issues with Rachel."

I looked at June, who looked at me with a knowing glance. The doctor, of course, was being diplomatic and was not about to break patient confidentiality by disclosing his real diagnosis of Rachel's mental condition.

June appeared to have an epiphany. She turned to me.

"That's it! She broke up with a boyfriend. Rachel had been going out with him for over a year. For Rachel that was an eternity. I couldn't get to the bottom of it, her reason for breaking up, I mean. She doesn't do long term relationships. But it seems to have affected her. I know she took up with another guy, but this was sort of hush-hush. Well not really, it's just that I'm not in her league anymore. I don't mean that in any snotty way, but this new guy is some hot shot in the City. I hope I'm not right, but I fear she may have swapped true love for the high life. Er, Vishti, do you know anything about that? I know she confides in you."

"Yes, I did know about her change in boyfriends, but I hadn't realised, or rather it hadn't occurred to me that this was causing her any distress. On the contrary, I thought she was enjoying the *high life* as you describe it. But to be fair, I hadn't really discussed her feelings for her old boyfriend."

I turned round to the doctor.

"Is there anything else? Is there any way that we can help you further?"

The doctor shook his head.

"Well, we would like to see her, if that's possible."

"Yes, if you'd like to stick around. They are doing a few more tests. I'll ask the nurse to come to find you and you can go through then."

The doctor got up to leave. I turned to June and handed her a twenty pound note.

"June, could you get us a drink? I'll have a cup of coffee. I'm parched. Get yourself anything you want."

"Of course."

June got up and headed towards the counter. I touched the doctor's arm to attract his attention, as he now had his back to me.

"I didn't want to say anything in front of June, but there is a bit of a history. I don't want to exaggerate, but could any of this be akin to self-harm?"

"Why? Is there a history of self-harm?"

"No, but there were problems in her childhood. I wouldn't want to say more, but if you are suggesting counselling I'm sure they would be able to get to the bottom of any psychological issues."

"Between you and me, we *are* recommending counselling."

I thought to myself: *And good luck with that!*

June and I sat and chatted for about another 20 minutes. It was slightly awkward, I think, for both of us, because we only wanted to talk about Rachel and, yet we both had concerns about how much each of us should reveal about what we knew about Rachel and her past.

As we were guided by the nurse along the corridor, I was quite pleased to see that she was in a private room. I don't think that would have been automatic. I think it would have been a request from Rachel, which showed me that she was able to make decisions. I could hear her thinking: *I've got the money, why shouldn't I? Bugger that! I deserve it!*

As we were about to enter her room, I touched June's arm.

"June, would you do me a favour?"

She nodded.

I continued, "Would you mind going in first without me? Take as long as you want, and we can swap when you're ready. It's just that I'd like to spend some time alone with Rachel."

"Of course. I understand. Give me 10."

When I walked through the door, Rachel turned away. I was a bit taken aback. She could not have been surprised to see me since June had told her that I was waiting outside.

There was only one reason why she would turn her face away from me. June stayed a few moments more, made her excuses and left. I told her how appreciative I was of everything she'd done. I asked her if she'd mind updating Dixie.

I approached the bed and sat on the chair and took Rachel's hand. I knew she'd have to turn to look at me and I was fearing the worst.

There it was. Her hand was over the left side of her face, well, actually just covering the left side of her mouth. She looked at me, tears welling. I looked at what remained of her *trademark smile.*

We sat in silence and looked at each other, occasionally looking down and then into each other's face. Then our faces broadened into a grin. Then looking down before looking up again at each other. The dance went on. It may have been 10, it may have been 20 minutes. I was reminded of the first time I had suggested that she used silence in a negotiation. First one to open their mouth loses. She'd explained to me, that, at least in business, or rather with clients, the slogan had served her well. But we were not in a negotiation, or, at least, I didn't think we were.

Negotiation or not I broke first.

"They say you can make a full recovery."

"They've said a lot of things."

"Well, you'll have to do the physio."

I was waiting. Here it comes. Why do you think I didn't want to start the conversation? But I continued:

"Sorry about that. You know you are very dear to me. I want to see you back to your old self again."

"Don't worry, I'm going to do the physio. I can handle that. I won't let you down. My *trademark smile* will be back in action. And don't think that's for you, Vish. That's purely business, so I don't lose clients."

We shared a laugh, but I knew what was coming next.

"But if you tell me to see that shrink, I will bloody well press the panic button, tell them you tried to rape me and never let you near me again!"

"Here's the deal. Let me give you my psycho-babble. Answer my questions, let me get to the bottom of this until *we* have a solution. Then I won't mention the shrink again."

"Sounds like a plan."

She tried to extend a hand to shake mine but it was all wired up with tubes.

"OK, Sigmund, come up with your magic."

So I started to describe what the popular view, as espoused by June, was:

"You haven't got over your breakup with Gus, who you are still passionately in love with. You were beginning to have doubts about going off and swapping the true love you had with Gus for the high life you've got with Jack."

Rachel looked at me and smiled.

"Oh, yeah, June certainly got that right!" she commented sarcastically.

"No, not Gus. Actually, it was Richard. I met a guy, fell in love, had great sex, you know, Vishti level, dumped him, had a breakdown, stroke, or whatever. I did all of that on my own, without you, Vish. Aren't you proud of your Cindy? She can have relationships all on her own without running to Uncle Vish for help! Aren't I good? Aren't you proud of me?"

"Stop, stop, Rachel, stop beating yourself up."

I reached for some tissues. Her face was drowned in her tears. I started mopping the tears, gently. She took my hand away from her face to give me the half *trademark smile*. She looked at me and gave me a slight nod, to indicate that she was ready, emotionally, to carry on.

"Well, I am enjoying Jack, there's no doubt about that. No, not Jack exactly, but the lifestyle he provides. He's moved further away from Ellie Mae. I'm not a wife stealer. The marriage was really finished when she realised that, with his new job, he wasn't coming back to New York. I think she's filing for divorce. That's not really relevant, other than the fact that he's now taking me to his business functions, as his arm candy and plus one. And that's so much fun. The other week, I went to one of these charity dinners or political fund-raisers, you know £1,000 a plate. You've probably been there…"

"Something similar, not sure I've ever reached the £1,000 a plate league, but, yes, I know they can be fun, if you enjoy that sort of thing."

"Yes, well, but for me it was a first. That sort of scene. The people I met. They're not all snobs. Some of them, not many, admittedly, some of them are actually real people, not cardboard cut-outs."

We shared a knowing smile.

"He insisted on buying me a new frock. Well, I suppose, a ball gown. He is a bit of a control freak, but he's not one of these guys who buys you a dress because he likes it. No, Jack just gives me a budget. He asked me if I had a favourite store. Of course, we have an account at Harrods anyway. He was very direct: *Spend what you want on the dress. I want you to look great and the sky is the limit, except anything over £5,000 comes out of your pocket.* He wasn't joking, but £5,000 was more than enough. I bought a very sheer velvety thing, body clinging, virtually backless, showed off my figure and oozed sensuality. I think I was the belle of the ball. I didn't think I could fit in to these events. Little old me. Grand-daughter of an immigrant an' all. But I was lapping it up. I was also lapping up the attention from the men at our table. And again Jack, not the jealous type, was pleased that his companion outshone the other women at the table. We decided at the outset that our relationship would not be exclusive. Obviously, he is still married, but in any case, he is still banging his escorts. From my side, he accepted that I might want the occasional younger man. But the irony is that I'd kept faithful to him. Well, until Richard."

*I paused for breath. And to think of Richard. And what I had given up. My sacrifice. Sacrificing my life to rescue Richard's family. Giving up my lover for the sake of his daughters.*

"OK, Jack's not the best lover. At best, the sex is average, I'd probably put it at 4 out of 10. No, that's an exaggeration. He's a selfish lover. But he makes up for it in other ways, like the auction."

"The auction?"

"Yes, you know, it's all for charity so everybody bids over the odds just to show off how wealthy they are. They're all these City types there. Jack said they expected to raise a million that evening."

"I get the idea, but, Rachel, I think you're now definitely out of my league."

She looked up at me, held a hand up to cover half of her mouth and flashed me what remained of her *trademark smile*.

"So, a week at a ski lodge in Courchevel came up for auction. Some toff had donated it. He owned the lodge so it was costing him nothing. Of course, everybody gave him a big cheer when the prize was announced. The guide price was £7,000. I almost put my foot in it when I looked around at the others on the table and said I thought I'd seen it on AirBnB for £2,000. One of the lasses at the table remarked that she had been there last Easter and she'd love to go again. So I piped up that I was just kidding. I looked at Jack with pussycat eyes and asked if he'd bid for me. He took a paper napkin off the table, scribbled something on it and handed it to me, as he said: *Go on, you do the bidding*. I looked at the napkin and he had written on it: *Don't go above £20,000*. I thought he was joking, so I looked at him to ask if he was serious. The bidding was already up to the guide price. He said to go on or I'd lose it and whispered in my ear: *I don't like to lose*. I can't tell you the feeling. I wouldn't say an orgasm but I was actually getting wet with excitement as the bidding went up £500 pounds at a time. The hammer went down at £15,000, to the lady in the velvet dress on table seven. For Jack, the money was nothing, like tipping the waiter."

"Well, you might say: *Tipping the Velvet.*"

We started laughing out loud. She forgot to cover her face, so I saw the damage the TIA had done. I momentarily looked perplexed, and she quickly put her hand up to cover the droop.

"The people at the table clapped, but, of course, Jack had to have the final word: *You'll have to buy your own skis. I'm not made of money.*

I gave Rachel a smile, followed by a more serious look, as if to say: *Can we get down to the serious business?*

"What is that expression you always use when I start going round The Wrekin: *I digress*. Ok, here's what you want to hear. I miss Gus. No, not as a lover. What we had was a normal boyfriend-girlfriend relationship. I miss Richard more. Do you remember you painted a scenario once, about finding a life partner? It could have been him. He was someone that I could spend a quiet evening with over a glass of wine. Like in 10 years' time when sex won't be the be-all and end-all of my life. In the meantime, the sex was great. So he did tick all the boxes, but, of course, I couldn't be with him.

I looked at Rache, quizzically.

"His kids. I couldn't let those innocent children end up in a split marriage. Look what it did to me!"

I was going to remind her that it probably wasn't the divorced parents, rather the abusive grandfather, but I hesitated. Probably not a good time to raise that.

"So I'm left with Jack. But Jack and I never sit down for a quiet evening. It's his private jet, it's his charity do's, next month it's the start of the Season."

"The Season?"

"Oh really, Vish, what planet are you on?"

Then, putting on her best accent, straight out of the Shires: "Lahdies Day at Arscot, Centre Court at Wembledon, corporate hospitality at Heynley. Isn't that what everybody does in June?"

"And you used to think that I was posh."

We shared a laugh.

"It sounds delightful."

"It is. I'm not kidding around, I love it and I wouldn't want to give it up. But do you want to know what I do when I'm not with Jack? I mean, when I'm not working, that is."

"Of course, go on."

"I said we're not exclusive, I could go out on the pull. But at the same time, he does expect me to be at his beck & call. He says to go out, have fun, but then he wants to know where I am 24/7. I don't mind. He really does give me enough socially, and, you won't believe me when I say this, though I miss good sex that is not the main problem."

"So, what do you do when you're not with Jack?"

"I sit in my smart Chelsea *pied à terre*, with a bottle of wine, watching Netflix and eating a bag of Doritos, and whatever crap Deliveroo will feed me. I binge on shit. I never thought I'd say that, but I'm a couch potato. I don't think it's healthy."

"Are you shitting me?"

Rachel looked up sharply. I don't usually use such language. That was straight out of Rache's playbook, but I needed to get the message across.

"That's what gave you the fucking stroke!"

Up to that moment, I don't think she'd realised. Of course, the doctor had explained to her, as to us, the impact of poor diet, alcohol, and lack of exercise on her blood pressure. But I really don't think she'd realised, until I spelt it out in such stark terms."

"You mean, I did this to myself. What do you want me to do? I'm bored. I'm bored with my shitty life!"

"I'm not going to tell you what to do. You'd only tell me to mind my own business."

"You're probably right, but I think I'd be a bit more graphic in my language. You'd tell me to give up Jack, and find another Gus, or a Richard, or go off and find wherever that walking holiday was where I'm supposed to amble along the lake with that faceless impoverished lecturer? Yes, I would go tell you to fuck off and mind your own business."

"Rache, you're killing yourself!"

"Well, that's up to me, isn't it? You're just jealous. I knew if I did well you'd be jealous of my lifestyle. Yes, I'm telling you to go fuck yourself. Go, get out of my room, my private fucking room and you go back to your ordinary life. Leave me to enjoy what time I have left."

Tears were streaming from her eyes. I wanted to hug her but the stupid tubes in her hands were stopping me from giving her anything more than a squeeze on her shoulders. That wasn't going to shake her out of her state.

I got up to leave. I turned my back and started to walk out of the room.

"That's right, fuck off and leave me here. Abandon me to that fucking shrink. You'll let them lock me up and throw away the key. What do you care?"

I walked towards the door and stopped and stood there with my back to her. If I walked out of the door, I wouldn't be able to help her. But I couldn't turn around until she'd calmed down. A few minutes passed and finally she stopped her rant.

"Well, aren't you going to say goodbye?"

I turned and walked back to her bed. I sat down on the visitor's chair.

"Of course, Rache, of course, I'm going to say goodbye."

We sat looking at each other. Silence. Until her lips silently mouthed the word: *Sorry*.

I shook my head and put my finger to my lips to indicate not to say anything. *Sorry* was not what I wanted to hear.

We sat and played the silence game. First one to speak loses.

This time, I couldn't afford to lose. Not if I wanted to save her.

So we did our dance. She kept wanting to speak and I kept putting my finger to my lips, thinking: *Hush, you're not ready yet.*

Just as before, 10 to 15 minutes. Then she put her hand over the drooping part of her face and gave me the half *trademark smile*.

She nodded to me, to indicate that she was ready, and I nodded back to confirm that it was now time to talk.

"OK, Mr Psycho-babble, give it your best shot. This had better be good. You've got my attention!"

"Given that you want to stay with Jack, it seems to me that you really have very few options. First, you've got to get back to the gym."

"I don't have a gym in Chelsea."

"Then join one. Better still, have you still got Greenwich?"

She nodded.

"Spend the days you're not working at the Greenwich flat so you've got the gym on hand."

Her eyes lit up: "You're brilliant, Greenwich has a 50 inch, fuck you screen. My Chelsea flat has a miserable little TV."

I wasn't sure whether she was joking.

"No! No more Netflix!"

"But I'm bored!"

"*Her Centre.*"

"What?"

"You told me that you give money to the shelter. You said you even pop in, once in a while, to help out."

"No biggie, so what?"

"So, volunteer."

"I don't understand."

"You don't know what I mean by volunteering?"

"No. I don't understand how you think that if I go there and work for nothing on a regular basis that would help. I work bloody hard at Fi's and am entitled to a few days' rest."

"And you enjoy it?"

"Don't start me off again, Mr Morality! Yes, I bloody do, but it's still hard work."

"And fulfilling?"

"What!"

"Full-filling?"

"Yes. Filling my mouth. Full of cum!"

We looked at each other and both started cracking up.

"Here's the, how would you say it, the skinny? I promise you that if you spend a day at *Her Centre*, or half a day, whatever you want, but do it regularly, weekly, and not as a casual drop-in, you will come away feeling good about yourself. You said you're bored. Fill up your time at the shelter."

"Helping to mend broken souls?"

"You'd be brilliant at it, but, to be honest, there is only one soul that I care about mending."

"Do you really think it would work?"

"No!"

"I knew you were playing with me."

"I don't *think* it would work. I *know* it would work."

"What am I supposed to do there? Pour them soup?"

"I don't know. It doesn't matter. Maybe some paperwork. Yes, maybe serve food. They need volunteers. One day you'll sit down and start chatting with one of their visitors, what do they call them?"

"Clients."

"OK, you'll be sitting with this woman, and she will be pouring out her heart to you, not thinking you're a shrink, but just a shoulder to lean on. She'll tell you how much better she feels just to have someone to talk to. You'll go home, maybe emotionally drained, but feeling good about yourself."

"You're saying it will do me good."

"It will build up your self-esteem. It will give you a sense a purpose. Of course, it won't be raising the big bucks, like Jack at the charity auction, but that's guilt money. This will make a difference; you'll feel that you've done something worthwhile."

Then she told me about getting Jack to donate £500,000 to *Her Centre*. I asked her how that made her feel.

"Pretty good, actually. I felt I got one over on him."

"No, I mean feel about what you were doing for the charity."

"Pretty chuffed, I suppose, but I can't get Jack to donate half a mil every week."

"You don't have to. Like I said, you can do good at the Centre by just sitting and talking to people."

"And, and there's got to be more."

"Yes, Rache, of course there is! Of course, there's more!"

I paused. I hesitated for dramatic effect, until she was getting impatient, and saying with her eyes: *Go on then.*

"Just think of the £10.99 a month you'll save when you realise that you can cancel your Netflix subscription!"

# 44
## Mickey re-visited

My TIA was a wake up call. And, of course, Vish was right.

The lifestyle change was easier than I expected. I took Vish's advice and stayed over at Greenwich on the days I wasn't working so that I could use the gym and pool facilities. As soon as I started resuming some form of exercise regime, it became easier to slow down on the junk food and cut back on the vino.

Being back at Greenwich also meant that I was closer to *Her Centre*. Again, responding to Vish, I started volunteering. My mission to save Mickey was well on the way. I was soon able to catch up with her again at the Centre.

None of this addressed the underlying cause of why I'd let myself go so badly. I knew that I was going to have to address that sooner or later. I was developing my plan.

But in the meantime, I was serving soup at the soup kitchen. Though not literally.

At *Her Centre*, Mickey and I were sitting together in the canteen before addressing that day's tasks, which included some cleaning chores as well as getting chairs ready for the evening event. Mickey was participating in a round table discussion, entitled *Life After*, which was intended to show some of the inmates, as we liked to call the clients, how it's possible to rebuild their lives after years of abuse.

"I miss you at Felicity's. The only reason that I was reluctant to recommend the job was that I wasn't sure you'd be able to get out once you started."

"I'm not really sure that I understand. My goal was to earn £20,000 to pay off the gang-masters and buy my freedom. Once I'd achieved that and was free of them, I knew that I was ready to follow my dream and become an artist."

"I suppose that's why I'm still there. I got used to the money. You saw what you could earn. You could have worked two days a week and still earned more than the national average. For me, I've gotten used to the money and the lifestyle. But I don't have that sort of interest, you know, like you and art."

"That's really what I'm going to tell them this evening. If these other women have got an interest, a passion, they will be able to build a new life for themselves. In many respects I'm lucky: my daughter is being looked after by her grandmother back in Romania. It's a cultural thing. I know that a lot of the women here have got young children. When they leave the abusive relationship, maybe a husband, partner, or casual boyfriend, they're on their own. They are insecure. They rely on the Social because, they tell themselves, they need to stay at home to look after the kid. The benefits system here is supposed to provide a lifeboat, but it often results in a lifetime of dependency. They're not working. Home all day with their kid. The first thing they will look for is a man to help them through their loneliness and bored existence. They think he will provide them with some financial support and assist in bringing up the kid. But, almost inevitably, the cycle returns. They end up with another man and, predictably, as before, they make poor choices. It's easier for me. The kid is with my mum. I've learned to become an independent spirit. I don't need a man in my life. And, unlike many of the women here, my experience in the brothel has left me totally numbed with respect to seeking any kind of sexual relationship. So you see, I'm lucky. I can pursue my interest in art. If I make pennies from the sale of my art that is enough for me to survive. I've discussed this with Eileen. I explained to her that I don't think I'm a role model, again because of the cultural differences. I'm not sure how my decisions could be replicated by most of the women here."

I was just blown away by Mickey's understanding, not just of her situation, but how her life was so different from most of the women here. She was so perceptive, but I think Eileen's take would be that if just one member of tonight's audience took Mickey's words and converted them into action, that would be enough.

But Mickey's words were also an inspiration to me. I knew that I had to get out of *my* abusive relationship. I nearly had a stroke, thanks to the man who buys me things. I knew it before my TIA. I didn't need Vish to tell me. My couch potato lifestyle was all because of the man who buys me things. It's not fair to say that he abuses me. He does the only thing he knows how. Everything has a price. I am a bought woman. But I had gotten used to the lifestyle. Getting out, for me, was not to live in an artist's garret. I would have to deal with the man who buys me things in my own way. In such a way so that I could sustain my lifestyle and move on to even better things. Unfortunately for me, moving on to even better things means keeping the things he buys me, the material possessions. They are the only things that I know how to value.

If I could have been with Vish, my life could have been filled with a spirituality that only he could give me. With him I could have dwelt in my equivalent of the artist's garret. Without him, my destiny was just to buy and acquire more things.

I hadn't realised it, but I had started to say all these thoughts out loud. Mickey was looking at me a little confused. I could see she wanted to comfort me. I think she felt my distress. She just seemed to have that empathy, to experience other people's suffering. But I couldn't let her in.

"Mickey, you are so wonderful, and I'm so proud of what you achieved. I can't stay for the talk tonight, but I wish you well. Just keep doing what you're doing."

I got up from the table and we hugged. Tears in my eyes. There's always tears in my eyes. Mickey was able to smile at me. But her face, as ever, would not show the emotion she felt inside. The numbness that she referred to. The result of her abuse was not just numbing her on the sexual side. Tragically, like me, she would never be able to enjoy a stable relationship with another human being.

Far from my helping Mickey, I found that *she* was helping *me* to understand myself, to come to terms with myself, and to exorcise my demons.

Vish, my soulmate, you always knew. You knew that volunteering at *Her Centre* was never about what I could do for them. It was part of your mission in life to rescue me.

# 45
## A business proposal

"Hi, Vish."

"Hey, what have you been doing? It's been a while."

"Oh, you know this and that. Sorry, I've been really busy."

It sounded like a bit of a brush-off. Rache called me when she wanted something, but she had her own life, and I suppose it had always been one-sided. I was always more interested in her life and what she was doing than she was in mine. I'd called a few times. She took her time to get back to me and then she'd be too busy to meet, even for a drink. So I was fascinated to hear what this call was about.

"You don't have a million pounds floating around, do you?"

I thought she was joking, so I gave her a flippant reply.

"Sure, but if you want the cheque, you need to see me for a drink."

"No, I'm actually serious. Fi has offered me the business for a million pounds."

"And I'm serious. Not about the cheque. If you want to talk it through, we do need to discuss it face to face. But do you really want to buy it?"

"That's why I called. I don't know if I do or not. I don't have that sort of money and, even if I did, how do I know how much it's worth?"

"How much do you have?"

"About 200K."

I noted the 'k'. She'd always used the slang 'grand' for a thousand pounds. I wondered what other changes I'd notice since we last met.

"So, let's meet, if you're not too busy, that is."

"OK, Vish, I haven't been returning your calls. *Mea culpa*. Tell you what. Dinner. And I'm paying."

*Mea culpa?* Where did that come from. Rache seemed to be just a little more mature in her discourse. I wondered if it was new friends she'd met. Had she turned her life around since her TIA? We'd spoken, but she hadn't really opened up about any real changes to her lifestyle. I was curious.

"I'll take you up on your offer. Where?"

"I know the Renaissance. Just for old time's sake."

I smiled.

"Dinner's on you. Room's on me."

I knew that she knew I was just kidding.

"Don't tempt me. I'm still waiting to find someone with a better tongue."

"You're too kind, but I know you're flattering me."

"Actually, I'm not. And it's not for want of looking. I can't pretend that I don't miss the sex we had."

For once I wasn't sure whether or not she was kidding or propositioning me.

We had both moved on, and I knew that neither of us wanted to go back there, but there was this lingering thought. Should I book a room, just in case? I quickly dismissed the thought as the musings of an old man trying to regain his youth.

Those days were gone. I drifted momentarily back to Felicity's and the *blue door*. The day I met Cindy. Had I really made a difference to her life? I know that for me, the experience was transformational.

********

Rache was early. She was waiting in the roof top bar. The same one about which she'd been so scathing. The roof should be on top of the building: *sky high, not on the first floor so we're breathing the fucking car fumes.* I smiled as I reminisced at her quaint, if crude, description.

She was quite stunning. I'd always appreciated her looks, but this was a new Rache. No more student attire. A sophisticated, attractive woman, and she'd clearly made an effort to impress me, or seduce me. I had to wonder. She was wearing a black dress, not the mini dress I'd bought for our first assignation at the hotel. This one was knee length but with a slit on the side.

She was seated at a table in the bar and got up to greet me. I moved to kiss her on the cheek, but she turned so our lips met.

"Was that dress just for me?"

"You remembered."

"How could I forget? But you're wearing tights. I remember you trying on the dress in the room and I asked you to leave the tights off. I said I'd get turned on if I knew you weren't wearing panties underneath when we went downstairs to the bar."

"Vish, your eyesight must be failing you. These aren't tights, these are hold-ups."

And as she said that she crossed her legs and allowed her dress to rise up so I could see her bare thighs above the black stockings.

"And who said I'm wearing panties?"

And she proceeded to uncross her legs, and spread them slightly, but, of course, I couldn't see whether or not she was going commando.

There was a bit more banter and sexual innuendo, and I was beginning to regret not booking the room. After our drinks, we moved to the restaurant, ordered our meal and Rache opened with:

"OK, let's get down to business. Fi has cancer and she wants out. She reckons the business grosses £350k after her split with the girls, and nets £300k after paying rent, website, and supplies. I was surprised, because I've cut myself back to ten days a month, but I still account for about a third of the business, though she has four other girls. I know you'll want to know about the lease. There's two years left, but Fi said they can't kick her out. I wanted you to check that because I'm not sure if she's bullshitting me or not."

"Yes, depends on whether it's under the Landlord and Tenant Act, but I have to warn you there's always a morality clause, which they might get you with if they can prove sexual services were being offered."

"Tantric massage?"

"Hmm, it's a grey area legally, but you probably wouldn't want to take your landlord to court over it. Rache, can I say something – you've blown me away."

"I did dress to impress."

"No, not that. You look amazing, of course, but the last time I saw you, you were a college drop-out enjoying the fast life and talking about holidays, fast cars, and clothes. Now you're all business numbers, lease terms. I wouldn't be surprised if you've got a spreadsheet in your handbag."

As I said that she unclipped her bag.

"You're kidding me."

She smiled. The *trademark smile* was still there.

"Yes, just kidding, no spreadsheet, but I'm serious about the business, so I've done some homework. As for me, still fast cars. Thanks to the flat, and I'll be forever grateful to you for pushing me into it, I'm still spinning at the gym with the City hedge funders and investment wankers. I have to keep up and read the Financial Times every day, so I've got something to talk to them about. I make a point of watching Bloomberg while I'm on the exercise bike. I can't remember if it was your idea or mine, but I kept up the BS about being a financial journo. Even Jack uses that line when he introduces me at his business functions. And, don't laugh, but I even met a broker so I can profit from all those stock tips the guys give me, thinking it'll earn them a shag. Haven't used the broker yet. Have to shag him first, to make sure I can trust him."

*So you haven't changed*, I thought. Always transactional.

"Still with Jack, then?"

"That's a story for another day. Let's get back to the business proposal."

I'd gotten over the shock of how Rache had matured, so I turned to the business.

"A million sounds way off the mark. Start negotiating at one year's earnings - £300,000. And don't go to more than £400,000. You've got to play on Fi's weaknesses. But not the health issue. You both know it's there and it won't play well if you use it against her in your discussions. If the lease is under Landlord and Tenant, that's a plus, but even so you're going to have to face a higher rent in two years. But let's talk about if you really want it."

I then went into the ins and outs of running a business. Unless she wanted to take over Fi's role, she was going to need a receptionist, probably two part time, to cover a seven day week. The cash is a major problem. I explained the two issues with cash. Would she be ready to go in every day to pick the cash up. If not, who is would she trust with the money?

"The second issue is laundering, and I don't mean the towels. There's a limit to how much you can stuff into your deposit box."

"I can get a bigger one. I've already checked."

"No, I don't mean the physical size. If the business goes well in a few years you could have a million stashed away, but you won't be able to spend it. You either get into bed with the money launderers, metaphorically speaking, or you move away from cash and swallow the tax. That could be a problem for the girls because they'll see their take home pay drop. It might also be a problem for some clients who want anonymity unless you start taking crypto."

"Really, could that work?"

"Maybe for your City types but not your average Joe. You'll have to work out a system to launder the money, so that you can show it in your bank account. What's your long game in this?"

"I thought a million was a nice round number for an FU nest egg, and then walk away. I could buy the flat for around that figure, but renting seems a better deal and I don't want to be tied down."

"What, five years?"

"Yes, sounds about right. I'll be in my thirties - time for a second career. Don't laugh, but what with reading the FT every day and the tips from my City friends, I was thinking about becoming a professional day trader."

"Rache, be careful with your money laundering and insider dealing, I don't want our get-togethers to be visiting time in Holloway."

We talked some more about the pros and cons of being a business owner. I gave her some ideas about the money laundering and then her final question, which I'd been waiting for.

"Would you stake me?"

"On one condition; we have sex."

"Done!" The *trademark smile* hadn't left.

"No, seriously, the condition is that I'd have to know you were committed."

"I checked my box. I've actually got £230,000 saved, so depending on what I have to pay I might be £200k short. Here's my commitment. If you stake me, I'd up my days back to four a week until I paid you off. With my earnings and the business' profit, I reckon that could be within six to nine months. Your idea of running some of the cash through that property management company you own, that makes sense to me. I'll pay you 10% for your trouble if you think that's fair for being my partner in crime. Better than 50% to the tax man."

Where had I heard that before? How did Rache know 10% was the going rate? I'm sure she didn't mix in Arthur's world.

"What more do I have to do, bat my eyelids?"

I took my mobile out of my pocket and started tapping.

"Hey, what are you doing? Calling an Uber? Bored with me already?"

"No checking my banking app to see how much spare cash I've got."

"Deal?"

She stretched out her hand. I moved mine across the table to shake hers.

"Deal!"

Rache smiled contentedly and announced:

"Glad you said that. It would be a shame to waste the room I booked."

She led me out of the restaurant to the lift lobby.

\*\*\*\*\*\*\*

I'd hoped, but it was beyond my wildest dreams. I think we both knew that this was a last hurrah. Rachel was unaware of my health issues. This was not a moment for me to share them with her. This was a moment for nostalgia.

I had to wonder whether she was just doing this for me. Everything Cindy does is transactional. I had to think that it was just a *quid pro quo* for the business loan. But part of me wanted to believe…

I told myself it shouldn't matter. Pleasuring an old man, another client, that should be enough for me.

I knew I could still pleasure her. The orgasms I gave her with my tongue. I knew they were genuine. I was confident I could still please her. But with all her dramas, the wild claim that I was her soulmate, I never really believed that that was the truth. I sincerely believed that Rachel thought it was her truth. However, I always thought that her soul was so damaged that she never really knew where the truth lay.

For all my psycho-babble, my amateur analysis, there was one thing of which I had no doubt. Until Rachel could banish her Cindy alter ego, her Cindy demon, her soul would never be at peace.

I knew that the only way I could mend that soul would be to exorcise that demon once and for all. I also knew what that meant. She had to face up to the challenge.

She was lying on the bed. Not completely naked; that would not have been seductive. Not with her legs spread; that would have been too crude. She was wearing a satin gown but with just enough of her nudity exposed to tantalise. Her legs to one side, ready to move slowly for me to admire, parting gradually with just a flash to expose her mons, before putting her legs together again and laying back on her other side.

She repeated the process, each time revealing just a little bit more, each time drawing me closer with her *trademark smile*. Imperceptible, I think only I would know, but just a very faint reminder of her TIA on the left side of her face. I hope I didn't give anything away.

"I'm not sure what you're waiting for. Either you've already gone gaga but your mouth is not drooling, or you don't fancy me anymore. Please don't tell me you've gone woke on me and swapped your gender."

I shook my head and smiled. "There's just …."

But she wouldn't let me finish.

"Oh, fuck!"

She sat up on the bed.

"Oh, fuckety fuck. It's worse than that, isn't it? I could take your not fancying me anymore. Even gay shit, but it's not that. It's far worse isn't it?"

I nodded.

"OK, let's get it over with. But I can't promise the after, whether I will still be in the mood. I'm getting better at my tantrums, honest I am. But, you know me, you could set me off and I'd end up in a flood of tears running through the hotel lobby starkers. But go on, lover, do your worst, punish me, give me shit!"

"Well, as you put it so eloquently, and as you seem to be sitting comfortably, I would just sit beside you and hold your hand, if only to stop you getting up to run through the hotel lobby."

*Trademark smile.*

"OK, come on, seriously, I think I'm ready."

So I started, first by asking if she had ever, if Cindy had ever, come out to play while Rachel was still present. I could tell just by looking at her face that she had been there before. I asked her to describe the experience and she relayed how Cassandra, who she described as a female version of me, had managed to get her to come while in a 69. How she achieved a simultaneous orgasm between her and her partner by basically having Cindy pleasure Cassandra while Rachel could lay back and enjoy her partner's tongue. I thanked her for sharing that experience and reassured her that we were really more than halfway to achieving what I had in mind.

When I explained to her what had to be done, she took it well. Not just as a good student understanding the wisdom of a teacher, but more as a colleague, an equal, absorbing by osmosis.

"I hope I haven't completely put you off."

"Well, I'm not going to run through the hotel lobby starkers But, if you think I'm going to let you near my clit after that lecture, you're in Wonderland."

"I do understand. I didn't know how you were going to react. If there's coffee in the room, I'll have a cup and then leave."

She gave me her *trademark smile.* I wasn't sure what was coming next. I was now standing, but she was still sitting on the bed. She grabbed my hips and pulled me closer to her. She started to unbuckle my belt. She slowly and seductively removed my trousers. She left my underpants on, while she massage my penis through the pants, then my testicles. She then removed my underpants, first dropping them to the floor and then carefully lifting each leg. She then looked at my erect member.

"Thank Christ! There's still a bit of life left in the old codger."

She took me in her mouth and did what Cindy does best and only Cindy knows how. I'd forgotten. It had been so long. Her tongue circling, twirling around the glans, sucking hard and deep. She was holding my hips so she could control the thrust. She paused for breath.

"I'm going to swallow it. I'm going to swallow it whole. I want to taste you. I want your seed inside my body."

She continued, increasing the pace, forcing my throbbing member deep down her throat. I could feel her tonsils. I could feel her controlling her gag reflex. I was shaking. She was waiting, waiting for me to come.

At that moment, as I spurted inside her as she promised, instead of withdrawing, she bit me hard and swallowed everything I had to offer. She pulled me onto the bed. She was on top of me, our faces were staring at each other. She started to kiss me passionately. Our tongues met, but hers was forcing itself into my mouth.

She pulled herself away and, with that irreverent charm, asked, "Ready for coffee yet, or is it my turn?"

Now I knew she was ready. We had done this so many times before, but today was different, not just because it was to be our last session, our last sexual experience together. Our last, but the most important. She now knew there was one last thing we had to do.

*He explained it all to me, and as usual, so annoyingly, he knew exactly what he was talking about. He read me like a book but, when I opened the pages, they were blank.*

*So I needed him to nurture. I needed him to guide. That's what he was now ready to do. I'd given him his fond farewell. I thought swallowing his cum was a nice touch. I hoped he appreciated it as a final* hey ho. *But now, I was ready. Then I felt his tongue, the only tongue, and that includes my lover Cassandra, includes Richard and all the others, Vishti's was always, and ever, the only tongue that knew its way deep inside my soul.*

*But he had explained that today was going to be different. So I lay back and tried to enjoy as his tongue was swirling, nibbling, and sucking my lips, circling my clit. Now he was sucking, I was working with him, helping him sense my feelings. I was responding so he knew exactly, exactly where, exactly when, exactly.*

*Wriggle, just a small adjustment, and then right back, right on the button. He was working and I was getting more excited. But now I was focusing on his words. Yes, I could feel Cindy coming out to play with all her guile, her mischievousness, her bitchiness, her street smarts. And, yes, Rachel was here in the present, submissive, just ready to be pleased and ready to be taken.*

*And the tongue, Vish's, Vishti's tongue was still doing its work, was knowing its way, and there he goes, he knows I am ready. But also he knows that I am not. So he takes me down, by nibbling, sucking to keep me hovering, to bide my time. But this time, like never before, I have to focus. I have to stay in the moment. I have to speak to Cindy and tell her what needs to be done.*

*I've always loved you, Cindy, but now I must take control. As I start to come and my body is jerking and in a spasm, no need to tell Vish, my 30 seconds will be provided. My contractions continued. His tongue still lingers, until my full orgasm is complete.*

*I hear Cindy shout out and I see tears in her eyes. Rachel is calling for her to submit. And Cindy is resisting. She still wants her freedom.*

*But Rachel now knows that it is only in this moment, this moment of passion, this moment of bliss, that she can finally exorcise her demon.*

*And Cindy now knows that from this moment on, from this moment of passion, from this moment of bliss, Rachel will hold the key to her freedom.*

# 46
## Monty

Spending the night with Vish was just like old times. Yes, he was older but hadn't lost his tongue touch. We both knew it wasn't to be the rekindling of an old flame. Face it, the flame was never extinguished, just flickering a bit, in the wind. Neither he nor I expected a repeat. Vish, my soulmate for then and forever, but destiny required that we should never again be together as a couple.

After the moment when my demon was extinguished, Vish explained that Cindy had not ceased to exist. It was simply that Rachel needed to know that Cindy was only another side of her character. My issue, Mr Psycho-babble had explained, was that following my childhood abuse, Cindy had become a separate and dominant personality. That I really was two people, and that made me a nutter. (Don't think he put it in quite those words.) All I had to do, what Vish, in that moment of passion, had helped me to achieve, was to merge two souls, so Cindy was back where she belonged, a part of Rachel and part of Rachel's personality, but not a separate character in Rachel's life. Of course, Vish also explained that I could have done all that in a few sessions with a proper shrink if I hadn't been so obstinate, to which Cindy replied: *Yeah, but it was more fun this way, Vish.*

But I had work to do if I was going to be ready for the showdown that I knew was drawing near.

I called Monty, or should that be Monte, third in the line of succession to the inheritance of 5,000 acres of forest in Westphalia, the beneficiary of a trust fund that owns a vineyard. A vineyard that still has, in its cellars, the only remaining bottles of their 1928 Chateau bottled Malbec. Overseer of the €3 billion investment fund, for what they quaintly describe as the Family Office. But to me, a European. An aristo. And the younger brother of the woman who has become my closest female friend, and lover.

He was expecting my call. Cassandra had prepped him.

"I must say, as I told Cassie, that I'd be not only willing to help but it would be nice to catch up again."

"Cassie? Oh you mean Sandy!"

"Who?"

"Sorry, forget it! Private joke. I'm suggesting lunch but insist that I pay. I'm picking *your* brains. It's the least I can do."

"No, that would be ungentlemanly."

"Please, don't embarrass me. It's not up for discussion."

"OK, but only on one condition."

I was hoping, but I still didn't know the guy, so maybe he wasn't ready.

"You let me buy you dinner, in exchange."

Yes. He's bitten!

"OK, but I'm going to take you somewhere special. I promise you, it will be a first, a never to be repeated treat. I expect you to choose somewhere at least as nice for dinner."

A few more back-and-forth comments, and we set the time and place. I wasn't sure where to take him. How do you impress a European aristo that was used to Michelin-starred restaurants for breakfast?

I spoke to Vish. He was more worldly than me. He'd know of a good place, and then Monty would need to think twice before he chose the reciprocating venue for our dinner date.

"He's going to be staying in a hotel up West, but I'd be more comfortable at my end of town. Smart, yes, but cool, one of these new fash places that have a three-month waiting list... This week. Of course, you're right; they'll all be fully booked. What! Are you serious? Really? Do you think? Brilliant, I knew you'd come up with the right place. I would never have thought of that."

I couldn't wait. Vish's inspiration. He was so on the money. He knew that I had to make the right impression with Monty, but at the same time, I had to be within my comfort zone. Of course, there was only one place, it was so obvious once Vish had suggested it.

I met him outside the underground station. He greeted me with the customary kiss on both cheeks. European. Aristo.

"It's literally a few minutes' walk."

He looked around in anticipation.

"Could you do me a favour? Park your backside on that bench over there."

He looked behind him. Took out a handkerchief, I assume silk, brushed the dirt from the bench, and sat down apprehensively.

"Don't worry, I cleaned the bird shit off before you got here. Now tell me - mustard *and* pickle?"

Once he'd gotten over the shock, he took it all in good humour and munched on his salt beef on rye. Then we got down to business.

"I've read up on all the background, but it's more the technical side that I'm not too clear about."

He then took me through the procedures for setting up an offshore account, starting with how to register a company in the British Virgin Islands or BVI, what due diligence they would do before they would *onboard* me as a new client, and how the bank account would work. He then explained how the holding company would only own shares in other companies. It wouldn't hold the cash and property directly.

"I'm not sure I understand what difference it makes having one company own shares in another company that actually owns the property. It all sounds unnecessarily complicated."

He explained:

"It's all about the shuffling of assets. Look, supposing I wanted to sell you my Trump Tower apartment in New York. There'd be paperwork, and escrow and lawyers and such like. You'd either need to sign the paperwork yourself in New York or appoint an attorney. Now, in fact, that property isn't in my name. It's in the name of Montagu137 Inc. My holding company (I'd rather keep the name of that confidential) owns the shares in Montagu137 Inc. All I have to do is email my BVI administrators to transfer the shares to.... what did you decide you wanted to call your holding company?"

"Dycin."

"Yes, Dycin Inc" They transfer the shares in Montagu137 Inc to Dycin Inc and, hey presto, you are now the new proud owner of the Trump Tower apartment."

"Doesn't sound very safe or secure."

"Of course, there are safeguards. Let me show you.

He took out his phone and started to tap.

"I've promised Cassie that she can have the stables I own in County Kerry."

"Ireland?"

"Yes, the Republic, the South. I inherited them, but never go there and Cassie is the horse rider. I was going to wait till I got back to Switzerland next week, but here, let me show you how easy it is."

I was quite intrigued, but this had a serious purpose which I was not prepared to share with Monty or anyone else for that matter.

"Here, I e-mail BVI. I put in my password, best to keep that under wraps."

After tapping in his password, he passed me the phone. Obviously, the password was not visible.

The e-mail read: *Please transfer the shares in Montagu33 Inc to Assand77 Inc.*

"Here, tap send."

We waited no more than 30 seconds.

His phone pinged. It was an SMS with a 6-digit number.

"Oh, like my bank. OTP (one-time passcode)."

"Well done, spot on, but here's the clever trick."

He pulled out a bunch of keys from his pocket. Attached to the key ring was a gizmo-type thing.

He handed me the key ring and invited me to tap in the 6-digit OTP, then told me to press a button, and the gizmo generated another 6-digit OTP. Back to his phone, I'm now inserting that new number and pressing send. We waited, again, couldn't have been more than another 30 seconds. He shows me the e-mail that has just come through which read: *All done, do you want us to send your sister a confirmation?*

"Cassie doesn't know it yet, but she, or rather one of her companies, now owns Montagu33 Inc, which, as you will have guessed, in turn owns the County Kerry stables."

"Wow! Like magic."

"A bad actor would need to know the password, have control of the mobile phone, and the gizmo. So you see the system is foolproof. Not only that but, because no one can see the property has changed hands, there's none of this interfering by the IRS or HMRC."

"What, you mean no tax?"

"What do you call us? Aristos? There was a socialite hotelier called Leona Helmsley who famously said: "Only the little people pay taxes.""

"Not the fucking aristos."

"Exactly! You're about to join the elite set!"

"Euro-fucking-pean aristos?"

Monty laughed out loud.

"No – not that set, the other exclusive club – tax dodgers!"

I was going to tell him about my own small foray into that world via my cash earnings from Felicity's but thought better keep that to myself. Even though I'd be taking a step up, if I ended up buying the business off Fi, this was still small beer compared with the mega-millions that Monty was hiding from the tax people.

*One day Cindy! One day!*

"*So* what happened to that hotel woman?"

"Well, she ended up in jail."

"Murdered her husband or something?"

"Tax dodging!"

"You mean even the aristos get their comeuppance."

"Well, she was rather, how would you say it, taking the piss. Difficult to win the sympathy votes with the jury when you've…"

"Shat on them."

He smiled at my coarseness.

"So we prefer discretion."


There were a few other things I needed to know, so we covered a bit more of the ins and outs of offshore banking, then before parting company, he asked:

"What was the name again?"

"Dycin. D-Y-C-I-N"

"Yes, Dycin Inc. I'll ask our BVI people to set it up immediately. They will require the normal ID, passport, and proof of address. I can certify all the documents which will save couriering stuff through to them."

"Passport?"

"Yes, you do have one, don't you?"

"Of course, but in my name."

Cassandra knew my real name. She'd said: *You don't look like a Rachel.*

I remember now letting that pass because I didn't know if I was being overly sensitive.

Having decided that Cassandra could know my name, I had no problem with telling Monty. But he sensed my initial hesitancy.

"Look, it's none of my business. I can simply introduce you to the BVI administrators and don't have to be your middleman. Really, that's not the object here. I was just trying to save you time."

"Of course, I'll give you my passport. And stuff. Maybe I can bring the papers when we meet for dinner."

"In about three weeks when I'm back in London?"

"Oh, when are you leaving?"

"Tomorrow. Catching the afternoon flight to Zurich, home in time for dinner."

He could tell that my face dropped.

"Unless this BVI thing is urgent. I'm free tonight if you have nothing else to do."

*Trademark smile.*


*******

*Cassie had warned me that Cindy could be a little unconventional. When I called my sister to tell her about the Irish stables, I mentioned the lunch venue. She just laughed:* That's what I mean. That's what I love about her. You never know what to expect.

*I couldn't match her for a like-for-like venue, but I'd received a personal invitation to Richard Caring's pre-view soft-opening of Bacchanalia, his new restaurant five minutes' walk from Claridge's, where I was staying. I hadn't intended on going as I was packing for my departure the following day, but Cindy seemed keen to get this BVI thing sorted.*

*I thought she'd be impressed to be one of the few people invited to this exclusive event. Richard, originally a Caringi before the name was anglicised, was looking for branding advice for his new venture. He went to his Italian roots to find the branding consultancy which happened to be a joint venture with our Italian relatives, where I sit on the board. The agency took his concept and, perhaps unsurprisingly, came up with a Roman twist: Bacchanalia – A Mediterranean Odyssey. I ended up as one of fewer than a hundred people to receive an invite.*

*I should have listened to my sister. Cindy seemed completely unfazed, and, while she was OK to eat there, she insisted that we have drinks at my hotel first. Her rationale:* I want to give you those papers first and doing it at the restaurant doesn't seem the right place.

*When she arrived at the hotel bar, she didn't disappoint. She turned heads as she waltzed past the other guests in a backless Valentino green silk cocktail dress and matching Louboutins with 9-centimetre heels. She may have appeared indifferent to attending the exclusive dinner, but she would still want to impress the billionaire restaurateur.*

"You never know when I might be in the market for a new sugar-daddy. If the name of the new restaurant is anything to go by, I think Richard and I are going to hit it off."

*I'd half hoped the Valentino was to dazzle me, but I'd come to learn that Cindy was always on the make. She may only have been half-joking about a new sugar-daddy.*

*I asked what she was drinking. Instead of responding, she waved at the waiter, who came across to our table. She flashed him a most provocative smile, as she ordered a* Martini, with an olive, make that dirty! *The slightly embarrassed waiter inquired:* Gin or vodka?

*Her response took me aback. Completely deadpan:* If you have to ask, you'd better tell the bartender to come over to take my order.

*I looked at her. Smiled at the poor young man:*

"The lady will be having a gin martini."

"Cindy, can I ask you a very personal question. Please don't take this the wrong way. Where do you get it from?"

"Cassandra. When I first met her, I was in total awe. She appeared to me as so sophisticated, so self-assured. So European aristo. I have to admit, I copied her. But you have to believe me, that if I'm down the Crown & Anchor in Greenwich, I put my airs & graces in my back pocket and you're just as likely to find me half legless offering to snog the winner of a game of pool."

*I didn't really get the scenario. I think she was playing with me, and simply telling me that she can mix with the best and worst in Society.*

*She'd hardly been there for ten minutes, her drink still half full, when she suddenly got up:*

"Sorry Monty, I have to ask the Concierge something. Here's all the paperwork. Thank you again."

*She walked out, without looking back, leaving me speechless. After 5 minutes, I started to get worried. After 10 minutes, I got up to speak to the Concierge.*

"Young woman, wearing a green dress. She said she was coming out to ask you something?"

"Oh yes, she asked me to send something up to your room, left this note for me to give you, in case you came to see where she was. The gift is waiting in your room, sir."

*I was completely off-balance. Cassie told me not to be surprised by anything Cindy did, but the Richard Caring preview? There are people who'd pay serious money just for a seat at that table.*

*I opened the envelope and read the message:*

Really sorry to disappoint. Please apologise to Richard. Tell him another time. I left something in your room. It would be nice if you would open it before you go off to your FU-look-how-wonderful-I-am-Richard-Caring-Snobfest.

*I wasn't sure if I upset her. I sent a text to Cassie:*

"Think I've upset Cindy. She's left a present in my room but has blown me out for dinner. Any thoughts?"

*Cassie replied instantaneously:* "Don't worry. She's a tough nut. I'd suggest picking up the present first, then play it by ear."

*I went up to the room, not knowing what to expect. When I opened the door, my silk dressing gown was draped over the couch, which was odd, as I usually hang it in the bathroom. Then it moved. For a split second, I thought Cindy had left me a rattlesnake until I heard a familiar voice:*

"What took you so long, lover? I was getting ready to leave."

\*\*\*\*\*\*\*\*

When I told Cassandra, I knew she'd be up for it. I just didn't know if I could pull it off. Of course, she knew the Concierge, but I loved how she handled it:

"I told Carlo that it was Monty's birthday, and that I'd arranged an escort for the evening who would give him a codeword, what, let me see, Vade Mecum, yes, that would work. I said that she'd tell him her name was Cindy and give him the codeword. I asked him to please be an absolute darling and let her into Monty's suite!"

I was still a little anxious. He'd made such a big thing over the Richard Carling pre-view. You know, just 100 guests and all of them *royalty*. That was his word for the nouveau riche. The children of pop stars and the like. He meant the new guard who had taken over from his type - old money. I think he despised them, no breeding, unlike his class. European aristos. But nevertheless they were the new royalty so he would want to prove that he was still a player on the London social scene. I thought he might very well go to dinner on his own and miss out on what he could eat back in his suite.

When I heard the door open, I pulled the gown over me, it swamped my tiny frame, so he wouldn't see me lying on the couch, face and body hidden.

"What took you so long, lover, I was getting ready to leave."

"I... I... er..."

"Oh, just come over here and eat my pussy. I'm so damp with anticipation."

"Can we go into the bedroom? It might be more comfortable for you."

"Don't you remember what I said downstairs? Half legless, snogging on the pool table, that's me. I think the couch will do fine."

He started to laugh.

*Thank fuck!* I thought. I was beginning to wonder whether he really was from the same gene pool as Cassandra.

He came over to me and picked me up into his arms and, as he carried me into his bedroom, he quietly crowed:

"I think it's time for this European aristo to take control."

I am now on the bed, the gown open, revealing my nakedness. Now he is down between my legs. I only really have one thought: *I can't expect better, but will he be as good as...*

His tongue knows its way to the playground. I quiver as soon as it touches my clit. I almost come there and then. I am already horny. I have been playing with myself while waiting for him. The anticipation, and the slight anxiety, not knowing whether he would come up, has heightened my excitement. Now he is inside, licking the walls of my vagina. This is a first.

His tongue seems very long, and I thought for a moment that perhaps he was really trying to lick my G-spot. European aristos, even Cassandra, had never tried that one! He removes his tongue and goes back to the clit. Oh, I get it. He is using that trick to slow me down. Must remember that. He works my clit until he can feel I'm ready, then tongue fucks my pussy to take me down. *God, keep doing that.* About three, four more times, and I have to intervene.

"I'm gonna come. I'm gonna come. I'm coming. I'm coming."

I was going to add *don't stop,* but I don't need to. I can't believe they shared notes, but it was as though Cassandra had said: *By the way, once she's come, continue for 30 seconds, she'll need to pass two or three more contractions, to make sure her orgasm is complete.*

Fuck! Good. Certainly up there with the best. No, not in the Vish league, and I didn't want to bring him down a peg, but no match for Cassandra. But certainly good enough for me to want to give him his *quid pro quo.*

I was on my back. He was on top of me. His erection was rubbing against my mons. Knocking at the door, so to speak, waiting to enter. I needed to wriggle to get into position, to let him in. Getting ready to let him penetrate me. I wanted him deep inside. I wanted to feel his hard cock. I was ready to submit. My juices were flowing. I was ready for him to take me.

I looked at his face. Rugged. Charming, Romanic. He smiled and I suddenly froze.

How could I have been so stupid? I pushed him off me. I turned over so that I was lying on my stomach, my legs slightly apart, my butt cheeks on show. I raised my belly slightly: *European aristo. Euro-fucking-pean aristo!*

And I let him take me from the rear.

# 47

# 1928 Macallan

My meeting with Monty had been the prep for what was about to unfold. Jack and I had been together for almost five years. Nobody would have given it that long, certainly not me. I went over to his penthouse apartment, about 5,000 square feet overlooking the Thames. Must have cost about £10 million. I really wanted to be on neutral ground because I knew what was coming and I didn't want to give him the upper hand. But he insisted that I came over because he had something very special to show me. If I'm honest, I was curious because he seemed really excited. When he opened the door he greeted me with an indifferent kiss, but he looked like a kid in a toy shop.

"I've got something to show you. You will be so impressed."

It was a bottle of Scotch. A bloody bottle of Scotch.

"Are we having a drink?"

"You have to be kidding me. Do you know how much I paid for this?"

I thought, humour him, build up his ego, "Oh, I don't know £1,000."

He stared at me with a look of disdain, as if to say: *You stupid bitch*! He really upset me when he looked at me like that. I just felt so disrespected. When I think about what I'd given him in our five years together and now, I was his constant companion. OK, not his exclusive lover, but then, we'd never been exclusive. But I'd given him pleasure, which was rarely reciprocated. I'd never really loved him. It was always contractual. He knew that. That didn't mean I didn't take the sex seriously with him. On the contrary, I always gave him my best, even though I needed to go elsewhere for satisfaction.

So, he gave me this contemptuous look, before telling me his story about how he had won the auction. Some charity do where this bottle of whisky had come up. He knew it was coming:   Macallan, 50-year-old anniversary malt, 1928 Speyside. He read to me directly from the auction catalogue:

*Distilled 1928. Bottled 1983. #003 of 500. Natural cask strength 38.6%.*
*Comes with a letter of authenticity from Alan G Shiach - Chairman*
*Macallan Glenlivet Distillery.*

*In presentation wooden leather box.*

I asked to see the label. He thought I was interested in the scotch, but I was curious about the year. What was it about 1928? First it was Cassandra's Malbec and now Jack's Scotch Whisky. There was something about 1928. Were the gods trying to tell me something?

So, Jack then proceeded to tell me about the auction. There were only two bidders left – him and a business rival sitting at the same table. The bidding went up to £70,000, and each bid, after the guide price of £40,000 had been reached, was received with raucous cheers.

Jack went on to describe how he was bidding against his rival. It was going up by £2,000 a time but when it got to £70,000, he scribbled on a piece of paper which he slid across to the rival. His rival in the bidding, and in his business world, unfolded the paper and folded it back again. Jack then shouted £75,000. The auctioneer looked at the rival, who shook his head. The hammer went down. Everybody clapped and cheered. £75,000 for a fucking bottle of whisky.

Jack was enjoying the tale. There was no mileage in me spoiling the flow. I asked him the question that he wanted me to ask:

"What was on the paper?"

"Oh, it just said Madeleine with a telephone number."

This was getting tedious. He was like a poor comedian spinning out a shaggy dog story for dramatic effect but losing the audience. I was getting fed up, but I had to suffer his idiocy.

"Don't keep me in suspense. Who is Madeleine?"

But I could guess what was coming.

"Madeleine was his mistress. It was an open secret, but his wife said if she could ever get hold of that woman, she would make sure to end it."

"So you were just telling him, showing him that you had control."

"Exactly, it was all about control and who was the Master of the Universe. He may be my business rival, but in my market I always win."

"Would you have given, you know, the phone number, to his wife?"

"We will never know, will we?"

He gave a devilish smile, trying to ape a Bond villain.

"I had budgeted £75k for the Scotch. I knew I had to win."

I didn't want to spoil his party, but if there were only two of them left bidding, couldn't he have slipped the paper at, say, £50,000 and saved himself 25 large in the process? It seemed a little churlish, so I kept shtum.

"So, if you're not going to let me have a shot of your pricey number, what are you saving it for? Don't tell me, I know. You will open the bottle after you've *done your Mae West*, you know, the deal of all deals, the one you've been waiting for. What is it, some £10 billion IPO? You'd want something like that to celebrate your deal."

"You mean the unicorn I'm working on? It's just $3 billion, actually. No! No, this remains an investment. It can only go up in value. But I have pledged that if the day comes, when I'm knocked off my perch, when one of those young Turks who work for me, or some other fucker, steals my glory and takes over as numero uno... When I am no longer Master of the Universe... When, and I know that day might come, when I lose the edge... Because, in this business, if you don't have edge, if don't have ego, if you don't have the self-confidence, you can't pull it off... I fear the day may come, and I've often imagined it will come from the most unlikely direction. But if it does, I hope I will be able to take it with grace, I hope I will be able to look my opponent in the eye and pour myself a glass from my £75,000 Macallan and toast their success."

Enough of this shit. Jack had changed since I first met him. He was only supposed to be in London for a few years before going back to New York. As luck would have it, he had been offered a CEO position at a boutique hedge fund based in the West End. His career went from being the top dog in a leading US bank to becoming Master of the Universe. His ego and share options meant he couldn't spend his money fast enough. Even his pending divorce would not eat into his quite considerable wealth. The marriage was already over before he told Ellie Mae about the new job. As he was staying in London indefinitely, their separation was now final and she filed for divorce. She'd always known about his shenanigans. Not about me, but I happened to bump into her on one of her infrequent trips to London. Purely by accident, I discovered that we shared a manicurist at the hair salon at Harrods. She confided that she had known Jack was seeing escorts on a frequent basis.

My role had changed. Ever since their estrangement, I had become his companion. He'd set me up in a *pied à terre* in Chelsea. I'd accompany him on business trips. But above all, I was his arm candy at corporate events. The average age of the hedge fund guys was mid-thirties. He was the elder statesman, but when it came to their wives, girlfriends or plus ones (or pluses one, as we used to joke), when it came to them, he could wheel me out with pride.

But was it enough? We had never been exclusive. I never wanted to offer him that, and if he was on a trip without me, he'd always played away and nothing was going to change. I'd never wanted to replace Ellie Mae but now I was the stable partner, and, when he wanted a bit of variety, a bit of excitement, he looked elsewhere.

I'd had enough of the small talk. It was time to get down to business.

"Jack, it is time for me to tell you what I want, what I need, from you."

"I don't understand. What *do* you want? My enduring love? I thought we understood. No commitments. That's what you said."

"That's right, but isn't there a price to pay?"

"For what?"

"For you getting between my legs while you're still smelling of your last lady of the night."

"Is that what this is about? I've been seeing Belinda off and on for years, since before I met you. If I remember correctly, you were busy that night. That mystery man, the Indian guru you won't tell me about. Business you said. Did he come through for you, by the way?"

"As a matter of fact, he did. A loan of £200,000 for my new business venture."

Jack laughed but it wasn't a *ha ha* laugh. It was a mean laugh.

"200K? Chump change! I would have given it to you, not lent it to you."

"No, you wouldn't! You would have asked me what it was for. You would have got one of your analysts to run their spreadsheet over the business plan before dropping a dime. Then you would have presented me with 101 changes to the business model to improve the return on investment."

"And what's wrong with that?"

"Nothing, but that's your world, not mine."

"And the Indian guru just sits on his magic carpet and manifests the money out of thin air. Sorry, Rachel, we take investment seriously in our shop."

He was the only one who calls me Rachel. Even his friends and colleagues respect my preference and drop the "L".

"He respects my opinion, my decision."

"I respect you."

"No, you don't, not where it matters in the business world, the corporate world."

He just burst out laughing.

"Of course, I don't respect you in my world. I'm talking £200 million deals and you're messing around with £200,000. You're not in my league, Rachel, so please don't give me that shit!"

"Don't do this, Jack. Don't make me spell out my terms for staying with you."

"Your terms. Your fucking terms. I own you. OK, tell me what you want. Another diamond ring? A fur coat? Oh that's right, fur isn't PC. Another pair of Louboutins then. Send me the invoice. Deal done! Now, can we get back to normal?"

"I want to buy my flat."

"Chelsea?"

"No, the flat in Greenwich. My rental. It's come on the market."

"How much?"

"One two."

"More than a million for a bachelor pad in Greenwich. That's where you met Gus, isn't it? He was a neighbour and then you jumped ship when something better came along."

"It doesn't work with me, all the put-downs."

"Sorry, darling, I won't let you buy it for one point two. You're being ripped off. But here you are. Just to show no hard feelings, I'll give you a mil, go buy something else."

"It's a million two. I like the flat. It's got a nice view of the river."

"OK, one two. Well negotiated. See, I respect you in business."

"Don't be sarcastic. Are you serious, can I put the offer in?"

"OK. Done deal. £1.2 million for the flat. After the divorce is through. Cash is a little tight, and Ellie Mae will take me for at least $20 million. Six months. I'll give you the £1.2 million. No strings."

"I need it now. The flat won't be there in six months. I've set my heart on it."

"Look, I'm not bullshitting you. I would if I could. Honestly, if I had the free cash and didn't have to put it all down on paper for the divorce settlement, I'd write out the cheque here and now."

"I never know when you're serious."

"I am serious, in six months I will give you the money."

"Let me ask you straight. If put a couple of pieces of paper in front of you, for you to sign, here and now, as you say, which meant I could buy the flat without waiting. And you wouldn't have to part with any money for six months, would you do it? Here and now."

"God's honest truth and hope to die."

"I'd rather you hadn't phrased it like that."

He looked at the chequebook I was sliding across the table to where he was sitting.

"Sign here. You'll recognise that."

"Where did you get that from?"

"Oh, Jack! You just leave things lying around my Chelsea pad. Shall I write the date, six months from now, and the amount? That's one piece of paper for you to sign."

"Well done, Rachel, pulled one over on the old guy."

He grabbed the cheque book lying on the table between us. He scribbled on one of the cheques and slid the cheque book back to me.

"There you are. Man of my word. Signed and dated, six months hence. Still don't see how you're going to get the flat, though. Mr Guru's magic carpet again."

"Please, Jack, just sign the next piece of paper. This one won't cost you a penny."

"OK, and what's this?"

He looked down at the single sheet of paper I had just slid across the table, so it was now lying in front of him.

"A guarantee?"

"Yes, it's called a personal guarantee. That's where, for example, you say to the bank, if Rachel doesn't pay this loan back, the bank can ask you for the money."

"I know what a personal guarantee is. Don't play games with me!"

"It's not a game, Jack. The bank are giving me a £1.2 million pound loan, for six months. And the beauty is that the bank will never have to call the guarantee, because, hey presto, I can bank the post-dated cheque in six months' time."

"Which bank? Even with my guarantee, no bank would do that without checking me out. No one's asked me for a reference."

"Didn't need a reference. I went to see Gus at your old bank. Always good never to burn bridges. Of course, he knew you were good for one point two so he didn't need to take up any bank references."

"And the interest? How on earth can you afford the interest?"

"Oh, don't worry about that. That's what my business meeting was about the other day. I'll be pulling in enough to cover the interest and more."

Jack started to clap slowly in mock congratulations.

"You're still not taking me seriously, are you?"

"Why, is there more? Don't think I have anything more left because of the divorce. Between you and Ellie Mae, you've cleaned me out proper."

I thought: *I haven't got started yet, kiddo*, but realised it was best to keep that thought to myself.

"No more paperwork to sign. I promise you. I won't ask you to sign any other scraps of paper this evening. But, yes, the divorce. You know I bumped into Ellie Mae purely by chance the other day. It appears we share the same manicurist at Harrods. She was here visiting her U.K. lawyer. Something about depositions. She didn't mention numbers, but rather implied that she thought you had some assets stashed away."

"Cow. This was supposed to be an amicable divorce. She's getting about $20 million, plus $10 million in trust for the kids."

"The apartment in Barbados. Port St Charles. You said you won't go there again. Too many Canadians."

"So?"

"I loved it. The last time we went there you said I could go there anytime."

"If I remember correctly, I said you could go there *anytime you wanted a break from me*. Still stands. It's yours."

"Thank you. That's all I wanted."

"To visit the apartment."

"To have the apartment."

"You are kidding me. That's $7million."

"The last one sold for 6.5 and that was on a higher floor than yours, so I really think 7 is a bit high."

"You're serious, aren't you?"

"Yes, I had to make sure I could afford the service charge, it's a ridiculous $20,000 a year, but with my new…"

"I know, your new business."

"Yes, I needed to make sure I could cover the expenses on the property before I asked you to transfer it to my name."

Jack laughed. He was taunting me again. He told me that if I'd done my homework, I'd know that the property wasn't in his name, so how could he transfer it.

"Jack, why won't you take me seriously? I did do my homework. Sunny Hills Properties Inc."

"How the fuck!"

"Jack, you think I'm just a ditzy blonde, an air head. You leave stuff lying around. Papers. Bank statements. Files open on your lap top."

That threw him.

"You bitch, you've been spying…"

"Jack, please don't get emotional. This is purely business. Barbados. It's not too much to ask. I hope you'll agree."

"You are shitting me. I think you'd better leave before…"

"Before what? Come on, Jack! Before I phone Ellie Mae and give her the details of some of those offshore accounts. Some of those BVI companies that own those hidden assets. How much, Jack, how much are you hiding from Ellie Mae? I reckon you've got several hundred million hidden away."

"About half a bill, but I've got some investment partners."

Shit! I hadn't factored them in. But I'd gone this far so I had to carry on:

"She knows that you lied on your deposition, but she's got no proof. If she did, what would that mean, Jack. Five years in jail for perjury?"

"You fucking bitch. You're blackmailing me. Go on, give it your best shot. You try that, sunshine. See where that gets you. You think I haven't done my own homework on you? You think I don't know that you're a ho on the side. Wanking people off for a tenner."

"Oh, Jack, I never wanted to go there, you're forcing me."

"You fucking cow. I'll never give in to blackmail. I'll swing first."

His steely eyes, cold and piercing. I had to calm him down.

"Please don't use that word. I'm just suggesting that I continue to use the Barbados Property, which you'll never miss. You said you doubt you'll ever use it."

"You're not asking just to use it; you want to own it."

"Well, technically, I won't own it. Dycin Inc will own it. Actually, let me be precise. Your holding company which owns the shares in Sunny Hills Properties Inc, whose sole asset is the Barbados property, will transfer the shares in Sunny Hills to Dycin."

"Who the fuck is Dycin?"

"Oh sorry, it's a BVI company that I don't own, just like you don't own Sunny Hills."

My plan was coming together. Monty had set up the company for me. So far, so good, but how far was Jack going to push me?

"Fine," he said, grudgingly. "Well done, so you now know how to set up a BVI company. So, assuming I was prepared to give in to your blackmail, how do you propose I make the transfer?"

"Is that a deal?"

"What do you mean?"

"Well, if I can tell you how you could make that transfer, here and now, without signing any more papers… Remember when you kindly helped me to buy the flat about 10 minutes ago, you asked if there was anything else and I said that I'd promise I wouldn't ask you to sign any other scraps of paper this evening?"

"Your words entirely."

"Yes, I know, Jack. I prepared for this. If there were no more papers to sign, then could I have the apartment?"

He looked a little puzzled. I could see he was wondering what was coming next.

"No, not quite, Rachel. Two conditions: the first, show me how I can transfer to you a $7 million apartment without signing any paperwork. Do that and you're half way there. Second condition, and the reason I won't give in to blackmail, your blackmail...."

"Please don't use that word."

He ignored that interjection.

"Blackmailers always come back for more. I couldn't trust you. Today Barbados, tomorrow the 1,000 acre farm in Australia."

"Thank you. I didn't know about that."

*Almost, Jack, you almost cracked a smile.*

"Rachel, I'm serious. Those are the conditions. The first is a test to see if you've done your homework. The second condition, I don't know how you can meet that. How you can demonstrate to me that it's all over, no more twisting my arm for more money?"

"Are you ready? Sit down. I need you to focus."

He'd been very fidgety, since he realised that I knew more about his offshore assets than he could ever have imagined. That that could cost him tens maybe hundreds of millions in his divorce settlement, and worse, jail time. He had lied under oath when he disclosed his statement of assets to Ellie Mae's lawyers, and that was perjury. He sat down and faced me across the table.

I then proceeded to tell him what he already knew. All he had to do was email his administrators in the BVI and instruct them to transfer the shares. No paperwork for him, no signature required. Of course, for the email he would need his password. The one only he knew. Then he'd need his phone, because the people in the BVI would send a one-time passcode to his mobile, like most banks use. Here was the clever bit. He'd need that gizmo that he keeps with his car keys. He had to enter the passcode from the BVI into the gizmo which would generate another number, and it was this number that he'd send back to the BVI to confirm the transaction.

I told him exactly how he could do it, to prove that I knew. Monty had shown me all that when he set up Dycin for me. I've got my own gizmo, just like Jack's.

I looked at Jack.

"Are you impressed yet? Are you ready to concede that I am no longer the bimbo, even if not your equal?"

His look had changed. His look now seemed to be saying: *I've underestimated you. OK, you're good, but not that good.*

But I hadn't finished. Oh, Jack, I didn't want to blackmail you. I didn't want to bring you down, but you're going to push me, I could tell. You're going to push me to the point of no return and then there will be no going back. You're going to push me like you did when you asked me if I really enjoyed sex with you and bullied me until I had to tell you the truth.

I remember so clearly telling him:

"I can't say I don't enjoy it when we fuck, but to be honest it's never great. You'll never be a great lover. To be a great lover, you have to learn to give."

Then he replied that he gives me gifts all the time and I said:

"I mean give of yourself when we have sex."

"I like to be in control."

"It not about control, Jack. You can give and still be in control, like when I give you head. You enjoy that, don't you?"

"Are you kidding? You're the best there is."

"When I give you head, I give it my all, I give myself to you completely. Everything I do when I'm sucking you off is for your pleasure, for your satisfaction. But I never lose control. Quite the opposite, I stay perfectly in control. I'm the *best there is*, as you kindly put it, because I stay in control. I will stay focused while I'm sucking, while I'm licking, At each moment, feeling, sensing your reactions, circling, nibbling, until I can sense that you're coming, then edging you two or three times until I know you're ready. Then giving you an explosive orgasm. All the time doing this selflessly, for you, giving my all. So you see, Jack, it's not about control – it's basically that you're a selfish fuck. Always were, always will be, but *hey ho!*"

I surprised myself. Jack was dumbfounded. No one had ever spoken to him like that. I'd shaken his ego a bit, but he soon recovered and was back to his old arrogant self. What he didn't know was that this was different. *This time, if you force me Jack, this time, there can be no mercy. Please don't make me. Please don't make me do it.*

Jack continued. He was looking at my face but he had not heard my thoughts and he certainly didn't know what was coming.

"Well, I have to admit you really surprised me with your research and knowledge. Well done, but there were two conditions and you only passed one. I don't see how you can persuade me that you won't come back for more."

"There is no more, Jack. It's all gone. I won't come back for more because there is no more. But, if you do the right thing, the honourable thing, and give 50% to Ellie Mae, then you'll get the other 50% back. I didn't know about your investment partners. I'm not a thief, Jack, you'll just have to believe me when I say I'll make them whole."

"I don't know what the fuck you're talking about, but if you think you're going to mess with my offshore accounts. Actually, you try! They're password protected."

Oh, I had to laugh. I wanted to stay professional, but he was behaving like a cartoon villain.

"What's so funny?"

"You are, Jack, you are! You have two daughters, don't you, Jack?"

He looked puzzled but nodded.

"Kate, 10th April 2004, and Alison, 17th of October 2006."

He was still looking puzzled but his expression was changing. His face was getting flushed. I think he knew what was coming.

"You see I got a bit confused that day when you asked me to download a file from your laptop and I needed your password: Kate041004. But then I realised the Americans switch the month and the date. It was fairly obvious really but I just had to try it out: Alison101706."

He was beginning to get visibly angry. He picked up his phone. "Security, I need someone removed from the penthouse."

"Jack, no, Jack, please let me finish. This is the good bit. Now, Jack, please, tell security you made a mistake."

As I spoke I was waving my gizmo at Jack. The one that looked identical to his. The one that generated a unique OTP.

He looked at me in bewilderment. I motioned to him to call off security. He dutifully obliged.

"These gizmo thingummies all look the same, don't they? This failsafe system works pretty well until you fall asleep next to your lover, next to your mistress, with your phone and gizmo left lying around."

Now he's checking to see if the gizmo on his key ring really is his or mine.

"Don't worry, that's your gizmo. I don't need it any more. There's nothing left. Game over, Jack. I cut a deal with Ellie Mae. She said I could have the Barbados apartment. She's not greedy, Jack."

"I think you've said enough. I know people. Serious people who do serious things. Don't make me hurt you."

I was starting to get angry and for the first time raised my voice.

"When are you going to get it, Jack? It's over. You said earlier that you thought that when it came, you know, being knocked off that pedestal, you said it might come from an unexpected direction. This is the direction, Jack. It's over! You're over! If you play nasty, you end up skint with your investment partners breathing down your neck. Co-operate, and there's more than enough to go around. Your partners will get their share back. You'll still have enough to live on. Just that no one will ever want to do business with you again. Try and accept defeat gracefully."

He got up from the table and turned away from me. He was shuffling, no more stride in his step, shuffling like an old man. He kept shuffling over to the bar in the corner, picked up a bottle, put it down, picked up another, scotch, gin he didn't seem to care. Never a real drinker, but in need of consolation, if only from a bottle of booze.

I was staring at a broken man. The man I had broken. I felt no sense of satisfaction, no sense of pride. The ditzy blonde, the flower girl from dahn the Old Kent Road had picked up this Master of Universe, picked him up like a clump of damp laundry to be wound through a mangle and squeezed dry. No sense of satisfaction, no sense of pride, as the clump of laundry, now paper thin and lacking any shape, was ready to suffer the final ignominy of the pressure of the steam iron.

He had two glasses in his hand when he came back to the table. He opened the bottle carelessly and poured more than half a glass. He touched the other glass and looked at me to see if I wanted to join him.

That was a first; Jack made a point of always making me pour his drink. I could be sitting on the loo and he would shout, "*Fancy a drink, kiddo?*" Whether I said yes or no, I'd come out of the loo and he'd be waiting there, waiting for me to get him the drink and pour it for him before pouring mine. Ever the slob, never a gentleman, but he explained to me that it was a master and slave thing. For him to pour me a drink, or even offer to pour me a drink meant that I had won. In his own small way, he was acknowledging that I deserved his respect.

So, I nodded and he poured me a generous double shot. He wasn't being mean, only pouring me a double when he had half a glass. My double shot was in celebration, his half glass was there to drown his sorrows.

He raised the glass and I raised mine and as the glasses clinked together he toasted:

"Here's looking at you, kiddo!"

I sipped my drink, feeling confident and assured, pleased with what I had just achieved, but no sense of satisfaction, no sense of pride, yet with some remorse, not for Jack, but for Cindy, knowing that this phase of her life was over.

I glanced across at Jack, who was looking at his now empty glass, a broken man, and pouring himself another oversized measure. As he put down the bottle, which was now barely half full, I glanced at the label – Macallan Anniversary Malt 1928.

# 48

# Sitting on a Yacht

Things were never quite the same after my triumphant conquest. I don't mean with Jack but overall. My life. I felt I'd come so far. Now I had everything: the financial security and a steady business.

I had handed the day-to-day over to June, the new Fi. She was glad to get out of the treatment room and was quite content to give up the hand jobs and blow jobs, or whatever went on in her treatment room. She was happy to swap that for the position of overpaid receptionist. No salary, but a third of the take, pulling in £100K a year. The other two-thirds went straight into my bank account. We were quite legitimate now, well, almost, if you ignored some of the shenanigans that went on in the treatment rooms. Financially legit, I mean. When I told Vish about my *coup de grace* with Jack, he suggested - well, implored might be more accurate - that I should start to pay my taxes. What were his words: *Think of it as your debt to society, and, in any case, it means you can stop relying on those shady money launderers.* I took his advice. I remembered Monty and his story of that hotel women who ended up in jail.

My idea of becoming a professional day trader hadn't really come to fruition. Instead my BVI administrators had introduced me to a bank in Barbados. They looked after my portfolio. Apart from the Barbados property, Ellie Mae gave me a nice bonus, so the income from my portfolio took care of my regular expenses. That left the money from Felicity's, which my banker turned to good use, introducing me to some more speculative investments that were, so far, paying off handsomely.

Time to move on, to the next phase of my life.

I'd already hit the big three zero, and something in me had changed. I still enjoyed sex, but it no longer dominated my life. When I met a new guy, I stopped wondering what he would be like in bed. I was more concerned about his thoughts, whether I could have a sensible conversation with him, whether he valued my opinions and I valued his. Vish had told me to find someone I could spend an evening with, in front of the TV, me reading a book and him flicking through his e-mails, both knowing that we didn't need to say a word, just enjoying each other's company, each other's energy.

Vish had told me that I'd know this guy when I met him. There would be a sign. I would know, there and then, that he would be my life partner.

Of course, Vish and I had stayed in touch, the occasional dinners, less frequent now, almost down to birthdays and anniversaries. His birthday, my birthday and of course the 6th of September, that chilly autumn afternoon when he first stood outside the *blue door*.

*******

I was sitting sipping a dry martini on the yacht which was moored opposite my apartment in Port St. Charles.

"Could you make that dirty when you top me up?"

I glanced across at the bronzed Adonis, in his budgie smugglers; my boat boy, who was under strict instructions to always keep my yacht spick and span and his body always ready for action.

"You want dirty?"

He had a slight Bajan accent. He was the product of a rather beautiful local girl (I'd seen old photos) who was swept off her feet by some Canadian millionaire when she was 17. Their love child had grown into quite a stunning young man, but his mixed race had resulted in almost Asian features. South Asian, Indian. I pictured him as how Vish might have been when he was younger. Probably not, but it made for a more interesting time when I bedded the boat boy.

"Yes dirty martini. Do we have brine from an olive bottle?"

Poor boy, I'd lost him, but my mind was back at Jimmy's house, challenging him to make a dirty martini without troubling the butler, and our stupid cocktail guessing games, and Cassandra's tongue, and.... my fist... had I really done that? Certainly never found anyone else to do that with...

I was suddenly woken out of my daydream. I looked up at the side of the mooring and saw a guy standing there wearing this stupid boat captain's hat. He wasn't at all my type. He was probably in his mid-forties, and he had a very prominent birthmark almost like a half moustache, a flattened mole across his upper lip. It really stood out. I thought, I bet he was self-conscious about that when he was a kid. That probably accounted for his slightly awkward manner as he started stuttering his words. I thought, please not another wally with a pathetic pick-up line. But there was something about that mole. I thought I'd seen it before but couldn't place it.

"I say, I know this is terribly forward of me, but we're neighbours; I'm renting the apartment next to you. I'm only here for 10 days. Please don't think I'm stalking you, but I saw that you spend most of your time on your own, and I thought maybe we could share a cup of coffee sometime."

"Or a chocolate milkshake," I tried to brush him off.

He look confused but smiled.

"Well, you don't know if I drink coffee, so that was fairly random. You might just as well have picked a chocolate milkshake."

And I thought, should I or shouldn't I? No, not the coffee, you know what I mean, should I flash him? I was still wearing the same bikini from Bali. I could afford better now, but it held so many memories.

No, please don't be so crude, I didn't mean flash him my tits! I meant, of course, flash him my smile…

My *trademark smile.*

He smiled back. The *trademark smile* that Vish had first mentioned. It was natural, I hadn't invented it on purpose, but Vish had explained to me how to use it. How it could melt the hearts of any man.

But, then it happened, suddenly there and then, as I looked up at him, at his odd birthmark across his upper lip: I was back on that lakeside path, hand in hand with the man with the pixelated face. And I could hear Vish explaining that I couldn't see his face in my mind because my future had not been written. *You'd know when you meet him* was Vish's prophecy. I remember trying so hard to see through the pixelation on his face, but couldn't see his eyes, couldn't see his nose, none of his features, just what I thought was a light brown moustache, but now I realised it was a flattened mole resting above his upper lip.

# Epilogue

I had to go to the funeral, but I couldn't be seen. Pathetic really. This man who came into my life for a bit of slap and tickle, had become my mentor, but more, my soulmate. He had stepped into the role of father, mother, priest, and banker. Shit! Vish, I'm going to miss you so much. I was standing in the cemetery pretending to look at someone else's grave about fifty feet away from the funeral cortege. I stood there while the small group of mourners were watching the coffin being lowered into the grave. I could see his widow in black with her head lowered. I'd never seen her before, but from the body language and demeanour of the other mourners, it was obviously her.

I wondered whether, if she had been more open, if she had satisfied Vish sexually, would I ever have met him. What would my life have been then? How would I have ended up? I owe it to you, you son of a bitch. Why did you go die on me? What I am, what I have achieved, it was you, you did it. You took a screwed-up kid and nurtured her into a mature, independent woman. And now you've gone. But thanks, thank you, thank you a million times for what you've made me into.

I watched the mourners leave until Daphne was left alone, with, I don't know, a family friend. I saw her talk to the friend and then start walking away while the friend stayed by the grave. Daphne was walking towards me. I froze. I was going to turn and go but something made me stay and watch her approach. She was standing in front of me now, staring at me with cold tearful eyes. I couldn't read her expression. Why was she staring at me?

"Hello, Cindy."

I shuddered. No one had called me that for years. I was going to protest. Tell her that wasn't my name, but, I thought, what's the point?

"How long have you known?"

Her facial expression changed to one of resignation.

"Since the beginning."

She turned around and walked back to the grave.

# The Cindy Speak

My Ed suggested this. He said sometimes I talk funny, and people wouldn't understand. The Yiddish and some of the old slang came from Mum. The new slang you'll probably know anyway. But it's the made-up words where people might need some help. I don't really know when I'm making them up, or when I use a real word or phrase but the wrong way. *Rocking my boat* is a good example. I use it where other people say *Floating my boat*. I prefer my meaning.

I hope *The Cindy Speak* will make it easier to read the book if some of my words or phrases aren't familiar. I put in a few words that aren't even in the book, just for a bit of fun. You might like to use them in your conversation, then people might think you also used to be a flower girl from dahn the Old Kent Road.

Ed wanted to call it a Glossary, but I didn't see the point of titling a section about the words I use with a word I'd never use.

*********

**Bell-end** = Shmuck

But only in the sense of "stupid idiot".

The literal meaning of *bell end* is the glans, or rather the bell shaped bit at the top of the penis. Whereas the literal meaning of shmuck is the penis as a whole. I know it's a bit confusing when the two words mean the same colloquially but not literally.

**Blow job** = Fellatio.

That's how I use it anyway.

The Urban Dictionary is a little more descriptive: *Something stupid school girls will do in an attempt to be popular or to get a boyfriend. Never works, all it ever accomplishes is to get the stupid girl labelled a ho or slut and possibly get her a case of herpes.*

I think my definition is much simpler and non-judgemental, and to be honest I don't think it's the Urban Dictionary's job to moralise like that. Maybe I'm lucky, I blew a lot of boys behind the bike sheds at school for a couple of fags, and never got herpes. Plus I never got called a ho or slut, not to my face anyway. The lads knew that if they called me names, they'd still be singing in the church choir way past their bar-mitzvah.

### BDSM =

Before I tell you what it equals, I'll tell you what I told Ed. "You're kiddin', right? No one ain't goin' to be reading my sh*t if they don't know what that means." So he told me to look it up. He was dead right, as usual, 'cos I didn't know, I mean not proper like:

BD= Bondage & Discipline:
DS= Domination & Submission:
SM= Sadism & Masochism.

Bet you didn't know that. So really it should be BDDSSM, only no-one says it like that.

### Cf. = Compare

It's Latin. I put this in as a joke. I didn't use the term in the book, but you'll see it used further down here, in *The Speak*. I'm just taking the piss out of my Ed because he's always using this and other Latin words. I call him an intellectual snob, but I love him really.

### Chuffed = Well pleased.

But it can also mean the exact opposite. I never knew that. Look it up in the OED (Now I'm a proper writer I'm allowed to use the initialism instead of saying the Oxford English Dictionary.)

I'm actually enjoying putting *The Speak* together. It's taught me a lot about the meaning of words. You could say *I'm dead chuffed*

### Chutzpah = nerve, cheek, audacity.

I explain the meaning in the book. It's used quite a lot by people who aren't Jewish. The problem is, unless you're Welsh, you won't be able to say it properly, Gentiles pronounce the *ch* like in *chat* but if you're Welsh and you can do the guttural sound, like when you're saying *Llandudno*, you'll be getting close. I think gentiles who use the word but say it with a *ch* sound have got, how can I describe it, I think they've got a lot of *chutzpah*

### Come = To reach orgasm (either sex).

For a man, ejaculation. For a woman, you don't usually see the ejaculate, so it just refers to reaching orgasm. For a woman, we call ejaculation squirting. You're lucky if you can do it. I've only done it a few times. I can't squirt to order, like porn stars.

The point is that I'd never say a man squirts. Maybe you'd say spurts, but not squirts.

Mind you, it doesn't really matter what you call it, I just get a kick out of seeing any man throw out the daddy sauce.

**Cum** = The ejaculate or spunk.

I might use it for women's juices when they're wet after an orgasm. But not if they're squirting, when I'd use the word squirt, as in: *I drank her squirt*. But I've only done it a couple of times so I'm not sure if I really know the difference between cum and squirt. Sometimes there's a bit of pee in the squirt because it comes out of the same place. Believe me ladies, you'd know the difference between squirt and pee.

**Dahn** = Down.

Ed says this isn't really for *The Speak*, because it's just writing the word the way I say it. But if you don't get my cockney accent, you wouldn't know what I'm saying, so we agreed to leave it in.

**Down-low** = It's supposed to mean secret information, or stuff not generally known. I just use it to mean any information, so it doesn't have to be secret, just something you won't talk about a lot. e.g. *Doc gave me the down-low about STIs.*

**Diss** = Disrespect.

I think this is universal now. Sometimes words start to get used because it's so obvious. The proper word is so long that it was hardly used. Then when it was shortened everybody uses it. Or maybe, before, people were more respectful, so you didn't need to use the word a lot, but nowadays everyone *disses* everyone, so you need an easy word to say it.

**Frig** = Before I tell you what this equals, I want to say putting *The Speak* together has been fun because of the stuff I've learnt.

I know how we all use *frig* to mean masturbate, when we say *frigging off*, but a lot of people just use *frig* to mean *fuck*.

But here's the fun bit. When I looked it up it says it meant *fuck* first from the 1550s and then masturbate from the 1670s. I've got a daft mind, but when I read that I thought they were saying it took over a hundred years of fucking before they learnt how to masturbate. I know that's just me being daft, but also it tickled my fancy. Like I pictured these two guys in the 15 hundreds trying to masturbate but it wasn't working for them so they said: *Sod it! Let's frig!*

**Hand relief** = Masturbation of a man. It's a technical description. I'd never use it outside the treatment room. So if I told my boyfriend I wasn't in the mood, I would never say: *I will give you hand relief.* I think he'd freak. I'd just say: *I'll toss you off if you like.* Then there'd be a bit of argy-bargy while he would try to up the ante to a blow job, but I'd stick to my guns, and he'd settle for a quick wank.

**Happy ending** = Another technical term for when a masseuse brings a male client to orgasm. I don't think you'd say that about a masseur and a female client. (Q. for Ed: Why do you think that is? My answer is just look at their faces. The stupid grin on a man's face after he's come. *Happy*, yes, I'd go with that. But look at a woman after she's come. I'm talking real orgasm, ladies, not the fake like you might do to please your man. I mean, I might pass out, but even if you don't, the look will be of bliss, of total relaxation, of deep, deep, satisfaction. *Happy* just don't cut it.)

Anyway, you wouldn't say a *happy ending* if you were tossing your boyfriend off. As I said, it's more of a technical term we use in the profession. We professional masseuses have our own professional jargon. Same as the medical profession, like they'll say they're going to examine your breasts, never your tits. That's what I mean by a *technical term*.

**Hey-ho** = It doesn't have a meaning.

We professional writers call it a filler. (Sorry I keep mentioning *professional writers*, but if *you* started out as an erotic masseuse, being able to genuinely say you're a *professional writer* would give you quite a kick too. I know Sami wrote the books, but she used the bits that I wrote and I get some of the royalties). Plus *The Speak* is all my own writing.

As I was saying, it's called a *filler*. You use it in conversation to signal you're pausing but not finished. I never realised I did it, but if I'm talking and I haven't got the words, I'll slot in a *hey-ho* to give me time to think. When I'm writing, I don't really need it, but it is how I speak so it made sense to leave the filler in the text to give you a better idea of how it would sound if I was saying my thoughts aloud.

**Introflective** = A cross between introspective and reflective. If you look up the difference on the web it says:

*Reflection is a process of weighing the pros and cons of an action thus helping people to arrive at a solution that is better in all respects. Introspection, on the other hand, refers to analysis of one's own actions, thoughts, and behaviour and how it affects others. In a sense, introspection is self-evaluation.*

Gotta be honest, I'm not sure I can get my head around that. I just like the way my made-up word sounds.

**Jerk** = see Toss. It's also the same as *toss* in that, unlike *masturbate*, you can't use it as an *intransitive* verb (that was Ed's contribution, don't ask me). But it has a wider meaning, so you can, for example, *jerk* someone around. You don't mean you're tossing them off, you're saying that you're messing them around, as in trying to waste their time.

That's what I like about English. There are so many different words that you can use for a simple act like jacking off (see what I did there).

**LBD** = Little Black Dress

Obviously, most of my women readers would know that, but I guess the men might not be familiar with the term. So, if you're a man you might wonder why the dress is so universally popular that everyone just uses the initials. I can't really explain it to a man but I'll try.

You have a wardrobe full of socks. You're going somewhere special and you take out a pair of socks to match your tie (I know no-one wears ties nowadays but stay with me here). You're wearing your favourite orange tie, so orange socks to match. But you're going to a formal do, and you think: *Orange works for the tie, but the matching socks will be too flashy.*

So you take out a pair of burgundy socks, more understated. They go with anything - except the orange tie. You're worried it might clash. Now you're thinking of patterned socks because they have some orange in the pattern, but you're not sure. Your S.O. comes into the bedroom and asks why the hell all your socks are strewn over the bed. You're in such a tizzy.

You end up wearing your old standby - a pair of black socks.

I'm not sure if that makes sense, but the ladies will know exactly what I mean.

**Mano o Mano** = Face to face. This is a Cindy-ism, where I deliberately use a word the way I want to. *Mano o Mano* actually means *Hand to hand,* and you use it when you are talking about two people fighting. In my job, there's a lot of hand work, and I work face-to-face with the client, so I think my version works better.

**Mae West** = I thought everyone knows rhyming slang. Normally, you drop the second word, like just saying *apples* for *apples and pears* = stairs. But I think saying someone's the *Mae* sounds funny so I always say *Mae West* = *Best*

**Mish mash** = A confused mixture.

It comes from the Yiddish word mish ( מיש ) or German misch, which means mixture or jumble. *Mash* also means mix in English, as in a *mash-up*. So you've got two words that mean the same. Ed says that is either a *tautology* or *pleonasm*, he wasn't too sure. He's not Jewish, so I wouldn't expect him to know Yiddish.

**Pussy** = Vulva or Vagina.

I actually use the word *fanny*, but I had to change that because Ed told me it would confuse my American readers. Across the Pond, *fanny* means *butt*, so I can see there might have been some confusion. As I talk a lot about *fanny action*, people might think the whole book was about gay sex.

*Dahn* Petticoat Lane, when it was like a food market, mum told me they'd talk about *fanny merchants*. It was like a *double entendre*, 'cos the guys would think you meant it as a compliment like you thought they could give you great sex, whereas the gals were just calling them an *arsehole*.

Thinking about it, I wonder if that's why the Yanks started to use *fanny* for your *butt* instead of for your pussy. (Note to Ed. Can you look up the history to test my theory? A lot of Yanks came over during WWII so could have picked up the slang then, but if they used *fanny* like that before the war, then my theory doesn't work.)

**Quim** = Vagina, but I use it to mean your juices down there, *cf. snail trail*. I've got plenty of other words to refer to the cunt, so I use this as the female equivalent of *gism*.

**Rimming** = *cf.* Tossing Salad

**Rock my boat** = Turns me on something rotten.

The normal meaning is the opposite. If you think about stepping into a rowing boat, when other people are sitting in it, you're disturbing the balance. So you could say, for example, *I was getting dressed up to go to the party and then my boyfriend rocked my boat by telling me it had been cancelled*.

That's not how I use it. Think about when people say: *That's real bad, man!* And they mean it's very good.

**Romanic** = When I'm talking about someone with Roman features who I fancy, and I'm thinking *romantic.*

Ed had to tell me this is a Cindy-ism because I didn't make up the word. It's a real word, but it means something entirely different.

**Shag** = Fuck

This was another one I was going to leave out of *The Speak* because I thought everyone uses it. But I looked it up in the Urban Dictionary which said: "A British slang term for sexual intercourse. Used by people who think the term *making love* is too innocent and *fuck* is too coarse. First, I didn't know it was just a British word. Second, what they said about *fuck* being too coarse is right, or at least it used to be. When I was a kid, the girls would always talk about *shagging* but we'd leave it to the boys to say *fucking*, which wasn't lady-like. Nowadays, I watch these kids roaming the streets, girls as well as boys, and it's all *fuck this* and *fuck that.* I'm sorry to have to say this, but I think a lot of the girls today think it's clever to act the slut. I don't like it. Lucky I didn't have kids. I could see myself slapping my daughter if she told me to fuck off. Horrible that I think like that. It would be so, so wrong. Her saying *fuck off,* I mean, not me slapping her.

Just kidding!

**Shag a monkey** = Sorry I ain't got a clue about this one. But it's one of those expressions we use, normally when we've had too much to drink. *E.g. I got so pissed last night I could have shagged a monkey.* But it's also supposed to come from calling someone a *shag monkey* when they're so pissed that you try to suck up any alcohol from a deep pile shag carpet. I think this must be one of Mum's phrases. No one has shag carpet anymore.

**Shlepp** (also shlapp) = Carry.

It's Yiddish. Even people like me who don't speak Yiddish can get that these words have more meaning than the literal translation. So, for example, you might *carry* your shopping home every day, but on Friday when you've just shopped for the weekend and you have three heavy bags instead of one, that's when you're *shlepping* the shopping home.

Btw, you can say *Yiddish,* the language that Jews used to use a lot when they lived in Eastern Europe. It's a kind of mix between German and Hebrew. But you're not allowed to use the Y word anymore, it's like the same as the N-word. Unless you are one, of course, when you're talking to one of your own, then you can call him what you bloody well like.

**Skinny** = a bit like *down-low*, where there's supposed to be something secret, but again, for me, secrecy isn't the issue. It's when you want the details, so usually it's "all the skinny" like don't leave anything out. I don't know where that comes from. You'd think, if it meant *all the information*, we'd say: all *the fatty* but no one says that.

**Snail Trail** = Vaggy juice.

I saw a definition saying: *a viscous streak of vaginal lubrication left on the surface.* I wouldn't say that for two reasons. First, you might misread it like I did. I thought it said *vicious*, which made no sense to me. Second, they're trying to be clever, thinking the trail is a streak. I sort of understand because snails leave trails like that. But for me, *trail* refers to the smell trail of your vaggy juice and not what it looks like.

**S.O.B.** = Well everyone knows what it means, but I used it in the book when I was annoyed with Vishti, and I really didn't think it was fair to call him that, so in that place, just in that place, in the book, it stands for *Stupid Old Bastard.*

**Spunk** = Semen

When Americans talk about *spunk*, they mean courage or determination. They don't use it in the other sense.

I asked Ed why, if I had to change *fanny* to *pussy* so as not to confuse my American readers, shouldn't I use a word Americans would understand. He gave me some options: *cream pie*, jizz, *cum*. I do use *cum* but, now that I'm a *professional writer*, it's good to change the words around otherwise it gets boring.

In the end, the issue with *fanny* is that, if you're American, you'd just keep picturing the wrong end of the action, so to speak, whereas *spunk* is a masculine attribute anyway. So we decided you'd easily adjust to reading, for example, *I swallowed his spunk and it tasted sweet.*

Btw: this would be a good place to apologise to my American readers because, in the book, I use the term *Yank*. My Ed has a *sensitivity squad* to spot stuff that could upset people. It's mostly for the *woke* brigade where I had to put in Trigger warnings. A lot of the time I told them to *fuck off.* I told Ed that you can't put trigger warnings on every page; that would be just stupid, especially in a book that has lots of sex. Anyone who buys the book knows there's going to be a lot of *cunt* spread around.

Anyway, back to my use of *Yank*. I don't mean nothing bad, so get over it. I'm just *yanking your chain.*

**Squeeze** = Some people just use this to mean boyfriend or girlfriend, but when we use it, it might mean someone regular or casual, but only if sex is part of the relationship. If you're referring to a friend where there's no sex, I'd just use China (China plate = Mate).

Talking of squeeze, a Squeeze Box was the term commonly used for an accordion or concertina. Mum used to play me this old track from the Who called Squeeze Box. It's a hoot. Here's a taste:

"Mama's got a squeeze box, she wears on her chest.
And when Daddy comes home, he never gets no rest.
'Cause she's playing all night, and the music's all right.
Mama's got a squeeze box, Daddy never sleeps at night."

**Suck off** = Fellatio or cunnilingus. I wasn't going to put this in, because it is pretty obvious, but I thought it worth explaining that it really applies to the whole process, not just the sucking. I could come with just a tongue licking me. The sucking is more to prolong the action, to stop me coming too soon whilst keeping me aroused. So if someone had brought me to orgasm just by licking my clitoris, without any sucking, I'd still say: *they sucked me off,* but the chances are I'd follow that up with *but I came too soon.*

**Tapped out** = Fully satiated after sex.

I thought everyone uses this expression, but Ed told me that its proper meaning, well not proper because it's still slang, is when you're completely out of money. Maybe, but if you watch some gals playing with themselves, they actually tap their clits, or rather they tap over their lips but the pressure connects with their clits. They speed up the tapping and they can make themselves come like that. I don't do it that way. I'll always rub and pinch a little, but I've seen a lot of women that do it like that, and not just in porn where it's fake.

**Tickle my fancy** = Provoke amusement.

I don't think this is in the book, but the phrase itself tickles my fancy, so I put it here. Fancy can just mean someone you like, but come on, we all know that it means your fanny - sorry, pussy. So it's a kinda naughty way to say someone made you laugh, like you might say *you laughed so much you wet yourself.* I dunno. When you wet yourself, it's peeing a bit by accident. We've all been there, but for me when I talk of being wet down there, I'm always talking about being horny.

**Tossing salad** = Rimming or Anilingus.

If you think I spelt that wrong go look it up. R.I.M. Just kidding! I dunno why, I know it should be analingus, with an *a*, it's just not.

It's supposed to come from prison. Never been there, but it turns a lot of guys gay because there are no chicks around. Or were they gay already but just didn't know it until their cellmate decided to poke them around? Well, in prison, when they do it, they are supposed to use salad dressing to hide the taste. That makes no sense to me, 'cos there's always vinegar in salad dressing, so I think I'd prefer it unseasoned, so to speak.

Honestly, this is not really my bag. Receiving OK, although I'm not even into that. But giving, not in my backyard. But you'll read in the book that, just a few times with the right person, I'd tongue fuck their arse. I think it's like the ultimate show that you'll do anything for them, so, for me, it's gotta be with someone special. As I said, never been in a male prison, so I wouldn't know what they get up to. Never been in a woman's prison either, but if I was, I wouldn't need no salad dressing, I'd be *tipping the velvet* any day of the week.

**Tipping the Velvet** = Cunnilingus

It's all about tongue. I thought it should have been tapping because some people like to have their clit tapped instead of rubbed. Personally, I'm a rubber or pincher, except in BDSM. If I really trust the guy, I'll let him lash or slap my clit, with a whip or paddle, but gentle like. Got that wrong once. He took the piss and really hurt me. So I kneed him in the balls and that ended the session.

Anyway, tipping is a better word, because you can take it to mean the tip of your tongue or like when you give someone a tip, which is either money or a good suggestion, so *tipping* is always about getting something nice.

**Tosser** = Literally one who goes around masturbating but it's normally used just to mean a fucking idiot. You can use wanker in the same way.

**Toss off** = Masturbate but, unlike masturbate, you always have to say who you're doing it to. Just as you can just say: I'm masturbating but you can't say: *I'm tossing.* You have to say, for example: *I'm tossing myself off.* I just think these words sound better. So if my boyfriend walks in on me while I'm pleasuring myself, it would sound odd to say: *Fuck off, I'm masturbating.* I'm more likely to say: *Come in and fuck me.*

**Trademark smile** = Cindy's unique smile, beguiling, tantalising, seductive, sexy. I know it's daft putting this in *The Speak*. Everyone knows the meaning. But I argued with Ed, the whole thing, my whole life is defined by my smile. Without my smile, there would have been no book, no volumes, no trilogy. He let me keep it in, but he insisted I explain my reason for wanting it in *The Speak*, so that's what I've just done.

**Wank** = Masturbate.

It can be a noun or a verb, whereas *tossing* will always be a verb. Like you can say: *I have a wank every day* but you can't say: *I have a toss every day.* I mean good luck if you do, but you just can't say it.

It's quite a versatile word. I can say: *I just had a wank.* But if you use the real word, you can't say: *I just had a masturbate.* Maybe: *I just had a masturbation,* but it doesn't sound right.

So I always prefer *wanking,* if you get my drift.

**Wagatha** = Word made up by a journalist. (Ed says it was Dan Atkinson of the Guardian. I dunno, but he's usually right about these things.)

I thought the whole world knew about this, but Ed said I might have readers in Scotland.

It's a clever play on words. First, you gotta know that *W.A.G.* stands for *Wives and Girlfriends.* Then you gotta know that Colleen Rooney and Rebecca Vardy are both married to English Premier League Football (soccer) players. Then you have to follow what's going on in the English High Court because Becky Vardy sued the Rooney bird after she dissed her on her social. Then the Rooney bird did some clever detective trick to prove Becky was telling tales out of school. Finally, you need to know who the fuck Agatha Christie is.

That's why no one in Scotland would get the clever play on words:

1. They have their own Premier football league, so won't have heard of the husbands Wayne and Jamie.

2. They have their own legal system, courts and stuff, so why should they know what goes on in the Old Bailey?

3. They have their own newspapers. I don't know if you can even buy the Guardian in Scotland.

4. Scottish broadcaster and comedienne Susan Morrison has gone on record saying she hates Agatha Christie.

*Hope you enjoyed The Speak – just a bit of fun.*

*Lots of love*
*Cindy x*

# Acknowledgements

Neither Greenwich College, Her Centre, the developers of Upper Riverside nor lovehoney.com have participated directly in contributing to this novel. Nevertheless, the author wishes to acknowledge their contribution, in so far as using real organisations as a backdrop provided a more authentic context for the story than creating fictional institutions.

So, with the acknowledgements, there comes a disclaimer. The author has no reason to believe that Greenwich College is anything other than a reputable educational establishment, and no individuals, upon whom the characters in this novel are based, have any connection, direct or indirect, with the College.

Similarly with Her Centre, although the author hopes that, by drawing attention to their good work, this may provide a small boost to their fundraising for such an excellent cause.

It is not expected that the Upper Riverside project will suffer from the indirect promotion of the scheme in these pages. But, again, readers should not imagine that the residents of that luxury project are anything like the characters in this novel. The author does not know any of those residents, so has no reason to believe that they get up to the sort of shenanigans depicted in the novel, notwithstanding that they may well work in finance in Canary Wharf. If any reader should happen upon one such resident, they should be sure to first ask whether their apartment has a *River View*, before committing to invest in conversation.

As for lovehoney.com, not one of the toys used by the main protagonist failed to function so the author hopes this purveyor of erotic equipment will consider all references to such products as a bit of free publicity.

The novel could not have, would not have been written without the inspiration of one very special person, the one with the *trademark smile*, who probably will never know how much she has contributed, not just in the hours of interviews about her life experiences, but also in helping the author to understand Cindy.

A penultimate shout out to my Ed. Without the many linguistic corrections, highlighting the malapropisms and generally improving the readability, this Volume was at risk of turgidity (as evidenced by the fact that Ed never reviewed this paragraph).

Finally, the author thanks their life partner for the endless patience, devotion, and tolerance, and for providing the space that has allowed the mind the freedom to wander. They're the author's very own Vishti, the soulmate whose pearls of wisdom have helped to exorcise the author's own demons.

This is the sole work of the author, though some readers may recognise the influences of the author's literary heroes, influenced by, but no reflection of, their far more accomplished literary prowess.

# A message from the Author

I hope that, through these pages, Cindy has given to you what she has given to me – an insight into the workings of her mind – a chance to share some of her feelings of pleasure and pain – as well as a few moments of erotic fantasy.

If you would like to know how Cindy's life progresses, and, if you think you can keep up with the pace of her new adventures as she continues to explore her own sensuality, rocking through a jet-set lifestyle, you are invited to read:

**Cindy's Diaries**
**Volume II**
**XO**
**RACHEL GOES HOLLYWOOD**

Sami Goldhurst

# About the Author

Sami Goldhurst grew up on England's South Coast and was educated at a local grammar school before studying Philosophy & Psychology at Cambridge University.

An initial career in international private banking provided exposure to the excesses of wealth and greed. A decade-long sojourn in the Far East offered direct experience of an exotic lifestyle. The early adventures in Sami's life are reflected in the *Cindy's Diaries Trilogy*.

Sami's time is now divided between the tranquillity of a Thames-side river view residence and the cosmopolitan playground of Marbella, echoing the bi-polar world of the epic tale's main protagonist.

Sami's narratives are based on real encounters embellished with fantasies born out of vivid imagination, creating believable, if flawed, characters, and relishing their exciting, if edgy, existence.

With a down-to-earth, hard-headed, matter-of-fact writing style, Sami's novels aim to engage, stimulate, amuse, titillate, startle and surprise.

Printed in Great Britain
by Amazon